New York Times Editors' Choice

Continued Praise for *Rock the Boat:*

"The perfect summer beach read for anyone who craves a smart story with a happy ending."

—*Oprah Daily*

"[A] witty, heartfelt debut novel about a belated coming-of-age. Dorey-Stein . . . spins a diverting yarn about friendship and family."

—*The New York Times Book Review* (Editors' Choice)

"A lively, intelligent read that confidently renders everything from a busy back bar to the slow process of grief."

—*People*

"It'll hit you right in the feelings. Beck, will you please write a sequel?"

—*HelloGiggles*

"A sizzling summer read . . . Whip-smart and perfectly capturing that delicate balance between your younger and adult selves, Dorey-Stein's book will have you—*gasp!*—craving a reunion with your high school pals."

—*EOnline*

"Following up on the success to her Obama White House memoir *From the Corner of the Oval*, Beck Dorey-Stein is turning to fiction with her debut novel, filled with similar coming-of-age themes and circumstances. Protagonist Kate Campbell returns to her New England hometown for the summer, finding she needs to reevaluate a few things in her life before she is ready to move back to Manhattan. Of course, that's *if* she moves back, after diving deep into some of the relationships and secrets that consume her seaside community."

—*Fortune*

"In *Rock the Boat*, Beck Dorey-Stein has given us the perfect summer read—sharp, irreverent, and compulsively readable—about how the best stuff in life is always what you didn't plan."

—Lauren Weisberger, *New York Times* bestselling author of *The Devil Wears Prada* and *Where the Grass Is Green and the Girls Are Pretty*

"Beck Dorey-Stein's buoyant first novel is about finding out who you are and what matters most when everything tips sideways. It's about rediscovering what love costs and finding your way back to the people who truly mean home. Funny and effervescent, hope- and heart-filled, *Rock the Boat* is a breath of delicious and utterly fresh air."

—Paula McLain, author of *The Paris Wife* and *When the Stars Go Dark*

"Brimming with wit and warmth, and peopled with a terrifically vibrant cast of characters, *Rock the Boat* is a delightful, whip-smart page-turner with an expansive heart."

—Claire Lombardo, author of *The Most Fun We Ever Had*

"What a cocktail of a book, topped with frothy, delicious wit. Beck Dorey-Stein nails the pathos and comedy of that slippery, sideways path to (sigh) adulthood. We can be awful to the people we feel safest with—those who love us and who have known us the longest—and Dorey-Stein captures that truth beautifully. I'm wildly grateful to have discovered a novelist who delivers this amount of sheer pleasure on a page."

—Judy Blundell, author of *The High Season*

"*Rock the Boat* is the warm, wonderful escape I've been wishing for. A novel with gorgeous sentences and complex, kind characters set in a Garden State beach town—what more could you want? Mix yourself a Paloma and sink in. . . . Dorey-Stein's debut novel is sheer delight."

—Amanda Eyre Ward, author of *The Jetsetters*

"A witty and endearing escape, a summertime must-read."

—*Booklist*

"The author perfectly captures what it means to come home again and rediscover yourself in the process. Make room in your beach bag for this cozy summer read."

—*Kirkus Reviews*

ALSO BY BECK DOREY-STEIN

From the Corner of the Oval

Rock
the
Boat

Rock
the
Boat

A Novel

Beck
Dorey-Stein

The Dial Press
New York

2022 Dial Press Trade Paperback Edition

Published in the United States by The Dial Press, an imprint of Random House, a division of Penguin Random House LLC, New York.

THE DIAL PRESS is a registered trademark and the colophon is a trademark of Penguin Random House LLC.
RANDOM HOUSE BOOK CLUB and colophon are trademarks of Penguin Random House LLC.

Originally published in hardcover in the United States by The Dial Press, an imprint of Random House, a division of Penguin Random House LLC, in 2021.

LIBRARY OF CONGRESS CATALOGING-IN-PUBLICATION DATA
Names: Dorey-Stein, Beck, author.
Title: Rock the boat: a novel / Beck Dorey-Stein.
Description: First edition. | New York: The Dial Press, [2021]
Identifiers: LCCN 2020051561 (print) | LCCN 2020051562 (ebook) |
ISBN 9780525509172 (trade paperback) | ISBN 9780525509165 (ebook) |
International edition ISBN 9780593244159
Subjects: LCSH: Friendship—Fiction.
Classification: LCC PS3604.O7364 R63 2021 (print) | LCC PS3604.O7364 (ebook) |
DDC 813/.6—dc23
LC record available at https://lccn.loc.gov/2020051561
LC ebook record available at https://lccn.loc.gov/2020051562

Printed in the United States of America on acid-free paper

randomhousebooks.com
randomhousebookclub.com

1st Printing

Book design by Elizabeth A. D. Eno

For anyone lucky enough
to have seen a sunflower in full bloom—
which is to say
for everyone lucky enough to have known
Sophie Christopher.

O enchanted land of my childhood, a cultural petri dish from which regularly issues forth greatness. New Jersey, in case you didn't know it, has got beaches. Beautiful beaches. And they're not all crawling with roid-raging trolls with reality shows. I grew up summering on those beaches and they are awesome. Jersey's got farmland, beautiful bedroom communities where that woman from *Real Housewives* who looks like Dr. Zaius does not live nor anyone like her. Even the refineries, the endless cloverleaves of turnpikes and expressways twisting in unknowable patterns over the wetlands, are to me somehow beautiful.

To know Jersey is to love her.

—Anthony Bourdain

Part I

Road to Nowhere

Kate Campbell opened her eyes but couldn't see a thing. It was the middle of the night and, like a young Miss Clavel only less French and more ginger, she knew something was not right. Recalling the details of the previous evening, however, she realized it was just the opposite—nothing was wrong, and everything was finally about to be extremely right.

Kate smiled in the dark as all the evidence accumulated to form an arrow pointing at a singular fact: Thomas would propose to her in the morning. Wriggling back under the covers, Kate grinned as she imagined what everyone would think besides *It's about time.* Of course it was about time; it had been twelve years.

Despite—or maybe because of—the countless, candid conversations they'd had about how and when to get engaged, Kate was shocked that Thomas would spring this on her. It was impressive, really, to still surprise someone after more than a decade of dating (never mind those two rocky breaks when he was stressed in med school, or those six months his first year of surgical residency, or this second fellowship). They'd agreed forever ago that the only real incentive to marry would be if they wanted to start a family, and they hadn't even discussed children in the last six months because Thomas's fellowship was basically *Kill Bill* only in long, white coats and with far more blood.

But the end of the fellowship was finally in sight with an offer at the same hospital, and their conversation the night before was undeniable evidence of an imminent proposal. They'd been in a cab crossing back over the Brooklyn Bridge, Kate watching the fare tick up and up, when Thomas had asked if she'd like to go to brunch at Norman's in the morning.

"Before New Hampshire?"

"Mm-hmm," Thomas said, looking at his phone.

"With Aggie and Marta?" Thomas's sister and sister-in-law lived above them in the building Thomas's grandparents owned. They would carpool to New Hampshire together for Easter Sunday, just as they'd done every Easter since they were twenty-two.

"Just us," Thomas had said, as he continued to stare down at his phone. This calculated attempt to plan a casual brunch without Aggie and Marta seemed odd to Kate, like inserting a key only to find the door already unlocked. It momentarily jostled her out of her midnight stupor, but she had been too tired to explore what Thomas's suggestion might mean—until now, hours before dawn, when his odd behavior had, poof, turned into proof.

But proposing in *April*? Kate wrinkled her nose. April in New York was horrific—an open sewage drain of a month with damp clothes and nagging colds, everyone trudging through the office as bedraggled and psychotic as the Times Square pigeons. Kate had assumed that if this was going to be the year, Thomas would have waited for May, and asked while they were on vacation with his friends.

As the sun rose, however, Kate warmed to Thomas's strategy: He would pop the question now so they could then drive up to New Hampshire to celebrate with the Mosby clan over Easter. She hoped but doubted that

Thomas had thought to include her family in some way, which was not his strong suit, only because his family was big and fun and . . . a lot. All three generations and extended branches of Mosbys lived here in the city, mostly on the Upper East Side but everyone in Manhattan, or what Thomas jokingly referred to as "the only island that matters." It was easy enough to forget that Kate did come with her own small family of four from a tiny beach town in New Jersey. Technically, Sea Point was only a three-hour drive from the city—the same distance as New Hampshire—but it felt worlds apart from her life in New York because the rest of the Campbells found the city as daunting as Thomas found Sea Point "quaint."

Kate closed her eyes and hoped the sleepless night wouldn't show on her face when they asked a stranger to snap their picture after she'd said yes—or maybe Thomas had hired a photographer to hide in the bushes for candids? She wondered if he had thought to size his grandmother's engagement ring just before emitting a low groan: She had become the kind of person she despised, and she wasn't sure whether to blame her work, her generation, or herself.

As a rising star at Artemis Public Relations, Kate's craft was bending stories into taglines. Recently, she'd caught herself treating her own life like a client's portfolio, and her online profile reflected her professional life's permeation into the personal—her photos were flawless, her captions simple and clever. Kate envisioned colleagues, acquaintances, and ghosts from the past viewing her engagement photo with envy, even googling Thomas. In two days, she'd post a cute photo—the ring tastefully included but not prominently featured—with a low-key caption, something along the lines of: *We did a thing.*

Three hours later, Kate encouraged Thomas to take his time in the shower so she could strategize her caught-off-guard look. Each hanger held a jacket or sweater that wouldn't be good enough for her future mother-in-law, Evelyn, who would apologize to her friends for Kate's poor taste as they pinched her phone screen and zoomed in to inspect every inch of the engagement photos. But here, this wasn't bad—a blue-checked dress Thomas had once said made her look like a sexy Raggedy Anne. The dress showed effort without letting Thomas know that she knew.

"Almost ready?" Kate yelled through the bathroom door.

"Done yesterday," Thomas called over the high-pitched groan of the pipes. The water pressure was barely more than a sad dribble, but Kate wasn't about to complain after four years living rent free. Then again, Kate thought, maybe she could raise the issue once she became a Mosby.

Running a brush through her hair and a rake through her thoughts, Kate found herself feeling triumphant rather than joyful—or maybe joyfully triumphant. She'd put in so much time, given all of her twenties to this relationship, and endured a decade's worth of saccharine smiles from ancient strangers inquiring, "So when do you think you'll . . . ?"

The imminent proposal felt validating in a way that probably wasn't especially feminist, and yet, wouldn't anyone feel victorious when they finally saw the big return on their risky investment? And it had been downright dicey at times—after twelve years, the bottom had dropped out more than once, usually in direct correlation to where Thomas was in the medical gauntlet. Even last night at the party, Kate had worried they were heading toward the red when she'd gestured to the spinach stuck in his front teeth and Thomas had rolled his eyes before skulking off, leaving her alone in the kitchen.

Now, Kate gave herself a once-over in the mirror: Her strawberry-blond hair rippled down in obedient, tame waves, the freckles across her nose were visible but not chaotic like they would be by mid-June. The dark, pronounced eyebrows she'd hated as a kid were cooperating today, and after she'd drawn a bronze rim around her wide green eyes, Kate took private delight in the double takes that her heart-shaped face so often invited.

Just last week, she'd been confused for the breakout actress from that Netflix show while ordering at Barney Greengrass. Kate no longer blushed when she disappointed strangers bold enough to approach her—in fact, she wore big black sunglasses to encourage such speculation. Tourists came from small towns like hers to gawk at the city's glamour and so Kate indulged in their celebrity-sighting fantasies not only because it was fun but also because it proved just how far she had come since arriving in New York fifteen years ago as a college freshman.

The toilet flushed and the bathroom door opened.

"You look nice," Thomas said, checking his hair in the mirror. "Where's my putty?"

Kate handed him the hair product half hidden under her brush—it arrived every month from a tiny shop in Vancouver and cost more than their utility bills—but he wouldn't know that. Thomas dropped his keys twice before successfully tucking them into his jacket pocket. *Nerves*, Kate deduced, flashing him a well-glossed grin. "We haven't been to Norman's in ages!" she announced to Thomas's reflection in the hallway mirror.

"Back to where it all began," he replied, slipping his bare feet into the walking loafers to which the entire Mosby clan subscribed.

The spring of their junior year of college, Kate and Thomas had met in the bathroom line at Norman's just after two a.m. According to Kate, he'd complimented her purple Shark watch and according to Thomas, he'd made fun of her purple Shark watch. Several hours later, they'd staggered out of the diner and straight into each other's world.

Now, as Kate clutched Thomas's hand on the walk back to where they'd first met, she surrendered to the overwhelming affection she had for New York, the greatest of cities that she'd come to see as hers. In the West Village, beautiful strangers swirled around her like gorgeous pieces of moving furniture—enriching the milieu with their statement pieces, their curated indifference. The anonymity among other well-heeled intellects is what Kate loved the most—even more than that woman's vintage handbag as they crossed Greenwich. Her hand in Thomas's, Kate smiled at ten-year-old twins clad in thousand-dollar down jackets and beamed with the knowledge that she'd never felt more at home than she did here, among the ambition and creative genius that charged the city with its own electricity. Joan Didion had been right when she'd written, "New York was no mere city. It was instead an infinitely romantic notion, the mysterious nexus of all love and money and power, the shining and perishable dream itself."

Kate knew that each one of these power-walking New Yorkers would arrive at the café or yoga studio or sound bath and untuck their scarves as they shed their aloofness, exchanging it for the cultivated mindfulness they'd been practicing in therapy. Changing identities in New York was easier than renting bowling shoes in New Jersey, though both would give you break-in blisters. The birthplace of the rebirth, the key to making it in Manhattan was believing you belonged—along with easy access to a dependable dry cleaner.

"I'm so sorry to bother you but aren't you—" a tourist in her early forties asked as she grinned at Kate while they waited to cross Hudson. The woman was gripping her phone and Kate saw her camera app already open, the lens in selfie mode.

"No, she isn't," Thomas interjected; he had zero tolerance for out-of-towners, except for his West Coast friends and the easily placed Eaton type.

Turning the corner and spotting the diner's iconic neon sign, Kate sped toward it, appreciating how her future was waiting inside her past—she'd have to play around with that idea for subsequent content captions or maybe even her vows. Like the city itself, the best thing about Norman's was that it weeded out the weaklings. The diner achieved this through an impossibly heavy glass door that, like everything else at Norman's, hadn't changed in the last seventy years. If you were a regular and of a particular age, the hostess would hit the handicapped automatic button from the inside—if you were anyone else, you were on your own. Kate ignored Thomas as he swore under his breath and used both hands to yank open the door. Inside, while Thomas massaged his shoulder, Kate scanned the room and approached the hostess stand with a request: "May we have that corner booth?"

The hostess followed Kate's finger past the servers and bussers racing around with big brown trays, narrowly avoiding collisions. Thomas had once joked that navigating Norman's reminded him of driving in Rome—harrowing, and safer to do a little buzzed.

"You know them?" she asked, looking at the two willowy blondes sipping coffee through straws, occupying the booth to which Kate pointed.

"No," Kate ceded, "but we'll wait. We've done it before. It's kind of our booth."

At this moment, Thomas looked up from his phone and met the hostess's disgust with an apologetic smile. "Kate, they haven't even gotten their food yet."

Acquiescing only to disguise her comprehension of what today meant—would mean forever—Kate followed the hostess to the vacant, freestanding table by the jukebox, closest to the restrooms. "First time for everything," she sighed, forcing a smile and ignoring a man's phlegmy cough at a neighboring booth.

Glenda, the notoriously grumpy server who seemed to despise Kate as much as she adored Thomas—who was never Thomas but always *Baby* or *Honey* or *Honey Baby* on especially frisky days—asked Baby what he'd like to drink and walked away without looking at Kate. Until *The New Yorker* had featured what they termed "The Glenda Phenomenon" in their "Shouts and Murmurs" column, Glenda had been unaware that she'd starred in so many ungraduated short stories that the NYU English Department had unanimously voted to place a moratorium on the use of her likeness.

Glenda returned with two coffees, two orange juices, and the infamous attitude that made her so vital in preserving the city's folklore. After ordering their usual, Thomas leaned forward and said he needed to ask Kate something.

"Are you," Thomas began, reaching across the table for her winter-white hand. Her caramelized skin from Mexico, Kate silently lamented, had blanched as soon as they'd touched down at LaGuardia. "Happy?" Thomas stared at her, waiting for her response, with the bluest eyes Kate had ever seen. Mayflower blue, she liked to joke, because his grandmother never missed an opportunity to mention their Plymouth forebearers.

"The happiest," Kate crooned, arching her back to sit up straight, basking in the moment like a cat in afternoon sun.

"Really?" he said, drawing slow circles on the back of her hand with his thumb.

"Really," Kate said. "I am the happiest."

She felt Thomas's hand retreat to retrieve the ring from the pocket in his jacket. But he didn't reach for the pocket. He just sat back, his eyes so wide that they became two Mayflower blue islands surrounded by an ocean of white shock.

Thomas held out his hands again and she met him halfway, ignoring some primordial sense of panic. He flipped her right hand over and traced the lines of her veins across the pale underbelly of her wrist. Kate waited. She felt light-headed before realizing she hadn't taken a breath since she'd said "happiest." Leaning forward and speaking slowly, in a low voice that would haunt her for months, Thomas confessed: "I'm not happy. I'm really, really not happy."

Six hours later, Kate's parents flanked her as they walked out of the Jane Street apartment and toward their parked car, which offended passersby with its flashing hazard lights and yellow Jersey plates. Buckled in the back, Kate closed her eyes and tried to understand what had just happened, how this implosion of her life had occurred.

In the diner, she'd actually laughed when Thomas had said he wasn't happy. She'd almost said, *This is a weird way to start a proposal*. But then Thomas's eyes had welled with tears and instead of asking "Will you," he'd said, "This isn't fair."

That's when time had sped up and stood still.

Kate had swallowed vomit before bolting from the booth and pushing through the hulking diner door like it was nothing but a string curtain. On the street corner, she'd put her hands on her knees and her head between her legs as Thomas stood behind her and calmly explained he would go to New Hampshire as planned; he was using his vacation days to stay up there for the week so she would have time to pack her stuff and figure out next steps. They'd walked up Eighth Avenue in silence, too stunned to speak. When a subway grate blew the city's bad breath up Kate's dress and Thomas looked embarrassed for her—like they were no longer on the same team, no longer a we—Kate broke into a run only to arrive back on Jane Street and realize the apartment keys were in Thomas's pocket.

Waiting on the steps, she'd called her sister.

"Can you go to a friend's place?" Bernadette asked. "You shouldn't be in that apartment by yourself—oh, Christ, and tomorrow's Easter."

"My friends are his friends," Kate whimpered.

"Is it Nora?" Bernadette dared.

"He swears there's no one else."

Bernadette scoffed and muttered a string of uncomplimentary expletives under her breath before saying she'd figure something out. They hung up just as Thomas rounded the corner and reluctantly offered that she could come to New Hampshire for Easter, as long as she could keep the weekend drama-free since his grandmother was in remission.

"He wants me to go with him," Kate lied.

"No, he doesn't," Bernadette said just as Thomas cleared his throat and clarified that he needed to be alone, that New Hampshire was only an option if she had nowhere else to go.

"Stay there," Bernadette growled. "Or book a train home and I'll pick you up."

After unlocking the front door, Thomas grabbed a pre-packed suitcase he'd hidden behind the white couch, kissed Kate's forehead, and explained he was being cruel to be kind before asking her to drop her Jane Street keys in the mailbox when she left. An hour later and alone in the apartment, Kate had cried herself to exhaustion. Staring up at the ceiling, she listened to the rhythm of the raindrops and Rolodexed her regrets:

She should have said yes to that puppy Thomas had wanted the previous summer, yes to another hour at the party the night before, and no to that early SoulCycle class when he'd been sleeping off his week of overnight shifts. The regrets poured down as the rain picked up, and the incessant tapping against the window reminded Kate of her least favorite client, Hal, who liked to express his annoyance by impatiently drumming his manicured fingernails on the conference room table.

Kate groped for her phone, ignored the incoming call from Bernadette, and composed an email to her boss and her boss's boss at Artemis PR, who just so happened to be Evelyn Mosby. In three lines, Kate quit her job. She didn't even bother to read through the memo before hitting "send." It was over. She'd lost the big investment so it was time to burn it all down. The momentary flex of independence felt good, like the warm licks of a bonfire—until everything inevitably turned to ash.

"You did WHAT?" Bernadette yelled into the phone five minutes later. Kate heard their parents, Sally and Dirk, gasp in the background when Bernadette relayed the latest bit of breaking news. "Write back and apologize or—wait, no, just put your phone down. You're out of your mind. Hold on—okay, Mom and Dad are going to drive up right now, but no more emails."

It was only when Dirk and Sally Campbell appeared on the Jane Street front stoop and her mom said "Oh Katie" that she let her body go slack and allowed her parents to organize the evacuation. Kate curled up in the corner of their queen bed that she realized was now just Thomas's and watched the clumsy pile of wire dry cleaner hangers spill off the down comforter and onto the hardwood floor. As her father loaded luggage, her mother worked to dismantle her closet, while Kate pored over Thomas's social media presence, trying to understand who could have infiltrated their life when Thomas worked all the time. Kate had met the other fellows in his program and felt a shred of comfort that they weren't his type before realizing she had no idea what Thomas's type was if it wasn't her.

From the closet, Sally scoffed about the kind of people who hung their jeans, knowing full well Thomas had turned her daughter into that kind of person. Locking herself in the bathroom, Kate secretly texted Thomas. If Bernadette had come up with their parents, she would have confiscated Kate's phone upon arrival to avoid this very situation, but Bernadette was at home with her daughter and so Kate was in the bathroom texting. Thomas replied immediately, proving to Kate that he still loved her and that this was just another dramatic hiccup. Taking a deep breath, Kate opened the message and saw it was the automatic reply she'd set up for him years ago so that he wouldn't be tempted to text and drive.

Three suitcases and countless overstuffed trash bags later, Sally barked out directions from the passenger seat like a Marine on a rescue mission as Dirk navigated their way out of the West Village. A sign above the Holland Tunnel warned in flashing lights and far too late, STAY ALERT! The city disappeared behind them and the road ahead narrowed into darkness.

It took several moments for Kate's eyes to adjust to the blur of white tiles erasing the life she'd built for herself. Leaving the city this way—worried parents in the front, all earthly possessions in the back—felt like a permanent sentence. Driving under the Hudson, away from New York, was the equivalent of crossing the river Styx, only without the romantic promise of an afterlife.

Emerging from the tunnel, the GPS mechanically welcomed them to New Jersey with as much enthusiasm as one could muster for the state. Dirk and Sally let out a joint sigh of relief as they merged onto 95 South. The sun had set and hundreds of red taillights idled in the stand-still traffic, reminding Kate of worker ants. Fifteen years in the city and she'd never had to commute.

Merging onto the Garden State Parkway, Kate listened to the steady grunt of her parents' rusty SUV that was bad for the environment but good for moving two daughters in and out of dorm rooms, group houses, and apartments. She let her forehead thud against the window with every bump in the road and watched with envy as oncoming traffic headed north, toward the city, toward the epicenter of everything. One car's high beams temporarily blinded all of them and her mom squawked: "It's like they're shining a flashlight directly in our faces!" Sally Campbell didn't know, how could she, but at the mention of a flashlight, the memory rushed at Kate without warning. She closed her eyes and allowed the curtains to lift.

She'd been dating Thomas for six months when he'd surprised her with a trip to his parents' vacant ski lodge in New Hampshire the first crisp fall weekend in October. Kate had expected the lodge to smell musty, a thick layer of dust making her sneeze every few seconds, the cupboards bare except for mouse droppings. But when Thomas opened the front door, the exposed wood beams sparkled and a crackling fire in the great room beckoned. This wasn't anything like her uncle's double-wide in the Poconos, which he'd optimistically called his lodge—this was what happened when Martha Stewart masturbated to pictures of John Muir for a week and then designed a rustic-themed mansion accordingly. It was outdoorsy-chic, a cozy-rugged cabin meant for early-morning ski runs and twenty-person dinner parties. It was beautiful and all theirs for the weekend.

"I called ahead." Thomas shrugged nonchalantly before explaining that the caretaker had swung by.

After fooling around in the living room, under the direct supervision of a mounted moose head, they got dressed and bundled up for a walk through the idyllic gloom. Thomas wanted to show Kate the boarding school campus where he'd spent his formative years—a stunning hundred-acre sprawl that seemed more like a movie set version of a school than an actual institution. As they walked, Thomas tossed a flashlight to himself like the sweet Eagle Scout he was—he'd brought it so they could find their way home in the dark because an Eagle Scout was always prepared.

The school's gothic architecture, beginning with the twelve-foot-high stone wall that surrounded the campus, was designed to intimidate. "Our kids will go here," Thomas had said, hugging his arms around the flagpole in the center of the quad and grinning at her like a schoolboy with a crush.

"Our kids?" Kate smirked. They were twenty-one. *They* were kids. But

the vision of her own children attending a place like this . . . she could feel
her insides shift and the throbbing wound from her own high school experience, buried yet still raw after all these years, seemed to finally quell
as she imagined crossing this quad as a mother in a responsible green
cardigan and espadrilles, a familiar figure heading to the school play, a
contributing member of this community. She would belong.

"Yeah, our kids," Thomas affirmed. Kate could barely make out Thomas's outline as he launched himself from the flagpole, pulled Kate into a
hug, and nuzzled his face into her neck. She heard him rustling in his
pockets right before he pulled out the flashlight and held it below Kate's
chin, clicking it on with his thumb.

"What are you doing?"

"I want to see your face when I tell you," he murmured.

"Tell me what?"

"I love you," he whispered. His lips against her ear as he said it, the way
he sounded out of breath, and smiling. She couldn't see him but she
knew the sound of his smile, and because he'd put that dumb flashlight
under her chin, he saw that she was smiling too, maybe even tearing up
because this was a moment she would remember forever—she knew it
then, even as it was still happening. "I love you," he said again, squeezing
her even tighter, "and we are going to make the most beautiful children,
and they'll attend Evergreen, and they'll have your right brain and my left
brain, so they'll all be valedictorians. But mostly"—Thomas gripped
Kate's shoulders and spun her around so she faced him—"I love you. And
I will always love you. Like Whitney Houston will always love you, but
with blueberry pancakes and morning sex, even when we're in our nineties." He scooped her up just then and carried her across the quad like a
groom whisking his bride across the threshold, bellowing "I Will Always
Love You" so loud that his voice ricocheted off the stone walls. Thomas
had shined the flashlight ahead of them through the woods and back to
the cabin, their path clear and bright.

At the end of the weekend, Kate had grabbed the flashlight and taken
it back to New York. It was sturdier and more pragmatic than an engage-

ment ring, but it promised the same thing: *I will always love you.* For years, they kept the flashlight on their coffee table, a centerpiece they hoped guests would ask after, which they did, until it disappeared during their New Year's Eve party the previous year.

"Dirk!" Sally shrieked as the entire car swerved, jolting Kate out of the memory.

"There was a turtle!" her father yelled back.

"Did you hit it?" Kate asked reluctantly, peering past her own reflection to outside the window. The Garden State Parkway had narrowed to two lanes and was empty. Tall, narrow trees stood guard on either side. They must be driving through the Pine Barrens now.

"Sure didn't," her father said proudly. "And he was almost to the white line of the shoulder, so I bet he makes it."

"Oh, so it's a he?" her mother asked. "How very twentieth century of you."

As her history-teaching parents sparred about pronouns, Kate tried to nestle back into the memory of visiting Evergreen for the first time, but she couldn't—it felt as awkward as trying to wriggle back into a wet bathing suit.

Now they took the exit for Sea Point, passing the billboard that reminded tourists in peeling turquoise paint: NEW JERSEY'S BEST-KEPT SECRET! The lighthouse illuminated the raindrops on the windshield so they shimmered like diamonds before continuing its revolution through the darkness. The salt in the damp air and the sound of the crashing waves were undeniable: Kate was back where she'd began. In real life, and in one day, she'd lost Thomas, quit her job, and returned to her least favorite place.

"Lots of construction happening," her father said as they coasted through the sleeping town. Kate peered out at the shops and restaurants—the windows that weren't still boarded up from the most recent hurricane were dark and empty—everyone somewhere warmer, better, until the high season.

MVP

For as long as Ziggy Miller could remember, Easter in Sea Point was an aggressive publicity stunt to resurrect the town like it was Jesus's only stop on his comeback tour. This was the first year, however, that Ziggy found the annual endeavor humiliating. He was sick of pandering to tourists, sick of everyone using his hometown as an escape from real life. Sea Point was not Disneyworld or the front cover of the Williams Sonoma Easter catalog, no matter how many papier-mâché eggs occupied the front lawns of the gingerbread houses on Ocean Avenue.

They did the same thing at Christmas, when the town took its cues from the likes of Bedford Falls and Whoville and hosted a meet-and-greet with Mr. and Mrs. Claus, a tour of the elves' workshop, and a highly competitive Shirtless Santa 1k on the beach that usually ended in a Shirtless Santa brawl on the boardwalk. Tourists came from far and wide for the big holidays in the off-season, eagerly escaping to this little fantasy beach town at the edge of the world.

Carrying a large rock through the empty church the night before Easter Sunday, Ziggy dropped it too close to the ball valve, almost breaking the new filter. One inch over and he would have busted the waterfall he'd spent all night building. He told himself to focus on the project—as ridiculous as it may be. Even if Sea Point was the only town he knew of that had an Easter pageant that included a waterfall and a Bruce Springsteen a cappella group, it was still a real place where real people lived and, as he knew all too well, real people died.

Ziggy couldn't believe that Walter Beam, the youth pastor who also ran the Sea Point Theater Troupe, had asked Ziggy to build the waterfall this year. Alone. But Walter had asked, and Ziggy had agreed, "Because yes is easier than no," Ziggy's mother used to say the night before school bake sales. She'd open the oven door, squint into the 400-degree heat, and pull out a fifth batch of brownies while explaining that volunteer work rarely involved volunteering but rather preying on those with the greatest sense of obligation or lowest tolerance of guilt. But that had been in another life.

Stepping away from the project, Ziggy wondered, how was a waterfall any sort of priority? Didn't Jesus live in the desert? Wasn't an Easter pageant that included a crucifixion a little intense for kids, even if the Springsteen a cappella group sang "Tougher Than the Rest"?

Emerging from St. Mary's Church well after dark, Ziggy cursed the sudden rainstorm as he hustled to his truck. Fiddling with the radio while waiting for the heat to kick in, Ziggy watched a silver Porsche SUV with Pennsylvania plates pull up and honk impatiently. He couldn't make out the driver's face in the glint of his rearview mirror, but Ziggy did see two white hands hovering above the wheel, fleshy parentheses of frustration asking the usual question of an idling car in a packed parking lot.

Ziggy gave the silver Porsche an apologetic wave before backing out and flicking on his turn signal to make a left onto Ocean Avenue. In February, he'd moved out of his apartment above the surf shop and back into his parents' house—or, rather, his mother's house—which meant he now had to drive across town, from West to East Sea Point, instead of walking a block to the little oasis he'd given up when his dad had dropped dead. But he had no choice, considering that only last night Bev had attempted to cut her hair again, most likely around four a.m., when the sleeping pill had partially worn off. Before heading out to work this morning, Ziggy had sat across from her at the kitchen table and mustered the grace to dub her hack job "very rock and roll" when it was actually very disturbing.

Now driving past two teenagers skateboarding with boogie boards tucked under their arms, Ziggy felt a wave of nostalgia. In spite of himself, he loved Sea Point. He loved that he'd grown up by the ocean, surrounded by nature he was free to explore without parental supervision. As a kid, he'd adventured alone or with a pack of boys via feet, bike, or board all over town, and during the off-season, if it got too cold or too dark, they'd wave down an oncoming car that undoubtedly belonged to a familiar face. He loved that, from an aerial view, the town appeared as an inverted heart—as if all elements of the natural world had conspired to illustrate just how special Sea Point was.

Of course, he hadn't always felt such affection for his hometown. Like most local kids, Ziggy had learned from the older boys in the back of the school bus that he'd grown up in what appeared to be the ball sack of New Jersey, America's armpit. In fairness, their interpretation was not wrong— an inverted heart shared a scrotal likeness. But most adults described the geography as an inverted heart. Some even capitalized on it: Every summer during the high season, Sea Point sold hundreds of thousands of dollars of merchandise emblazoned with a red heart stitched upside down, which had felt particularly apt to Ziggy since February.

Driving home alone in the dark, Ziggy considered his life's trajectory and instantly felt his shoulders tense from the particular weight of carrying a legacy. Miller Values Plumbing (MVP) had served as a pillar of the Sea Point community for three generations, beginning with Ziggy's grandfather, who'd returned from Vietnam a staunch believer in isolationism, daily vacuuming, and not dying in Hammonton, the town where he'd been born. When an army buddy offered him a job renovating a bar at the edge of nowhere, Ziggy's grandfather loaded his wife and nine-year-old son into a rusted-out truck and gunned it down the highway toward the family's fate.

"Before I could read a clock, I knew it was only a matter of time before I took over the business," Zeke used to say. The MVP origin story had played like a pop song throughout Ziggy's childhood, a track consistently introduced at every new client's house. Bored housewives, mesmerized by the handsome handyman, would linger near the leaking sink or ancient boiler and listen to the chorus line Ziggy knew by heart. "I started keeping my father's books when I was twelve and never stopped," Zeke would say, impressing young and old women alike, and making Ziggy beam with pride. His father could fix anything, and he'd taught Ziggy everything.

Almost everything, Ziggy thought now, switching on his high beams to alert the possums, raccoons, and foxes that he was heading their way. He drove toward the lighthouse, its beam appearing and disappearing in slow, tired circles. An empty Ocean Avenue stretched out before Ziggy, and it was impossible not to see the rest of his life in the endless concrete that led him toward more darkness.

His father had taught him how to install gas lines, reroute pipes, and repair everything from dishwashers to septic tanks. But the billing system had felt so instinctual to Zeke that he put off showing his own son how to calculate estimates and factor in material and labor costs. "It's just faster for me to do it," was Zeke's response whenever Ziggy asked about a customer's payment plan. "We're too busy," Zeke would say. "You have the rest of your life to learn that stuff."

And then, two months ago, at the age of fifty-four, Zeke dropped dead of a heart attack. He left his thirty-four-year-old son without an understanding of the books or a plan for the business. Every morning since February fifth, Ziggy had woken up with a metastasizing mass of grief at his center. He'd walk along the boardwalk and wonder at all the people laughing—how could they do it without Zeke Miller among them? Existing in the void of his father's absence felt like drowning in a black hole, except the gravitational pull was inside Ziggy, drawing him away from the world, toward nothing.

Imagining Zeke beside him was how Ziggy coped in the After. Here in the truck, his dad sat next to him, window down and cursing the bad radio reception before asking Ziggy if he was hungry, which is how Ziggy realized he'd never eaten dinner.

Pulling a U-turn and parking right in front of the Wawa, Ziggy found himself waiting in line, dazed, with a turkey hoagie and SunChips. He watched the hot dogs perambulate in their own grease before he opened his wallet and let his gaze travel lazily over the information on his driver's license: thirty-four years old. Five foot nine. One hundred seventy-six pounds. Blue eyes. Blond hair. Organ donor. Eyeing the king-size Butterfingers on display above the conveyor belt, he tried to remember what it was like to crave something. In the Before, he'd eaten a Butterfinger every night, a ritual he enjoyed in the privacy of his own apartment above the surf shop. Now just looking at the orange and blue wrapper made him feel queasy, which explained why he was no longer 176 pounds. In fact, Ziggy had lost so much weight since February that the only pants that still fit were his Carhartt overalls—and they didn't so much fit as hang from his shoulders.

"This it?" the cashier asked. Chipped white nail polish, brown hair, black eyeliner, and big blue eyes. She was new at the register but her face was familiar. They figured it out at the same time: Yates Academy. She had been in the grade above him, but since they hadn't seen each other in nearly twenty years, Meredith—that's right, Meredith Travers—looked much older now, haggard even, with crow's-feet and teeth the color of cornmeal. She'd played field hockey, an All-American, if Ziggy recalled correctly. On her left index finger sat a silver band with an empty setting, naked prongs jutting toward the fluorescent lights holding nothing but its breath. Ziggy told himself it was probably fine, she was probably fine. Maybe it was some sort of political or fashion statement. Not everyone was a disaster.

Ziggy accepted the change from his $20 and told Meredith it was good to see her, which it wasn't because she looked the way he felt. He stepped outside to eat on the green bench in front of his parked truck. The hoagie was even soggier than he'd dreaded.

"Nice night," Meredith Travers said a minute later, lighting the cigarette between her lips. He looked up and she smiled at him, her eighteen-year-old field-hockey star smile, and asked what he was up to the rest of the night—she'd just finished her shift.

"Summersault is still open," Ziggy suggested. "Want to get a drink?"

"How about your place?" she asked, eyeing him up and down. "You've gotten cuter since high school."

Ziggy patted his flat stomach. "Dead Dad diet," he said, stretching his arms above his head. No one wanted to talk about his father, but everyone was eager to comment on his weight. The consolation prize for losing his best friend, his mentor, his hero, *his dad*, was that he was finally getting attention from women. Ziggy wondered if Meredith could smell the grief on him, if it clung to him the way the tobacco clung to her. Grief in his hair, his fingernails, the cabin of his truck.

"Sure," he said. "Follow me?"

Ten minutes later, Meredith's sedan followed Ziggy's truck down a long seashell driveway that led not to Ziggy's house—where Bev was probably passed out in front of the television—but to Daffodil Cottage, one of the few surviving Victorians in Sea Point.

Most of the original Sea Point mansions had been razed after years of neglect, but Ziggy and his father had spent the better half of the last decade restoring Daffodil Cottage for the owners who were almost never there. Technically, the Miller men were just plumbers, but off the books, they could build anything. "We're dream-makers," Zeke had once said.

Daffodil Cottage now boasted both nineteenth-century charm and twenty-first-century luxuries, including a sauna, a small home theater, and a climbing wall for the children who preferred to summer on the Amalfi Coast. Zeke and Ziggy had been in the middle of renovating the basement—the owners wanted "the world's most savage man cave"—when Zeke had dropped dead. Ziggy was now trying to finish the project himself and just this past week had installed the six-by-six steam shower the owners had asked for by sending a link to one they liked in *Private Air Luxury Homes*.

Incredibly, the owners' ever-growing wish list had yet to include a security camera—they found the town's trusting community, its open-door policy, positively charming. They believed in keys, a standard alarm system with a type-in code, and local eyes. "The last thing we want to do is change the ethos of the neighborhood with security apps and floodlights," the owners had written in an email to Zeke and Ziggy years earlier. "We love Sea Point for its quaintness, and we trust you to watch over Daffodil Cottage for us."

Not everyone shared the owners' laissez-faire approach to security or their desire to preserve "its quaintness." In more recent years, a developer named Harry Leeper had discovered the untapped value of Sea Point and hastily purchased every empty lot to erect oversize houses. The new construction came with highly sensitive and extremely visible security systems, which was a quick way to illustrate the worth of the property without having to invest in quality materials or sustainable designs. It could be argued these added safety measures prevented break-ins, although the year-rounders would be quick to point out that burglary had never been an issue. Regardless of the reason, the fact of the matter was that no one had ever robbed Daffodil Cottage, even if Ziggy Miller broke into it most nights.

Since February, Ziggy was the only living local who carried the key and knew the code that opened Daffodil Cottage, which made it his house, his secret, and technically not a break-in. He told himself that it was just a little light trespassing. Totally harmless.

Ziggy inserted his key, punched in the code, and pushed open the front door. Flipping on the light switch, he listened to Meredith's predictable gasp as she took in the palatial living room, ogled the creamy cashmere throws folded over an immaculately white linen sofa, the plush shag rug that Ziggy would also describe as white but the owners would have been quick to specify was Mist. *Only the wealthy can surround themselves in so many shades of white without worrying,* Ziggy thought to himself, and not for the first time. Only the wealthy could pay other people to erase the tracks of their shoes, the trail of their dead skin cells, the history of their dirt.

"You've got great taste," Meredith said, and as she tossed him an All-American smile, Ziggy thought of all the girls before her who had said the exact same thing before collapsing into the exact same corner of the sofa. He crossed the room and as soon as he sat down next to her, Meredith climbed on top of him. "You know what's weird?" Meredith asked, unhooking his overalls before looking Ziggy in the eye. "For some reason, I always thought you were a scholarship kid, too."

SkyMiles

Sitting in the Delta lounge at San Francisco International Airport, Miles drained his coffee and ignored the incoming call from Ziggy. As his childhood best friend, Miles knew what Ziggy wanted, and since he couldn't do anything for him anytime soon, it was better to just avoid the situation altogether.

In the wake of Zeke's death, Ziggy had asked Miles to help him understand his father's accounting books—a stack of dog-eared composition notebooks kept in a cardboard box out in the garage next to spare plumbing parts. Ziggy had gently nudged Miles a dozen times in the last three months since he had agreed at the funeral to take a look, but now that he was back on the other side of the country, the thought of sorting through Zeke's records and seeing his awful handwriting seemed way too depressing.

Besides, he'd just taken a 10 mg raspberry gummie for the flight and could not be trusted with the careful handling Ziggy now required.

Miles's phone buzzed again. This time it was a text from Brozetomen. There was little worse in life than being pressured to have fun with people you'd long outgrown and would feel fine about never seeing again. After Josh Praetaker texted a picture of his business-class pod from LaGuardia, Miles muted the group he would be spending the next seventy-two hours with at a ranch outside Bozeman, Montana. They'd barely spoken in over a decade but Miles's sophomore year college roommate, Kevin, needed warm bodies to fill the tuxedos on his wedding day and what were fraternity brothers for if not heavily documented tribal gatherings with open bars?

In honor of "the best years of his life," Kevin's wedding would be held at Princeton, their alma mater, in the chapel, which made Miles kind of want to die. After graduation, Kevin had moved back to his hometown of Malvern, Pennsylvania, and eventually proposed to his high school sweetheart. They'd put a down payment on a four-bedroom house and another down payment on an unborn Labradoodle. They were doing the thing Miles had no interest in doing, much to his girlfriend Chloe's dismay.

Miles's bond with Brozetomen was anchored in one weekend the spring of freshman year, when they'd been locked in a basement for forty-eight hours with Miley Cyrus on repeat, two kegs to empty between eight pledges, and no food. They'd taken turns hoisting Ned, the smallest, on their shoulders to dump the bucket of feces and urine up and out of the single garden-level window. Years later, a knotted rope of nostalgia, loneliness, and an acute fear of aging lassoed them together at bachelor parties and weddings.

Another text, this one from Chloe asking if he'd made it to his gate.

Miles wrote back immediately—yes, with plenty of time. Why did even the most attractive woman at the company Christmas party devolve into an anxious, sexless camp counselor with a Pinterest clipboard full of neutral handbags after two years of dating? She followed up with a question about socks that was too much for him before his second cup of coffee, so he opened his email instead and did a double take at his mother's name.

Jo Hoffman rarely sent emails—everything could be sent over text or said on the phone. Granted, he'd put his mother on DO NOT DISTURB mode after she became apoplectic about Minnie Hastings's backhand—but he was not, nor would he ever be, the appropriate audience for commentary on women's doubles. Before he could talk himself out of it, Miles forced himself to click on the (no subject) subject line.

My Dearest Miles,

I've tried calling you several times but I keep getting your voice mail, which is full. You really need to clean that out in case of emergencies. More importantly, after much discussion and thoughtful consideration, I've decided the Wharf is not a monarchy but a democracy and, as such, my successor will be nominated by the board rather than appointed by me. Yes, I'm aware I am 52 percent of the board so in the end it will still be my decision, which is my preferred take on democracy. (Also: I took Kathy to see *Hamilton* for her birthday and even though it's a shame she didn't get to enjoy the original cast, the new Aaron Burr is delicious.)

Take a breath, honey. Eric was disappointed until I explained you two will keep your board seats. Now he is elated and planning a six-month vacation to South America. You will continue to benefit financially from the Wharf—you just won't be a shoo-in CEO, which makes sense since you live on the other side of the country with a full in-box.

Don't see this as a punishment but as an opportunity—you are now free to do whatever you want, to pursue any passion, travel to any corner of the world to find happiness. Making you CEO would have been clipping my favorite bird's beautiful wings.

All my love.

Miles stared at the letter. Was he so high that he was hallucinating? Was he too high to call his mother?

"But we *have* discussed it," Jo said on the phone, moments later. She was panting on her Peloton, trying to rehab her knee in time to beat Minnie Hastings in the spring doubles tournament. "Your go-to line when we talked in the Maldives was that you didn't care." It was true that Miles was not currently interested in working for Hoffman LLC, but that didn't mean he was ready to give up his birthright.

"I didn't care while we were *on vacation*," Miles stage-whispered, doubling over as he yelled into the phone. A middle-aged woman with thick-framed glasses sitting across from him, sipping a martini before their ten a.m. flight, looked up from her magazine with intrigue, so he cupped the phone. It was with his hand as a makeshift cubicle that Miles suggested maybe his mother had suffered a stroke that none of her underlings had been brave enough to tell her about. In the silence, he heard her smile. She was relishing his distress.

"Hold on," Jo said. "Let me conference you in with Eric and Vince."

Miles felt his whole body start to vibrate and it wasn't from the coffee. As his mother put him on hold, Miles couldn't decide if he was angriest at Jo, his brother, or Jo's lawyer who'd probably told her this new plan was a great idea.

Jo cleared her throat as she returned to the line. "You there?" she asked.

Miles sucked in his breath. "Mom, let's keep this between us. We don't need Vince to sort out our family shit and Eric is a fucking idiot."

Jo inhaled and began to call him honey just as Vince the lawyer offered an awkward hello, and that's when Miles heard the distinct, high-pitched laugh of his older brother, Eric.

"That was mad harsh, bro," he said. Thankfully, Eric never took anything too seriously, in large part because Eric was almost always drunk or high or both, even if Jo refused to acknowledge it. Unlike their dad, Ari, who'd fled to Florida years ago when the brothers were still in Velcro sneakers, Eric wasn't a mean addict but a dopey, low-functioning man-child. He'd shown the greatest professional promise this past year by failing to show up to work at the Wharf and instead sitting in Jo Hoffman's finished basement all day, playing videogames, dabbling in amateur poker, and waiting for food delivery. And because of Jo, who'd never not bankrolled him, Eric had decided this was a lucrative career. When Miles had pointed this out in previous conversations, Jo's response was always, "What do you want me to do?"

This was why Miles didn't go home. Although he still admired Eric from a historical perspective—the legend of a big brother casts a long shadow—Eric was a disaster and everyone in Sea Point knew it. Technically, he was a manager at the Wharf, but his corner office sat empty seven days a week, which was a relief to the other managers, who had enough work to do without managing their boss.

"Eric, hey, sorry," Miles said, running his sweaty, shaky palms on his travel-day black athleisure-wear pants. He was about to explain how this was all a big shock to him when he heard a loud buzz over the sound of running water and realized Eric had decided this conference call was the perfect time to brush his teeth.

"You'll still get plenty of money, Miles," Jo yelled over the buzzing.

Vince the lawyer echoed the sentiment and prattled on about shares and percentages. But they all knew it wasn't about the money, just as they all knew that Eric was gurgling Listerine, now spitting it out, now running a shower.

"We're so proud of you for all your success in real estate, honey," Jo purred, unaware of how condescending she sounded. "But the Wharf needs someone who has more business experience than a listing agent. At least for now!" She and Vince chuckled at this in a scripted way that made Miles think she'd made the joke before, behind his back.

"Of course, if you want to put Wharton to use," Jo dangled expertly, "that could change things."

Ten years ago, after graduating from Princeton and in direct response to his older brother's failings, Miles had followed in his mother's footsteps and aced his way through Wharton—the University of Pennsylvania's graduate business school. If he was honest with himself, the crowning moment of the experience hadn't been when he'd found out he'd ranked fifth in his class, but when his mother, an alum, had handed him his diploma onstage and said, "I'm so proud of you." But that had been a decade ago, and since then, he'd been dicking around in commercial real estate.

His phone beeped with another incoming call. Ziggy again. Miles ignored it.

"I'll come back before Memorial Day," Miles said to his mother, a plan taking shape behind the dark, handsome face that had served him well his whole life. In one swift cross-country move, he would win back his birthright, help his best friend, and slip away from his cloying girlfriend.

"Seriously, Mom, don't do anything before I get home."

As soon as he hung up, Miles sent Ziggy a text: *Can't talk but coming to Sea Point. Will take a look at your dad's books. See you soon, brother.*

For the first time in years, Miles felt adrenaline pulse through him—finally, there were stakes in his life. He had something to fight for, and no one was a tougher sell or a shrewder magnate than his mother. Only now did Miles see how he'd been treading water in San Francisco, waiting for what came next and praying it wasn't just the middle-aged paunch of resignation tucked into every pair of dad khakis.

This was it, and he was hungry. Jo would see how business savvy he'd become and he would honor Zeke by getting his financial accounts in order for Ziggy. Miles could use the Millers to further demonstrate what he could do with a flailing family business: MVP would have its most profitable year yet, thanks to Miles, and as a result, Jo would have no choice but to give the Wharf to him. Everything would pan out if Miles put in the work.

Plus, he'd heard Bell was back in town.

Big Things vs. Small Things

"**I** can't believe it's been three weeks since you called me," Bernadette said to Kate over the TV in their parents' living room. "It feels like yesterday but also kinda like a year ago?" Dirk and Sally were out to dinner at the Wharf, just the two of them, and Bernadette was babysitting her thirty-three-year-old sister.

"How are the job applications going?" Bernadette asked.

Ignoring the not-so-subtle attempt to steer the conversation toward the topic of employment, Kate pointed out that her favorite actor in *Wives with Knives* was ambidextrous and married to a much younger man.

"Kate," Bernadette interrupted, "we have to talk about your future."

"No, we don't."

"Yes, we do." Bernadette, like most firstborns, didn't understand no.

"But I don't have a future," Kate said, taking a swig of her full wineglass before promptly crying over her pizza. Her future had been with Thomas—first on Jane Street while he climbed the surgical ranks and she the corporate ladder at Artemis, and then eventually in New Hampshire, having kids, sending them to Evergreen. Thomas had promised.

Bernadette patted her knee and said that this was for the best, she was better off alone. Kate rolled her eyes and searched for the remote control to turn up the volume. Her sister was oblivious to the offensive nature of such platitudes because she'd never had her heart broken. Bernadette held up the remote like a hostage and added, "You know I never liked him," which, of course, Kate did know. In fact, four Thanksgivings ago, Bernadette had even drunkenly told Kate that Thomas was "the one before the one" and then felt compelled to elaborate by saying he was "an overrated rich kid."

But sisters could be uniquely awful, and that was the same Thanksgiving when Bernadette's husband, Rob, announced he was quitting law to develop an app, so Kate had assumed the comment was misplaced. Later that same evening, Bernadette had succeeded in persuading Rob to remain at Lucas, Collins & Nickerson, but she hadn't convinced Kate to drop Thomas.

"Maybe you should talk to someone," Bernadette murmured, popping open a fresh seltzer. Kate shook her head—she'd already explored and exhausted the idea. There were three therapists in Sea Point. One was Kate's retired high school gym teacher, who'd been gruff enough about her performance in badminton. The second Kate had seen once in college, who'd more or less suggested she develop an eating disorder as a means to control her anxiety. The third was a regionally renowned clinical psychologist who everyone raved about—Kate had once overheard a young woman croon in the Acme, "Jenny Kim is a lifesaver." Unfortunately, Jenny Kim was also the mother of Georgina Kim, Kate's ex-best friend, so that was a no-go.

"He's a real sociopath, doing it in public, at your diner," Bernadette stated, laying out the facts of the case slowly, painfully, and not for the first time. "But to be fair, Rob and I thought he was a sociopath from the beginning."

"He said it was to end where we began," Kate sniffled. "He thought closing the circle would be helpful in moving forward."

"He just didn't want you to break any of that artwork his grandparents bought wholesale from the Nazis."

Kate pursed her lips and twirled a spool of cheese around her finger before giving it to Homer, her parents' geriatric mutt. He consumed it quickly but kept his eyes on her, suspicious, and in her head, Kate returned to saying goodbye to Thomas on Jane Street. What she couldn't admit to her sister any more than she could confess to herself was that when she'd begged Thomas to reconsider—as she'd successfully done twice during med school, once during residency and yet again during fellowship—Thomas had looked her in the eye and said he couldn't mislead her any longer. "I love you but I'm not *in* love with you, Kate. I wish I were, but I'm not—and I've tried to be. But we're just . . . over. For real this time. For good. And I'm sorry but I know it's the right thing to do—for both of us."

"You're not eating," Bernadette announced like a verdict.

"And you're not drinking," Kate retorted.

"It's too early or I'd tell you."

"Tell me what?" Kate asked, batting her eyelashes and feigning innocence.

Bernadette stared at the TV, as if she were suddenly engrossed in the rerun of an episode that both sisters had seen so many times they compulsively said the lines aloud with the actors.

"Don't worry, I won't jinx it," Kate said in a wine-chugging competition with herself. "You're too fertile to be jinxed, anyway."

"How would you know?"

"Your supple thighs, your pillow lips, your fertile folds."

"STOP!" Bernadette shrieked. Perhaps the greatest curse for a big sister was the vicious memory of a younger sister. These lines were a direct quote from Derek Urgar, Bernadette's high school boyfriend who had been an aspiring poet. Ultimately, he had given up verse and followed in his father's dentistry footsteps—a more fitting profession, according to everyone.

"Fertile folds," Kate recited, this time as Sir David Attenborough. "Who knew that a creature as beautiful as a Bernadette Campbell, known for her aggressive demeanor in the courtroom, could also be in possession of such impressively fertile folds in the bedroom?"

Bernadette reached over and twisted Kate's nipple through her shirt. Kate shrieked, but instead of pinching her back, she wiped her greasy hands on Bernadette's jeans, the expensive black ones she knew Bernadette loved, which made her sister scream before grabbing Kate by her matted five-day rat's nest of a topknot and pushing her face down into the couch cushions.

If their parents had been home, Sally would have barked at them to stop it this instant, and Dirk would have dryly stated they were going to break something without looking up from his stack of grading papers. Alone, they were free to regress into teenagers.

It took a moment before Kate realized the two forces digging into the meat beneath her wing bones were Bernadette's kneecaps. Her thirty-eight-year-old sister was on top of her, using one hand to hold Kate's two arms behind her back and the other hand to shove her skull farther into the couch.

"What is wrong with you!?" Bernadette yelled from above.

Kate tried to respond but the cushion made for a surprisingly efficient gag.

"I said, what is wrong with you?" Bernadette snapped.

Through the increasing amount of blood rushing to her head, Kate could hear her sister ask a third time, which was when she stopped trying to regain control of her arms and instead let her body go limp.

"EVERYTHING!" Kate hollered, muffled, just as Bernadette hopped off her back. "EVERYTHING IS WRONG WITH ME!"

Surprised by Bernadette's silence, Kate sat up and looked at her imprisoner, who was laughing too hard to make any noise until she let out a sound so appalling, so jarring, so clearly a hee-haw, that they stared at each other before cracking up. The hee-haw—what their father called the Bernadonkey—was so off-putting that Bernadette had been careful to never let anyone outside the family hear it. It was music to Kate's ears as hot tears rolled down her cheeks. Her beautiful sister had the world's ugliest laugh and there was something so wonderfully just about that.

"Everything is wrong with you," Bernadette repeated, standing up and walking into the kitchen. "Truer words have never been spoken." She returned with ice-cream sandwiches and handed one to Kate. "You need a plan."

"It's April. In Sea Point. My plan is don't die."

"You could go on a trip."

Kate swirled her wine as if she hadn't just poured it from a box. How could she have known Mexico would be her last trip with Thomas? She hadn't expected any lasts and now she was drowning in them.

"From a financial standpoint," Kate said, "it would be more responsible to just stay here and freeze to death than go to some island only to drown or disappear or get sold for parts."

"But don't you have a ton of money saved?" Bernadette asked. "Since you didn't pay rent?" Her judgment floated to the surface of the question like an oily film.

When Thomas's great-aunt had died in the Jane Street apartment four years earlier and Thomas called Kate at work with the news, she'd promised herself she would use the opportunity to save up, but it had been hard because of—and here a sledgehammer T-boned her sternum—Thomas.

Throughout the course of their relationship, Thomas had paid for the big things—the mid-century furniture he loved that crowded their first apartment, fit their second, and begged for siblings on Jane Street. Because Thomas claimed to have stronger opinions about aesthetics, he didn't hesitate to put the bedframe, dining table, desk, sofa, and chairs on the credit card that then provided his free airfare in triple the points.

In their previous apartments, they'd split the rent and the utilities, but because it was Thomas's grandparents who owned the building in which they now hosted grown-up dinner parties, Kate had insisted she pay the utilities—before learning how inefficient the old building was. The water bill alone was a slap across the face, but she couldn't walk back the offer.

And then this weird thing tended to happen when they went grocery shopping or ordered takeout or dressed up to go to the new Thai restaurant Thomas had suggested they try, just the two of them: When it was time to pay the bill, Thomas would suddenly be on his phone, typing furiously about something sensitive and medical, something that his eyebrows telegraphed as life or death. As a result, Kate paid for the exorbitant groceries—Thomas loved doing taste tests with cheese—the gourmet dinners in, the shockingly expensive brunches out, the never-ending dry cleaning and cab fare. The cabs weren't bad in the beginning—Jane Street was conveniently located, after all—but then Thomas's friend Grady bought a luxury condo in Brooklyn with a roof deck that boasted 360-degree views that they loved to visit. It was right around the same time that Grady closed on the condo that Thomas decided switching subway lines was too much of a hassle.

Sitting in her parents' house with her sister, Kate realized how intimidated she'd been to talk about money—really talk about it—with Thomas. They'd had one conversation about it, early on, when they were a year out of college and still in their first apartment. Thomas had dragged Kate to see an Eames lounge chair and ottoman he desperately wanted and which cost a hilarious $5,500—except that Thomas wasn't joking. Kate still remembered how her mouth had hung open as Thomas made delivery arrangements with the sales associate, which is when he turned to her and said, "How about I get the big things, and you get the little things?" At the time, it sounded reasonable, and that one conversation had guided the next decade of shared expenses. The trouble, Kate learned far too late, was that the little things collected as quietly as the gum wrappers and receipts in the bottom of her bag until she realized the weight she was carrying around amounted to nothing. After all those years, she had no proof of the small things—the monthly Wi-Fi bill, the cab ride home, the $15 side of guacamole—but she was pretty sure they ended up costing more than the big things, and without any of the glamour that accompanies a white-glove delivery.

Bernadette exhaled and looked down at her hands. "If you're going to live here," she said, adopting her courtroom voice, "you need to A, get a job, and B, get your shit together so you don't kill Mom and Dad."

Kate considered this for a moment and said, "Clearly Mom hasn't informed you of her newest steps record."

In the past few years, ever since their father had given their mother his old Garmin watch, Sally Campbell had revealed a competitive edge that could only be rivaled by their father, Dirk, a triathlete for forty years. The high school sweethearts had become high school history teachers and, without any interest in retirement, the dynamic duo now completed a workout every morning before seven a.m. This was roughly four hours before Kate got up to eat the corners off saltine crackers and watch old episodes of *Arrested Development* unironically.

She refused to read. Reading reminded her of Thomas. They'd been in a two-person book club for the last three years and while she'd enjoyed nearly everything, Thomas had found each work lacking. He had scoffed at living writers for being too contemporary, dead writers for being outdated, and little-known writers as, "well, there's a reason they don't have much of a following." When she'd first returned home and reached for her favorite novel as a literary Xanax, Thomas still managed to sour the prologue as she heard him say, "They all try too hard."

"I'm serious," Bernadette said, turning off the TV. "I know you've taken a real hit here and I am one hundred percent on your team, but I'll resent you if you kill Mom and Dad with your grief."

"Trust me, they are way too into each other to notice my grief," Kate asserted with mild disgust. Only the night before she'd walked in on her parents rounding second base in the kitchen. "Besides," Kate added quietly, "sometimes people just die."

They both knew who she meant. Three months before Kate had come home, Zeke Miller—their neighbor and the town plumber—had suffered a heart attack and died in the back of an ambulance. His son, Ziggy—Kate's first friend—had been with him.

"Have you seen him?" Bernadette asked. "Ziggy, I mean."

Kate shook her head. "Only his truck backing out of the driveway. It seems weird to go over just to bring up his dead dad."

"It would be nice to acknowledge," Bernadette said. "Especially since I'm handling the probate. I wish you'd come home for the funeral—there must have been three hundred people packed into that church."

Kate nodded absently. She'd been on a tiny island in Mexico at the time of Zeke's funeral. Thomas's friends were "chosen family" as they constantly touted, and Thomas was their quiet, charming patriarch. They organized multiple group trips every year, which Kate bragged about on-line almost as much as she hated attending in real life. Even twelve years into the relationship, she still felt like Thomas's tagalong girlfriend who didn't understand the inside jokes from the Naked Dance their freshman fall. There was also the fact that Thomas's chosen family had all been in-volved with each other—couples and threesomes and allegedly, as they often alluded to with conspiratorial ambiguity, a fivesome. Although she and Thomas had never discussed it, Kate guessed the group resented her for removing Thomas from their seemingly endless game of musical, con-jugal chairs.

Sitting next to Bernadette on their parents' couch, Kate felt queasy: Instead of attending Zeke's funeral, she'd once again tried—and failed—to win over Thomas's pals. Rather than heading home to support her oldest friend, Kate had flown off to ingratiate herself. It should have been Kate who understood that Ziggy would be lost without Zeke, and yet it had been Bernadette who'd insisted on handling the probate, who'd quietly hired a babysitter so she could contact Zeke's bank and accountant with-out her three-year-old daughter Clementine screaming in the back-ground. Kate had never even sent Ziggy a sympathy card. At the time, her priorities had felt so appropriate—of course the group trip trumped Zeke Miller's funeral. *What did it matter*, she had rationalized, *since Zeke was already gone?*

Remembering that first night in Mexico now, she felt her chest clench with shame. Swaying with the breeze after they'd ordered drinks and apps at the hotel bar, Ashley had said, "It's so amazing how undiscovered this place is." The food arrived and Ashley, who said her allergies made eating practically impossible, took out her vape pen.

"Yeah," Jake agreed, reaching over Kate for the chips. "I'd say we should come back, but give it a few years and it'll be so Tulum."

"Tulum?" Kate had asked, assuming it was an adjective she didn't know.

"A town north of here," Thomas explained, rubbing her back. "I went in high school, before it exploded. It's the opposite of this place, which is still a secret."

"But it's not really a secret," Kate said slowly. "We're staying at a five-star resort. The iPad default setting is English."

Ashley, who'd been looking up at the palm trees, narrowed her eyes on Kate as a lioness might focus on an injured antelope. Kate stumbled as she tried to elaborate. "I mean, if we're here, you know, well, we—we know about it—"

"*I* knew about it," Bradley interrupted, tilting his head and glaring at Kate as if he'd only just registered that the oversize gnat next to Thomas could speak.

"Kate's got a point," chimed in Nora, nodding as she gulped down her margarita. "As inconvenient as that truth might be to your fragile little egos," she joked, swatting at Jake. She was the only one of Thomas's friends who didn't seem to resent Kate's presence. Back in New York, she would text Kate separately to invite her to her gallery's public events, even when she knew Thomas would be working. Yes, Nora wore thousand-dollar scarves into the ocean and routinely flew to Finland to "unplug for the weekend," but Nora was still the most grounded of the group.

Thomas squeezed Kate's knee as a peace offering and a reminder that they were on vacation, that she should play nice. "Either way, this is the most beautiful place I've ever been," she said, because it was true.

"Even more beautiful than New Jersey?" Bradley quipped, and the tittering that followed made Kate see herself as they did: a Jersey girl. That was the paradox about being a local somewhere—it made you an outsider everywhere else.

"But where are you from, really?" Jake had asked. "I have a cousin in Tenafly."

"That's North Jersey," Kate explained. "Sea Point is more South Jersey—it's shaped like an inverted heart."

"Never heard of it," Ashley said, squashing a mosquito on her bare shoulder and sounding bored.

"I guess that makes it more undiscovered than this place," Nora quipped, slipping a sly grin to Kate who nearly spit out her margarita. No one else laughed.

In a rare act of generosity, Bradley offered Kate his full attention. "Inverted?" he asked.

Kate nodded enthusiastically. Maybe she could finally get somewhere with Bradley, with all of them. "You've probably seen it on a sweatshirt and didn't realize." This, much to her surprise, made everyone laugh. And then Thomas coughed, and she realized that "inverted" was yet another inside joke among them, the college friends, that she could only reach toward through locked gates—like Gramercy Park, to which Thomas's family possessed a key, even though none of them lived on the park. From a red grosgrain ribbon the key hung on a hook to the right of their elevator door, and one either did or didn't know what it could unlock. Kate had made the mistake of asking once. Thomas's father had chortled— only a certain kind of rich white man didn't laugh but chortled.

And that certain kind of rich white man's children—these kids asking for another round of Mezcal—from SoHo and the Hollywood Hills— were citizens of the world, cultural plunderers who worshipped at the altar of self-realization and lit candles beneath their framed group portraits from Burning Man. While Kate spent her college breaks working, they planned hiking expeditions to Patagonia in the holy endeavor of disconnecting and chartered private cruises to the Arctic Circle where they captioned their selfies, "Because polar bears."

Kate was simple compared to them. She'd never been to Burning Man or Patagonia—or the Galápagos, or Lantau Island, or Carnival. It was fine, she told herself, they were Thomas's friends. But what she didn't own up to until after he'd dumped her was that when Bradley mentioned New Jersey and everyone had tittered, Thomas had laughed the hardest. It might have even been a chortle.

After one more episode of *Wives with Knives*, Kate and Bernadette retired to Kate's bedroom to check on Clementine and squeeze into the double bed.

"It's so unfair you still have your room," Bernadette whined, pulling back the blue cotton sheets, soft after twenty years' worth of cold rinses and low tumbles.

"You have a whole house now," Kate yawned. "A really nice house."

Five years ago, Bernadette and her husband had been successful, on-the-rise lawyers in Philadelphia. Rob was still a hotshot litigator and commuted four days a week, while Bernadette had decided the previous year that she wanted to try being a full-time stay-at-home mom after Clementine had broken her arm at daycare. Kate wasn't sure how well Bernadette's new career was going, especially when Bernadette showed up at their parents' house in a skirt suit and black pumps when her only meetings took place on the playground with other moms.

"It's not the same," Bernadette complained. "I don't get why as soon as I left for college, they jumped into reclaiming their space, but with you—they just did some light dusting to maintain your shrine."

"It's not a shrine."

It was totally a shrine. They both knew it. During her four years at Sea Point High, Kate had squeezed every ribbon, trophy, award, sash, and cash prize out of her school with the same zeal as that of a bully shaking down smaller kids for their lunch money. She had, in fact, been called an academic bully for her predatory performances during Model UN and Debate Club. Senior year, when Kate crossed the stage to be recognized for her excellent performance on all of her AP tests, the National French Exam, and for even being named a Scholastic Arts and Writing Award

National Medalist, it was rumored that she had corrected the principal's grammar as she shook his hand.

While Bernadette's achievements were more physical—four years on the varsity volleyball and track teams and named both homecoming and prom queen her senior year—Kate had followed in her parents' cerebral footsteps. Her intact childhood bedroom reflected not only Kate's bookish talents but also the legacy of her parents' own erudite ways. As two nerds, Dirk and Sally had no idea how they'd raised Bernadette—a spandex-wearing, volleyball setter prom queen—but Kate's accomplishments made immediate sense to them. Her interests were familiar to their own, which meant they were easier to celebrate.

Through heavy eyelids, Kate admired her sister's face. Bernadette had always been naturally breathtaking, but her recent Peter Pan haircut only accentuated the delicate perfection of her features. It was a startling, indiscreet beauty. "Only you can pull off that pixie cut," Kate murmured.

"I showed them that picture of Michelle Williams."

"Same thing," Kate sighed. "Only you and your famous twin can pull off that pixie cut."

Bernadette laughed and twirled a fistful of Kate's hair around her fingers. "I read that she keeps it short for Heath Ledger. Should we chop off yours? New 'do, new you?"

Kate shook her head. Thomas liked her hair long.

In the best dream she'd had since April eighth, Thomas wouldn't stop kissing her cheek, peck after peck after peck. It was so ludicrous that Kate giggled loudly enough to wake herself up and see Clementine leaning over her, mouth still puckered in her mid-kiss blitz. "Mommy says you have to get up."

As she was quick to declare to anyone anywhere, Clementine was "two and four-quarters" with cropped blond hair made entirely of cowlicks, Bernadette's wide-set brown eyes, and Rob's Betty Boop eyelashes, which were so dark and long that Bernadette had twice been chastised in the

Acme for putting mascara on her toddler. Kate adored every inch of her niece and took a particular pride in the fact that Clem had inherited the Campbell mouth—pouty rose-petal lips eager to turn upward into a devilish smile at the first hint of a dare, as it did now when Clem told her aunt, "We're going to the library."

This was news to Kate, who picked up her phone to text the despot downstairs. Bernadette had anticipated this reaction, however, and had already texted, *Just come.*

The library was a twenty-minute walk from the Campbell house—it sat on the corner of Ocean Avenue and Sunset Boulevard, right in the center of Sea Point. "The last time I came here was for SAT prep," Kate said as she pulled open the library's red door and received an immediate smack in the face. It was the smell of childhood: spilled apple juice and the distantly familiar odor that, as a kid, Kate could only describe as "weird," but which she could now identify as mold comingling with mildew under the industrial gray carpeting.

Although the library smelled the same as it had thirty years earlier, it sounded entirely different. Growing up, the library hummed along to its own soundtrack—the cheerful beeping of books being checked out; the crinkling of laminated covers being opened and closed, pulled and returned to the shelf; the whir of the photocopier as high school kids worked on research projects. It had been a bustling hot spot back in the day, a social hub where Kate could reliably run into three friends from school and at least one adult who would offer Kate a butterscotch or a ride home.

Now, the place appeared as dead as most of the authors whose work lined the shelves.

And smaller.

Since her last visit for SAT prep, she'd spent hours in the NYU libraries and then exploring the New York Public Library, which, as Thomas loved to tell visitors emerging from Penn Station, was ranked the second-largest library in the country and third-largest in the world. The Sea Point library wouldn't rank for anything, Kate thought now, except for maybe that new gigantic ant farm separating the two public computers from the non-fiction stacks. Kate walked closer to inspect. The ant farm was freestanding and the size of the whiteboard in the Artemis PR breakroom, maybe six by five, with four legs elevating the sheet of glass several feet off the ground. Who'd thought that was a good idea?

"I don't know why Patricia greenlit that," Bernadette said over her shoulder. They exchanged the most subtle of conspiratorial looks the way only sisters can. "Did you see your artwork has held up? Sort of, anyway."

Unlike the rest of the library's beige walls, the alcove on the other side of the checkout desk was a mural of rainbows, stars, animals, and recognizable literary characters, including Babar, Pippi Longstocking, Amelia Bedelia, and Arthur the aardvark. In high school, Kate had helped paint the mural as part of a community service project (for which she later won the award she'd banked on to round out her junior fall transcript). Kate smiled at Babar's faded green suit, and Pippi's red braids, which were now more of a sun-bleached orange. A commendable depiction of Roald Dahl's character Matilda sat in the corner atop a pile of books and below the floating quotation Kate had spent a week's worth of fall afternoons emboldening with black paint:

> "These books gave Matilda a hopeful and
> comforting message:
> You are not alone."

Bernadette gave Clementine an encouraging push on the bottom to go find a seat with the two dozen or so other cross-legged children who'd assembled on a big red apple-shaped rug. It was nearly time for Story Hour—the same Wednesday morning event Bernadette and Kate had attended as kids. Watching her bowlegged niece navigate the carpeted pecking order, Kate breathed a sigh of relief when a girl waved Clem over, having saved her a seat right in front.

Directly centered under the arch of the rainbow that Kate's ex-best friend had painted fifteen years earlier was a green velvet armchair that didn't look tired so much as exhausted. It was Ms. Rose's chair, as any local could tell you. And this morning belonged to Ms. Rose, who held Story Hour in this corner every Wednesday from ten to eleven a.m., just as she had done every week for the past forty years.

"Are you nervous to see her?" Bernadette asked Kate.

It was nearly ten o'clock now, and Ms. Rose emerged from the women's bathroom and settled into her chair, peeling off the crocheted doilies on the armrests only to place them back down in the exact same spot, clearly outlined by the silhouettes of dust. After smoothing out her long black skirt, Ms. Rose crossed her ankles, popped open her can of Diet Pepsi, and took several long gulps. She fluffed the black lumbar pillow she always brought before smiling at it, as if the pillow were a loyal pet, and ran a bony finger around her mouth to catch any stray pink lipstick. With a game-faced solemnity, Ms. Rose cracked all of her knuckles before preemptively licking her thumbs and pointer fingers for expedient page turning.

"She's exactly the same!" Kate gasped. Bernadette nodded, her smile smug, her eyes on the green chair.

With a disdainful sort of grace, Ms. Rose scrunched her nose, closed her eyes, clutched the gold cross around her neck, and whispered the Hail Mary prayer. When she finished and opened her eyes, she seemed disappointed that the kids still sat before her. Although no one understood why Ms. Rose loathed children, everyone knew why she continued to read to them—her contract from the late '70s was iron-clad, providing benefits and a steady annual pay raise, despite the fact that she now worked one-fortieth of the hours that she had when she'd started. But nobody said anything because, for some mysterious reason, all of the children at Story Hour worshipped Ms. Rose. The cost of retaining a local celebrity was easy enough for the library board to overlook.

"She's more Scrooge than Mr. Rogers," Kate observed as Ms. Rose looked out at her audience with palpable revulsion. While Ms. Rose went over the litany of Story Hour rules (No Talking, No Laughing, No Clapping, Certainly No Cheering, etc.), Bernadette nudged Kate and signaled with her eyes to look right. Over her shoulder, Patricia Higginbottom frantically waved from the checkout desk.

"Well, look who's back!" Patricia exclaimed, wrapping her arms around Kate. As Patricia gushed about how beautiful she looked—was her hair longer or shorter?—three massive black dogs emerged from behind the checkout desk and lumbered toward Kate. In contrast to Patricia's rail-thin six-foot frame, which was always as freshly tucked and starched as a luxury hotel bed, the three dogs were hefty and unkempt.

"Were they crossbred with bears?" Kate asked.

"They're Newfoundlands," Patricia answered, amused. "They're my therapy dogs—Oscar, Maude, and Babycakes. Oh, I love your bag."

The vintage leather tote had been a gift from Bernadette, who beamed as Kate blushed because Patricia had impeccable taste. It was one of several reasons she stood out in Sea Point.

Another: The sleuth of bears by her side.

Another: Her accent.

Patricia was quick to remind anyone who asked about her drawl that she was a proud southerner who'd just so happened to have spent her childhood in New York, her teen years in New Hampshire, and her college years in Boston. Like any foreign language student, Kate had learned to translate each of these clauses into conjunctions of wealth, but even after fifteen years of listening to it in New York, she knew she would never be a native speaker. You were either born fluent in affluence or you weren't.

Despite all her time in New England, Patricia retained a thick southern drawl that Kate found warm and intoxicating, like honey poured straight from the jar. Her first husband, Lyle, the son of a local commercial fishing king, had swept Patricia off her feet at a wedding in Austin fifteen years ago. She'd given up her penthouse to live in Sea Point with him, and to everyone's shock, when they broke up four years later, Lyle left and Patricia stayed. She'd since bunked up with Chad, the hot life-guard of Kate's childhood, who was now husband number two and still attractive and still lifeguarding. Every Halloween, he dressed as David Hasselhoff from *Baywatch* by sporting his red swim trunks, sans shirt, and handing out candy from a torpedo buoy he'd sliced in half.

"I'm so sorry about your ex," Patricia sighed sympathetically. Kate shot Bernadette an accusing glare, but her sister stared at Ms. Rose, apparently too enthralled by Story Hour to engage in conversation. "What a ding-dong dud to have given you up."

Kate had spent ten years at the same PR firm but no one had reached out to say a bad word about Thomas after the breakup—how could they? He was a Mosby. His mother ran the company. Hannah from one desk over, who'd often brought up the "toxic web of nepotism," had most likely celebrated Kate's departure by scavenging her top-drawer collection of mint gum.

"I heard you've moved back for good," Patricia said, ignoring Kate's wince. "Any chance I can tempt you with a job?"

Kate smiled. "Do you mean here or at the Jetty Bar?" Back when Kate spent summers slinging drinks, Patricia had been one of her regulars, and patrons of the Jetty Bar were more faithful than most spouses.

"Actually, I hear they could use the help too, but I could use it more," Patricia said. "My summer associate just won an internship in the city so I'm down a morning person."

Kate swallowed hard. She'd been one of those girls who'd earned a one-way ticket out of Sea Point, who'd never looked back. And now, here she was, back in town and not exactly a morning person. She surveyed the space and tried to see it objectively. Even without projecting her own sad narrative on the neglected room and the faded mural, the place was still depressing. Despite Patricia's personal charisma and physical beauty, the Sea Point library was barely limping along. Bernadette had told Kate on the walk over that it was always empty except on Wednesday mornings, thanks to Ms. Rose's loyal fan base of sporadic bedwetters.

"You'd just check books out, shelve returns, retrieve holds, easy peasy." Patricia smiled.

"That's a really nice offer," Kate said, stalling to find an excuse. "But don't I need a graduate degree?"

Patricia fanned the question away like a bad odor. "You only need a master's in library and information sciences if you're full-time, year-round."

"Oh."

"It's twenty hours a week," Patricia pushed. "Come back tomorrow and I'll have all the paperwork ready. You're going to be such a great fit, Kate. I promise."

The only person more overjoyed than Bernadette by Patricia's job offer was Clementine. On their walk home after Story Hour, Clem hopped up and down, energy fizzing out of her doughy little body as she chirped, "We'll be friends with Ms. Rose!"

Hot Men Plumbing

Running late to SeaSalt Inn, Ziggy floored the truck and ignored yet another call from Clyde at Ocean City HVAC. OCH was the monster company that was eating up every small business like a particularly hangry Pac-Man. They were closing in on Sea Point, which meant they were closing in on him. Clyde had left his first voice-mail while Ziggy had sat in his parents' living room, trying to translate Zeke's chicken scratch of an accounting book. Like a seasoned hyena circling easy prey, Clyde had been nothing but friendly in his message. "I know it's a tough time but let me know what's next for you," Clyde had said, practically licking his lips over the phone.

Ziggy had learned quickly that there was no life referee when someone died. No one blew the whistle or called a time-out or shook his mother out of her catatonic state. He kept waiting for his dad to appear and get things sorted, handle the business side of things like he always had, but instead random people he hadn't spoken to in ages would text him, *Let me know how I can help*—as if they had ever proven useful to him in the past.

The one person who would have known how to file a life insurance claim was the same person who had just died, which is why Ziggy hadn't taken any steps to figuring out finances until a week after the funeral when Bernadette Campbell crossed the street from her parents' house, wrapped her arms around him in the bitter February cold, and asked, "Who's handling the probate?"

Ziggy didn't have an answer because he had no idea what the probate was. His blank expression was just the invitation Bernadette needed to kick into high gear. Before becoming a full-time stay-at-home mom, she'd been an estate lawyer for over a decade, and from their many lengthy conversations that followed her driveway intervention—in which Bernadette spoke in clear bullet points and contingency plans—it was obvious to Ziggy that she had been a formidable attorney. This hardly surprised him. Growing up, Bernadette had always been confident, bossy, and unafraid of confrontation. When Ziggy and Kate had set up their first lemonade stand, she'd instructed them to charge fifty cents instead of twenty-five as she'd laced up her Rollerblades. "Just tell them it's worth it," she'd said with a nonchalant shrug. "If that doesn't work, mention inflation, and if that doesn't work, tell them to go to hell." The day had ended abruptly, Ziggy recalled, after Kate had told Mr. Nixon to do just that.

A week after she'd offered to help with the probate, Bernadette called with an update. "Technically, because your dad named you executor, I'm working on your behalf," she said in such a professional tone that Ziggy sat up straighter in his truck as if she could see him. "And so before we go any further, I just want to remind you that anything we discuss regarding your dad falls within attorney-client privilege." Ziggy stuttered, trying to figure out a gracious way to ask her about fees, but Bernadette cut him off and said this is what big sisters were for. "Your dad always put air in my bike tires—did he ever tell you that?"

Ziggy shook his head, though it hardly surprised him. "And then Clementine always asked to pet his truck tires," Ziggy said, smiling faintly. His dad had been absolutely smitten with Clem: She would approach the truck with her hand outreached, palm up, as if the tires were a strange dog she couldn't resist. Every time Zeke encouraged Clementine to tickle the driver-side tire—and then made euphoric Scooby Doo sounds when she did—Ziggy knew it was only a matter of minutes before his dad wondered aloud about how fun it would be to have a granddaughter.

"So here's where we are," Bernadette asserted. "We've filed the will with the probate court, talked to your dad's accountant, who said your dad is in good standing with his taxes, notified the Social Security Administration, his bank, the three credit card companies, and set up a new bank account for us to use going forward, to keep track of what comes in and what goes out." Bernadette took a breath here as Ziggy continued to hold his. "Everything is fine, I promise," she reassured him, "but there's a lot to go over and I'm going to tell you the bad news first."

Bernadette lowered her voice as she explained that she'd reached out to a cheerfully demonic representative at State Farm, who'd conveyed in an upbeat baby voice that Zeke had stopped paying his life insurance premium two years prior, which meant there was no point in submitting a claim. "So there's the bad news—there's no insurance money," Bernadette said, giving Ziggy several moments of silence to process the blow.

It was easy for Ziggy to think back to the last time he and his dad had discussed life insurance—it had been years ago, after Zeke's doctor told him to keep an eye on his diet, that his blood pressure was high. Over a lunch of salt-drenched fries at the Wharf, Zeke had cursed at his phone before explaining his life insurance premium had skyrocketed because of the high blood pressure. At the time, Ziggy hadn't thought to ask his father if he planned to pay it because it seemed irrelevant—his dad had no plans of dying.

"Looking forward, the next thing for us to tackle is your dad's assets," Bernadette continued. "We have to file an inventory of the estate's assets, but that's not a big deal. Per the will, he left the business to you and everything else to your mom—the house, all of its contents, her car, their savings, et cetera—no stocks, right?"

Ziggy shook his head before remembering Bernadette couldn't see him in his truck. His voice came out thin and raspy, more pathetic than he would have liked. "No stocks," he said, hearing his father disparage the fat cats in the big city, always cleaning out the desperate folk and never suffering any consequences. *In Atlantic City, at least they give you free drinks before robbing you blind*, Zeke used to say.

"So that's a nice silver lining," Bernadette continued. "I mean, in case you're thinking of selling the house or the business—those assets get what we call 'stepped up,' meaning you won't have to pay taxes on any gains until Bev dies." Bernadette kept going down her enumerated list before the silence on the other end reminded her that this was Ziggy's family and not just a fun exercise in her former career, the one she missed every day, especially when the conversation at the playground drifted into why Emily's toddler had such loose bowels.

"I'm sorry, Ziggy, I got caught up in the numbers," she said, just as Clementine emerged from her nap, signaling the end of her call and the use of complex sentences. "It's just I know how much you've poured into that house, and it's a rare opportunity to cash in without paying taxes through the nose. If you sell now, you and Bev can walk with the profit, which would be significant."

Bernadette was right, of course, but the Miller house wasn't just a residence—it had been Zeke and Ziggy's labor of love for more than twenty years. Together they had restored the rambling Victorian to its original glory and given it a second life with a thorough facelift and updated plumbing, electricity, and insulation. When Bev and Zeke purchased it, the grand house bore the endless scars of its abuse as a boardinghouse for international seasonal workers during much of the twentieth century before it had been abandoned altogether. More firetrap than family home when the Millers signed their names on the dotted line, the wraparound porch was rotted and Bev put her foot right through the third step to the second floor on her way to see what animal was scurrying above their heads.

Over the years and with every spare dime they earned, Zeke and Ziggy had peeled back and torn up the shortsighted solutions of previous owners—disposing of the wall-to-wall carpeting, the asbestos siding, the drop ceilings, the shoddy drywall partitions, and the plastic pink-tiled bathrooms. They'd unearthed the original moldings, constructed built-in bookshelves, and installed antique hardware salvaged from work projects until the home gleamed with integrity. It was, hands down, one of the nicest homes in Sea Point, a masterful blend of classic architectural charm with modern comfort.

Adding to the allure, the Miller home sat on an enviable acre just two blocks from the beach. Bev had unleashed her artist's eye on the house's grounds, treating the acre as a canvas and somehow threading together a fairy-tale aesthetic with a user-friendly front yard, fit for enduring touch-football games and impromptu wrestling matches. Pedestrians stopped and cars slowed, pointing to her hydrangeas, her vined trellises, her crepe myrtles and rosebushes.

Or at least, they had in the Before.

Before, Bev's flower beds had garnered blue ribbons in the Annual South Jersey Garden Tour. Before, Ziggy's mother went out for early-morning walks to the ocean with her easel. Before, Ziggy came over from his own apartment above the surf shop in West Sea Point and forked home-cooked dinners into his mouth as if they would never end. Before, Ziggy and his father would drive around in the truck and Zeke would make him listen to all the music he loved from around the world. Having never left Sea Point, Zeke traveled through sound waves and had taken up residency everywhere—in England with the London Symphony orchestra and in Zimbabwe with the Shona people. Zeke could spend hours lecturing Ziggy and their clients on the Shona people's mbira, or the erhu—a two-stringed fiddle from China.

Now, in the eternal After, the front yard was barren and Ziggy anticipated a spring and summer of understory strangulations. Bev never left the house and the stovetop hibernated beneath half an inch of dust-encrusted grease. Instead of Zeke's nonstop international concert on the stereo, Bev kept the television blaring throughout the day, an unsettling soundtrack of reporters yelling at one another through twenty-four hours of breaking news.

"Obviously it's up to you and your mom," Bernadette explained, treading gently. "But unless you sell the house or the business or both, prepare to be very frugal for the foreseeable future."

Ziggy rolled his eyes. As if he and his parents had ever not been frugal. They'd never gone on vacation, only went out to restaurants for birthdays, and put every paycheck they made back into the business. "And you'll have to go through his books," Bernadette added, interrupting his thoughts. "We need to know the financial standing of each project—who owes MVP and what MVP owes—in order to move forward with the assets inventory. You need to go through them because I took a look and I have no idea what the different initials stand for."

That made two of them.

Not only was Zeke's handwriting illegible, but he'd made up some kind of bookkeeping code as a kid that he'd never bothered to explain to anyone. They'd had plans to go over the accounts, but they'd had so many plans, most of which—canoe excursions, baseball games, the ongoing restoration of Daffodil Cottage—were far more exciting than understanding state and federal tax forms.

Slamming the driver side door outside SeaSalt Inn, Ziggy called out his apologies to Todd as he ran up the slate walkway. The massive B&B, looming in sophisticated hues of gray after a recent paint job, reminded him of that famous opera singer his dad used to drone on about, the one who'd recently retired—SeaSalt could still take anyone's breath away, but beneath that beautiful façade, her pipes were a mess.

"Just glad you're here," Todd said kindly, stepping off the porch and walking toward him in a crisp blue Oxford shirt and khakis. Extending his hand to Ziggy, Todd's brown, bespectacled eyes twinkled as he added, "Miraculously, everyone's still alive."

Like most lifelong locals, Todd Meacham had been friendly with Ziggy's father—they'd played football on the Sea Point High varsity team, just a few years apart. Now in his fifties, Todd ran a successful inn with his husband, Barry. Yesterday afternoon, he'd called Ziggy, flustered—there was a growing puddle of water in the basement without any obvious source.

"The guests have been good sports, for the most part," Todd said. "But I did have a couple leave last night because of 'unacceptable' water pressure."

"I'm sorry I couldn't get here earlier," Ziggy said.

Todd dismissed the comment by shaking his head. "You're going through a lot without my complaining," he said. "You're here now, and you've got to see what Barry gave me for our anniversary—he's outdone himself."

Before Ziggy could reply, he saw it: Above the reception desk hung a framed oil painting in which two Great Danes posed like sentinels on the front porch of SeaSalt Inn, wearing matching red cable-knit sweaters that barely stretched over their chests. Handsome and heavily jowled, Roger Federer and Rafael Nadal were the beloved mascots of Oak Avenue known for their seasonal woolens and fear of squirrels.

"Don't they look regal?"

Ziggy nodded. He took a picture of the painting and then realized he didn't know whom to send it to. Zeke would have loved it, would have spent the rest of the day chatting about it to anyone who would listen. Bev would find a way to twist the painting into an attack—why wasn't she painting and why wasn't she painting rich people's pets so that she could make a killing? Ziggy decided to send it to Miles—Miles liked dogs. He replied almost instantly with an eggplant emoji and Ziggy fought the twinge of annoyance at his generation's lazy-caveman form of expression.

Putting his phone back in his overalls, Ziggy followed Todd down to the basement. He sourced the leak, explained he'd need to replace about four feet of pipe, which would require a trip to the hardware store. Todd followed him back down the walkway to the curb, his hands stuck in his pockets. "What's the damage?" Todd asked. "I'll write you a check while you're at Holloway's."

"Um, what did my dad charge you last time this happened?"

Tilting his head and stuffing his hands farther down into his pockets, Todd squinted at Ziggy like he was an IKEA furniture manual. "I'll have to check," Todd said slowly. "But this seems like more work? And more materials? And last time you guys just reinstalled a sink after Barry had tried and failed to do it himself?"

Ziggy nodded and tried to focus his eyes so it seemed like he was crunching numbers in his head, but all he was doing was waiting for the moment to end.

"I'm sure you've got a ton of people offering you free advice," Todd said, interrupting Ziggy's humiliation and bending down to pick at a tuft of crabgrass sprouting in a crevice of an otherwise pristine walkway. "But Barry and I are here for you, okay?"

Ziggy moved his head up and down, resisting the urge to just get in the truck, drive away, and never come back.

"Obviously I'm not sure what the finances are, but Barry was a big money guy back in the day, so if there's any way he can help you figure out all that stuff, because we know it can be confusing, and overwhelming, and your mom—"

"I appreciate that," Ziggy said, cutting him off. The idea of Barry, a guy he barely knew, going through his dad's financials—it made his stomach knot up.

"We could set up a time for you guys to talk things over? I mean, if you're planning on keeping the business—or even if you'd prefer to sell it?"

So that's what Todd was doing, Ziggy realized, he was gauging the future of MVP.

"I don't know if you've heard," Todd continued, "but there's another local kid trying to get into the business, which, depending on how you look at it, could—"

Ziggy scoffed. "Good luck to him—Ocean City HVAC is taking over faster than that stuff." He nodded at the backyard, which was a thick forest of twenty-foot-high bamboo stalks.

"Don't get me started—I could kill him for that," Todd said. "Barry thought we could create a Japanese garden—no research, no idea that bamboo is all about world domination."

Ziggy laughed and took a deep breath before sharing his big announcement. "Actually," he said slowly, "Miles is moving back, so he's going to catch me up to speed about the business side of the business—you know, share those Wharton skills."

"Miles Hoffman?"

Ziggy beamed as he nodded. His best friend was coming home to back him up, save the day, be the good person Ziggy had always known he'd had the capacity to be.

Clapping his hands together, Todd reached over to grip Ziggy's shoulder. "Well, that is fantastic news! If business is anything like ice hockey, which I think it is, I know you guys will do great work together."

"Let's hope so." Ziggy shrugged with false modesty. During their tenure, Miles and Ziggy had led their club and high school teams to multiple State Championships and been named co-captains their senior year. When Miles went on to play hockey at Princeton, he'd called after the first day of preseason to say the Princeton goalie was "absolute garbage" compared to Ziggy. "I'm going to get worse here, without you to shoot on," he'd complained.

"It'll be interesting, that's for sure," Ziggy said now to Todd, feeling the muscles in his face begin to ache—this was the most smiling he'd done in months. "How about I get back to you about the bill after Miles helps me reboot the business?"

Barry nodded with so much enthusiasm that Ziggy adjusted the strap of his overalls to avoid looking at him. It was hard not to feel pathetic when a client acted excited to receive an invoice. "This is terrific," Todd said. "I give it six months before you guys have your own reality show on Bravo!"

Ziggy laughed as he headed back to the truck with Todd on his heels. "I'm serious!" Todd yelled. "Just don't forget about my pipes after *Hot Men Plumbing* surpasses *Real Housewives*!"

STD

On the first Saturday morning in May, four weeks after arriving home, Kate sorted mail in the kitchen while her parents completed their "long run." The ritual and banality of sorting was soothing, just like her mom had promised it would be a month ago, when Kate couldn't tie her shoes without crying.

The night before, Bernadette had formally announced that she was pregnant and Kate, surprised by her own genuine excitement about a new niece or nephew, had said as much. "Well, hopefully you'll be around to take Clementine on dates after the baby comes," Bernadette had said. "She apparently has some 'concerns' about expanding our family." The idea of still living in her parents' house in six months was too grim to fathom, so Kate had smiled and said she would visit often.

Now, she sang Destiny's Child's "Bills, Bills, Bills" as she tossed an envelope from Sea Point Power atop one from the Freedom Bank of New Jersey and tried not to think about the state of her ovaries. They were fine, she decided, and definitely not shriveling—she just needed to bide her time until Thomas came around.

And then she saw it. An envelope of disaster, innocently tucked between a spring catalog and a Verizon bill: "Kate Campbell and Guest."

As lethal as a legal summons, she'd been served a Save the Date.

Thomas had called them STDs, and although Kate had scolded him at the time, attending a wedding without him now struck Kate as far more painful and embarrassing than a case of the clap.

She should have known from the weight that this STD was from Vanessa "Nessie" Drew, everyone's favorite, wealthiest shlocal, who was getting married the first weekend in August. A shlocal was a summer local, a part-time resident during the best months. The Drews' summer home was beachfront in the nicest part of town on the same block as Jo Hoffman's house. Nessie and Kate had become friends the summer after third grade when they both participated in the Junior Lifeguards program, the only girls in a pack of half-naked boys with countable ribs and impressive lungs. After surviving Junior Lifeguards, they'd tried sailing, soccer, tennis, and art camps together, solidifying their friendship as pen pals through the winter, when Nessie returned to the far-off land of Gladwyne, Pennsylvania.

The summer after freshman year of high school, Kate was thrilled to watch Nessie fulfill her dream of taking the stand to become a real lifeguard, which came with a whistle, an official navy blue Speedo, and complete authority of the beach, jetty to jetty.

By that point, at age fifteen, Kate was best friends with Georgina Kim, and they'd agreed to wait tables at the Wharf together because that's where the real money was. On the rare day off, Kate and Georgina would spread their towels next to Nessie's stand and watch her perform her duties with flirtatious aplomb—she was a strong swimmer and her hand signals were excellent, if always a little suggestive.

By the time they graduated from high school three years later, the only evolution in any of their summer careers was that Nessie's signal for "No ball throwing" was downright dirty. Kate and Georgina were still waiting tables at the Wharf, holding out for when they would finally be able to bartend. And while Jo Hoffman didn't bend the rules about minors handling alcohol, Mike the bartender did, which is why he never questioned Nessie's fake ID on the nights she'd roll into the Jetty Bar with her lifeguard buddies and order lemon drops for everyone. As Kate and Georgina sweat through their shirts with their hands full of dishes, Nessie would corner them on their way to the kitchen and try to give each of them a shot glass, which was always sticky and half empty from Nessie's friendly jostling through the crowded bar. "More for me," Nessie would slur when they demurred. After a few rounds, she would physically force Kate and Georgina to stop what they were doing so she could say how much she loved them, and had she ever told them how much she loved them? "You're just so georgeous," Nessie slobbered in Georgina's face one night, and despite Georgina's blush and best efforts, the name "Georgeous" stuck.

What no one had understood back then, Kate realized now, was that Nessie took her schoolwork seriously and her future seriously—just none of them. Sea Point wasn't real life to her; it was a summer escape to have fun and make out with boys at the local bar. After graduating from Stanford, Nessie stayed in Palo Alto for a year of research and then veterinary school, where she'd met Rye Moffett, the man she deemed worth taking seriously in sickness and in health. Kate had learned about Rye from Nessie's parents when she'd come home for her father's birthday the previous fall. Mr. and Mrs. Drew were still dedicated Sea Point shlocals with their own engraved bench in front of the Wharf—because sometimes the line was long and the Drews wanted somewhere comfy to sit while they waited.

Examining the STD like evidence of her future death, Kate stared at the "and guest" on the envelope. Nessie must have either assumed Kate was still with Thomas or she had found out they'd broken up and wanted Kate to bring a date. Just the idea of bringing some faceless mannequin was devastating. Thomas as her built-in plus-one for life had been a luxury she had taken for granted. The anvil of her new reality had already landed on her head and yet it kept pushing her farther down in the dirt.

Kate's phone rang and she reached for it, assuming it was Bernadette, who was the only person who ever called her. But it wasn't Bernadette, it was Thomas. Kate stared at the name, the vibration of the phone no match for the thunder in her chest.

She picked up.

"Kate!" His voice. It rushed back into her ear like high tide at daybreak, the first ice-cold sip after a long-ass week. She pressed her head into the phone so his voice could sound the way it used to when he woke her up in the middle of the night, muffled from pillows and deep sleep.

She'd siphoned off all good thoughts of him for the past four weeks, blocked him out. But here he was. And just like that, all her defenses flew off their hinges.

"Don't worry, everything's fine, I'm fine." He started talking but she just wanted to hear his voice, fall into that blanket of reassurance. Something about his parents' anniversary but she didn't care, she leaned into the sound without listening to the words. Between each of his calculated pauses, Kate ignored her survival instincts. She let his voice unstitch the wound he'd made of her.

As he told her about Aggie and Marta's fertility woes, Kate suddenly remembered a cold, rainy Sunday from the previous October—they'd ordered ramen from the place around the corner, and while Thomas picked up dinner, she'd fished out beers from the back of the refrigerator and put their favorite hot sauce on the coffee table before reaching for the remote to queue up their show. She was wearing his Evergreen crew team sweats but when he came back from picking up the takeout, soaking wet, he'd stripped naked and stripped her too as the ramen cooled, still in the plastic "Have a Nice Day" bag on the floor. They fell asleep in the warm cocoon of each other's heartbeats and woke up slowly, happily. Kate still remembered snuggling into Thomas's bare chest that night and feeling almost overwhelmed by the realization there was nothing she wanted that she didn't already have.

"But you know how that goes," Thomas said now, chuckling. She missed that chuckle, how his laugh tickled her ear, the full weight of him behind it.

"So I wanted to give you a heads-up about something, and I'm hoping we can be adults about it." Kate would replay this moment in slow motion, how she was still untangling the hasty knot of words as Thomas forged ahead, not waiting for her reaction.

"How's this for a small world," Thomas said. "Your friend Vanessa is marrying a guy named Rye Moffett in Sea Point the first week in August."

Kate squeaked acknowledgment as her eyes landed on the Save the Date sitting in front of her.

"As it turns out," Thomas continued, "Rye is cousins with a woman named Wally."

"Wally?"

"Short for Walton," Thomas said, exasperated. Kate imagined him rubbing his eyes like he did whenever he started to lose patience. "Her mom wanted everyone to know that her daughter has Walton blood even if her last name is Moffett—it's a whole thing."

"What's a whole thing?"

"It's not important," Thomas snapped. "But she asked me to go to the wedding with her."

Before Kate could comprehend the detonated grenade he'd just casually lobbed, she said the only thing she knew to be true: "Wally's a cool name."

"Um, yeah," Thomas answered, thrown off, not understanding that Kate's blood had stopped circulating. Her soul hovered several feet above her. "So I'm coming to Sea Point for that wedding in early August. And I assume you're going too, so I just—"

People always talked about their heart hurting, but when love's evil twin nailed a blindside tackle, the pain hit lower, in the gut. Thomas kept talking for what might have been thirty seconds or three minutes, feeling the need to fill her in on the "aggressive" new coffee spot around the corner from his apartment (his, no longer theirs).

"Well, I should let you go," he said suddenly, meaning he wanted to hang up. Kate heard a woman's voice in the background saying hi to him over the rustling of bags. "We'll see you in August."

It had been one month.

One month and it was serious enough to assume he'd be attending a wedding in August with this girl?

One month and he was already speaking as "we"?

Googling Wally Moffett was a bad but inevitable idea, as was the petroleum fire that incinerated Kate's stomach when she saw that Wally was a yoga instructor at the studio Thomas had attended religiously for the past, what, year? Two years? "Oh my God," Kate said aloud in her parents' empty kitchen, realizing the latitude of the timeline. Wally had started before they'd ended.

In her black-and-white teacher photo, Wally wore her thick blond hair in a high bun and appeared unbearably petite, with chiseled arms holding up the rest of her in some impossible contortion. Kate couldn't achieve that pose while lying on her back—she couldn't even break down the physics of it. Meanwhile Wally stared back at Kate with a thousand-watt smile that seemed to say directly to her, *This pose is a blast! Try it sometime, just play with it, and also, by the way, Thomas Mosby wasn't wrong to have fallen for me, only human, ya know?*

Kate's eyes pulsed with fury as she skimmed Wally's bio, looking for ammunition. She'd grown up "at the foot of a mountain in Montana," where she'd cultivated a lifelong appreciation for the natural world. She'd since become an activist to "elevate mindfulness surrounding climate change" through her volunteer work at a sustainable yoga studio in the Peruvian Amazon, but her true passion was music. An award-winning cellist, Wally had been honored to perform with the likes of Arcade Fire, Patti Smith, Nick Cave, and even Prince when she was in high school. Zooming in on Wally's face, Kate understood high school hadn't been too long ago.

Bernadette's phone went straight to voicemail before Kate remembered she and Clementine attended tumbling class every Saturday. Shoving feet into sneakers and dog bags into pockets, Kate grabbed Homer and his leash. They walked to the beach with purpose, as if life had provided poor customer service and it was time to speak with the manager.

At the sight of the crashing waves, Kate knew she'd met her match. She let Homer off leash and watched him run to the water's edge before following him, wishing she could walk in and sink, descend into the salt water until she no longer felt this terrifying anger, but she looked to the right and saw she had witnesses.

Two barefoot teenagers sat with their legs outstretched in front of them and their blue jeans rolled up to their knees. She couldn't tell if they were dating or siblings, but from the downwind whiff she got, she was certain they were high. Kate watched them dunk their hands into a pink bucket nestled between them to make a drippy sandcastle. Leaning back to admire their creation, the boy yelled, "This is magnificent!"

Kate stormed in the opposite direction of their giggles, down the beach toward the closest jetty. For a moment, Kate thought of calling Thomas back and ripping him apart, telling him that she knew what he'd done, she knew he'd cheated, she knew all about Wally's homewrecking backbends—but what good would that do? The only thing Kate had left was her quiet dignity and the fact that she had left the city without stirring up any drama. According to her social media, she was still in New York, living her dream life, and Thomas hadn't untagged himself in any photos of them together or posted anything new. It was thus fair to deduce that he still loved her. And while Kate's public-facing self would need to wait out Thomas's twelve-year itch, her Sea Point self was ready to scratch off her own skin.

She ventured out on the rocks. In the summer, a lifeguard would have blown his whistle and signaled for her to get down—climbing on the jetties was strictly prohibited. But this was the off-season, and she was a local, and Kate was going to walk to the edge of the rocks.

Homer clumsily trailed her, splashing in the shallow pools and slip-

ping on the slick sea moss. Ocean spray spit in Kate's face so she closed
her eyes and, much to her surprise, opened her mouth and screamed. She
screamed from the absolute center of herself. She screamed as Homer
licked her balled-up fists. She screamed and she screamed and she
screamed. She thought she just might scream forever.

In response, the ocean roared, white caps swirling, waves breaking on
her soaked sneakers, reminding Kate of her unsure footing just as an all-
encompassing tidal thunderclap swallowed up her voice. A five-footer,
Kate realized, would easily knock her off the jetty and into the jagged
rocks below, and who would she have to blame? Kate unleashed one more
yell and the ocean absorbed her indignity with its own violent wailing.
Her lungs gave out and, in the middle distance, she saw a wave swiftly
beginning to build upon itself. Kate yelled at Homer to run. She sprinted
off the jetty, eyes one step ahead of her feet, adrenaline guiding her back
to safety.

From the sand, breathless and rattled, Kate watched the gigantic wave
grow to a terrifying six feet before breaking on the rocks where she'd just
stood. She saw herself standing out there, screaming into the wind, consumed. A few moments longer and her story would have been forever
changed. That was the thing about the sea—it went from a commiserat-
ing audience to a merciless anarchist in seconds. It was as predictable as
life itself.

The Acme

Waiting in line at the Acme with her gray hoodie up and celebrity sunglasses on, Kate assessed the basket of the man in front of her: four apples, a six-pack of toilet paper, and a package of bacon. It was a small bounty—a bachelor's bounty—compared to Kate's overstuffed shopping cart, and so she discreetly nudged the romaine to hide the three boxes of macaroni and cheese.

"What kind of apples?" the cashier asked, holding up the candidates in question.

"Isn't there a sticker?" the man in front of her asked.

"Must've fallen off," the cashier shrugged, putting the apples aside and flipping through a thick black binder full of SKU numbers.

Reaching for the yellow plastic divider before loading her own haul onto the conveyor belt, Kate heard an almost inaudible whisper. "They're Pink Ladies," the guy murmured, and as Kate watched a rash of crimson crawl up the back of his neck, she missed New York more than she knew possible. How had she come from a place where a man was too embarrassed to accurately identify his apples if he had to say the word "pink" or "ladies"? She wanted to be back in Manhattan, where she would walk past the New York Times Building on her way to lunch with a potential client before meeting Thomas and his mother at the Guggenheim for an exhibition preview. She wanted the infinite array of culture, faces, styles, and desires compressed, against all odds, within 22.7 square miles.

"Kate?"

A deep voice pulled her out of her dinner-and-a-show daydream. The Pink Ladies man stood at the end of the conveyor belt, in the bagger's station, staring at her.

"Ziggy!" Kate threw her hands up in the air, momentarily thrilled before the mortification hit: How could she not have recognized him? And even worse, how had she not reached out after Zeke had died? Trapped in her too-lateness, she struggled to find words that would redeem her, but what was there to say? Kate pushed past her cart and hugged him.

"My mom said you were back," said Ziggy. "How've ya been?"

Kate forced a smile and then decided she didn't need to pretend. "Oh, pretty shitty."

Ziggy's face lifted into a grin—his eyes crinkled in the corners and his mouth stretched wide to reveal confoundingly white teeth. It was the teeth that made Kate take a step back—they looked too big for his face. She tilted her head, diagnosing the stark difference. He must have lost what, twenty, maybe thirty pounds.

He read her face, patted his flat stomach as if it were still a bowl full of jelly, and said, "Same here. Rough winter."

She nodded, taking in his tan overalls, steel-toed workman boots, shaggy hair, and beard stubble. He looked, oddly enough, objectively attractive.

"I'm so sorry about your dad," Kate finally said, as the cashier rang her up.

"Thanks, yeah, me too."

"And I'm sorry I couldn't make it to the funeral. It was—"

"Don't worry about it," Ziggy said, cutting her off. "He got a great turnout—more than three hundred people! We went to the Wharf after and Jo sent out free drafts of Stella and chicken wings—everyone had a good time. I think he would've approved."

Looking at Ziggy and seeing her sandbox secret keeper under all that scruff, after all this time, Kate couldn't believe she'd gone to Mexico instead of coming home for Zeke. An acidic mix of heartbreak, loss, and shame sloshed in her stomach.

Ziggy didn't seem to notice. Instead, he helped bag her groceries and asked, "You'll still be around Labor Day Weekend, right?"

"Maybe," Kate said. She hoped she'd be back in New York by then, back on her feet and in the center of things.

"Well, you'll appreciate this," Ziggy said, waiting for Kate to swipe her card before helping her with her bags so they could walk out together. "My dad wrote in his joke of a will—it was literally on the back of a Wawa receipt—that he wants a Rock the Boat party thrown in his honor on the day after Labor Day so that all the locals can attend."

Every year on Labor Day, the Sea Point ferry transformed into Rock the Boat—an all-day party on the water complete with a DJ and a dance floor—to support a local charity. Last year, they'd raised thousands of dollars for the children's hospital; the year before that, it was for the wildlife center. It was the summer swan song and the best way to keep tourists in town through Labor Day—no one could afford to miss the fun and drama of Rock the Boat any more than they could resist collecting the coffee mug party favor. Like an original black-and-white Delaware license plate with a low number, owning a collection of Rock the Boat mugs spanning the decades was a point of pride and prestige. Wealthy shlocals displayed their mint-condition, chronologically-ordered mug collection on the floating shelves of their open-layout kitchens. It was the same coded nod of elite insider status as an ACK bumper sticker.

In true local fashion, Ziggy's parents hadn't attended a Rock the Boat party since meeting at one in the early '80s. In even truer local fashion, Ziggy had never been able to go—he was always working on Labor Day, just as all Sea Pointers were. "He wants everyone to go out on Rock the Boat, like when he met my mom," Ziggy explained in the parking lot. "We're supposed to go back and forth to Delaware the whole day, just drinking and dancing and telling stories about him."

"Oh my God," Kate laughed, opening the trunk of her mom's car. "That's amazing."

"Yeah, who knew my dad was such a partier?" Ziggy joked, leaning over to help her unload her bags. He straightened up and put his hands on his hips. "What's amazing is *that* was the extent of his will," Ziggy said, shaking his head in disbelief. "The only thing he planned for after his death was a Rock the Boat after-party."

By Labor Day Weekend, as Kate and Ziggy knew from firsthand experience, most locals were punch drunk with exhaustion. They were delirious from ten weeks of traffic jams, double shifts, lobster-red tourists complaining about the sun, and French Canadians ignoring American tipping culture. August, in particular, was an incandescent lightbulb everyone dreaded though no one dared mess with—revenues from that month alone would need to last through the off-season—but even if the tip jars dried up through the fall, everyone lived for September. Labor Day Weekend was the last big weekend for tourists until Halloween, which meant the Tuesday after Labor Day was the first day that locals could drink coffee in their pajamas, take a shower, and catch their breath.

"Hey, I should—" Kate fished in her bag for her phone and was about to ask Ziggy for his number when a sudden gust of wind gave way to the force that was Jo Hoffman.

"My eyes must be playing tricks on me!" her radio-smooth voice announced from two cars down. Swathed in the neutral tones of Eileen Fisher, Jo's attire was the only thing calming about her. Her clout stretched her petite five-foot-three frame several inches taller. She raised her arms toward the sky as if she'd just won *The Price Is Right* and waited for Ziggy and Kate to exalt their local celebrity.

"Mrs. Hoffman!" Kate mustered, dropping her phone back in her bag and rushing toward her former boss. Jo offered her a cheek to kiss and Kate used the opportunity to inhale perfume she'd never be able to afford—it smelled of gardenias, sea spray, and influence.

As everyone in Sea Point knew, Jo Hoffman had put herself through Wharton business school in the early '80s by waiting tables at the IHOP near campus. And, $25,000 in loans later, after graduating at the top of her class, she convinced her husband, Ari, that they should move to the shore where real estate was relatively cheap. Unlike her classmates, who made a beeline for New York and San Francisco, Jo didn't choose the promise of an international city but instead bought a boarded-up dive bar in a little-known town in (gasp!) New Jersey. At their five-year class reunion, Jo's former study group confessed they'd assumed she'd suffered a mental breakdown upon hearing she was taking her talents to Sea Point. They'd been wrong, of course, but their suppositions were founded in reality—no bright young woman would choose to move to the edge of nowhere, let alone a bright young woman with a newly minted MBA from Wharton.

At the time, those who knew Sea Point at all understood that Sea Point was for the desperate. The town's industry consisted only of a defunct bar, a restaurant with one working burner, a fishing shack that sold creative interpretations of bait, and a wharf that drove the meager local economy.

As she liked to mention whenever she found herself standing behind a lectern, Jo had discovered Sea Point by accident. After a classmate's bachelorette weekend in Atlantic City, Jo had made a wrong turn on the expressway and landed in Sea Point, where ambitious visions of the future instantly zapped her hangover. Driving through the sleepy town, what caught Jo's eye were the smattering of nineteenth-century mansions that seemed both random and perfectly situated. The breathtaking architecture, Jo soon learned, had spilled over from the popular Victorian tourist destination down the road. Some of the more adventurous tycoons of the late 1800s had constructed a cluster of stately summer homes and one lavish sixteen-room inn—the Bluebell Hotel—along the Jersey coastline before deciding they preferred the established getaways of Southampton and Newport. Aside from these few structural displays of grandness, however, Sea Point had remained untamed throughout the last century, a last frontier in which Jo saw endless potential.

Even if the ramshackle bar—Skip's—needed to be gutted, its location was outrageous, and Jo understood the value of waterfront property in a seaside town. Geographically destined to lure summer vacationers, Skip's became the Wharf when Jo bought the building and the large parcel of land on which it sat for next to nothing. By the mid-1990s and ever since, the Wharf ranked first on every list about visiting the Jersey Shore. The wait list for a wedding extended two years out, and that didn't include the premium dates in August, when the price inflated to the same mind-boggling rate as that of a college education. Even so, those four Saturday slots were impossible to lock in unless one had extremely deep pockets *and* a direct connection to Jo Hoffman.

"Kate Campbell," Jo purred, "please tell me you are the angel I've been waiting for. Hi, Ziggy dear."

Ziggy smiled and Kate asked what sort of angel that was.

"The kind that can come work at the Jetty Bar so I can finally replace the world's worst bartender—don't even get me started, but let's just say he was there maybe a month and not only did we have a Me Too situation but we also had a Me Three, Me Four, situation."

"Yikes," Kate and Ziggy said at the same time before jinxing each other like they were six again.

"I have Jerry working seven nights a week by himself and it's just not right. He's got a bad back, you know. We have some decent college kids coming back for the summer, but you would be the absolute dreamiest dream, especially since you're here now. It's these awkward in-between weeks before Memorial Day that are ruining my life—and Jerry's. I heard you were home so I was giving you a little time to settle in before I began my campaign but I'm desperate and—oh, I'm sorry about that boyfriend, sounds like a real monkey's ass."

Kate ignored the last bit but wondered how everyone in town already knew about Thomas and then she remembered where she was: In Sea

Point, everyone knew everything that happened—sometimes even before it happened.

"Speaking of monkey's asses," Ziggy cut in, steering the conversation away from Kate.

Jo smiled. "Miles says he'll be back before Memorial Day Weekend and staying through the summer."

"He told me the same thing," Ziggy said, holding up a hand for Jo to high-five, which she did with an amused indulgence. Jo Hoffman was many things, but an avid high fiver she was not.

"I'll believe it when I see it," Jo sniffed. "I'm only his mother, but what can you do? You raise a kid to be independent and then you're disappointed when he's actually independent."

Kate forced herself to nod and not say that Miles had never and would never know about financial independence. Also, Eric lived in her basement and popped pills like Tic Tacs. Jo was a successful businesswoman, but a successful parent? Her boys were not far from forty, and Kate had a feeling Jo still paid their phone bills. Then again, Kate wasn't one to talk. An hour ago, her mom had given her a credit card and car keys to buy groceries.

"Well, I'm excited that he's coming back." Ziggy grinned. "He's going to go through my dad's books for me. And, for the record," he added, winking at Jo, "I think he'll be a real asset to the Wharf."

Jo shook her head at Ziggy and turned to Kate. "What do you say?" she asked, light brown eyes sparkling.

Kate forced a smile, though she couldn't muster one with teeth. She hadn't bartended since college. For the past ten years, she'd attended black-tie fundraisers with views of Central Park. Now she was back at home and instead of her name always being on the most exclusive of lists, she was being asked to mix drinks behind Jetty Bar. Kate could smell the sticky sweet grenadine and feel the weight of the no-slip rubber mats as she lifted them off the floor to hose them down at the end of the night—she was supposed to be past that part of her life.

"I'll let you choose your nights!" Jo Hoffman shouted in a one-person bidding war.

"Now, that's an offer!" Ziggy interjected with an auctioneer's bravado.

"I'll definitely think about it," Kate ceded. "Patricia just asked me about a job at the library, so I don't want to overcommit."

"Look at this one," Jo said, nudging Ziggy and pointing at Kate. "Playing hard to get. Smart girl. If Georgina's around, you can both work the bar, just like old times."

The mention of Georgina sucked all the moisture from Kate's mouth. "Georgina's in Colorado," she forced herself to say. "At least, last I heard."

"Oh my, she always was adventurous. Stop by to fill out the paperwork. I assume you'll want Fridays and Saturdays?"

As Kate searched for a gentle synonym for "no," Jo Hoffman suddenly excused herself to speak with Mr. Nixon, who had been trying his hardest to enter the Acme undetected. "See you tomorrow, Kate! Bye, Ziggy!" and then she was off, but not before yelling over her shoulder that Kate should get an oatmeal facial to help with the bags under her eyes.

"She certainly hasn't changed," Kate muttered.

"Only in Sea Point can you get a job offer and three boxes of mac and cheese in the same place." Ziggy grinned, tossing her an apple from his grocery bag before polishing one for himself.

Kate took a bite and, still chewing, asked, "Why'd you get weird about the Pink Ladies?"

"Oh, you saw that," Ziggy said, nervously scratching his eyebrow. "They're my dad's favorite type of apple." Guilt plumed in Kate's chest. She swallowed hard and forced herself to meet Ziggy's gaze. "He'd give one to my mom and say something dumb like, *A Pink Lady for my old lady*, which no one thought was funny, but now he's gone so everything is a mind fuck. Anyway, sorry about the boyfriend."

"Oh God, I don't need your sympathy," Kate said. "Don't you have a job to get to?"

"Yeah, but it's good to see you." They looked at each other and Kate

felt an ache at the grown-up version of her childhood friend—it was his
new broad shoulders and that old mischievous grin he'd had as an eight-
year-old, when he'd proposed they pull out Kate's two loose-ish front teeth
so they could use her tooth fairy money to buy a bag of Twizzlers.

"You should come over sometime," Ziggy said. "My mom would love
to see you."

When Kate made a noncommittal throat clearing, Ziggy doubled
down. "I'm serious, stop by whenever—we're not fun, we're actually pretty
shitty, but misery loves company."

"I'll bring some ice cream," Kate ceded. "Mint chocolate chip still
everyone's favorite?"

Ziggy nodded. "Impressive memory."

"It's easy to remember when nothing changes."

"You say that like it's a bad thing." Ziggy's phone buzzed and he
glanced down, explained it was work. "But here's this," he said, opening
his wallet and giving her an MVP business card. "My cell is the second
one." Kate nodded, recognizing the third number listed as the Miller
house phone—she still had it memorized, the only one she knew by heart
besides her own. The first number must have been Zeke's.

After saying goodbye to Ziggy, Kate climbed into her car, exhaled, and
let her head thud against the steering wheel. Seeing Ziggy had made
Zeke's death real. Since February, she'd been too busy to process that Bev
and Ziggy had lost the third leg of their steady tripod and that they'd all
lost Zeke. She'd lost Zeke. Thomas suddenly felt so temporary, so fixable,
compared to what Ziggy would miss for the rest of his life.

Returning to Sea Point as a half-hatched adult, Kate had expected the
daily mortification of explaining why she was back in town—or rather
why she wasn't still in New York. She'd prepared for the always-awkward
bump-ins with what's-her-name's-daughter and Mr.-who's-his-face. But
she had not anticipated the heartache for a place she'd chosen to leave or
the staggering nostalgia for the people she found herself missing. It left a
dull throbbing in her bones, a kind of emotional arthritis. Here she was
and everything was the same except everyone was gone. Zeke Miller was

dead, Georgina was in Colorado, the ramshackle bungalows on First Street were now million-dollar fortresses that absorbed the sun like four-story black holes. Maybe it was just all the gray gathering for the impending thunderstorm, but it seemed like each human she encountered in Sea Point was walking around with trauma stuffed into their pockets like dirty tissues.

In her rearview mirror, Kate watched Ziggy back out of his parking spot. And there it was, gloating beneath the brake lights of his father's pickup truck. It knocked her sideways, the sight of that familiar, bold red lettering: GO JAGS!

Kate rolled down her window and waited for the gut-punch nausea to subside. It had been so many years ago and yet Yates could still do this to her, blindside her as badly as Thomas had on the phone. If only she had gone to Yates, she would be the kind of girl a guy like Thomas would marry; a woman who wintered in Saint Bart's, who fit in seamlessly with the Mosbys and Thomas's chosen family. She pressed down on the thought as if it were a bruise she could mitigate by feeling all the pain all at once.

In eighth grade, after Kate had been kicked out of her friend group for the inexplicable reasons of middle-school girls, Mr. Voy called Kate into his office, folded his hands on his desk, and recommended that Kate sit for the PSAT. Mr. Voy, the cute guidance counselor everyone liked, explained that the PSAT would take two hours and twenty-five minutes, administered after school, and it would cost $16. Kate had barely suppressed a laugh—why would she pay to take a long, optional test?

"Have you ever considered applying to Yates Academy?" he'd asked nonchalantly, as if the private school were a potato chip flavor and not the emerald city of academic excellence in New Jersey. Mr. Voy was new, which meant that he was the only adult Kate had encountered who had not known Bernadette. He had noticed Kate's high performance across all disciplines and explained that if she were to test well, her score might open doors, including those to Yates.

Kate's green eyes grew bigger as she envisioned attending a different high school than all the girls in her grade who'd stopped speaking to her except to ask for her homework. The possibility of surpassing them felt like a fantasy. Better still, attending Yates meant avoiding four years of drowning in her big sister's backwash at Sea Point High. Bernadette had already been crowned volleyball captain and homecoming queen, and everyone said she'd wear the prom queen crown that spring. To eighth-grader Kate, Yates wasn't a school; it was a life raft.

On a particularly hectic Monday morning, Dirk wrote the $16 check without asking what it was for, and several weeks later, Mr. Voy summoned Kate back into his office with a shit-eating grin because, don't you know, she'd scored in the top 1 percent of eighth graders in the nation. A letter soon arrived from Yates Academy, inviting Kate and her parents to visit the campus and meet with the director of admissions, who was thrilled to offer her a place in the incoming class.

A few weeks later, Kate had been snooping through Bernadette's closet, looking for the perfect outfit to wear for the Yates campus tour, when her parents summoned her to the kitchen and explained in apologetic but certain terms that she would attend Sea Point and not Yates. "We practice what we preach," Dirk said. "We believe in public schools."

"Yes, we do," Sally said, reaching for her husband. His jaw was clenched, but his hands trembled. Kate had never seen her father so upset. He wasn't angry, she knew this, even if she couldn't understand what was going on. "We like teaching at Sea Point but we also like giving you and your sister opportunities to make your own decisions."

"Great," Kate jumped in. "I choose Yates." In the ever-growing list of reasons to attend Yates, Kate had added only minutes earlier that Yates had a better mascot: the jaguars. She could see herself already, in the bleachers at a basketball game—"Go Jags!"—which was only about a billion times cooler than the Sea Point Herons.

"But unfortunately," Sally continued, ignoring Kate's declaration, "you can't make this decision because it's a financial one."

"Huh?"

"We spoke with the admissions director and they've offered you a place, which is an incredible accomplishment, truly a feat. It's so competitive, Kate, you should be very proud of yourself. But they haven't offered enough financial aid for us to really consider it, especially with Bernadette going off to Rutgers in the fall, so it—it's just not possible for us, as a family, to send you there. And we're so, so sorry about that."

"But Ziggy gets to go there." A year older than Kate, Ziggy was a freshman at Yates and his dad was just a plumber. If the Millers could afford it, the Campbells should be able to, too. Even though they hadn't been friends since elementary school, Kate and Ziggy still waved to each other when their paths crossed, which happened less and less. Kate had been looking forward to telling Ziggy she'd be joining him at Yates—maybe he'd even say that she could carpool with him and Miles Hoffman.

"Yes," Dirk muttered. "They offered Ziggy a financial scholarship and somehow Zeke and Bev are swinging the rest. I'm not sure how but— well, it's easier when you only have one kid, I guess and—" Dirk was rambling, talking to himself, as if he'd just woken up from a bad dream and was trying to remember the strange, disconnected pieces of it. "I mean, really, it's not like we know the details of their situation, and even if we did, it's none of our business, but good for Ziggy."

"He didn't even score that high on the PSAT," Kate said, without having any idea if this was true.

"They can't say it's a scholarship for hockey," Dirk sighed, rubbing his temples. "Athletic scholarships, like academic scholarships, aren't allowed at the private high school level. Not officially, at least. But the reason why they sought him out and offered him such an attractive package is most likely because Ziggy is a tremendous hockey player."

Kate sat back in her chair, disgusted with her parents. This was her shot. She'd taken a test, aced it, and Mr. Voy had said that if she did well, her performance could open doors for her—doors that were shut even to Bernadette. But no, she was trapped. She'd done everything right and she was still going to Sea Point, where sleeping with any starter on the football team counted as a varsity sport. She'd done everything she could and been stopped dead in her tracks by a dollar sign, a bottom line beyond her control.

Driving out of the Acme parking lot, Kate pushed her foot down on the gas and floored it to her parents' house. Ever since eighth grade, she'd known she was smart enough and ambitious enough to succeed on a larger stage than Sea Point.

She thought of the day when the thick packet had arrived from NYU, offering her a full ride. It had been the redemption she'd dreamed of for four years. She thought of her meteoric rise at Artemis. At any point since eighth grade, Kate might have given up, but she always climbed her way to the top—at least, she always had in the past. Right now, she felt too exhausted to start over, like she'd already given life her best shot, but what choice did she have? It was either surrender to an inconsequential existence in Sea Point or lift herself up and fight for what she wanted, what she deserved.

When Kate returned home, she locked herself in her room, took out her old journal, and wrote down some resolutions. The stream of manifestations that poured from her fingertips culminated in a three-point plan to take her from Jersey Zero to New York Hero just in time for Nessie's wedding. She'd win back Thomas. She'd return to New York. She'd land the job of her dreams. With patience, guile, and tact, she would emerge from this summer enviably employed, engaged, and en route to the city where she belonged.

The following morning, Kate heard the recycling truck's double honk outside her window, and then Ziggy's voice. She peered through her window because that's what you did in a small town: You spied and called it keeping an eye out.

"Early start for you!" the recycling guy yelled to Ziggy.

"Nah," Ziggy called back, looking down at his keys. "Just got here."

"Oh hey now!" Roger yelled, impressed. "Good for you! Get it while you can!"

Ziggy laughed before shifting to the somber discussion of the NBA playoffs. Kate went back to bed and wondered if Ziggy had a girlfriend or if he was just sleeping around—half a dozen times since she'd been home, she'd seen him pull into the Miller driveway early in the morning or back out of the driveway late at night.

He's not the only one making moves, Kate determined, looking at the page of fresh ink staring up from her desk.

She remembered from the yoga website that Thomas's new fling had a rock-solid core, but there was no way she had Kate's guts. *Namaste, Wally, but your chaturanga is not ready for this*, Kate thought with no small amount of glee. Reviewing the offensive plays, she prepared to execute:

KATE CAMPBELL'S THREE-POINT PLAN

1. Fortify bank account.
2. Build résumé.
3. Procure plus-one.

If she could successfully complete this three-point plan, Kate knew that Thomas would combust with jealousy before Nessie and Rye had cut the cake. Imagining the victorious scene, Kate almost pitied Wally, who would learn along with everyone else that Kate was ruthless, ambitious, bossy, controlling, and all the other things the patriarchy turned into dirty words about women. She was a driven alpha, a competitive opportunist, a single-minded monster, a freaky freakazoid.

Wait.

Kate listened for her parents, but they'd already left for work. She opened the YouTube app on her phone and searched "Freaky Freakazoid."

As everyone in the world now knew, Ruthi Jones was the teenage wunderkind from Dallas, Texas, who'd upended the idea of genre by making the music she wanted to hear. Having grown up bouncing around foster homes, Ruthi was now a household name, an outspoken pop star with grit and proud Latinx roots. "So many people helped me along the way," she told *Rolling Stone* magazine after her album *MetamOrphan* hit number one on the Billboard charts. "But my own voice is what saved me."

Ruthi had most recently broken the Internet on a visit to Kensington Palace where the young princes and princess begged to learn how to "bake the cookies"—Ruthi's signature dance move in the *Freaky Freaka-zoid* music video. Ruthi broke down the steps for them in the Royals' kitchen, where they were also, quite literally, baking chocolate chip cookies. In the clip that the Duchess of Cambridge posted the next day, Princess Charlotte begs, in her posh British accent and patent-leather Mary Janes, "Please, Ruthi, might we bake the cookies as we bake the cookies?"

If Ruthi Jones embodied self-salvation, *Freaky Freakazoid* served as an anthem, protest, victory lap, clap back, and a choreographed masterpiece. In the music video, women of every size and color twisted, jerked, ripped, dipped, and flipped their bodies with such force that the world's biggest singers, critics, and dancers agreed it was revolutionary, and when it cleaned up at the Grammys, Beyoncé herself hailed it as "an urgent call to arms . . . legs, hips, lips, truth, and love."

Kate threw on clothes as she pulled up a video on YouTube. She watched a famous dance coach give a tutorial that was nine minutes long, start to finish. "Before we get started," the chiseled choreographer said to the camera, "I want you to relax your face, loosen that jaw, shake it all out. This is hard work but ultimately, you've got to make it look like fun, so practice like you're having fun from the outset."

Kate relaxed her face. She smiled because the instructor told her to, but then she smiled because this was her secret. She could conquer this dance without anyone ever knowing. As she fumbled her way through the first few steps, Kate laughed at herself in the full-length mirror. She was horrific, like a Canadian goose trying to find rhythm, which only made her laugh harder as she tried over and over again. It felt so good to be so bad at something. When was the last time she'd given herself permission to be absolutely atrocious?

Restarting the video, Kate caught herself being patient, even encouraging, to the woman in the mirror. Her attempts to bake the cookies were mortifying, but so was life. Maybe failing was just a way to make room for redemption, like a litter fire in the forest to allow for more growth.

"Feeling good?" the choreographer asked into the camera. Kate grinned, shaking out her arms. As ridiculous as she looked trying to master the bubble waffle, this was the best she'd felt in weeks and her whole body was already vibrating with soreness.

Kate restarted the video. After another run-through of *Freaky Freakazoid*, Kate had enough endorphins pulsing through her to pick up the phone and initiate steps one and two of her three-point plan.

Walk-Off

It had been so easy that Kate scolded herself for not acting sooner. After ten minutes and two phone calls, she had increased her employment by 200 percent. In service of the three-point plan, Kate had accepted two job offers so that she could save enough money to move back to the city by the end of the summer.

First, Kate would work at the library five mornings a week—shelving books, greeting patrons, helping out Patricia any way she could. From eight to twelve, Monday through Friday, she would be busy and, with a bit of the creative finesse for which she'd been known at Artemis PR, Kate could manipulate "seasonal part-time library associate" into something résumé-worthy—senior account executive of literary strategy?

Second, Wednesday through Sunday night, Kate would step up behind the Jetty Bar, slinging drinks and earning an ungodly amount in tips. There was also résumé-building potential there, Kate mulled, she just needed to elasticize the verbiage for tending bar. It meant waiting on the public and being responsible for everyone's well-being—public servant?

Jo Hoffman had punctured Kate's eardrum on the phone, immediately belting, off-key and at the top of her lungs, "Wind Beneath My Wings." Kate's head was still throbbing from the serenade, but it had been invigorating to feel so desired by Jo and Patricia after such a demoralizing month. These two women had missed out on the last decade of Kate's life and yet they saw her, loved her, understood and appreciated her. A long time ago, she'd demonstrated she could do the work, and she would prove it again. The calls had felt like sinking into the ancient leather couch her parents kept in their shared office at school—a warm hug that held her in all the right places when she'd needed it most.

On the heels of these two calls and the promise of future paychecks depositing into her forsaken savings account, Kate finally felt buoyant enough to do what she'd been putting off since February. With a renewed sense of self-worth, she dialed the third number listed on Ziggy's MVP business card: the Miller family landline.

"Kate Campbell!" Bev announced, holding her front door open later that evening. "Come on in, the house is a mess." Bev's hair was shorter than usual, cut in irregular, jagged pieces, like broken window shards, and the faded black hair dye was growing out with pure silver threads coming in from the roots. The shimmery gray suited Bev, but Kate knew Ziggy's mom liked going to the salon, loved pretending to be a young Joan Jett with the curtain of raven locks touching her shoulders. Or at least, she had.

"And you brought ice cream! Let me see your face." Bev stopped Kate in the hallway to the kitchen and held her head in her hands. They were the same height, but as Kate stared straight ahead into Bev's hazel eyes, she felt like she was towering over this fragile, bird-boned woman who seemed to almost tremble with sadness. Bev's warm hands still holding her cheeks, Kate lunged at her before she could stop herself. A physical form of apology, Kate squeezed her long and tight to telegraph her remorse: *I'm sorry for your loss, I'm sorry for not coming back, not going to the funeral; I'm sorry for not visiting you sooner, for not writing a letter, for not even acknowledging that your life got blown apart. I'm so, so sorry.*

"Oh honey," Bev murmured into Kate's shoulder.

It had been a lifetime since Kate had last stood in the front hallway, but the classic Miller house smell of fresh laundry swaddled her in nostalgia. Bev led the way through the living room, where Kate stifled a gasp at the sight of Zeke's blue pleather La-Z-Boy chair, still in a 120-degree recline, an eerie homage to the man who was supposed to be home right now. She imagined touching the chair and finding it warm from his body, and the thought brought so much comfort that Kate pretended Zeke was just in the kitchen, poking around for a handful of honey-roasted peanuts that Bev would say he didn't need.

"I know, I know," Bev said, holding her hand up as a stop sign to the chair as she passed it. "I just—I haven't dealt with that yet."

Kate only now realized the neglected grounds outside reflected the sad state of affairs inside the Miller household.

"These need a rinse," Bev said, picking a dead fly out of one of the ice cream bowls Kate recognized from childhood. Given that the bowls were now bug tombs, Kate surmised Bev and Ziggy hadn't enjoyed ice cream since Zeke had been around to complain about Bev's scoops being too small. "Sit here, Kate," Bev instructed. "Ziggy should be coming down any minute—just showering off the day. Tell me how you are."

"Oh, you know," Kate began. She thought of Thomas—*I'm really, really not happy*—and said, "It's nice to be home."

"Sounds like that ex was as slippery as they come."

Kate nodded. As she accepted the bowl from Bev, she stared at Bev's engagement and wedding rings, sparkling in the dim light.

"I can't take them off," Bev said without meeting her eye.

Kate nodded. "Why would you?" she mustered.

Bev gave her a meek smile and, when she turned her back to scoop more ice cream by the sink, Kate studied Bev's easel in the corner. She must have been working right there when she'd gotten the call about Zeke. The brushes hadn't been washed; gobs of paint were still smeared on the palette. Ziggy had told Kate in the parking lot that Bev hadn't lifted a brush in months. Her husband was gone and had taken her creativity with him.

Ziggy entered the room just then, greeted Kate, and sat down across from her with the ice cream Bev handed to him, his hair still dripping. They sat in silence until the sound of metal spoons scraping glass forced each of them to look up. Kate hadn't even tasted the ice cream; all she could comprehend was Zeke's absence.

Clearing her throat, Bev asked, "Would anyone like to play Trivial Pursuit?"

An hour later, the three of them were doubled over, refilling one another's wineglasses and laughing uncontrollably at Ziggy's argument for why the Scots should reconsider their national animal. "A unicorn isn't real!" he shouted. "And the red deer are red! Gingers! They're such a better representation!" Kate was reaching for a new card when her phone vibrated in her back pocket. She ignored it. It shook again and Kate wondered if it was her parents asking for help with the new remote control, so she looked. It was Nora. Thomas's Nora. A missed call and now a text.

NORA: Cannes isn't the same without you!

Kate dropped her phone on the carpet and stared at the rectangle of metal, glass, and identity. It had weaponized against her. First Thomas's call, now this Taser of a text. Cannes was happening without her—of course it was. For the last several years, this was the week when she'd wake up next to Thomas in the Majestic Hotel just as room service arrived. Thanks to Nora's famous mother, Thomas's group of friends had attended the film festival every May since sophomore year, and Nora had extended the invitation to Kate the spring after they graduated—an offer that Kate wouldn't have been able to afford except that Thomas said his credit card points could take care of the flight and hotel, no problem.

Kate's first time in Europe had been to the French Riviera with Thomas and his chosen family. After more than a year of dating, she loved Thomas, but she was aware—even back then as she stepped off the plane—that she was also in love with the jet pack he'd strapped to her back to launch Kate around the world. Never in her wildest fantasies had she imagined attending Cannes, but because of Nora, who was because of Thomas, Kate had sat across from her handsome boyfriend in her fluffy white hotel robe eating the most perfect chocolate croissant of her life.

Now Kate was sitting on the faded green carpet in her neighbor's living room, playing Trivial Pursuit. And Nora was in Cannes, which meant Thomas was in Cannes, which meant Wally Moffett was in Cannes. What if Nora had known about Wally the whole time? What if Nora liked Wally more than she'd ever liked Kate? The spiral of what-ifs began to feel a lot like vertigo.

Unlike the rest of Thomas's college posse, who treated Kate as Thomas's unfortunate pet, Nora had seen Kate as a kindred spirit. Over the years and throughout the annual trips, holidays, and events, Nora and Kate had developed their own rituals within the group's traditions. At Cannes, the two of them woke early to walk along La Croisette before the crowds took over. One time, they bumped into Nora's mother's agent, who treated them to coffee and then mentioned multiple times that he was waiting on a call from "Leo"—as if he needed a reason to be sitting alone at a café on the French Riviera. Last year, after Nora had complained to Kate for the better part of an hour about how the rest of the friend group made her feel claustrophobic, they'd spotted their favorite director, an edgy young woman, boarding a yacht. When they called her name, she'd waved to them like friends and they'd shrieked with delight before doubling over in preteen giggles.

Kate didn't doubt that Nora's experience of Cannes did feel different without her, but it wasn't not like Nora had extended an invitation this year, or even reached out in the month since the breakup. Nora had chosen Thomas—their shared history, their convenient, co-dependent social set—and Kate could hardly blame her. The unsung trauma of a breakup was all the collateral damage inflicted on the most platonic of friendships.

And yet, regardless of intent, the text was an act of terrorism. How were people allowed to just intrude on your life without permission? Bogarting someone's attention required nothing more than a phone and an unchecked whim, probably inspired by the bottles of champagne Nora's mom sent to each of their rooms the first and last night of the trip.

Kate tried to take a deep breath to excise the dizziness, but she couldn't look up at Bev and Ziggy, whose eyes were on her, waiting for an explanation, or at least to read out the blue Geography question. Continuing to stare down at her phone, Kate saw Nora texting more, those dot, dot, dots on the move, but then they disappeared.

Years ago, Thomas had taught her that "holding" was a foul in football, but in twenty-first-century communication, Kate thought, there should be a penalty for withholding valuable information, especially if it had to do with your ex-boyfriend's new girlfriend. Nora owed her ten yards—or at least one biting remark about Wally.

"I've got to go home," Kate announced, her voice sounding far away from her skull. After delivering a perfunctory hug to Bev and a quick shoulder pat to Ziggy, Kate walked outside, too in her own head to hear the slap of the Millers' screen door behind her.

"Yo!" Ziggy called out. "What happened?"

Kate glowered into the darkness and started to walk past her house and down the street. Over her shoulder she fumed, "Nora texted me to remind me they're all in France."

"Who's Nora? And where are you going?"

"For a walk."

"Want company?" The concern in Ziggy's voice made Kate bristle—it reminded her of her own mother's pity and so she kept walking in the dark toward nowhere. But then she heard his footsteps grow louder and faster as he ran up behind her. Catching his breath, Ziggy said, "We don't have to talk." He kicked a pebble and it skipped down the street, dot, dot, dot.

Kate watched the rock disappear and thought of what Ziggy's father had told her when he found her crying in her front yard, the day Dirk and Sally had informed her she wasn't going to Yates. "I heard the bad news," he'd said, and before she could react, Zeke had reassured her, "We don't have to talk." He spoke to her like an equal, Kate remembered. Squinting up at the bright spring sky with his hands on his hips, he'd asked, "You know the cool thing about herons?" When Kate had shaken her head, still too upset to talk, Zeke hadn't told her so much as shown her, flapping his arms like wings until her tears had turned into laughs. She'd never thanked him for that and now it was too late. Her whole life already felt too late— that's what they'd put on her headstone.

Kate and Ziggy headed toward the duck pond in silence, but when they arrived, ten minutes later, they tacitly decided they weren't done walking, so they kept on, to the lighthouse. Ziggy kicked another stone, which skittered down the empty road and landed under a streetlamp's circle of orange light, like a showcased gem. Kate wondered what willed Ziggy to kick a rock—the same question she had about most sports objectives—until she approached the orange circle and kicked the rock as hard as she could. To her surprise, something inside her jostled loose and made her want to do it again. Harder.

"Get your own," Ziggy said, smiling in the dark.

They kicked their own rocks to the sound of cricket chirps and frog burps for half a mile—their bodies meandering the width of the empty street to chase their stones but keeping pace with each other. At the light-house, the wind picked up and Ziggy broke the quiet by saying the breeze felt good. Kate nodded. They passed the entrance to the nature preserve and were about to pass the newest Harry Leeper monstrosity when Ziggy stopped midstride. Kate assumed he was going to make a disparaging re-mark about the Creeper McMansion but tonight he was full of surprises.

"This here's a white oak. It's my favorite tree in Sea Point."

Struggling to find an appropriate response to Ziggy's impromptu show-and-tell, Kate nodded.

"I mean, in general, my favorite tree is a sassafras, but this particular tree, this exact white oak, is my favorite," Ziggy prattled on. "Like, if we had a tree draft, this would definitely be my number one pick."

Kate looked at Ziggy and saw the white teeth of his goofy smile, his chipped canine from her ninth birthday party piñata. He was trying to cheer her up.

On the heels of Nora's thoughtless text, Ziggy's kindness infuriated Kate and she imagined kicking that favorite tree of his, right in the trunk—anything to release the surge of red venom firing through her body, anything to make him understand the rage, the indignity of being her.

"Hey, you know who just popped into my head?" Oblivious to her wrath, Ziggy strolled over to his white oak and reached up to stroke a thick, low branch like it was the warm muzzle of a horse.

Before Kate could ask, or not ask, because she didn't really care, he said her name.

"Georgina Kim—where is she these days?"

It was a right hook Kate didn't see coming.

"Boulder," she forced out of her mouth. Boulder didn't hurt because Boulder was a fact, and facts were indisputable statistics on the back of a baseball card: Georgina was five foot five, thirty-three years old, a writer and adjunct professor based in Boulder, Colorado. Facts were accessible, inarguable.

The truths, however, could rip your heart out at any moment, anywhere. Truths were trickier, untethered to time, and entirely subjective. They were easy enough to conflate, confuse, and misconstrue. The truths about a former best friend were the words to the hit song that came out the summer you turned seventeen—impossible to unknow, and once they got in your head, they lived there forever.

Here were the truths about Georgina Kim: Kate Campbell thought of her whenever she was asked, "Cone or cup?," and whenever someone mentioned John Belushi, which was surprisingly often. She thought of Georgina Kim at the car wash, where Georgina had once described the mops as giant jellyfish. Every time Kate ordered a hot chocolate with extra whipped cream or passed a vending machine and saw those disturbing orange peanut butter crackers, she thought of Georgina. Even though the song came out after they'd stopped speaking, whenever Kate heard Taylor Swift's "Gorgeous" she sang it as "Georgeous" and cursed Nessie for giving Georgina that ridiculous nickname . . . right before she envisioned singing it to Georgina in some alternate universe where they were still inseparable.

The hardest truth to live with was that Kate Campbell thought of Georgina Kim every day, one way or another. Georgina haunted the most mundane moments, because if it wasn't free-range chicken eggs, it was crunchy peanut butter, and if it wasn't Jane Austen, it was *Hey, Arnold!* She was wild cherry slushies on Sunday and that Washington Capitals jersey she wore all through ninth grade, which meant that the mere mention of D.C., like Toni Morrison and Smartwool socks, immediately conjured Georgina Kim. She was Saves the Day and every Jersey punk band that almost made it big, any teenager loitering outside the arcade with blue hair. The truth was that Georgina Kim was the best and worst part of growing up because she was the best friend Kate had left behind.

"Yesterday I saw this little girl on a purple bike, just like the one she used to ride," Ziggy said, interrupting Kate's thoughts as they neared the lighthouse.

"Oh yeah?" Kate asked politely, feeling dizzy for the second time that night.

Ziggy nodded. "My dad used to call it the Campbell lawn ornament because it was always parked in your front yard. I hear Boulder is cool—bet she fits right in. Is she still playing hockey?"

Perhaps because of the day she'd had, or because she knew Ziggy was right and Georgina could fit in anywhere—but also stand out everywhere—or because he'd said her ex–best friend's name with such naked curiosity, tears sprang from Kate's eyes suddenly, inevitably, like they had the previous morning when she'd caught the sharp corner of a saltine cracker in the back of her throat. In an awkward attempt to console her, Ziggy tapped her shoulder like he was testing to see if the stovetop was still hot. Even through her tears, even in the shadow of the lighthouse, Kate saw that Ziggy was pale with concern as he asked, "Is she okay?"

"She's fine," Kate sniffled, before adding, "She's married."

Kate turned and began the walk back home, the stiffness in her walk commanding silence from Ziggy. Above them, the cold beam from the lighthouse appeared and disappeared, a revolving finger pointing blame through the darkness.

Finally, when their driveways came into view, Ziggy cleared his throat. "Same time tomorrow?"

Kate shot him a scowl he didn't deserve.

"To do this again," Ziggy clarified, gesturing back toward the dark street they'd just traversed together. "An after-dinner walk. Feels pretty good to get some fresh air, catch up, talk about the day's injustices."

"But we didn't talk about the day's injustices."

"Didn't need to," Ziggy shrugged. "We walked 'em off."

Golden Retrievers

"**B**ut what about Carmel?" Chloe asked Miles, sitting up in their king-size bed in their Presidio Heights apartment.

Miles had anticipated her surprise but forgotten all about Carmel. He was going to miss that part of this chapter, the Chloe chapter—her parents' secluded cottage in Carmel-by-the-Sea. He would miss the box seats at Giants baseball games with Chloe's younger brother and Chloe's healthy yet unbelievable cooking—she'd miraculously turned cauliflower into his favorite vegetable. The biggest loss would be the parties on the private beaches with Chloe's high school friends—the beautiful girls, the ubiquitous drugs, the fleet of Jet Skis and impromptu booze cruises—the unapologetic decadence of it all.

"I'm really sorry," Miles repeated, meeting her gaze and reaching for her hand. "But I think you know I have to do this."

Chloe smiled with her perfect mouth—the one all the actresses paid for but never quite achieved—and Miles saw what she saw. As an eternal optimist, Chloe thought he was changing, growing up. This charitable interpretation stemmed from her hours volunteering at the local animal rescue, where she routinely succeeded in rehabilitating neglected and abused dogs. If a pit bull trained to fight to the death could learn to trust and love humans again, Miles Hoffman could also change—he saw her thoughts scroll across her face like ticker tape.

"I'll come visit," she stated. "I need to meet your mom, anyway."

Miles nodded with the feigned investment he reserved for clients standing in building lobbies out of their price range. "Absolutely," he said, squeezing her thigh and leaning in to kiss her.

"Will you come back for River's wedding?"

Miles delivered a well-rehearsed grimace. "The Fourth of July is the biggest weekend of the summer," he explained ruefully. "If I'm not at the Wharf for that, I might as well not go at all."

Chloe stared down at her bare fingers, thinking about the wedding RSVPs, texting her engaged friends with crying-face emojis to say one guest instead of two, one vegan entrée instead of a couple. At the receptions, she'd sit quietly drunk in her white-padded seat and politely marvel at the tasteful centerpieces instead of working up a sweat with her boyfriend on the dance floor. It would be awful.

Miles watched the story line play out on Chloe's wrinkled forehead and saw two of the things he liked most about her—Chloe's inability to conceal her thoughts and her refusal to get the injections that most of her friends considered as life-changing as their Pilates classes. She'd never been a follower, Chloe touted, and she wanted to age naturally, gracefully—"like the French." (Her friends were quick to point out that Chloe's Swedish model of a mother was often assumed to be Chloe's sister, her face still brimming with the plump collagen that Chloe had surely inherited.) Nevertheless, Chloe's convictions were as honest as her face. She said exactly what was on her mind, whether it was that the tempeh was under-seasoned, Tessa's eyelash extensions were overdone, or that Miles's friends from Princeton were "especially douchey, even for Princeton."

Her outspokenness, her predilection for standing out rather than blending in, was also, Miles thought, the best indicator of how privileged she was. Before she could form complete sentences, Chloe had been assured that her opinions mattered and, as she grew, the world and its rules often bent to her whims. Her parents had encouraged her candor, even paid for it by sending her to small private schools and pricey summer camps. On opposite coasts, Chloe and Miles had grown up between the same bowling bumpers that encouraged risks, inflated confidence, and prevented consequence.

Now a physical therapist specializing in lymphedema and oncology rehabilitation at UCSF, Chloe charmed every person lucky enough to cross her path, whether it was in the post office or at a protest. As any colleague from the hospital or fellow rescue volunteer was quick to inform Miles when Chloe invited them over for a home-cooked meal, Chloe was kind but tough, blunt but hilarious, and so very generous. When Miles noticed they always included the word "generous," and pointed this out to Chloe, she had nodded thoughtfully, as if she'd observed this too. Over roasted artichoke hearts, she'd pondered aloud, "I think it's a gracious way of acknowledging the money I spend on my friends when we both know they can't afford to reciprocate. Right? Gross but accurate? It's probably why I'm throwing Lauren her baby shower, even though she was a total bitch in Palm Springs."

It was this self-aware spunk that made everyone love Chloe, and Chloe loved Miles. She wanted to marry him, she'd said it multiple times now—the first time drunk on their way home from her best friend's engagement party, but now she said it sober and on a regular basis, testing it out, watching his face. He'd kiss her forehead or squeeze her hand or overtly grope her to redirect the conversation. Just this past Saturday, Miles had cupped Chloe's ass in broad daylight as they waited to buy a French baguette at the farmer's market—the woman in line behind them had smiled broadly at Miles's hand and proclaimed how much she loved love. The woman may have been stoned, now that Miles thought about it, but Chloe had asked about her clogs and voila, just like that, he was off the hook—for the moment, anyway.

These physical reactions to her statements—because they were always statements ("I want to marry you, Miles Hoffman. In the fall.")—afforded him the latitude of interpretation. He wasn't verbally agreeing with Chloe about marriage but he wasn't snuffing out the idea, either. *Let her believe whichever narrative she wants*, Miles thought.

Chloe wasn't stupid—far from it—but intelligence had nothing to do with love. Miles had seen it before. The only thing he wanted to avoid more than marriage was hurting Chloe, which was why his summer in Sea Point had offered him the perfect solution: As long as Chloe didn't propose to him in the next week, he could avoid all the unfortunate business of breaking her heart.

The Prince of Sea Point had learned a long time ago that dumping someone was a lose-lose: He hated to be the bad guy. In college, Miles had even taken a women's studies class and learned all about agency and empowerment, the psychology of which he then applied to his love life. Since graduating, he'd empowered dozens of females by granting them the agency to break up with him and believe it was their idea. As a result, he was still on cordial terms with all of his exes, which was helpful for professional networking and even better for personal travel. After Chloe got over him, Miles hoped they could reconnect as friends so that he might stay at her parents' flat in London or their condo in Capetown. Instead of locking doors shut, Miles liked to keep every exit cracked for future entry. His nightmare was anyone disliking him, even an old girlfriend.

"You're being a coward," Chloe said directly, facing him with flinty eyes. "You're running home to avoid marrying me." He'd known from the moment he'd met her that she was trouble. Smart women were always trouble—it's what made them so appealing, before it made them so exhausting.

"That's not true and you know it," Miles scoffed. "I haven't been home in years. My mom's built a whole winter resort thing I haven't even seen except in *Travel & Leisure*."

"Right, which is why I don't understand the sudden urgency," Chloe growled.

"Because in case you don't recall, when I flew out for Zeke's funeral, I was only there for twenty-four hours because of that opening you said we couldn't miss," Miles answered coolly, losing his patience. "So I came back. But my mom has threatened to cut me out of the Wharf, and Ziggy asked me to help him with MVP because his dad, who was like a father to me, died out of nowhere. As inconvenient as those things might be for you and Carmel," Miles scolded, "I think you can agree they're important. I need to see Ziggy, and I need to see Wharflandia, which ends right before Memorial Day Weekend."

Miles was thinking about hot tubs in New Jersey when Chloe stood up and announced she was taking a shower, signaling the end of the boxing round. He rolled off the mattress and hit the hardwood floor for his daily push-ups. As he counted them out, he commended himself for navigating the Chloe–Jo Hoffman dynamic for this long. For two years, he'd been Odysseus, sailing between Charybdis and Scylla. He'd only survived because Chloe was so close with her family—Miles had spent the past two Thanksgivings and Christmases with them, enjoying himself immensely. The Chadwicks put on a great production—they were bighearted but low-key billionaires who loved to entertain as much as Miles loved to be entertained, which is why they still talked about the eight live reindeer Bob Chadwick had rented as a surprise last Christmas. Donner had peed in the corner of the living room and Vixen, true to his name, had nuzzled Annika Chadwick's ample bosom for most of the night.

Miles counted out his last thirty push-ups and decided to do an extra ten for good measure. He'd told his boss Buzz that his extended trip to Sea Point was a way to expand the Winston name on the East Coast, even if they both knew there was no need—Winston Commercial Real Estate was doing just fine. Since graduating from business school, Miles had collected an impressive salary from the company—plus options and quarterly bonuses—enabling him to drink top-shelf Scotch on balconies overlooking the Golden Gate Bridge. The best part was that he didn't have to actually sell real estate—he wasn't even a broker.

"People will want whatever your beautiful face tells them to want," Buzz Winston had told him at his Wharton graduation as he handed him a discreet white envelope containing an obscene signing bonus. Lawrence Winston, Miles's housemate during graduate school, was a nice enough guy to share a kitchen with, but his dad Buzz was the real go-getter, a showboat and a shark, just like Miles. They'd bonded instantly when they'd met in the clubhouse of Augusta National at the start of the Masters tournament.

For the last ten years, Miles's job as community director at Winston entailed nothing more than serving as the company's posterchild at the city's most exclusive rooftop cocktail parties and golden-ticket galas. Miles would be lying to say he didn't enjoy chatting with tech giants, hotel heirs, senators, and baseball owners while eyeing the lithe women in tight dresses who were a little disappointed that he wasn't some sort of mogul but absolutely devastated when they learned he had a girlfriend. They'd text him the following week with a project they thought he might be interested in, and Winston Commercial Real Estate would plant its flag a week later.

The men at the parties were worse—salivating over Miles's youth and murmuring truly heinous things about the brunette serving the tuna tartare five feet away. As they appraised the women like livestock and downed their second round of dry martinis, these men leaned into Miles as if trying to breathe in his vitality. Within their designated context, the men's performative vulgarities had amused Miles. But in the past year, their behavior had begun to unnerve him, even upset him.

The bottomless hunger of these powerful men had grown their bank accounts but destroyed their first, second, and third marriages. They were paunchy and yet so vain, pregnant with self-hatred but swollen with self-congratulation, and the contradiction of it all terrified Miles. He didn't want to turn into one of these sagging fleshbags in suspenders, clutching his arm, forcing him to look at lewd photos on their phones, all the while emitting a stink of garlic and imminent death. These were the men who insisted they loved women. These were the men who would text Miles the day after the black-tie event with a picture of the brunette server asleep and naked, with a follow-up text asking for Miles's email because he seemed like a good guy and there was a project in Parnassus Heights that he should consider. As Chloe was quick to point out, it was toxic masculinity at its finest, and for the past two years, Chloe had protected Miles from turning into one of these men by preventing him from going out with them. She had been his sexy, accomplished, vegan-cooking excuse. But it turned out that two years of dating in his thirties could not have been more different than two years of mating in his twenties.

Now Chloe was serious, and Miles wasn't interested in serious. Miles was interested in not becoming a disgusting old man, which meant a break from the city, a break from the steak dinners, a break from flirting with Buzz's twenty-three-year-old personal assistant. Fear was the push and now the threat of losing the Wharf served as the pull to Sea Point—one of two pulls, really, because there was also Ziggy.

In February, Miles had promised himself while sitting in the second pew at Zeke's funeral that he would fly home regularly to check in on Ziggy and Bev. Zeke had been a better father to him than Ari ever had, and although Zeke had never asked Miles for anything, Miles had sat behind Ziggy in that cramped church and imagined Zeke reclined in his blue La-Z-Boy in heaven, nodding his thanks that Miles would keep an eye on his family.

He'd meant to return sooner, or at least text Ziggy more often, but Miles's life on the West Coast didn't lend itself to such East Coast considerations—there were always great seats for the game and last-minute reservations at that new spot. And there was Chloe, who sometimes felt less like his girlfriend and more like a walking calendar of social obligations. Chloe expected him to attend her work events, her family events, her volunteer holiday events, and, worst of all, her friends' events. Regardless of whether it was an engagement party, a baby shower, or a charity ball to raise awareness for congenital dandruff, Chloe's friends ate up all his free time in an endless parade of self-congratulation.

Miles was over it—all of it—and Chloe would be fine. She'd meet some Golden Retriever from Marin County who worked in consulting and started most of his sentences with "essentially." It would work out for her, and for him—the world's systems were designed for their every success.

Anticipating his impending freedom, Miles texted Bell to let her know he was coming back to Sea Point and that he'd love to catch up. Within a minute, he knew she'd seen it, thanks to the "read" receipt under the text. Only Bell wouldn't have thought to turn those off.

It took Miles a moment to register that Chloe was back in their bedroom, her hair wet, her eyes red, her nose sniffly. Wiping her tears with her towel, Chloe collected her thoughts with a straight-A student's sense of agency and empowerment before declaring, "We need to talk."

Story Hour

Kate set her alarm for the first time in over a month but woke up throughout the night, worried she'd slept through it. Although the job was just a part-time gig at the library, she wanted to impress Patricia. As Sea Point's fashion icon, Patricia was as good a motive as any for Kate to finally unpack her two suitcases and three trash bags from Jane Street in search of her favorite work dress. She'd only worn it twice at Artemis PR before her life got punted to the ball sack of New Jersey.

"You have to tell me where you got that dress," Patricia said matter-of-factly when Kate walked through the door. "And then you have to forgive me for everything I'm about to show you."

Throughout Patricia's orientation, Kate felt like she was on the set of *The Music Man*: Not only did the Sea Point Library boast a spiral staircase to the second-floor stacks and a pulley system to transport books up and down, but the technological advances seemed to have stopped in the early 1960s. After teaching Kate how to access the convoluted digital system on what appeared to be the original IBM 610, Patricia led her into the staff office. "I know it's old school," Patricia acknowledged, stroking the antique punch clock, "like everything else in this place." Kate nodded as she

scanned the office and inventoried the overstuffed shelves, the row of fil-
ing cabinets, the three-foot-high pile of miscellaneous cords that made
Kate's OCD tendencies hit the fritz. The place wasn't old school—it was
outdated. Nursing homes invested more in the future of their patrons
than this library did.

It hadn't always been this way. As a teenager, Kate had viewed the library as a hub of action. Every Sea Pointer, from the Dungeons & Drag-
ons sort to the cheerleading squad, had found a reason to congregate
downstairs in the meeting room or upstairs in the stacks, even if it was just
to flirt or make out. Kate's SAT prep class had pushed the capacity of the
meeting room on Saturday mornings while several of Kate's teachers had
packed in for adult improv on Wednesday nights. The library had provided something for everyone. "This is where Chad and I met," Patricia
said, patting the Xerox machine where Kate had made copies of her college essay. "He asked me for a dime. Silver lining of this place is that the
photocopy is still ten cents."

"What happened?" Kate blurted out. "Sorry," she added, "but what
happened? Where is everybody?"

"They got smartphones and Nintendo Switches," Patricia explained.
"We also failed to keep up with the times, and now I'm just—well, I guess
I'm as guilty as anybody for letting this place turn into a relic."

"Not all relics are bad," Kate pointed out. "Look at Ms. Rose—she's a
rock star."

Patricia's laugh sounded like a *shhh* as she managed to clap her hands
noiselessly like the professional librarian she was. "That's the truth. Ms.
Rose is what keeps us relevant. Here, let me take you upstairs to the
stacks."

Although she knew the library well—their relationship dated back
thirty-three years—walking into the small staff office gave Kate the same
intoxicating tingles of trespassing into adulthood as her first sip of luke-
warm beer at a high school basement party. "You'll work behind the
checkout desk for the rest of this shift," Patricia said, "but first I want to
show you the secret storage room." Kate followed her up the spiral steps

and down an aisle to a bookshelf full of red encyclopedias. Patricia tipped the "L" volume toward her and the bookshelf popped open to reveal a hidden enclave. Kate gasped. The storage room they stepped into was just a nondescript closet full of cardboard boxes, but it had been there all along, throughout Kate's illustrious years of photocopying and SAT prep downstairs, and she'd never known. Patricia smiled before confiding, "This may or may not be where Chad and I consummated our marriage."

As time crept by and the library remained empty throughout the morning, Kate sat behind the checkout desk and began to wilt in her favorite dress. Just after eleven a.m., a stout man in red Lycra bike shorts burst through the door on such a mission that Kate assumed he was a lost professor in the throes of very important research. "Nature calls!" he announced over his shoulder as he beelined to the bathroom.

When the clock finally struck twelve, Kate felt a decade older and three shades paler than when she'd arrived. It had been a mistake, telling Patricia yes. The library was not only a graveyard but as much a professional dead-end as the rest of Sea Point. Kate couldn't even look for jobs during her shift because Patricia had a no-phone policy on the floor and the computer at the checkout desk had nearly crashed when she'd double-clicked on the "World Wide Web" icon.

Tuesday morning at the library moved even more slowly than Monday because it was no longer novel for Kate to watch her life crawl backward.

Wednesday morning, however, the library hummed with anticipatory energy as soon as Kate arrived—even the fluorescent overhead lighting seemed brighter and stopped flickering as Kate stored her bag behind the checkout desk. When Patricia unlocked the front door, the excited footfalls of children filled the air and the library was instantly alive with toddler giggles and flashes of OshKosh B'gosh as kids raced through the aisles and toward the Children's Corner. Ms. Rose's Story Hour provided enough reason for patrons to visit the library early and check out books afterward, milling about to say hi to one another and let the kids tap on the glass of the ant farm.

The last time Kate had seen Everett, the manager of Summersault, he had been chain-smoking on the back stoop of the dive bar, crying over the end of a summer fling. Now he was married with two kids and a nicotine patch on his forearm that he proudly showed to Kate. The next person she recognized was Daphne, a shy girl a grade above her at Sea Point High who'd suffered from eczema and always chewed on her pencils during AP physics. Over the past fifteen years, she'd taken over her father's shoe store and had two daughters. The only noticeable thing on Daphne's face now, Kate observed, was a toothy smile she was quick to share.

Story Hour served as an impromptu reunion Kate never could have imagined attending without feeling embarrassed about being back, but she didn't have time to feel like a failure because no one cared where she had been or why she had returned, only that she was here in the library with them. Kate couldn't be sure, but she thought she even saw Ms. Rose do a double take in her direction before giving her the same distinct scowl she only offered at the end of each Story Hour—Bernadette saw it too and agreed it was Ms. Rose's attempt at a smile.

The busy morning surprised Kate into a good mood as she rushed home to take a quick shower and somehow managed to show up ten minutes early for her first shift at the Jetty Bar. The physical movement, change of scenery, and quick interactions seemed to have rearranged all of her molecules as she remembered her junior-year social psychology professor lecturing about the importance of "flow." Pulling into the Wharf's employee parking lot, Kate understood that her previous attitude had been silly—childish, really—as if a temporary job at the library in Sea Point would be the only thing to define her.

"Look who's back!" Denise McKibben announced. The Jetty Bar's manager since its opening day, more than thirty years ago, Denise was mostly fair and plenty tough. She was quick to point out a poorly folded napkin or a barely polished martini glass, but equally eager to pay a compliment after a high-grossing night. The seasoned manager would pitch in every which way she could for her servers—delivering drinks from the bar, running credit cards, even bussing tables. She wasn't afraid of the dirty work—back in high school, Kate had once seen Denise on all fours in front of an eight-top, cleaning up a toddler's clam-chowder vomit.

Front of house, where she played gatekeeper next to the hostess stand, Denise was often overheard telling the cranky man who thought the service was too slow, or the disgruntled woman who found the menu too limited, that her favorite catchphrase, the one she lived by, was that "the customer is always right." At the end of another long night as her staff mopped the floors and ran their receipts, Denise would sit at the end of the bar with a glass of Sancerre and repeat her true catchphrase: "Fuck 'em." Even though Denise was gruff, Kate would never forget the time a table of college kids "dined and ditched" on her. Denise gave her an extra $100 that night, and it hadn't come from Jo Hoffman or the Jetty Bar.

"I'm not one for blessings but you doing this is a blessing," Denise said now, tossing a clean bar mop at Kate's face—the manager's version of a welcome wagon.

Half an hour later, Kate was reacquainting herself with the ins and outs of the kitchen, the bar, the crew. Denise showed her how the new computer system worked (so much easier than the one they'd had before), and soon thereafter Kate was welcoming customers and cracking jokes while sliding fresh cocktail napkins across the bar. Compared to waiting tables, in which a teenaged Kate had approached strangers in midconversation, poured waters, listed the specials, and instantly become their temporary subordinate, tending bar struck Kate as a more consensual meeting of the minds that tipped the power in her favor.

After so many years away, she'd forgotten what it was like to be the Jetty bartender, the high priestess of the sacred buzz. Kate poured absolution into rocks glasses and served forgiveness with a salt rim. The martinis were dirty but the clients were genuine, and as she racked up miles in the fifteen-foot galley, Kate considered how it wasn't about the alcohol for most of the people here. It was about congregating for a holy communion. It was about being seen, remembered, welcomed.

There was a stool for everyone at the Jetty Bar except Pretense, because he and his buddy Pride had a reserved corner table in the two-Michelin-star formal dining room. Halfway through her shift, Kate carded a couple visiting from New York and realized that if the Wharf had been in the city, she and Thomas would have been dining room regulars, gushing to out-of-town friends that the service was impeccable and menu brilliant in its simple sophistication. But in New Jersey, Kate knew better: A customer sitting at the Jetty Bar could order anything from the dining room menu if they'd been around long enough to ask. And as an employee, Kate didn't hate it when a customer sent back the scallops for being too browned for their liking because the only thing more delicious than scallops from the Wharf were free scallops from the Wharf.

By her third night, Kate was in cahoots with the servers, food runners, and kitchen staff. As they waited for Kate to make their cocktails, servers would wipe down the small beverage trays and gossip about their tables.

There were the day-trippers who tended to walk out once they learned popcorn shrimp wasn't on the menu. The condescending first-timers who found the cheap pitchers of beer offensive until their teenage children brought up all the celebrities who loved the Wharf—and then the pitchers were kitschy. It didn't matter to tourists that Jo Hoffman had promised her father in 1983 that she'd serve pitchers at her fancy resort, and that was how she still lured him to town for two weeks every summer. What mattered to the "just visiting" crowd was that if the rich and famous were okay with pitchers—Tina Fey, Will Smith, and even Oprah Winfrey, whose partner hailed from nearby Whitesboro—then it must be part of the Jetty Bar experience, like New Orleanian beignets and lobsters in Maine.

But Kate's favorite customers weren't the celebrities in their baseball caps and protective entourages. The people Kate waved to and shimmied for as they mounted their barstools were the Nightwalkers.

Nightwalkers were fellow restaurant folk on their night off who appreciated the artistry of Kate's cocktails and the multiple free rounds she sent their way because that's just what you did for your barkeeping kin. After all, the inside bartering among waitstaff was half the beauty of working in the industry, and so the Nightwalkers would pay their small tab and leave a fat stack of cash for Kate along with an invitation to their restaurant on her next night off.

Within the small world of Sea Point existed a smaller world of local hustlers who got by on curried favors and rumpled wads of green bills, always slightly damp from spilled drinks and sweat. The Nightwalkers took care of one another because everyone was busting their butts and no one was paying for health insurance. Even after a slow morning, week, month, fellow servers always left an extra $20 on the table. It wasn't code so much as a straight-up declaration that they had one another's backs. The cash was to compensate for the couple extending their passive-aggressive tactics to the service, and to cover for the patrons who left a $3 tip on a $47 bill so that it showed up on their credit card as an even $50.

"Why do they do that?" Kate asked the first time she experienced the egregious round-up method.

Denise had cursed at the receipt and muttered, "Because dinner is cheaper than therapy."

Behind this bar, she wasn't a Campbell or an almost-Mosby. She was just Kate the bartender, smiling to the honeymooners, sunburned fishermen, consulting bros down from the city, and exhausted dishwashers finally done for the day. Kate caught her reflection in the circle window of the swinging kitchen door and decided she was indeed a treasure in her own town. Because regardless of any fact about her former life, Kate knew with unequivocal certainty who she was when she tied on her black apron and put her hair into a high messy bun: a friendly face who could make a damn fine cocktail.

There was only one person in the world who would understand the euphoric frenzy of returning to the Jetty Bar, who'd stood beside her in this galley and wiped sweat with one hand and poured shots with the other. There was only one person who understood the highs and lows of gambling with large-party automatic gratuity, and Kate was desperate to talk to her. But she and Georgina had stopped speaking long ago.

Leeper the Creeper

Ziggy texted Kate the following Monday on her first night off from the Jetty Bar: *Walk-off?* The sudden immersion in the service industry had left her legs feeling like cinder blocks and the drawer of her nightstand flush with cash. She'd used this morning's tomb shift at the library to stretch her calves behind the checkout desk, but Kate had fantasized all day about a night to binge *Wives with Knives*. Ever since Thomas's phone call, she would watch her favorite show (which critics had unanimously panned for its gratuitous violence) and envision Wally as that episode's murder victim.

I can see you in your living room, Ziggy followed up ten minutes later, when Kate hadn't replied to his first text. It would have been creepy except that he used to call the landline to say the exact same thing when he'd been in third grade and Kate in second. It was an old, dumb inside joke that made Kate snort in spite of herself. Groaning at her sore muscles as she laced up her sneakers, Kate wondered if Ziggy would bring up Georgina again, but when she met him in the middle of the street, his mind was elsewhere.

"Miles gets in next week."

"Your Miles?"

"Yep."

"He's really coming back?" Just when she and Ziggy had started to re-connect, here came Miles Hoffman to steal him away. It was like middle school all over again.

"He sent me a screenshot of his flight," Ziggy beamed, holding up his phone. Kate squinted to read the ticket details—of course Miles flew first class.

"Well," she said, scanning the ground for a rock, "nice knowing you."

"Oh come on! He's not that bad!"

As they walked toward the lighthouse, Kate reminded Ziggy of all the reasons Miles was exactly that bad. In high school, not only had he cheated on every girl he'd dated, but he'd pulled a bunch of pranks that were dangerous. One year, Miles had soaped up the major stairwell at Yates and a pregnant teacher had been the first one to slip. She and the baby were okay, but if he had been anyone but Jo Hoffman's son, Miles would have faced actual consequences. Instead, his classmates voted the Prince of Sea Point their Class Clown, and no matter how many times he broke Parker Ryan's heart, her tan legs always appeared to be dangling out of his red Jeep after the Saturday night hockey games.

"That was high school," Ziggy argued. "He's got problems too, you know."

"Oh yeah?" Kate asked, intrigued. "Please inform me about the hardships in first class."

Ziggy hesitated, wondering if what Miles had told him was confidential. "Between us, Jo basically said he's out of the running for Wharf CEO." Kate interrupted him with a scoff so loud it echoed down the empty street. "Say what you will, but he's upset enough to come home and try to prove himself. Plus, he's going to help me with the books."

Kate nodded and twisted her mouth so she wouldn't say anything.

"I bet you'll like him now. Maybe I'll invite him to a walk-off."

"This is our second walk-off," Kate pointed out. "It's not a thing and we don't need to include the Prince, even if he is losing his grip on the Queen's coattails."

Ziggy stopped in his tracks and shook his head. "Kate Campbell, when did you start hating everything? My dad would be so disappointed in you."

Kate jerked her neck back as if he'd just attempted to swing at her face.

"Oh, right, meant to tell you," Ziggy said with a straight face, "I get to play the dead dad card whenever I want."

"What are you so giddy about?"

Ziggy shrugged, but he knew it was because Miles was coming back to town, and with his best friend around, and Kate Campbell across the street, he felt like Sea Point was on the verge of revival, a social and cultural renaissance. Instead of being left behind, he'd just been biding his time until everyone returned. He wasn't the stuck plumber but the proud local who'd known this whole time what his smarter friends had only just figured out: There's no place like home, especially when home is by the ocean. All roads led back to Sea Point.

"I've always loved that house," Kate said, looking up at the twelve-foot hedge that hid Daffodil Cottage from street view. "Have you ever been inside?"

Ziggy nodded. "It's as nice as you'd think. Maybe nicer."

"Tell me," Kate whispered, walking a few steps forward to the mouth of the long driveway and peering up at the house with uncharacteristic reverence.

"Pretty soon the front yard is going to be an ocean of daffodils."

"Tell me about *the inside*."

"I could show you," Ziggy responded without thinking.

Kate turned to look at him, and before she opened her mouth, he could tell by her curdled expression what she was going to say. "I know you're not actually going to go in there," he said with feigned nonchalance and gratitude for the starless night—he felt heat in his cheeks. "My dad and I did all the work on it. Right now I'm making them the world's most luxurious man cave."

"You know, if I were the trespassing type," Kate sighed, "I'd be very excited to see all your hard work."

Ziggy forced a slight smile, remembering back to when he too would never have dared. He'd only become the trespassing type in February. Despite the dozens of keys and combinations Ziggy possessed as part of the trusted MVP team, Daffodil Cottage was where he'd lost his breaking-and-entering virginity.

Ziggy understood, on some deep level he preferred to ignore, that it was Zeke's death that gave way to his trespassing habit. Acknowledging this, however, would have required looking directly into his past to understand his future, and that would have been no less debilitating than staring directly at a solar eclipse. So instead, Ziggy blamed Greg.

Greg had been more of an acquaintance in high school, but he and Ziggy had become friends after everyone else had abandoned their hometown for the big cities. Greg worked at the lumberyard and saved Ziggy useable scraps of wood, even let Ziggy borrow some of the shop's smaller machines. The morning of Zeke's funeral, Greg had shown up early and set up folding chairs in the back of the church because he'd rightly guessed there'd be substantial overflow. He was a nice guy who appreciated foreign films and microbrews.

A week after the service, Greg invited Ziggy to throw back beers at Summersault. It was a quiet night until a gaggle of bridesmaids entered the bar, click-clacking behind their queen bee, eyes already at half-mast from a full day of drinking. This happened often—girls wandering off Wharflandia's manicured campus to explore townie terrain. They'd quickly zeroed in on Ziggy and Greg, by far the most viable men there.

"Please save me from this," a bridesmaid had whispered to Ziggy. He looked over and saw a pretty girl with alert eyes. "I'm Camille," she said. "And I'm way too old for a penis crown."

And because he had been drinking, and because Camille was cute, and because he held the keys and knew the code, Ziggy determined that Daffodil Cottage was a more appropriate escape hatch than his mother's house.

Two hard turns and one hip check later, they were in. No need to grope for the light switch—muscle memory guided Ziggy's hand to where it had always been and, ta-da, he was in the foyer of Daffodil Cottage with a beautiful girl.

Touring the house while Camille gawked, Ziggy switched on lamps and wondered why rich people with huge houses so often attempted to downplay their grand lifestyle. Daffodil Cottage was no cottage—at least, not the way he thought of a cottage, which was a cramped little house where Snow White and the Seven Dwarfs slept in one room full of bunk beds. Daffodil Cottage was a six-bedroom house with five rain showers, two claw-foot bathtubs, a seven-hundred-square-foot kitchen, and a wet bar on the roof.

To his credit, Ziggy did a discreet walk through of the house first ("We trust you to keep an eye on Daffodil Cottage," the owners had said) while Camille scrolled through her phone on the white couch in the living room. And the next morning, after Camille had given him her number and a kiss goodbye, Ziggy watched *SportsCenter* until the dryer beeped so he could remake the bed with freshly laundered sheets. "An owner should never know we've been in their space," Zeke used to say, handing Ziggy the disposable blue shoe covers he insisted they wear over their boots before entering a client's home.

Throughout the morning, Ziggy heard his father's voice and the seriousness with which Zeke emphasized the importance of a client's trust: "Integrity is what makes us MVP and not Ocean City HVAC." Even though he and Camille hadn't spent any time downstairs, Ziggy went out to his truck and grabbed a pair of the blue shoe covers. He put them on before vacuuming the whole first floor. Just in case.

"They don't rent it?" Kate asked now.

"No, and they're almost never here."

"Well, does it at least have a grossly outdated kitchen? Or tacky art? That would make me feel better—tell me the whole place is wallpapered in *Dogs Playing Poker*."

Ziggy laughed. "It's amazing inside."

Seven years ago, on Skype from their Tuscan villa, the owners had spearheaded a complete remodeling of the kitchen. They'd FedExed sea glass from a beach in Praiano for their custom backsplash and put in a triple-paned wall of south-facing windows. When the shipment of black onyx was delayed for a fifth time and the tile guy disappeared, Zeke and Ziggy negotiated with the owners and installed the onyx kitchen floor themselves. The Miller men had spent a week in December on their hands and knees after work, alternating between beers and coffee to get the job done. In the end, the extra money paid for the cedar deck and slate walkway they built at their own house as a surprise birthday gift for Bev.

Kate took another awed step toward the driveway. "Tell me more."

"Leeper tried to buy it," Ziggy said.

"Of course he did," Kate scoffed.

If Sea Point tourists were asked about Harry Leeper, they might squint at the sky before giving up and saying, "I think I've seen that name on a sign somewhere?"

A local's reaction, however, would be a series of guttural sounds paired with a string of obscenities. In just ten years, Harry Leeper had torn down a dozen iconic bungalows, seven historic homes, including one with ties to the underground railroad, and the mythical Bluebell Hotel—all within a five-square-mile town.

With every Leeper purchase, a public desecration ensued. First, he bulldozed each lot so it was devoid of every suggestion of life, preferring the stark look of a landing strip to that of an active ecosystem. Then he built monstrosities with windows better proportioned for a child's playhouse and sold them to the highest-bidding out-of-towners who almost always paid in cash. For a few getaway weeks every summer, the buyers didn't mind the plastic siding on the brand-new $2 million home as long as there were as many bedrooms and bathrooms as possible to accommodate large parties. They wanted more house to compensate for being in New Jersey.

And so, in Sea Point, Harry Leeper wasn't a developer. He was the man destroying the town from the helm of his white pickup.

To be fair, he'd had help.

Donna McConnell, a hand-model-turned-real-estate-agent after an unfortunate incident at a mink farm, conveniently sat on the zoning board. She had used her dual positions to transform Harry from an unreliable construction worker to Sea Point's most successful and least respected builder. Known around town for her platinum-blond ringlets, hot pink leggings, and elaborate modifications to every restaurant order (no bread, no tomato, but always extra mayo), Donna's loud presence stood in stark contrast to her role as Harry Leeper's silent business partner.

In the early days of their clandestine enterprise, Donna tipped Harry off about owners who'd tentatively dipped their toe in the market by calling her realty office, and the very next morning Leeper would knock on their front door with the cunning charm and sparkling canines of a wolf just arrived at grandmother's house. He'd offer a signed check and assuage concerns about outdated kitchens, flood-prone basements and persnickety garage doors. "No need for an inspection," Leeper would tell the homeowners, caressing the nearest wall. "It has good bones." With a wink, he'd promise to care for their beloved home before clicking his pen, proffering papers, and explaining the deal expired in twenty-four hours. No local could compete with the cash and no seller could refuse.

Throughout Sea Point, it was quietly understood that Donna herself had fronted Leeper the capital to make these cash deals in the beginning of their joint business venture, and her foresight proved to be a sound investment. Harry Leeper's hefty profits on his first few houses cast him in an alluring golden glow to banks. Soon, he boasted access to multiple lines of credit, which meant access to big purchases, access to access. Although Donna kept the East Sea Point house she'd inherited from her parents, everyone knew she'd moved into Harry Leeper's house in nearby Ship Harbor. That was one more thing that drove locals crazy—Harry Leeper didn't care about demolishing Sea Point because he didn't live there.

With the onslaught of McMansions came the population who believed bigger was better. The new clientele opted to pay extra for the security alarms to be connected directly to the firehouse, so that each time a raccoon pilfered through their trash cans, volunteer firefighters were obligated to get out of their beds at three a.m. to go investigate the scene. The houses sat empty eleven months out of the year, even though the motion-sensing lights suggested otherwise. From two hundred miles away, the owners shook their heads as they monitored the increase in Sea Point's light pollution through an app on their phone, which also reminded them to meditate.

It was for these reasons that locals referred to Harry Leeper as "Leeper the Creeper." On evening strolls when they would look up at a new plastic castle that drowned out the stars, they would mutter his name under their breath, and every time they did, it sounded more like a curse.

Ziggy stared at the front door from the edge of the driveway and led Kate on an audio tour through Daffodil Cottage—the antithesis of a Creeper project. The master shower was its own greenhouse, Ziggy explained, with bouquets of eucalyptus hanging from the ceiling and filling the room with that tranquil, heart-slowing scent. It was the first bathroom where Ziggy had installed radiant heat without his father's supervision. "Fun fact: Daffodil Cottage was built the same year that the Bluebell Hotel opened and the *Titanic* sank—1912," Ziggy said. "A few years ago, the owners tracked down some of the original marble floor from the lobby of the Bluebell, so we got to install those tiles in the master bathroom."

Kate gasped. "Tell me you're joking," she whispered, as if speaking about something beloved, or holy, or deceased. The Bluebell was all three—its existence had been legendary, its demolishment devastating.

The Bluebell had been Sea Point's first hotel, a landmark in the sand, and its demise was widely considered the worst of Harry Leeper's countless transgressions. Built between 1909 and 1911 by one of the country's most prominent hoteliers, its creation had cost an astronomical $1 million. The lobby of the Bluebell was a replica of the *Titanic*'s ballroom, right down to the same Tiffany-style glass dome ceiling and double staircase bending to the second floor. On opening night in February 1912, the East Coast elite traveled to sleepy little Sea Point and danced on the roof of the Bluebell, only stopping to watch Henry Ford and Louis Chevrolet race their new inventions along the beach below. Leeper had razed it four years ago, infuriating the locals, who lined up on the beach to pay their respects as a twelve-thousand-pound wrecking ball turned history to rubble before their eyes.

"You know that's where my great-grandparents met," Kate gushed. "On my mom's side. Opening night. They reached for the same champagne coupe from a floating tray, and that was it. What did it feel like—resurrecting all that Bluebell marble?"

Ziggy shrugged. "Hard to say."

"Okay, fine, what does it look like?"

"It's mosaic tile," Ziggy said with his professional-plumber voice. "It's really nice, but honestly, my favorite part of that house is the outdoor shower."

"The church of any devout believer in summer," Kate agreed. "Tell me."

"Normally," Ziggy began, scratching his elbow and looking at Daffodil Cottage, "we have to work within pretty tight zoning perimeters. But you know how that works. One day I saw Donna pulling into the Wharf in a new Lexus and the next day we get a call from the owners giving us the green light to go to town on the shower, make it beautiful."

"I'm sure that was just a coincidence," Kate deadpanned. "Do you remember how I used to ask for an outdoor shower every Christmas?"

Ziggy laughed as he nodded. "This one is pretty insane—two heads from opposite walls, and then there's a separate changing room with a vanity. The ceiling is thirteen feet high and made of a stained glass window we salvaged from St. Luke's before Creeper tore that down too."

Passing the duck pond on their walk home, Kate had to give Ziggy credit: Even if he'd never left Sea Point, or graduated from college, the boy next door could create just about anything with his bare hands. The only thing Thomas had ever created was a TaskRabbit account so he could pay two bald guys in mesh basketball shorts to mount his gigantic television.

Stealing a look at her old friend under the streetlamp, Kate ventured to see Ziggy in a new light, as an adult. What chapters had she missed? What was he too humble, too private, to ever tell her? Kate remembered that, even in middle school, he'd always pretended to be sick on award day to avoid walking across the stage to collect his "Best Athlete" certificate as voted by his classmates. Given how attractive Ziggy had become, Kate acknowledged that it was unlikely he was single, even if he did wear the same pair of too-big overalls every day. She flashed to that early morning when she'd overheard Ziggy telling Roger the recycling guy he was just getting in—who was the woman?

They reached their driveways and lingered. Kate opened her mouth to ask if Ziggy was seeing anyone but worried how it would sound. Instead, she said she'd see him later and watched Ziggy grab his trash cans from the curb. "Tomorrow night?" Ziggy asked over his shoulder as he dragged the cans to the side of his parents' house.

"Sure," Kate heard herself say.

Prodigal Prince

Miles took a red-eye from SFO and landed at Philadelphia Airport on the third Tuesday in May. After picking up his rental, a brand-new silver Porsche 911 Carrera S Cabriolet—because go big or go home, but also go big when you go home—Miles watched the convertible's roof pack itself into the trunk as he blasted the PRODIGAL SON playlist he'd curated on the flight. He stepped on the gas and exhaled.

Taking in the Philadelphia skyline from the Girard Point Bridge and grinning as the sports stadiums came into view, Miles ceded the fact that he had a West Coaster's adventurous spirit but an East Coaster's loyal heart. He was excited to head home, to be back in the land of Philly sports teams and their insane fans, even if several frayed ends awaited him.

He stopped at a gas station for snacks and did a double take at the woman in line ahead of him—she looked just like his childhood au pair. When Miles entered Yates Academy in kindergarten, Jo hired "Valentina from Argentina" to drive him the thirty minutes each way and insisted they listen to the Spanish tapes she'd purchased. Miles had so resented Valentina, who spoke too quickly in words he didn't understand, that he'd tried to fire her from the back of his father's Mercedes. He'd still been in a car seat at the time, and Jo had not been amused when she'd found out. "You'll thank me someday," she'd said. "Spanish is the language of the future and you're a lucky boy to learn it early from a native speaker." Only now did Miles realize Valentina must have been barely twenty when she'd spent two hours a day driving him to and from school. He had no idea where she was now. The woman in line really was a spitting image of her, but as she'd looked three decades ago—Valentina would be in her fifties now. Nothing crystallized the impossible speed of time more than going home. Miles suddenly felt old and exhausted. He stepped out of line to grab a huge cup of coffee.

Back on the road and feeling the blissful buzz of caffeine hit his system, Miles saw two texts come in. He ignored the one from Chloe who, as planned, had broken up with him but seemed committed to "staying friends." Miles tapped on the one from Ziggy: *ETA? Bev wants to make you lunch.* Miles's mouth curled up into his signature three-quarter smile, a semi-grin that had ruined multiple marriages and ended one engagement. Nothing could be more of a homecoming than a Bev Miller lunch: a turkey sandwich with lettuce, tomato, and spicy mustard on wholewheat bread, cut on a diagonal, with ruffled Utz chips and a pickle from the Coffee Cow.

Within the hour, he was pulling into the Miller driveway. "You brought the sunshine with you!" Bev exclaimed, holding open the front door with one arm, the other raised in an expectant hug. And here was Ziggy, rushing past her like a dopey dog, galumphing toward Miles with half the body fat he'd had in February.

"Dude," Miles sputtered, "you look like a lost Hemsworth."

Ziggy didn't respond but instead kept grinning as he embraced Miles. "I'm so glad you're here," he said in a prolonged bear hug. His voice was thick, on the verge of tears, which didn't surprise Miles. Ziggy was his father's son—a sensitive soul, thoughtful, and proof that Miles wasn't a total sociopath if they'd been best friends for this long.

"Get over here already!" Bev yelped from the porch, stomping her feet.

"It's my turn!" Miles took the steps two at a time to Bev and scooped her up, lifting her off the ground. "You're finally home!" she squealed. "Do you know how much we've missed you?" The last time they had been together was at Zeke's funeral. Before that brief, heart-wrenching trip, Miles hadn't visited Sea Point in several years.

He didn't dare look at Ziggy just then. These Millers made him so emotional, and suddenly Miles's life on the West Coast felt far away and farcical. The house smelled like fresh laundry that had been hung outside on a line to dry—that crisp, clean scent that had compelled Miles to huff his pillowcase every time he'd slept over.

Walking through the house, Miles noted each mark of beauty, each artistic touch. Bev's medium was oil paint but her creativity nestled into every crevice, just as it always had. She moved through the world in an ongoing dialogue with nature: windowsills served as blank canvases meant to display a glass vase with a single bud or a robin's egg rescued from the road, a shed snakeskin, a smooth green rhombus of sea glass. Jo's home, meanwhile, was filled with art acquired from well-established New York City galleries, professionally framed and hung on the walls by Jon Bon Jovi's interior decorator. Both mothers were collectors, but what they pocketed, what they treasured, could not have been more different.

With her long, quick-twitch fingers, Bev swept up an ancient brown apothecary bottle from the nearest window ledge and insisted that Miles smell the dried sage.

This felt like home. And yet, sitting down at the kitchen table with the promised lunch before him, Miles felt his stomach lurch. He realized he had subconsciously been waiting to hear Zeke's heavy boots clunking down the stairs, his arms swinging in his faded flannel shirt, eyes glistening like wet pebbles above that oversize grin dominating his face as he announced, "Oh look! My favorite delinquent." Rinsing the sandwich down with a glass of milk, Miles forced himself to pretend that Zeke was just out on a job, not gone. He couldn't lose it in front of Bev.

The dark thought that had been haunting him since February, since

Ziggy had called him sobbing, curled up in Miles's chest and burrowed. He was a bad person for thinking it, even if he never said it. Why Zeke? Why not his own deadbeat dad?

Miles took a deep breath, inhaling the lemon Pine-Sol Bev used to clean the kitchen counters. These smells were as transportive as any psychedelic drug. He felt the singular peace he'd always experienced between these walls and also the twinge of guilt that accompanied being here and feeling this way when his own childhood home was across town in West Sea Point.

"Care for another?" Bev asked, already halfway out of her seat and reaching for the loaf of bread.

Miles looked at Ziggy. "Wanna go halfsies?"

In sixth grade, Ziggy and Miles had met at a pickup ice hockey game on the frozen duck pond in East Sea Point, just a few blocks from Ziggy's house. It had been a snow day and, after the game, as Miles waited for that year's au pair to show while hail pelted his bare head, Ziggy had asked if he wanted to walk back to his house.

Removing his sweat-soaked pads in the hallway for the first time of millions, Miles heard the Rolling Stones blasting from the kitchen, where Bev was cursing the sensitive smoke detector on the ceiling and waving a broom at it. He followed Ziggy, who dutifully stirred the chili on the stove, and called his mom to tell her he'd be having dinner with a friend from hockey. "Sure, honey," Jo had said, distracted. "Just let Paulina know when you want to be picked up." Miles hung up, wondering if he'd ever want to be picked up as Bev asked him to set the table. Miles still remembered how grateful he'd been to have a task, how folding those napkins gave him a place in the Miller family. At his own home, Rene the housekeeper did everything and forbade him from sitting in the kitchen while she cooked. After that first Miller dinner, Zeke had scooped four bowls of mint chocolate chip ice cream, and Ziggy had asked Miles the best question one sixth grader can ask of another: "Want to sleep over?"

When Miles was growing up, the ongoing drama at the Hoffman house—

his father's erratic disappearances, his brother's penchant for school suspensions—resulted in Miles's fondest memories taking place at the Millers'. In the kitchen now, Miles admired Bev's paintings hanging on the far wall. She used to rotate them every few months, but these were the same ones he had seen in February after Zeke's funeral. Ziggy had said that Bev had stopped painting, but Miles hadn't believed him until now.

"That's my favorite," Miles said, pointing with his sandwich to the smallest canvas across from him. Bev mustered a weary smile. At first, the painting appeared abstract, a half-moon of blue, narrow bars of gray over a swatch of pink, with a yellow background filling in the rest. But any local knew it was an off-center close-up of a table setting at the Wharf—the blue the plate, the gray the fork tines, the swatch of pink the cloth napkin and the yellow the Wharf's signature yellow linen tablecloth. Every artist in town sold paintings of the Wharf, scenes of the busy dining room, or the crowded Jetty Bar, or the line of chefs in their funny chef hats and checkered pants, but only Bev had thought to zoom in like this, to make a familiar scene both strange and intimate, engaging with the observer, waiting for the click of recognition that might never come.

"Take it," Bev said, opening the refrigerator door.

Miles looked at Ziggy, who gave him a "this is what it's been like" look.

"I'm serious," Bev added. "But really we should give it to your mother, don't you think?"

Miles shrugged and bit into his second sandwich to buy time. "Probably, yeah. That would be nice. Besides, I want a fresh Beverly Miller."

Bev made something of a squawking noise while Ziggy beamed, the corners of his eyes crinkling so that Miles knew he'd said something genuinely funny.

"What? It's a reasonable request. Every clown-around knows about the old Beverly Millers, all the priceless canvases that stay priceless because you won't sell them."

Bev patted his shoulder and kissed the top of his head before he stood up to pour himself more milk. "I haven't been painting," she said, and now, up close, Miles saw all the new lines in her face, the bruise-colored bags under her eyes, the prominent silver threads above her ears.

"Yeah, that's the word on the street," Miles said, reaching his arm around her and pulling her in for a hug. Ziggy shook his head from across the table, biting down on a grin that crept out all the same because he knew exactly what Miles was trying to do. "But I have so many people I need to impress, so could you just *consider* painting something new for me? Maybe one of all the cute new lifeguards in their blue two-piece Speedos?"

"You've always understood my aesthetic better than anyone," Bev said dryly, her words muffled by Miles's gigantic arm still wrapped around her. A client had once told him that he didn't give bear hugs so much as anaconda squeezes. "In other news," Bev said, switching the subject, "did Ziggy tell you about his father's ridiculous last request?"

Miles shot Ziggy a questioning look.

"I still can't believe it," Bev continued. "He up and dies on me, and then it turns out he's pulled this whole stunt in the will about a party on the ferry. AND THEN!" Bev looked at Ziggy, who was examining the black crud under his fingernails, before returning her gaze to Miles. "I get to the second paragraph on the Wawa receipt, where Zeke's requested a full-blown re-creation of the Rock the Boat party, just like the one we met on a hundred million years ago, so that everyone can find their soulmate somewhere between Sea Point and Delaware."

"He thought it would be a nice tribute," Ziggy offered quietly.

In the silence that followed, Bev looked at Ziggy, Ziggy looked at Miles, and Miles looked out the kitchen window, preoccupied with Bev's garden shed. "I know you don't want to hear this, except that you do," Miles finally said. "I find it *Notebook*-level romantic, what he did. He's basically saying that his biggest accomplishment was meeting you on that ferry, what, thirty-seven years ago?"

Bev nodded soberly while Ziggy slouched deep into his chair. For the first time in years, Miles felt he was in the right place, doing the right thing.

"Speaking of boats," Miles said, nodding out the window before look-ing at Ziggy, "you have time for a quick trip?"

Leaning against Bev's shed and covered in a blue tarp visible from the kitchen window rested the red canoe Zeke, Ziggy, and Miles had built the summer after sixth grade. Ice hockey may have brought the boys together, but it was their weekend canoe trips that bridged the rift of attending dif-ferent middle schools. Thanks to Zeke's vigilance over the years, the canoe was still in perfect condition.

"I can't go today," Ziggy said, blowing out a defeated sigh. At Miles's indignant gape, he explained that he was already behind—he needed to keep working on the man cave at Daffodil Cottage and, more pressing, Jenna at the yoga studio had texted him multiple times in the last hour about replacing a showerhead.

"She needs a plumber to do that?" Bev asked.

"Definitely not, and I told Jenna that, but she insisted." Since the start of his dead dad diet, Ziggy couldn't help but notice that Jenna Lobiak's yoga studio was suddenly always in need of his assistance, which was funny, since Jenna Lobiak had ignored him his entire life. Turning to the Sea Point Prince, Ziggy asked, "Mi-guy, come with? I can give you the books too."

"Why don't we just FaceTime Jenna on the way?" Miles riffed, know-ing Jenna had always loved him. The thought of seeing Zeke's handwrit-ing made his stomach lurch. He wasn't ready to dive headfirst into decoding financial records. "I'll tell her I kidnapped you—or do it when we get back? I've got to be at the Wharf by six for dinner with Jo."

They both knew Jenna would be far happier to receive a FaceTime call from Miles Hoffman than a new showerhead. As Ziggy mulled it over, Miles stood up and loaded their sandwich plates into the dishwasher.

"I can't," Ziggy decided. "I've got to get to Daffodil Cottage if I ever want to get paid. Let's go tomorrow—that way we won't have all these time constraints."

"The only constraint here is you," Miles joked, before rubbing his hands together with excitement. "All right, party people," he announced.

"I think it's time we start painting some new paintings and getting the canoe back out on the water where she belongs."

Ziggy grinned the adorable grin he'd always had, only now, Miles admired, Ziggy's dimples were deeper and his eyes bigger, almost bluer, as they shone in his slimmer face. "You've been home an hour," Ziggy mused, "and already you're making demands."

With the same lightning quickness that had earned him First Team All-Ivy every year at Princeton, Miles thrust his arm around Ziggy's neck and put his best friend in a headlock. "That's right!" Miles yelled as Ziggy yelped, littermates reunited. "Get used to it, Zig—the Sea Point Prince is back, baby!"

Like any coastal town that historically served as a port for sailors and fishermen, Sea Point's most popular resort had a bordelloed past. Before it became the Wharf, even before it was Skip's, the original structure had no sign out front but was referred to as Frank's by those in the know. After Jo bought Skip's for a song in the early '80s, she spent the next ten years culling investors from her Wharton network to spend nearly $20 million on rehab. By the mid-'90s, the Wharf was pristine, with the exception of four rooms.

The Wharf's business offices above the kitchen were in Frank's original rooms—still with numbers on each door—that had been rented by the hour early in the twentieth century. During every stage of renovation, Jo insisted that these four rooms not only remain but be preserved. No matter how many times the ghosts made her jump, she liked the physical evidence of what came before her: the wallpaper with its peeling rosebuds, the black stains on the ceiling from wall tapers burning too high, the wide floorboards that creaked like bedsprings, the spirit of a drowned sailor's angry bride who roamed the hallways, opening and closing doors at odd hours looking for her husband, but only when Jo was up there alone.

In her office overlooking the ocean, Jo had shoved her desk into the corner where a bed had once been, rust etched into the rosebuds. Women had been marketed within these walls and now a woman was here, making the deals, cutting the checks, deciding what happened next. The men had had their time.

"You're late," Jo said, her eyes still squinting at the spreadsheets on her computer screen.

"Sorry," Miles apologized, combing his wet hair back before hugging his mother. He would have been on time if he hadn't showered, but then he would have smelled like Jenna Lobiak, and he couldn't see Jo smelling like desperation. Jenna had been a good palate cleanser after two years with Chloe, the carnal page break he'd needed before the next chapter in his romantic life. "I ran some work errands with Ziggy."

"Of course you did. Are you hungry?"

Miles nodded and they descended the narrow staircase, waving to the staff as they cut through the kitchen. A nervous teenager tripped over his own feet as he led them to a back corner table of the dining room. Beyond their window, moonlight glittered off the ocean.

"What a view," Miles admired, pretending to read the menu since he already knew he'd order the Surf & Turf—another palate cleanser after two years of Chloe's veganism. "The staff seems extra scared of you these days. Are you still on that cannibal diet?"

"Very funny. That old sous-chef had to go. And can I just say"—Jo began, folding her hands as Miles held his breath and waited for the onslaught of criticism, the repeated assertion that she'd made up her mind about the future of the Wharf—"it's so nice to see your face in this dining room. I know it's you who just arrived and yet, honestly"—Miles did a double take as she dabbed her eye with her napkin, the gallery of diamonds and sapphires decorating her fingers catching the candlelight—"being with you here, well, it feels like a homecoming for me."

Spilman arrived just then, the Wharf's general manager. "I don't want to interrupt, but I thought bubbles would be an appropriate way to celebrate Miles's return," he said, displaying the French label before muffling the pop of the cork with the dexterous mastery of a professional assassin. Miles stood up to greet him with a hug, as much to demonstrate his love for his favorite Steve Buscemi look-alike as to relish how uncomfortable it made poor Spilman. The general manager seemed better suited for a life as a Beefeater than a human fire extinguisher, which is what GMs were, if they were good at their job. Spilman was excellent at his job.

"Cheers to you, my Miles," Jo said. "Welcome home, honeybear." The nickname would have been heartwarming if Miles didn't know for a fact that Jo also called her contractor honeybear—and her fishmonger, and her hostesses when she couldn't recall their names.

"And cheers to you, Mother dearest," Miles said, playing along. "The Wharf has never looked so good."

"Wharflandia," Jo corrected. "It's Wharflandia until Memorial Day Weekend. The hot tubs are open until then."

"You don't say," Miles said, beaming at Jo as he took his first sip. "Well, I should probably experience those firsthand, for R & D, of course."

Jo laughed as she hailed a server and ordered their appetizers. "It's always been my dream to have you take over," she said. "And then I realized my dream shouldn't dictate your life. I'm trying to set you free. You get that, don't you?"

"But I want to learn," Miles asserted, maintaining eye contact. "I came back, didn't I?"

Jo looked down at her lap and twirled the rings on her fingers, a tell that only Miles knew. It was her trick for resisting the impulse to cry—she'd learned early on that the all-male board did not respect her tears. "Mom?"

"I don't want to get my hopes up," Jo said to her lap, "only to have you disappoint me." Miles balked but said nothing. It was unfair, though not new, that, because his father and brother were disasters, Miles was expected to compensate for their bad behavior. Jo looked up from twisting her rings and smiled at him through wet eyes. "Let me guess: the Surf and Turf."

"Oh yeah," Miles said, sighing it all out and reaching for his glass. "I've only been thinking about it for the past ten years," he confessed, smiling sheepishly. Jo let out a genuine laugh and reached over to pat her son's hand.

"Explore Wharflandia and see what you think," Jo offered. Miles nodded and said he'd love to. From the West Coast, it was easy to forget the kinship he shared with his mother, but up close, Miles took pride in their parallels, how they could keep up with each other as they swung from subject to subject like monkey bars. Jo and Miles cackled with their eyes closed over a second bottle of Bordeaux as they finished their steaks and did impressions of the long-dead family cat, Marbles, who'd suffered an unfortunate underbite in addition to being severely cross-eyed.

"No, no," Jo gasped, "it was worse than that," and Miles stuck out his bottom teeth even more until mother and son were both doubled over and causing a bit of a scene. In spite of themselves, Jo and Miles luxuriated in each other's company. They relaxed into who they were as the dining room looked on with envy at the Sea Point royals catching up in the back corner of their past, present, and future.

The Pine Barrens

Early the next morning, Ziggy and Miles drove the fifty-four miles to their spot. On a map, the canoe launch was a nondescript speck on the Mullica River inside the green swath that was Wharton State Forest, within the expansive Pine Barrens. Larger than most national parks, with 1.1 million acres to its name, the extent of the Pine Barrens remained widely unknown outside of New Jersey. Despite its vast beauty, the Pines still felt like a local secret, hiding in plain sight as it stretched across seven counties and comprised 22 percent of America's armpit.

As Ziggy's truck made the familiar left onto the dirt road, Miles thought of old Joe Wharton. The same nineteenth-century industrialist who founded the Wharton School of Business—where Jo Hoffman had shed her working-class background and gained the tools and contacts needed to build a resort out of sand—had also acquired ninety-six thousand acres in South Jersey with the hopes of exporting the Pinelands' clean water to Philadelphia after the city's shortage of potable water had led to a spike in typhoid fever. This protected land later became Wharton State Forest—

the playground of Zeke Miller's early childhood. He'd spent his first nine years on the outskirts of Hammonton, the Blueberry Capital of the World, until Ziggy's grandfather had returned from Vietnam and decided he'd rather be a plumber in Sea Point than a picker in the Pines.

Now, more than a hundred years after Mr. Wharton was laid to rest, Ziggy and Miles embodied his philanthropic legacy in their every step. The boys pulled into the high grass next to the riverbed. They left their phones in the truck, wallets too, and hid the keys atop the front left tire, just as Zeke had always done. If the Pine Barrens was unknown to most Americans, this canoe launch that Zeke had discovered as a little boy was the sub-rosa rendezvous point nestled within that larger obscurity.

Pushing open the MVP truck's rusty passenger door, Miles waited to hear Zeke clear his throat and mumble something about WD-40. He would comment on the beautiful day before quizzing Ziggy on the bird that just flew overhead. It was strange, how present and absent a person could be. Strange and comforting, because even though Zeke was gone, he was most definitely here among the pines.

With every step away from the ceaseless work calls, Ziggy felt lighter and allowed his arms to swing loosely, almost jauntily, as he walked to the back of the truck. A playful whistle slipped past his lips—some tune without a title he knew by heart that his dad used to whistle in this very spot. The song floated above their heads while their footfalls kept the beat, a steady crunch along the carpet of pine needles. Miles reached into his back pocket to snap photos of the river only to shake his head, embarrassed by the immediate sense of loss, the phantom limb of his phone. It took a minute, adjusting to this old life.

The launch was muddy, as expected, and Miles threatened to turn back at the sight of a snake, but once they were settled in and rowing, both men felt their muscles melt into a natural rhythm. Relief saturated their bones like a much-needed summer storm. The only sound was paddle pushing water, wind swishing through half-dressed trees—the leaves still unfurling with the longer-growing days.

"You should be up here," Miles called over his shoulder.

"You're always up front."

"Yeah," Miles agreed, "because up until now you've always weighed more."

"Did you hear about the two-headed rattler?" Ziggy asked. Nothing chastened Miles quite like a snake story. "It was all over the local news. There was a baby timber rattlesnake with two heads—they called it Double Dave because the guys who found him were both named Dave."

As expected, Miles shuddered and begged Ziggy to drop it. The boys leaned into the quiet of the Pine Barrens and the deep breaths of their own thoughts, which were the same: Zeke had been the one to tell Ziggy about Double Dave, and he would have told Miles too—teased him about it, more likely—if he'd been around. But Miles had stayed away for so long, too long. The only time he'd deigned to see his own mother was when Jo paid for an exotic getaway vacation at a five-star resort five thousand miles away, and the Miller family, as far as Miles knew, had never taken a trip anywhere outside New Jersey except once—to the Outer Banks when Bev's brother married.

Miles dipped his paddle into the river and rowed the way Zeke had taught him, using economic strokes and not "drilling for oil," as Zeke used to tease. On either side of the narrow river, pitch pines and blackjack oaks reached for each other from opposite banks and created a cathedral ceiling above the red canoe so that the sky didn't appear blue but an electric, verdant green.

"Check out that sassafras on the right," Ziggy said. During their middle school years, after Ari had left for good, and Jo had a very public, very clichéd fling with her tennis instructor, Zeke had taken both boys out every weekend, enlightening them about New Jersey's flora, teaching them how to identify each tree species, first by the bark, then the leaves.

"I forgot how hot you get for a good-looking sassafras," Miles teased.

"If my dad were here, he'd be flirting with that white cedar."

Miles's laugh skittered down the river like a dragonfly just as the Mullica opened up into a clearing and the sunlight, no longer inconspicuous behind the spring boughs, beat down on the boys with a long winter's worth of pent-up heat. Shards of light reflected on the water's surface and mirrored the trees above the canoe. It was warm for May, and then it was hot.

"Want to capsize?" Miles asked over his shoulder.

"That's the theme of the year," Ziggy replied. "Let's do it."

Together, the boys leaned hard on the starboard and began to rock their weight. Canoes were difficult to capsize, but Zeke had taught them how to do it on a clear summer day the year they turned thirteen, when Miles became a man and his dad reappeared at his bar mitzvah with his masseuse-girlfriend, Florida tanned and oblivious to the destruction their presence caused. "I'm teaching you how to flip for two reasons," Zeke had explained from his kayak. "One, it's fun, but two, if there's a storm and you get flipped, you've got to know how to turn the boat over and get back in."

As the boat rocked, Ziggy felt the taut exhilaration in his gut, the roller-coaster thrill, that moment of maybe. And then he was under.

Allowing himself to sink, Ziggy closed his eyes and listened to the shrill silence of the river and wished he could stay down there in the peace forever. Opening his eyes to the murky yellow haze under water, he heard his dad's voice, and so did Miles, as they both swam toward air. How many times, over how many years, had Zeke told them the same thing, the Mullica mantra, whenever they'd slipped under the surface: *Look for the light and then kick like hell to reach it.*

The first half of the drive home was spent listening to a podcast, but after a stop at Wawa for gas and snacks, Miles felt the energy return to his strongest muscle: his mouth.

"I don't know how you've been doing it," he said, opening a bag of Doritos. "Being back makes me miss him so much—I keep waiting for him to show up and announce the Phillies score."

Ziggy nodded, keeping his eyes on the road.

"Do you ever think about going somewhere else?" Miles asked. "Maybe just to get away, but also, like, moving? I don't know how you can stay in that house and drive in this truck and not drown." When Ziggy didn't say anything, Miles continued. "I just wonder how you're going to balance it—like, how do you honor him but not get stuck in the past or, I dunno, haunted by it?"

"I guess we're just gonna have to figure it out," Ziggy said, biting into the first Butterfinger he'd had in months, excited to discover it tasted amazing. "And I can't do anything until I get the business in order, which is why I need you to go through the books."

"And do what, exactly?"

"Decode his billing and budget system so I know who to pay and who needs to pay me. And then, once we figure that out, I was hoping you could show me how to move it all online so it's easier to track going forward."

"Right," Miles agreed, craning his neck to look at the stack of composition books in the narrow storage space behind his seat. "I should be able to get to them this week. Just don't make me deal with any of those clogged drains." He shivered at the thought. In the canoe, Ziggy had told Miles his most recent horror story about snaking a shower drain at the local gym. The image had made Miles gag and he nearly dry-heaved just thinking about it now. In fact, Miles determined, looking out the window at the field of goldenrod, the next girl he dated would need to have short hair to avoid any such follicle catastrophes in the future.

Like Bell.

But Bell wasn't responding to his texts, even though they were both in Sea Point—he'd driven by her house and seen her car. Even if she was playing hard to get now and ignoring his blue-text blitz, Miles knew her well enough to know she'd eventually text back if he played it right. First loves rarely lasted but they never died.

As Ziggy drove over the bridge into Sea Point, Miles surreptitiously checked his phone. The messages to Bell were all unanswered. He scrolled up to evaluate how pathetic he looked, this full-court press, and read back down to his most recent one, a photograph of the red canoe. It was a good photo—artsy, but not over-the-top. Admiring his work, Miles suddenly registered the three dots that popped up on her empty side of the conversation. She was typing, and then, just as suddenly, she wasn't.

Still staring at his phone, Miles asked Ziggy, "Want to go out this weekend?"

Holloway's Hardware

There was something so encouraging about a hardware store on a Saturday morning. In every bin, on every rack, and along every aisle, a solution presented itself—you just had to know who to ask and where to look. Kate found Holloway's particularly soothing because her parents had DIYed their way through the '90s, and so she could anticipate the happy jangle of the bell above the door and instinctively knew which floorboards creaked in the shop where she'd spent much of her childhood, sitting cross-legged and building castles out of copper washers, while her parents debated paint samples and wood finishes.

Gus and Gertie Holloway were comically garrulous siblings in their early sixties with the same wiry bowl cut of gray hair. They'd inherited the shop from their parents forty years earlier and it was rare to see only one of them wearing denim overalls over a green Holloway's Hardware T-shirt. Contrary to any stranger's cursory glance, they weren't twins—Gertie was a year older and don't you forget it—but they preferred the same unofficial uniform along with black thick-framed glasses that they'd been tickled to learn were currently considered "hip."

Now that Kate was living with such responsible, initiative-taking housemates—her parents—she rarely had a reason to visit the hardware store, but they'd asked her to grab a new lightbulb for Roy before her shift at the Jetty Bar that night. The yellow-slickered sea captain lamp in the living room was the fifth member of the family, and Roy's permanent look of intense consternation—did he see whitecaps ahead or something more existential?—provided the Campbells with endless amusement. Growing up, Roy had served as the family therapist—"Have you talked to Roy about your science test?"—as well as the family mediator—"Go talk to Roy about your allowance." Kate had told her parents that, yes, she could pick up some lightbulbs because even between her two jobs, she needed more distractions if she was ever going to stop stalking Thomas's new girlfriend online.

In the past month, since Thomas's phone call, whenever Kate talked herself into googling Wally Moffett like an addict justifying one last hit, she would emerge from the dank quagmire hours later feeling not only sick but physically battered. Among her many irrelevant findings, Kate had learned that Wally loved to watch YouTube videos of household cleaning tricks. Across her online platforms, she'd consistently listed "discovering innovative and organic cleaning hacks" as her favorite hobby. So that was a thing. It felt like a win for Kate until she remembered all the times Thomas had counted up her water glasses, one on each surface in the apartment, and balked, "Would it kill you to be a little neater?"

Kate pulled into the Holloway's Hardware parking lot five minutes after they opened. Smiling at the familiar sound of the bell above the glass door, she froze in her tracks at the sound of yelling: "Oh for Pete's sakes, how many times do I have to tell you!"

"It's unsanitary!" Gertie yelled at her brother from her post at the cash register, where she was scanning SKU numbers on half a dozen red mailboxes.

"But it's not a cat colony!" Gus insisted, his hands in fists. "It's a cat *community*!"

Kate tried to stifle her laugh as she backed toward the door but the bickering siblings whipped around. Much to Kate's delight, they were wearing their matching overalls.

"Kate," Gertie appealed, "will you please tell my Looney Tunes brother that his cat colony is out of control?"

Gus lived next door to Kate's parents on a secluded triple lot, well hidden by wild shrubbery and massive trees. Years earlier, he'd towed a defunct, rusty school bus into his backyard and set up a bunker for cats he'd rescued.

"Listen to me," Gus said, abandoning the paint-mixing station and walking toward Kate, "a colony is a place run by a foreign ruling power—we can all agree to that, right?" Kate nodded with reluctance. "But cats have been in Sea Point longer than we have, and they're all fixed, so no one is getting knocked up." Raising his voice over Gertie's cackling, Gus continued. "It's a sustainable situation and, more importantly, it's a *community*. It's *consensual*. If the cats don't like it, they can leave, but I think it's pretty clear that they appreciate being part of a collective."

"Well, you've got at least one raccoon in your *collective*," Gertie sighed before turning back to Kate. "What do you need, honey?"

"Lightbulbs."

"Second aisle, halfway down on your right."

Gertie was the go-getter, the businesswoman who made sure people shopped at Holloway's and publicly shamed those who had their hardware needs shipped from the Internet. She lived above the store and made the rounds at Sea Point's bars and hotels, giving business to get business.

Gus preferred to work in the back with the paints. The fact that he knew Kate's name was a bragging right since Gus chose to ignore most patrons including, infamously, Sea Point's mayor—the cringey footage of which had briefly trended on Twitter. Shy with a bit of a stutter, Gus didn't like many people, but he sure did love his cats.

The door chimed, signaling the entrance of another customer as Kate wound her way around to the front of the store. She smiled as she handed her lightbulbs to Gertie and saw Ziggy fiddling with something near the register. "It always smells so good in here," she said wistfully, giving Ziggy a nod hello.

"Like wood and topsoil and Gus's stinky farts?" Gertie asked.

"I heard that," Gus yelled over. "And you're a child."

"Did your folks get that letter from Leeper?" Gertie asked as she scanned the lightbulbs.

"What letter?"

Smacking her lips and rolling her eyes, Gertie explained. "Our dear friend Mr. Leeper wrote a letter oh-so generously offering to buy our parents' house—the one Gus lives in, on the triple lot."

"Wait, what?" Ziggy asked.

Gertie continued: "Apparently everyone on the block got one of these Leeper letters, and you know, he's offering just enough to make people really consider. He's an asshole, but he's not an idiot."

"My parents haven't mentioned it," Kate said, grabbing her lightbulbs and slowly walking toward the door. "They'd never sell to Leeper, anyway."

"Me neither!" Gertie declared. "I may hate Gus's cat colony but I hate Leeper infinitely more. What about your mom, Ziggy? Has she mentioned anything?"

Gus walked over from his paint-mixing station without saying a word. Closing the space between him and Ziggy, Gus asked with a solemnity usually reserved for feline urinary tract infections, "How's she doing?"

Ziggy shrugged. "Hanging in there."

"She's one of my favorite customers, you know."

"We all know," Gertie yelled over from the cash register.

Gus ignored his sister and spoke to Ziggy and Kate. "Beverly—she comes in here, and she basically knows what she wants. But when she's narrowed it down to two choices and can't make the call, she asks for my help. I assist her, we talk about the profile of each paint option, we reach a decision, and then she leaves."

"Great story," Gertie said, breathing on her glasses before polishing the lenses on the sleeve of her T-shirt.

"That's probably my favorite thing about your mom," Gus said, using a paint mixing stick to poke Ziggy square in the chest. "She doesn't linger like most people. She knows when it's time to go."

"Speaking of which," Ziggy said, taking a step back from Gus, "I should get going."

"Yeah, me too," Kate piggybacked, waving goodbye to Gertie.

Exiting Holloway's together, Ziggy asked Kate about her plan for the day.

"Pretty packed schedule until my shift at Jetty Bar—I have to stalk my ex-boyfriend's new girlfriend while listening to John Mayer."

Ziggy nodded as if this was the answer he'd expected, such were the common symptoms of Kate's affliction. "Didn't you and Georgina used to make fun of John Mayer?"

"It's part of the masochism."

Ziggy grinned, and just as Kate wondered why she hadn't seen him all week, he announced, "Miles is back and we're going out tonight. Wanna come?"

"Like, *out*?" Kate asked. She hadn't been out since the night before Thomas dumped her. The idea of drinking outside of her house seemed exhausting. "I have to work."

Ziggy squinted at her, trying to x-ray her thoughts. "Can you ask Jerry to cover? It might be good to get out." At Kate's hesitation, he added, "Plus, my dad died."

"You're sick," Kate said.

"I bet Jerry would appreciate the offer," Ziggy continued, ignoring Kate's diagnosis. "It's a Saturday night—it'll be worth his time—especially since it's the last Saturday night of Wharflandia. They're moving all the hot tubs from the dock on Monday to get ready for Memorial Day Weekend."

Kate knew Ziggy was right, but it seemed impossible to already ask for a shift swap. After she nodded ever so slightly, Ziggy grinned and gently patted her on the shoulder as if more physical contact might break her. "I'll text you but probably around eight—it'll be a drive-off instead of a walk-off. Or maybe a drink-off? We'll see."

"Can't wait," Kate said, tossing the lightbulbs into the passenger seat and wondering what Roy would make of all this.

After Jerry had texted back saying he'd happily cover her shift, Kate settled into the worn corner nook of the living room couch for an afternoon of reading under Roy's fresh light. Among the few perks Kate had discovered since beginning her job at the library, perhaps her favorite was the fact that she was able to preview books before their publication. Lauded editors at all the major publishing houses wrote letters and sent Advanced Reader Copies (ARCs) to librarians around the country in the hopes of generating buzz, landing their projects on each season's Must-Read list, and positioning their books face out on every library display table.

Those publishing houses, which still loomed large in Kate's mind with the gilded mythology of an unattained dream, now needed Kate the way democracy needed voters in order to succeed. Although she was just one of thousands of library associates in the country, she had the power to make a difference in a book's fate. She could encourage a patron to pick up a debut memoir—or guide them to an established novelist, a commercial thriller, or a provocative collection of essays. Librarians had steering power, Kate realized, and connecting readers to their new favorite book was the strongest intellectual high she had experienced since working with her college thesis adviser.

Turning the page of the ARC, Kate found herself wondering what she should wear for her night out with Ziggy and Miles Hoffman. She couldn't think of Miles without saying his whole name, like he was a movie star or a band. A dress seemed aggressive, like she was trying too hard, but she needed to compensate for her return to Sea Point. Of course, Miles Hoffman would be a hypocrite to judge Kate since he was also in town, but rich kids could afford to live within all sorts of contradictions.

Ziggy texted at four to say to meet him outside at eight and to wear a bathing suit. After replying with a green nauseated face, Kate returned to her book and read the same paragraph three times before giving up. Her nerves were winning and required distraction. Climbing the stairs, Kate decided to excise her anxiety with a few run-throughs of *Freaky Freaka-zoid*. She got in position, forced a smile, and let the beat drop.

At 7:59 p.m., Ziggy was outside when Kate closed her front door. "You're early!" she shouted, walking toward him. She'd settled on a simple black dress she'd borrowed from Bernadette—or, rather, that Bernadette had forgotten in Kate's apartment when she'd come up to New York to visit. Four years ago.

"On time is late," Ziggy replied, which struck Kate as a Zeke-ism. The bright lights of Miles Hoffman's car zoomed up in front of the Miller driveway just then, hip-hop blasting so loud that Kate felt her ribs rico-chet. It took her a moment to realize it wasn't actually the music's volume that made her body shake, but that the current scene had trip-wired a long-buried memory.

On a Friday night her junior year of high school, Kate had waited on her front steps for Georgina to pick her up. In the dark, she heard the ca-cophony of teenage testosterone battling for airspace before she saw the group of boys emerge from Ziggy's house, laughing and playing a game, which Kate quickly identified as *Marry, Chuck, Fuck*. In an inexplicable, cruel twist of timing and fate, the boys loaded into a red Jeep just as Miles declared at an oblivious volume, "That's too easy: Fuck Princess Leia, Marry Ms. Gilmore." In the slow motion of a bad '80s movie, Kate watched Miles under the streetlamp throw a head nod in the direction of her own house. "And chuck Ziggy's snobby little ginger neighbor."

Now, seventeen years later, Kate lifted her hand to wave at the convert-ible idling in front of her, and Miles Hoffman gave her a wave back. "Hi!" Kate yelled, half a second *after* Miles had turned down the stereo volume with the practiced wrist flick of a devout SoulCyclist. He could slice a pizza with the blade of his jawline, and she was suddenly sixteen and chuck-able. But then, much to Kate's surprise, Miles threw the sports car into park and hopped out. He ran around the hood in a goofy, elbows-out jog, to give her a hug.

"Kate Campbell! Great to see you!" he said, taking a step back but keeping his eyes locked on hers. "I'm glad we get to catch up."

Kate wasn't sure how one caught up with someone they'd never really known in the first place, but he sounded genuine. Her body thrummed from the warmth of his gaze before she realized the charm was real. Miles Hoffman could fly out to Los Angeles tonight and land a movie contract tomorrow while the plane was still taxiing. His features were so startlingly cohesive—each asset highlighted every other, so that Kate found herself admiring his earlobes, which looked so supple and buttery, and created such an exquisite contrast from his dark five-o'clock shadow.

As Miles teased Ziggy for his oversize bathing suit, Kate studied his profile and decided he could succeed anywhere with that beautiful mug of his. But he was here, with her, in Sea Point, and that fact not only justified Kate's nerves all afternoon but also made the whole evening ahead of them sparkle like a compliment.

"Dude," Ziggy said, staring at Miles's car, "what are you driving?"

Miles rolled his eyes. "Just renting but yeah, they sweet-talked me. It's a cabriolet. A Porsche cabriolet."

"Interesting," Ziggy said, leaning over the convertible to stroke the leather interior. "Because it looks like a premature midlife crisis."

Kate felt a strange rattling emerge from the base of her throat and realized she was laughing. How long had it been since she'd laughed like that? And then Miles Hoffman did the most remarkable thing: He beamed at her. If the rug pulled the room together in *The Big Lebowski*, Miles Hoffman's true smile pulled his face together in a devastating and unjust way. He was cruelly beautiful.

"I've got the cab," Miles said, scrolling through his phone and placing the call. "Summersault or straight to Wharflandia?"

"Let's Summersault first," Ziggy said definitively. Kate opened her mouth to say she'd rather not go to Wharflandia at all since she'd asked Jerry to cover her shift, but she stayed quiet. The less she said now, the better. She wanted Miles to like her, and men like Miles liked women who spoke seldom — Kate knew because she'd dated a man like Miles for twelve years.

When the cab arrived, the three of them piled in, Miles volunteering to sit up front since he was the tallest. He immediately began to flirt with the fifty-something-year-old driver, who turned out to be the mother of a girl with whom Kate had attended Sea Point High. As Miles asked the driver what she did for fun, Ziggy turned to Kate in the backseat. "How was your day, post-Holloway's?" he asked. Kate silently thanked him for not mentioning her plan to stalk Wally in front of Miles.

"It was good," she offered. "What have you guys been up to all week?" She hoped that Ziggy didn't notice how closely she'd tracked the direct correlation between the days since Miles had arrived home and the nights since Ziggy had reached out for a walk-off.

"I've been mostly working," Ziggy said. "But we did get up to the Pine Barrens a couple of days ago."

"I forgot how special that place is," Miles added, turning around in his seat and leaning unnecessarily close to the driver as he looked at Kate. In the near dark, his brown eyes still glimmered with light. "It's amazing how undiscovered it is."

Kate thought of Thomas and his friends during that dinner in Mexico, the debate about undiscovered vacation destinations, and their derisive chortling about New Jersey. She'd never learned the origin of their inside joke about "inverted," but who cared? Suddenly Thomas and his "chosen family" seemed far away and miserable.

Wharflandia

They drank too fast at Summersault on account of Rooney the bartender insisting on shots of tequila, and then more shots of tequila, and then, to hell with it, more shots of tequila. "The boys are back in town!" Rooney announced, raising his own glass. "You too, Kate," he added, a little too late. Kate would have felt self-conscious, but the comped Patron had all but obliterated her five senses by the time they stumbled out to the curb, into a cab, and then back out into the salty air and stared up at the white mammoth that was the Wharf Resort and Hotel. To the left and right of the valet stands were the two vintage Hollywood spotlights on full blast, searching the sky for answers.

Compared to Memorial Day Weekend next week, the resort was operating at a low buzz. It was about to undergo its biannual costume change and transform from winter wonderland ("Wharflandia") to summer destination ("the Wharf"), which was why Miles had insisted they go out that night. He wanted to get a sense of this relatively new off-season enterprise so he could speak knowledgeably about it with his fellow board members.

Seven years ago, long after the Wharf had become the perennial number one summer wedding destination in the tristate area, Jo set her sights on turning a profit throughout the winter, which developed into Wharflandia. She visited winter resorts in Tahoe, Aspen, Stowe, and Sugarloaf. Sea Point was entirely flat—she couldn't rationalize the expense of building a bunny hill, let alone a slope, but she tapped into the sexiness of a ski lodge, the coziness of a winter cabin. Jo ventured to the Faroe Islands, Iceland, Denmark, and Norway. According to her general contractor, Jo called him from Newark Airport having just landed, still on the plane, seatbelt still fastened, but with the sketches, time line, and a budget for Wharflandia.

During the financially dry months of November through April, Jo proposed, she would turn the Wharf into a winter wonderland perfect for couples, groups, and corporate retreats. On the back hump of land she owned on the other side of the Wharf's gigantic parking lot, Jo would build eight rugged-chic cabins that inspired thousands of Pinterest pages and encouraged maids of honor to book a trip to Sea Point instead of some place up north or out west. Jo modeled the cabins after A-frame ski lodges and named them after the eight types of bears. ("Because bears understand hygge better than anyone!" she had joked in an interview with *Brides* magazine.)

The cabins, which could each accommodate up to a dozen guests, sat in a horseshoe around the small ice rink Jo had installed over the parking lot. On each cabin's back deck sat a twelve-person cedar hot tub. Most important, there were only eight of these beautiful, state-of-the-art cabins, and so while the coziness would appeal to the masses, it was the exclusivity, Jo believed, that would ensnare her targeted demographic. The best way to reel privileged people in was to threaten to shut them out. She slapped on an outrageous price tag, wait time, cancellation fee, and insurance policy. The saddest part about being filthy rich, she'd learned after all these years, was that you never felt quite wealthy enough—the proof you'd really made it was always one luxury vacation away.

Jo Hoffman knew her idea would be successful, but she had no idea winter in southern New Jersey could print money the way that Wharflandia did the moment they booked their first bachelorette party. The revenue started with the eight cabins and quickly spread to the two hundred hotel rooms that were suddenly fought over as overflow. If there were too many bridesmaids, or the best man had failed to book far enough in advance for the bachelor party, groups would settle for the honeymoon suites and even the standard Wharf rooms above the restaurant. The draw was so great and so widespread that last year they'd invested in a "cedar hot tub village" so that standard-room-renters could pay extra for a hot tub out on the back patio overlooking the water.

A surprising hit had been the dozens of professional groups that turned out for Midnight Bingo (the popularity of which could be credited to its cash prizes and conjugal Hail Mary—if you didn't close at Midnight Bingo, you weren't going to). But what Miles still couldn't believe was that Jo had resurrected the light-up dance floor she'd originally designed twenty-one years earlier for his bar mitzvah after-party and turned it into yet another cash cow. What had been the basement of the Jetty Bar was now The Basement, a speakeasy that was jam-packed Thursday through Saturday nights with bachelors and bachelorettes looking for one last one-night stand or at least a sloppy make-out on the dance floor to the sweet beats of '80s pop. Packs of sequined women celebrating their thirtieth, fortieth, fiftieth birthdays loved The Basement, as did swinging suburbanites and fantasy-prone book clubbers desperate to cut loose.

The outrageous revenue from Wharflandia allowed Jo to model her own business after much bigger, women-owned businesses she'd studied and admired from afar. She was able to offer better health benefits, a family-planning package, and an expansion of the Wharf's Pre-K and Childcare Center. It was impossible not to admire his mother's nonstop workhorse attitude as Miles looked up at the spotlights and gave their cabdriver a flirtatious wave goodbye. Miles told himself he would need to memorize growth trajectories to impress the board members, but that was in the future. Right now, he just wanted to relax in a hot tub and see if Wharflandia lived up to its hype.

Kate knew from working at the Jetty Bar that the hot tubs closed at ten. She took out her phone, pretty sure it was after eleven, but it was hard to focus her eyes after that last shot of Patron at Summersault. Nevertheless, Miles pushed through the glass doors, and Kate and Ziggy followed him through the grand lobby, past the spa, dining room, and Jetty Bar, and then through the French doors that led out to the wharf itself, where they plunged into a sky full of stars amid fresh ocean air. The trio found themselves on an empty veranda and Kate heard one of the boys whisper "Whoa" as they took in the view. Under a patchwork of constellations and one nearly full moon, the hot tub village beckoned with swirls of steam and glorious vacancy. For a moment, Kate worried about breaking the rules, but then she remembered that Miles made them. This was completely bonkers but also entirely kosher.

Miles stripped down to reveal abs that made Kate want to die—or at least remain fully clothed. "Last one in has to buy the drinks," Miles shouted as he and Ziggy raced toward the hot tub. Kate had no choice but to kick off her shoes, fling off her dress, and try her best not to think about how she looked in the black one-piece she'd bought for Mexico. Thankfully, the lights in the hot tub village were dim; Jo Hoffman had spent the better part of a month inuring herself to headaches for the sake of finding the perfect, most flattering light that still allowed guests to get back to their rooms safely. As usual, she'd succeeded. Kate moved through the May air feeling like a satin shadow of herself, barely more visible than the cool breeze that made her submersion into the hot tub transcendent.

"This is amazing," Ziggy sighed, sinking into the water and looking up at the sky.

"Spilman!" Miles announced like a game show host.

"Good to see you again, Miles," Spilman said, bowing his head. "I've brought robes that I'll leave here. Jerry heard you were drinking tequila at Summersault so he has sent these palomas, as well as a few snacks."

Miles waded across the hot tub to take inventory of the tray while Kate tallied the bill in her head: three palomas, grilled shrimp, crab dip, a rack of ribs, and the charcuterie plate—all comped for the Prince. She'd need to remember to throw $30 in the Jetty Bar tip bucket for Jerry before they left. Those palomas weren't especially fun to make. Kate bit her upper lip and waved to Spilman, who gave her the quickest of nods before disappearing back inside. That was fine by Kate because the charcuterie board was the size of a pizza box and her stomach was grumbling.

Miles handed Kate a frosted rocks glass. Jerry's palomas were beautiful and, because she hadn't made them herself, tasted particularly glorious. "To friendship," Miles said, extending his own glass and locking eyes with her, then with Ziggy.

The rest of the night could be measured in brined fingers. An unknown number of hours disappeared as Kate half-listened to Ziggy and Miles talk about people from Yates, the Wharf's room rates in high season, Bev's paintings, and the weird sound Ziggy's truck was making. At some point, the boys determined it was time to leave and Kate ambled after them, eyes half closed, relaxed, her whole body literally letting off steam as they walked through the lobby and out to another cab Miles had ordered while she'd licked clean the crab dip ramekin.

It was only on the ride home, when Ziggy asked the cabdriver if he could borrow the aux cord to play his favorite song, that Kate remembered Nessie's wedding, and Thomas, and Wally, and the fact that she was sitting in a damp hotel robe in the back of a stranger's car with two boys she hadn't seen in over ten years. She hadn't remembered to leave a tip for Jerry and the boys hadn't either. Kate cursed in her head and decided she'd leave him an envelope with cash and a note during her next shift. Even if she was with Miles Hoffman, she was not Sea Point royalty. Only Princes could afford to expect everything for free.

"Here it comes!" Ziggy yelled, pressing "play" and turning the volume all the way up. Ziggy's song opened with a strange keyboard, the flow of notes sounding more like a guitar jam—"that's a mbira," Ziggy yelled over the music. "From the Shona people in Zimbabwe." Kate knew then that this was a Zeke song.

"Here's the best part," Ziggy said, pointing to the speakers. Kate almost told him to turn it down, but this wasn't her call, it wasn't her car, and it wasn't her choice how fast they were going as the teenage driver flew through the blinking yellow lights of First Street, down Sunset toward Ocean Avenue. The cab zoomed so that the streetlights all connected as one bright line that led home.

Outside Ziggy's house and without a word, the Prince of Sea Point hopped out of the cab and walked over to his car, still parked behind Ziggy's truck. Kate looked up at her parents' darkened house across the street—her bed was so close—as Miles lifted up the black mat lining the back of his trunk and popped open the secret compartment. "Emergency stash," he explained, tossing the neon pink fanny pack to Ziggy.

Stumbling up the wooden walkway, they heard the waves before they saw the ocean. The sand was so cold that, for a moment, Kate wondered if it was wet as they sat in a semicircle and looked out on their merciless queen. This was the ocean in all her angry candor, her unbridled majesty. There was no bad time to see her, but two a.m. was particularly magical, especially with the clear sky they admired tonight. Miles unzipped his pink fanny pack with a showman's flare, a natural master of ceremonies, and offered Ziggy the first hit. Kate traced Orion's belt until Ziggy nudged her, passed her the joint. Like Clinton, she never inhaled—except that, like Clinton, of course she did. Looking up into the Jersey sky, Kate marveled at the thread of unforeseen circumstances that had led her to this strange but enjoyable moment. She might have drowned in the swirl of stars and thoughts had Miles not called her Bogie and asked her to share the spliff.

Accepting the joint from Kate, Miles leaned back on his elbows. "Here's the thing about Sea Point," he sighed, exhausted from knowing everything.

It was too dark to meet Ziggy's gaze, but Kate could feel his head turn to face her. They couldn't see each other and yet they shared an eye roll through the ink-black night while Miles paused for dramatic effect. Only this guy, who'd been back for fewer than twenty-four hours after ten years away, would try to tell them about their town.

"I've been everywhere," Miles began. "And if this beach were anywhere else in the world, people would go crazy over it. Where we are right now is better than anything they've got up on the Cape or even over in California if you actually want to swim."

"Is that why you spend so much time here?" Ziggy teased.

"I'm serious," Miles said, staring out at the ocean. The world was nothing but velvet swaths of navy blue and twinkles of silver. "Jersey isn't supposed to be this beautiful," Miles said, "but it is."

An hour later and back at home, Ziggy saw the yellow glow of the kitchen light but assumed his mom had just forgotten to turn it off after dinner. Bev was never up this late—she was usually asleep before eight p.m., with the assistance of a little blue pill. Pushing the front door open, Ziggy did a double take: His mom was in the corner of the kitchen, standing in front of her easel. As Bev turned to face him, Ziggy registered her glasses, the ones she only needed when she was working in that corner.

"How's it going?" he asked, suppressing a glassy-eyed, tequila-inspired smile of hope.

"I couldn't sleep," Bev sighed, "and I just thought, what the hell?"

Ziggy gave a right-on kind of nod and made his way across the kitchen, sneaking a peek at the canvas before opening the freezer door in search of the ice cream Kate had brought over weeks earlier.

"I finished it," Bev said, eyes still on her canvas. "Sorry."

"Why can't you sleep?" Ziggy asked, pawing through the cupboards and coming up with a bag of chips he'd bought in the Before.

"Who knows?" Bev put down her brush and joined him at the kitchen table. "Actually, I do. It's that." She pointed to a piece of paper, folded into the thirds of an official business letter. "Harry Leeper wants the house."

Nodding, Ziggy sucked the salt off his fingers, marveling at how wrinkly they still were from hours in the hot tub. It already seemed like another life. This was his real life, sitting in dim lighting alone with his mother, trying to maintain a surface of calm in the wake of their shared apocalypse.

"Zig, I think we should do it."

"Very funny."

"I'm serious." Bev pushed her glasses to the top of her head.

"Bernadette said we could afford to keep the house—the accountant agreed with her."

Bev nodded. "We can. But it's tough on us financially and also, you know, spiritually, for lack of a better word. I think we need a fresh start. He would want us to be happy."

"The business is here—and when I finish the man cave at Daffodil, and get Miles to help me sort out the books—"

"We're on the same team," Bev interrupted. "I'm not going to do anything unless we're in full agreement. But this is a really good offer and the market is stable and this might be, I don't know, a gift from the most unlikely of places."

Ziggy didn't try to hide his disgust. "He'd tear it down. You know that, right? He'd tear all of this down, everything Dad and I worked on. And he'd rip up your gardens with a backhoe in one afternoon."

Bev began to say something but then reached over and crammed a handful of chips into her mouth. They sat there, chewing loudly.

"We don't need to decide tonight," Bev said.

Ziggy stood up and reached for the paper. He saw the trail of zeroes interrupted by commas. It was a good offer, very good, just like Gertie had said. The Creeper was an asshole but he wasn't an idiot.

After ordering his fourth cab of the evening, Miles arrived back at his mother's house in West Sea Point. Walking up the marble steps to the front door, Miles's phone buzzed with a new text. A twinge of dread if it was from Chloe, who still texted to say she missed him, but then he thought maybe, possibly, Bell had finally caved, and he rushed to get his keys in the front door so he could focus on his phone.

The text was from his mother: *Come to my room please.*

But Jo Hoffman didn't have a room.

Jo Hoffman had a master suite that took up the entire second floor, having converted Eric's room into a steam shower and Miles's room into a walk-in closet with a mini runway when they left for college. Regressing to high school, he wondered if Jo would be able to smell the alcohol on him. Even after all these years, she still worked twelve-hour days at the Wharf, and then clocked another few hours at her home office before bed.

"Spilman said you stopped by tonight," Jo said now, peering up from her hardback, her face shiny with French creams that had not kept her from aging nearly as well as the injections had, although when inquiring minds asked about her regimen at conferences, Jo only mentioned the lotions and never the quarterly appointments with Dr. Maska. Her face was an asset to her reputation, and her goal—as impossible as it might be for a woman hovering around sixty—was to keep her skin as wrinkle-free as the iconic yellow linen tablecloths at the Wharf. No matter the board was full of paunchy men half her age with comb-overs and coffee-stained teeth—there was a fine line between a woman at the peak of her career and a woman showing the wear and tear of what that ascent to power had required—and that fine line was the presence of fine lines. Jo believed the injections were just as essential, and no more a choice in her field of work than her newsletters to shareholders.

Miles stepped closer to his mother and inhaled the arrangement of gardenias on the mirrored dresser to his left. In front of him, Jo's king-size bed beckoned, an oasis of white down comforters that Miles desperately wanted to face plant into until tomorrow. But Jo's eyes were on him, evaluating him like he was a questionable oyster, and he remembered why he was back and summoned his professionalism.

"The place looks amazing—Wharflandia. I can't believe what you've done in just, what, seven years?"

"Eight," Jo countered. "Nine if you count the first trip to Glasgow, but that was before I knew what I was doing."

"Well, even Ziggy couldn't—"

"Miles, what are you doing here?" Jo interrupted. "I'd like to manage my expectations, which will require your assistance. If you're here to hang out with Ziggy and get drunk on my tab like overgrown teenagers, great, you have my blessing. But when we spoke on the phone, and at dinner your first night back, you seemed gangbusters about wanting to prove yourself."

"I am—I mean, I—I do," Miles stammered. The night's decisions were sinking in behind his temples and coagulating into sludge around his brain.

"If that's true, I suggest a new strategy."

Miles fought the urge to rub his eyes. Instead, he went into Jo's palatial bathroom and filled a crystal glass with water, chugged it, refilled it, and chugged it again.

"I'm here to learn the business, like I said. I want to understand how the Wharf runs, but I just got back, and Zeke died, in case you forgot."

Jo took off her reading glasses like a boxer removing her gloves.

"So yeah, I want to be here for Ziggy, but there's enough time to do both." Looking at his mother's stern face, Miles gulped. "Ya know?"

Carefully saving her page with a dried sprig of lavender, Jo closed her book and set it on the bedside table. "I hate to say this, but you're probably going to have to choose."

Miles stared at his mother with unabashed repulsion.

"I know, I know, it sounds horrible," Jo continued, "but just, logistically, I don't think there are enough hours in the day to be Ziggy's support system and a CEO-in-training. You're no good to me showing up at work drunk or hungover or some combination of the two. I already have Eric for that, and I just got him out of my hair for six months. Unless that was your plan—to come home and replace Eric."

The plush carpet absorbed the silence between them. Miles's fantasy of lying down gave way to a cold, sobering fact he heard beneath his mother's voice: He couldn't come home and disappoint Jo just like his father and brother had—like he had tonight.

A forgotten memory suddenly popped into his brain like an ancient film slide and projected behind his eyes with vicious clarity: a Sunday night in ninth grade, sitting shotgun in Zeke's truck as they drove toward his empty house on the other side of town, the front lawns and property taxes expanding with every block. "You have reason to be pissed at your dad," Zeke had said, turning to look at him, a yellow moon peeking over his left shoulder. "And it's okay to be pissed, to feel whatever you're feeling, and you can always come talk to me about it." Zeke reached over and turned the radio, already too low to hear, all the way off. "But I just want to tell you, between the two of us, you're becoming a good man, Miles. I see how you help your mom out, trying to make her life a little easier, take her mind off the hard stuff. Those efforts show you understand loyalty and those efforts are what make me so proud of you."

Miles blinked at the white shag carpet and the Zeke reel ended. He would need to stand down, grow up, and do what his mother wanted. If Zeke were alive, he'd tell him to get to work, and maybe that was the real reason why he hadn't come home in so long. Zeke would have seen what Miles hadn't: the rebellious spite that fueled his San Francisco life—and he would have told him to cut it out.

"It's very nice to have you back," Jo said to her lap, folding her arms. "It's so wonderful, miraculous, really, to see you here, standing across from me, even if you are higher than a kite." Miles pawed at his own face, embarrassed. "Like I said, you have my blessing either way, but you can't do both."

Miles thought of Ziggy and Zeke and the stack of composition books he'd taken with him from the cab of the truck to the study downstairs.

"I choose the Wharf," Miles said, standing up straighter, forcing his shoulders back. "I just need to go through Zeke's accounts and explain them to Ziggy, get him on track and online. I'll go through it this week, and then I'm all yours."

"But what I'm trying to emphasize is that it's okay if this isn't what you want. My dream doesn't have to be your dream—it just isn't your right, either."

"I know, Mom," Miles said, resisting the urge to roll his eyes. "This is what I want." After hearing his voice say it, Miles wondered if he could will the statement into truth.

"Okay then," Jo said, her face inscrutable, as it always was in these moments. The year of her divorce, she'd kept her countenance at full sail—without wrinkle, without waver, always moving forward. Reaching for her book, Jo kept her eyes on Miles. "Take care of all that MVP business tomorrow and we'll have a meeting at the Wharf on Monday morning, nine a.m. sharp."

"Monday at nine," Miles agreed, and turned around to begin navigating his way out of the suite and toward the stairs. The guest bedrooms were on the third floor, but Miles preferred the study off the living room, sleeping on the pull-out couch where his father had slept the last year of the marriage. Collapsing on the white sofa, Miles thought of the Brozetomen text thread and realized he was no better than those guys. Like all of his friends, who looked and behaved just like him, Miles didn't make decisions based on what he believed was good in the long run; he made them on what he was afraid to lose in the moment.

Kate Campbell, "drunk as a skunk," as her mother liked to say, dragged herself upstairs and jumped at the figure in her room before realizing it was her reflection in the full-length mirror. Examining herself in the white Wharflandia robe, Kate was surprised to find that she looked pretty. Her big green eyes stared back at her and she heard that voice from her past call them captivating. Holding her breath and reassuring herself it was fine, it was not a big deal, she texted three short words: *I miss you.*

Kate slept through the morning, mouth open and snoring with abandon, a river of saliva inching toward her neck creases. On the floor next to her bed, in the front pocket of the Wharflandia robe, Kate's screen lit up. The message waited there patiently, a provocation tucked in terry cloth.

Part II

"ZF"

A perpetual procrastinator, Miles was not a Sunday kind of guy. Over the years, he'd developed an acute discomfort around the amorphous slowness and then rapid disappearance of God's seventh day, and the morning after his night out with Ziggy and Kate at Wharflandia proved no different. He knew some obligation hovered above his throbbing head but it was only when he groped the floor in search of a water glass and felt instead the stack of composition notebooks that Miles remembered he was responsible for understanding Zeke's antiquated business accounting. Eyes still closed, Miles decided to give himself twenty-four hours to nurse his hangover before realizing he couldn't: He'd agreed to a Monday morning meeting with Jo at nine a.m. sharp. Miles would have to take care of Ziggy and MVP today. Sundays were the worst.

Dragging 190 pounds of parched muscle into the kitchen, Miles chugged two glasses of water before waking up the espresso machine. Unsurprisingly, Jo was nowhere to be found—Miles surmised she was either at the Wharf or on the tennis courts, testing out her knee against Minnie Hastings's backhand. He left the kitchen clutching his chipped

Rock the Boat '89 coffee mug and returned to the study. Easing back onto the sofa, Miles picked up the top book and flipped to the first page.

And there it was, without introduction: The sight of Zeke's handwriting was a sucker punch in the stomach. It was visceral and, Miles only just realized, it was trespassing. This was as close to journaling as Zeke Miller would have ventured.

Just get through this, Miles thought to himself, turning page after page, inviting comprehension to come to him. This temporary surrender to ignorance was the biggest difference he found between his generation and his parents'. Kids who grew up with computers and smartphones understood there was an inherent learning curve, that exploring new terrain and pushing wrong buttons were critical steps in understanding how things worked. Zeke Miller, like Miles's mother, cursed at the screen as soon as they felt the first ripple of uncertainty. The younger generations, born into an iCloud of technological chaos, were more comfortable navigating the gray and knew how to keep their knees bent mentally.

Thumbing through the book, Miles sipped his espresso and drank in Zeke's hand-drawn grids. He tried not to think about the time Zeke would have saved just by using Excel, let alone QuickBooks. The tables included six categories, which would be easy to transfer to an accounting program, Miles thought, even with the stack of mystery initials in the second, third, and fourth columns.

After the date, each account was identified only by the clients' initials. Under "Project," Zeke again had just used initials. At least the sums appeared straightforward, as did the balances.

Miles pushed down on his temples and tried to refresh his gaze. This was doable, even on a Sunday. He picked up a different notebook and noticed two consistent customers that appeared on every page: DC and ZF. DC was scattered down the page, but always there, whereas ZF was the last row on every page. The estimate for DC ranged each time—from $50 to $18,000, but ZF was always the same amount: $360. Oddly, Miles noted, ZF's $360 was in the total cost column, not the payment.

On the precipice of discovering a pattern, Miles returned to the stack of composition notebooks and opened up to the last page of each one, where he saw a different "ZF" sum—a gigantic one—boxed in with blue ink. As he traveled back in time, the huge number grew smaller and smaller, diminishing with every older book, in contrast to the consistent sum of $360 found on each page.

Despite the double espresso, Miles knew his hands were shaking because of a truth forcing its way to the surface of his consciousness: Zeke had accrued a significant amount of debt that Bev and Ziggy didn't know about—not even the accountant knew about it, since he'd told Ziggy the taxes were straight.

Whatever ZF was, it had the potential to ruin Zeke's memory, which meant Miles could never show Ziggy these accounting records—he'd rather light them on fire and brave Ziggy's wrath. The stack needed to be shredded yesterday, and Miles needed to reach out to his Princeton friend Mitch who'd gone into estate law, because this was nothing short of a shitshow. If these books were an accurate reading, and there was no reason for them not to be, they did not suggest but screamed that Zeke Miller was paying someone $360 a month for unclear reasons. He must have had a mistress somewhere, or a kid, or a gambling problem, or, given the outrageous number staring at Miles from the last page of the most recent book, all of the above. Zeke Miller was dead and now Miles's best friend was over a hundred thousand dollars in debt and didn't know it. Forget learning QuickBooks—Ziggy would be lucky if the bank didn't take everything he owned.

Frantically rummaging through the stacks of notebooks, Miles flipped through the front pages, checking the date in the upper right-hand corner until he found the oldest notebook in the pile. It was from forty years ago, when Zeke had first taken over from his own father. The "ZF" account hadn't begun yet, and the numbers declared in straightforward digits the success of the business. Miles reached for another ancient notebook, and again, the clients' names were spelled out and the numbers were good.

The numbers were good up until twenty years ago, when "ZF" appeared with a $36,592 sum next to it, boxed in with blue ink. Miles thought with a gust of hope that it was Ziggy's college tuition, except Ziggy hadn't gone to college. Or rather, he'd received a full ride to Cornell and, as soon as the ice hockey season ended his freshman year, he'd packed up his bags and driven the five hours home, still wearing most of his pads. The one time Miles had been brave enough to ask him about it, Ziggy had just said it had been too cold, too far, and too big a waste of time when he knew what he wanted to do with his life.

But if it wasn't Cornell—and then it clicked in Miles's head like one of Zeke's vinyl records kissing the needle. Yates. Ziggy had earned all kinds of scholarships, but the school had still asked the Millers to contribute some—he knew that, he remembered seeing the pile of paperwork next to Zeke's La-Z-Boy. Miles reached for another notebook, using his finger to scroll through dates until he found the year he and Ziggy would have been freshmen at Yates. There was the date in the upper right-hand corner, and "YA" was boxed in with $7,000. A few pages later, "YA" had grown to $7,560, and Miles recognized that the personal line of credit Zeke must have taken out from the bank had an 8 percent interest rate. He flipped to the following year and "YA" had grown to $15,725. Their junior year, Zeke owed $24,543, and by the time Ziggy graduated from Yates, his father was $34,066 in debt. Miles jumped forward a year and saw the sum associated with "YA" became "ZF." While Miles was a freshman at Princeton, his mother paying over forty grand out of pocket, Zeke and Ziggy were huddled next to each other under the sinks of Sea Point, a massive secret stretching the back pocket of Zeke's Carhartts. On the last page of that notebook, Miles spotted in Zeke's left-handed scrawl: Ziggy's Future.

ZF.

Paging through the hand-drawn tables, Miles was able to see that each month for the past twenty years, Zeke had put $360 toward Ziggy's high school education. But paying the minimum on a large line of credit was like using dental floss to wire shut a great white's jaw. No wonder Zeke's blood pressure had skyrocketed, no wonder his heart had given out. As a father, he had given all that he could to provide for his son, but with minimum payments on 8 percent interest, his best intentions were nothing more than chum in the water for Freedom Bank of New Jersey.

Miles bent over his knees and pushed the composition books out of the way in case he puked. This was his fault. He'd been the one to tell Ziggy about Yates, and he'd been the one to tell his Yates hockey coach about Ziggy, who'd reached out to their club hockey coach and the Yates upper school admissions officer during the winter of eighth grade. It had all happened from there. Miles had recruited his best friend to his private high school and led the Millers straight into the belly of the bank.

Miles's phone buzzed. He didn't need to look to know it was from Ziggy: *Last night was fun. Think you could look at the books today?*

When the acceptance letter from Yates arrived at the Miller house, Bev and Zeke had been so proud of Ziggy for all the financial aid he'd received. Miles didn't need Zeke's books or his own Wharton Business degree to know what had happened from there; shame boiled in his stomach before catching fire in his chest. Zeke was a proud man and he'd kept that ballooning debt a secret for a reason. He'd watched the minimum payment take a chunk out of his profits without putting a dent in the principal. He must have felt so helpless. He must have tracked the growing debt gain height and heat—like a bonfire hungry to ride the wind. Zeke must have known the bank would own him forever, Miles realized, and he'd refused to ask for help. If Bev knew about this debt, she'd have sold her paintings or figured out a solution. Zeke had chosen to keep it a secret, and now it was on Miles's shoulders to betray either his trust or his son.

Turtles

Half awake, Kate saw the terry cloth robe on the floor next to her bed, and the whole night came charging at her like a bull: the hot tub at Wharflandia, smoking on the beach, and texting—*No, no, no.* Kate threw herself on the ground and fumbled for the robe's pockets in search of her phone. Had she really sent that drunk text? Instead of seeing her own line, the new response stared back at her with bright-eyed clarity:

I miss you too.

Kate wanted to dive headfirst into those words and emerge with their meaning. What now? Where were they supposed to go from here? This was great news unless the text had just been a polite, indulgent response to her pathetic outreach.

Kate started to type half a dozen replies but they all fell flat, and when she thought about calling, the fear became too intense—what if it went to voicemail? What if it didn't? Kate didn't have any answers, only swarms of questions that buzzed inside her brain like aggravated wasps, and so she decided to hold off. Waiting might be good for them. As the text sat there, begging for a response, Kate turned up the volume and got in position for *Freaky Freakazoid.*

"Was your hangover as bad as mine?" Ziggy asked the following Tuesday as they started their evening walk-off. They hadn't seen each other since Saturday night—proof that the high season was revving up.

"Worse," Kate answered, thinking of that *I miss you too* still sitting in her phone like a mosquito on her skin, silently gnawing on her.

Just a handful of days before the Memorial Day Weekend onslaught and it was so hot that Ziggy had swapped his signature overalls for cargo shorts. They were not only outdated but several sizes too big. Ziggy appeared to have threaded a piece of rope through the belt loops to keep them up and Kate deduced that he'd lost so much weight that even his belts didn't fit.

"Weather like this makes me want to fast-forward to winter," he said, pretending not to notice Kate eyeing the rope around his waist. "Cold air, no tourists, and, best of all, hockey season."

Kate nodded, afraid of what was coming, as inevitable as a heat wave in a Jersey summer.

"How's Georgina these days?" Ziggy asked. "Every time I think about the duck pond freezing over, I see her tough little game face."

Earlier in the evening, when Ziggy had texted Kate about a walk-off, she had happily agreed to revive the tradition that Miles's arrival had threatened. But Ziggy's inquiry about Georgina made Kate wish she were working at the Jetty Bar, watching Mr. Crudder spit shine his dentures with a cocktail napkin—anything was better than thinking about her ex best friend.

Almost twenty years earlier, Kate arrived at Sea Point High School wearing her favorite yellow T-shirt and a newfound cynicism that didn't sit right on a fourteen-year-old. But Bernadette had just abandoned her for Rutgers and Kate was now stuck living with the same two people who'd prevented her from attending Yates, where the average class size was nine, and the cafeteria was referred to as a dining hall. Worse yet, Kate's parents appeared so beaten down with guilt that she couldn't lash out at them any more than she could kill a spider after reading *Charlotte's Web*.

To make matters worse, Kate's friends had voyaged to the mall the week before school started and pierced their belly buttons. In an uncharacteristic move to make amends, Dirk and Sally had granted Kate permission to get her navel pierced as well, but Bernadette had called from New Brunswick and told Kate that belly button rings were *so over, so tacky* and, knowing how queasy her little sister was, *so easily infected*. As a result, Kate skipped the mall and now her three friends weren't speaking to her, which would have been more upsetting except that Dahlia, Allie, and Bryce had been mad at her since finding out she'd applied to Yates the previous spring. The matching belly button rings were just the excuse they needed to exclude her.

And so Kate arrived at Sea Point High having constructed a narrative of her life: She was a victim of an unfair system that would always favor the rich over the talented, the popular group over the individual thinker. Despite her clear aptitude, Kate would be a heron, a dumb bird at this big dump of a high school.

Even though she was smart enough to be a jaguar. Even though Yates had invited her to join their ranks. She was enough but the money wasn't, and so here she was, staring at Layci Douger's leopard-print thong sticking out of her low-slung jeans as she drew an anatomically correct rendering of their principal on the chalkboard before the bell for homeroom.

"Well, that's impressive," an unfamiliar voice had said wryly from one desk over, and Kate looked right to see a new girl staring up at Layci's artwork with facetious admiration. "Is it me," she asked, now turning to Kate, "or are we in the worst John Hughes movie never made?"

Kate didn't know who John Hughes was, or this girl with the bone-dry humor, but she cracked a smile and introduced herself.

The new girl was Georgina Kim. She had just moved to West Sea

Point with her mother after her parents' divorce. "I think my mom is trying the whole *How Stella Got Her Groove Back* thing, but in New Jersey, which is a little sad, and"—here Georgina paused, nodded up at the chalkboard, where Layci was now sketching a woman kneeling in front of their naked principal—"at the grave expense of my education." Kate was still trying to figure out a clever retort when Georgina added, "You have the coolest eyes I've ever seen—they're like Harry Potter green. Are you his sister? You could be like the long-lost Harriet Potter." From that day forward, Kate loved her eyes.

"What do you have first period?" Georgina asked, pulling out her schedule. As Ms. Hesser entered the room and wiped down the chalkboard without comment, Kate and Georgina discovered that their schedules matched. This wasn't too much of a surprise—Sea Point High offered so few honors courses that every freshman who'd signed up for all honors would be in the same boat—it's just that Kate and Georgina were the only students to have done so.

When Ms. Hesser called out Georgina Kim's name for attendance, she asked Georgina to come up front and introduce herself—"but make it fun!" With her hands in her denim shorts pockets, Georgina said she was from D.C. and liked playing ice hockey and doing the *New York Times* crossword puzzle.

"Excellent!" Ms. Hesser said, clapping her hands together. "Who has a getting-to-know-you question for our Washington transplant?"

In the silent crater of disgust that followed Ms. Hesser's enthusiasm, Kate flirted with a dozen questions to ask just to save Georgina the embarrassment of the current crickets, but she was too scared to raise her hand. She watched Georgina stand up there alone, seemingly unbothered by the awkward quiet in the room or the scuffs of sound from the hallway as students greeted each other after their summers apart.

"How do you feel about being the only Chinese girl in Sea Point?" Jackson Smith asked suddenly, his voice three octaves lower than it had been two months ago.

Ms. Hesser hissed his name over the tittering but then Kate watched the teacher look at Georgina to see her reaction. The new girl answered Jackson Smith directly, looking him in the eye as she told him that her paternal grandparents were from Korea but her parents were American— her dad a Californian, her mom a Bostonian—and they'd met in Seattle at a work retreat and then moved to D.C. for his job.

"But you look Chinese," Jackson insisted.

"I guess it's confusing for you," Georgina said slowly, tilting her head, "because everyone here is white and inbred." Kate's heart stopped as Georgina's voice dropped to a formidable growl that remained frighteningly even when she deadpanned, "I'm not Chinese, but you're a dumbass."

It was as if the entire homeroom had been stun-gunned. And then Ms. Hesser remembered herself and gave Georgina a warning about name-calling amid a delayed onset of gasps, giggles, and *oh shits*. Kate didn't realize she was laughing until Dahlia, her former friend, hissed that it wasn't that funny.

Except that it was, and in one swift act, Georgina had validated Kate's presence at Sea Point High. If this public school was good enough for the fastest thinker Kate had ever met in real life, it was good enough for her. Georgina returned to her desk and mumbled under her breath so only Kate could hear, "So much for positive first impressions, huh, Harriet?"

The bell rang to end homeroom and Kate followed Georgina down the hallway. As they navigated the crush of bodies, Kate keeping her eyes on the back of Georgina's head, she saw their friendship span decades and stretch into their twilight years until they were liver-spotted and senile in joint rooms at a nursing home, Georgina's bony fingers filling in the *New York Times* crossword while Kate sipped her canned protein shake and yelled obscenities at the TV. She saw all this in their future even before they arrived at first-period Honors Bio and Georgina turned to her and asked, "Lab partner?"

Inseparable by second period, Kate and Georgina strategized how to best avoid the Navel Gazers, which is what Georgina called Kate's former trio of friends after Kate filled her in on their falling-out. But the most important development for Georgina occurred outside of school hours, when Kate accidentally introduced her to Ziggy Miller.

It was a Saturday morning and the newly formed duo planned to ride bikes to the Coffee Cow when Georgina first spotted Ziggy. He was throwing all of his hockey equipment in the bed of his dad's truck when Georgina crossed the street. Kate didn't have time to tell her that Ziggy was a year older, a sophomore at Yates, and that they used to be friends but they weren't anymore, and that it would be super awkward to interact with him now, because Georgina was already asking him where he played since Sea Point High didn't even have a hockey team.

"I play at YA but tryouts for my club team are in an hour," he said. "Way more competitive than school—our right wing lives two hours away." Kate cringed as she overheard Georgina ask for a ride just as Zeke appeared in the driveway and said of course. Kate gawked from her side of the street as Georgina waved goodbye, politely offering Zeke directions to her house so she could pick up her gear. That was Georgina—no hesitation, all action.

Ten minutes into tryouts, the head coach of the elite club team saw the promise of a state championship in Georgina's nasty slapshot. She was a quiet force of finesse with a palpable hunger to prove herself. Coach envisioned adding a gold cup to his trophy case even before Georgina faked out Ziggy, the all-star goalie, and lit the lamp to win the scrimmage.

Kate still remembered sitting at the Coffee Cow counter the following Monday afternoon as Georgina told her about the tryout, and how thrilling it was to be back on a team, back on the ice. While ripping her paper napkin into tiny squares, Kate asked Georgina if she felt weird about being the only girl and the only freshman on a team of sophomore boys, most of whom attended private schools. "What's that got to do with the game, Harriet?" Georgina asked before taking a deep slurp of her Oreo milkshake. "They're just dumb boys."

But Georgina and that pack of dumb boys did indeed go on to win multiple state championships, which meant that even though Kate had been Georgina's best friend, Ziggy had been her teammate, her co-champion, and her keeper, which gave him the right to ask after her now.

"We don't keep in touch," Kate said.

"But you guys were so close."

Kate nodded. "We can't all be—what were you and Miles called?"

"The Richard Brothers."

At Kate's raised eyebrow, Ziggy explained that Maurice "the Rocket" Richard and his younger brother, Henri "the Pocket Rocket" Richard, were the most accomplished siblings in hockey—they were both NHL Hall of Famers.

"Yeah, we can't all be the Richards," Kate snarked. She was surprised to hear Ziggy sigh instead of laugh. "What?" she asked. "Trouble in paradise?"

Ziggy shook his head and looked up at the night sky. He knew he shouldn't bring up MVP, but he also knew this was why he'd asked Kate for a walk-off. Keeping his eyes on the stars, he waded cautiously into the conversation. "Miles promised to go through my dad's books and help me move the business online."

They rounded the corner and Ziggy looked up at Daffodil Cottage, a source of pride in an ever-growing swamp of disappointment. Kate followed his eyes and asked him if she could see the key. Flipping through a thick set of keys until he pinched an ordinary-looking one between his fingers, Ziggy held it up for Kate, who swiped at it and yelled, "Hot dog!"

Ziggy knew Kate was trying to cheer him up, except that her pitiful Jimmy Stewart impression only served as a reminder of all the good days in the Before and how they were swiftly drifting away from him. He could play any of Zeke's records and listen to his favorite songs, but the husky grunt of his father's laugh was already beginning to elude him. Ziggy never thought having to sit through *It's a Wonderful Life* at the Campbells' as a bored nine-year-old would be part of a good memory, but for months afterward, he and Kate would greet each other from across the street by yelling, "Hot dog!" It had been one of a million silly little interactions that had given Ziggy not only a wholesome childhood but also a feeling of wholeness that had buoyed his existence until February. Only after his father died had Ziggy recognized his former life to be an infinite string of small delights that he could no longer access.

Ignoring Kate's expectant smile now, Ziggy met her bright eyes with a flat gaze and said soberly, "They keep a spare key under the conch shell on the back step, but you'd still have to know the security code."

"You're no fun," Kate relented, exhaling and letting her shoulders slump in defeat. They resumed walking. "What's going on with the other Richard brother?"

"He's been ignoring me since Sunday."

Pointing out that it had only been a couple of days, Kate emphasized that Miles had just come home; he was probably still settling in. The ease with which she was able to defend the Prince of Sea Point only highlighted what a bizarre time in her life this chapter was proving to be.

"Sure," Ziggy acknowledged, "but he has a lifelong habit of putting things off when they aren't of some immediate benefit to him. Our hockey coach used to joke that the way to spell Miles's name was M-I-A."

"Are you sure that wasn't just your hockey coach trying to spell?" Kate quipped, nudging a rock toward Ziggy's foot. "If the books are so pressing, why don't you ask someone else to go through them?"

"My dad was private about money," Ziggy huffed. "If I knew anything about finances, I'd go through the books myself to save my dad the humiliation, but since I can't, Miles is the best option. That said, I have no idea what to charge clients, who has or hasn't paid, if I owe any suppliers money, and if so, how much. I drive around town and wonder if people think I'm a scumbag because I haven't paid them or a sucker because they owe me."

"I kinda doubt any of that's happened," Kate said. "It's a small town— they'd call you out if they needed to. But if you don't want to deal with the business, couldn't you sell it?"

Ziggy shook his head, tired from life. Bev had said the same thing, as if his dad's legacy was something to be cashed in and forgotten. "I like being everyone's emergency call when a pipe bursts or a toilet clogs. It's like being a first responder."

Kate nodded, considering this comparison. She'd never thought of plumbing as being as noble as medicine, and yet, every day Ziggy answered emergency phone calls. Maybe they weren't life-or-death, but he could keep a clear head under pressure. He could be counted on, trusted.

"And maybe it sounds dumb," Ziggy continued, "but it feels like I'm honoring him, carrying on his legacy whenever I drive around, with MVP on the sides of the truck. But yeah, on a daily basis, I feel like I'm letting down a dozen homeowners and businesses because I can't be in twelve places at once. I haven't billed half the clients since February because there's not enough time for all the paperwork, even if I knew how to do it. So everything keeps getting backed up."

"*Literally*," Kate emphasized, eyes twinkling at her bad dad joke.

Ziggy groaned and they walked on in silence past the duck pond and toward the lighthouse, where they did a loop around the nature trail.

"What's that?" Kate stopped short and pointed.

A small dark creature blocked their path ten feet ahead, just before the footbridge. Ziggy stepped gingerly toward it while Kate hung back, wondering how long it would take to wash skunk out of her hair.

"It's just a box turtle," Ziggy declared, taking out a pocket flashlight. "You know the thing about turtles, right?" he asked, suddenly serious, as Kate crept forward. She shook her head. "If you pick one up—to move it out of the road—you have to make sure you put it down in the same direction as it was headed."

"Why?"

"Because turtles spend their whole lives going in one direction."

"What?" Kate stage whispered. How had she not known this? Box turtles were basically the squirrels of New Jersey.

"Yeah," Ziggy continued, "and human interference won't make them change their minds. They have these tiny territories that they're really attached to. So even if it means crossing the highway you just rescued them from—they'll turn around and cross it again because they're dead-set on sticking to their plan and going the way they were going."

Side by side, Kate and Ziggy watched in silence as the turtle labored over a well-trodden path of trampled reeds and disappeared.

"Sea Point is full of turtles," Kate scoffed. "Everyone just grows up, gets married, has kids and dies. Rinse and repeat and no questions asked."

"Maybe," Ziggy ceded. "Then again, New Yorkers are turtles too."

"Are you kidding?" Kate sneered. "We walk so fast!"

"I mean you all go in the same direction—climb the professional ladder while complaining about everything."

Kate cackled, remembering Thomas and his friends lounging in the Jane Street apartment and, with red wine–stained teeth, lamenting the crowded deli, the cost of the parking garage, the noise from the road repair.

"But you're not a New Yorker," Ziggy mumbled. "Not really."

Minutes later, they were circling back, past Ziggy's favorite white oak, which he once again patted like a horse's muzzle before they walked down Ocean Avenue.

"Why don't you pivot?" Kate asked.

Ziggy narrowed his eyebrows.

"You're so much more than a plumber, Ziggy."

"You realize how offensive that sounds, right? Since I'm a third-generation plumber?"

Kate waved him off. "You know what I mean. Just look at Daffodil Cottage. You could be a general contractor. I mean, you already are, unofficially. But you could expand MVP to include carpentry, even whole houses."

"Become Harry Leeper."

"Become the *anti*–Harry Leeper," Kate argued. "Restore homes. Develop good projects instead of eyesores. People don't hate Harry Leeper for building, but for building thoughtless piles of trash. You could show him how it's done. And people would love you for it. No one likes his houses. They just want a home in Sea Point. You could become a boutique builder."

"What's a boutique builder?"

"I don't know, but everything fancy starts with 'boutique.'"

As they turned onto their street and Ziggy slowed to a stop, Kate told him to think about it. He promised he would before checking his phone. Miles still hadn't bothered to respond to his text from Sunday. Of course he hadn't gone through Zeke's books yet. Ziggy should have known better than to expect Miles to have changed.

Taking off his steel-toed boots in his parents' house, Ziggy wondered if Kate was right. Maybe Sea Point was full of turtles who were dead-set on moving in one direction. Maybe he was one of those turtles. All Ziggy had ever wanted was to follow in his father's footsteps, and now the path he'd walked his entire life had left him utterly lost.

Training Wheels

The night after her walk-off with Ziggy, on the Wednesday before Memorial Day Weekend, Kate showed up for her shift at Jetty Bar and did a double take at the tall man standing behind the bar with his back to her, taking up space in her shrine. He wore all black, like anyone in training, but even from twenty feet away, he radiated an untouchable confidence—the blood-deep entitlement of a royal.

Over six feet of ropey muscles and too good-looking for his own good, Miles Hoffman waved to her with an enthusiasm that would have seemed desperate from anyone else. Flattered as she was, she could barely force a confused smile back. Miles Hoffman's plan to prove to his mother he could run the Wharf was to bartend?

The only person who seemed more confounded than Kate about Miles's presence was Denise, the manager. Standing behind the hostess stand and pretending to review the new menu, Denise explained to Kate with a ventriloquist's tight lip that Kate would be training him. "I just never saw this coming," Denise groaned, apologizing to Kate before wishing her luck.

"Yo! How great is this?" Miles asked, extending his hand for a high-five. Kate was about to point out that he should have taken down all the stools by now when his phone vibrated on the bar, highlighting his rookiedom. Jo Hoffman had a strict "no phones on the floor" policy that, like every other rule, Miles jettisoned.

"I thought you were supposed to be decoding Zeke's books."

Miles shrugged before asking, "Ziggy told you about that?" When Kate nodded, Miles ran a hand through his hair. "I'm still working on them—Zeke sure had one helluva system. Haven't cracked it yet." Kate watched with horror as Miles used a filthy dishrag to wipe down the bar. "But I'm also here to learn about the Wharf, get a sense of how things run. My mom thought it would be useful if I helped you out for a bit."

"Who is that helping, exactly?" Kate hadn't meant for the words to come out as disgusted as she'd thought them, but she'd just caught a glimpse of Joey driving toward the employee parking lot. Joey, the twenty-five-year-old barback, was dying to bartend and had been busting his butt for at least four summers to prove himself—he'd started as a dishwasher and was slowly working his way up when he wasn't paying his way through Cape Tech and earning a degree in sustainable energy. If Kate remembered correctly, he'd complete the three-year program in a few weeks.

Recalibrating, Miles tried to lighten the mood. "I mean, at least you don't have to deal with my brother and me at the same time," he joked.

Kate ignored him as she crouched down to inventory the roll-ups behind the bar. "Your brother does his best managing when he isn't here."

"We can agree on that." Miles grinned, but Kate didn't return his smile. Instead, she disappeared into the kitchen and returned with a small plastic bucket steaming with boiling water. Kate began to polish wine-glasses with admirable alacrity; doors opened in an hour and they were already behind.

"I'm just not sure who benefits from you bartending—besides you," Kate said, forcing herself to meet his eyes. Miles stared at her, his mouth a wide "O" that stood for Offended. "I just think you'd be more useful decoding Zeke's accounting books for Ziggy—like you promised you would."

Miles watched Kate as she inspected a wineglass for smudges, holding it up to the sunlight. For the first time since he'd arrived home, he ached for Chloe—she'd know how to handle this mess. But Chloe was out, and Kate was on to him.

Of all the people Miles Hoffman imagined confiding in, Kate Campbell wouldn't have even made the backup squad until right this second. After all, she was going to train him behind the bar, so it would be better to have her sympathies than her current animosity. More important, she loved Zeke and Ziggy too, and love was at the root of the problem. Love was what made this situation seem so impossible. Love was why he would let this secret burn a hole in his chest.

Miles reached for a knife in the dishwasher bin and began to wipe it down. "Don't use bar mops for polishing," Kate snapped. She handed him a starched white cloth napkin, folded into thirds. "The little white tufts cling—see that? Use a dinner napkin instead—we have to fold more anyway." She resented him, Miles realized, accepting the napkin. Maybe she always had, but as long as he was in her space instead of helping Ziggy, Kate Campbell would loathe him. It was a risk to tell her the truth but a workplace hazard not to.

"Can you keep a secret?" Miles asked, taking a step closer to Kate. She backed away and leaned against the bar, arms crossed and waiting.

"I did look at Zeke's books," Miles said, lowering his voice. "And the business is fucked, Ziggy is fucked, I have no idea how to fix it, and I can't tell him." The truth didn't trickle out of his mouth so much as gush.

"What are you talking about?"

Miles shook his head. "As far as I can tell, Zeke went into debt when he sent Ziggy to Yates. He took out a line of credit and the interest just . . . got out of control." Miles sighed and Kate thought of a wave crashing, the wave she'd felt on her back so often when she'd lived in New York. It was that growing swell of debt mounting, of not being able to pay off her first and only Visa credit card each month, of never feeling secure enough to check the box for autopay.

She thought of eighth grade: Sally and Dirk sitting at the kitchen table, explaining that they couldn't afford to send her to Yates but they would support her when it came time for college, and that there would be more financial aid, more grant money, for undergraduate study than high school. Her parents, who'd met in their master's teaching program at Rutgers, had explained that Yates wasn't her one shot.

Only now did Kate understand that Zeke Miller, who hadn't been allowed to attend college, who'd been forced to work for his own dad and had never traveled except through music, had viewed Yates the same way her younger self had. Zeke had believed Yates would provide Ziggy with a better life, and that promise had been reason enough for Zeke to have gone all in. He'd pushed every last one of his chips to the center of the table and, over the years, Freedom Bank of New Jersey had gleefully watched him fall behind. No wonder Zeke wrote illegibly—he'd been hiding the cost of Ziggy's four-year excursion into private education for the last two decades.

Kate felt dizzy so she headed to the walk-in, Miles on her heels. Using all her strength, she opened the 165-pound door, stepped into the refrigerator, and went to the back where she knew the industrial-size, nine-pound container of Dijon mustard was stored. She promptly pressed her forehead against the cold glass jar.

"You can't tell Ziggy I told you," Miles said, his face drained of color. "You're the only person who knows now, besides me."

"Thanks for that," Kate muttered. She closed her eyes and tried to focus. Her gut reaction was that Ziggy deserved better than to be strung along. Unless Miles could just write a little check and sign off on Zeke's secret debt, MVP would continue to sink a little bit deeper every day, under Ziggy's feet and without his knowledge.

"What's the final damage?" she asked, not opening her eyes.

"The total is $116,709."

"Fucking hell!" Kate yelled.

"My first thought was just to pay it, or ask my mom to pay it," Miles said. "But Ziggy still expects me to walk him through the books and I guess I could just lie about all of it but—"

"No," Kate interrupted. "You're right. Don't lie. He needs to know the truth. At least, I think he does. Does he?"

Kate knew what it was like to be left in the dark—to think you were going to New Hampshire with your fiancé only to end up in New Jersey with your parents. She thought of Thomas sneaking around with Wally, pretending that he and Kate were fine, everything was fine. In hindsight, the truth-dodging that led up to the truth-telling—that stuff hurt more.

"I know I just dumped a lot on you, but can I ask for one more favor?" the Prince of Sea Point asked. Kate cracked one eye open. Before he could stop himself, Miles instinctively flashed his three-quarter smile. "Can you teach me how to bartend?"

Kate was not entirely surprised that her first shift with Miles Hoffman began as a delightful disaster because Miles, the crowned Prince of Sea Point, had absolutely no idea what he was doing behind the bar and still managed to charm everyone, including her. As Kate hurried to prep her station before the doors opened at four, she felt Miles studying her like a hockey play he'd never seen before, his mouth slightly parted, his eyes shaped like question marks.

While Kate retrieved more limes from the kitchen, an older couple walked in right at four o'clock and ordered martinis, up and extra dirty. Kate returned just in time to see Miles stirring the contents of a cocktail shaker with a steak knife, like the Jetty Bar was his fraternity's kitchen. *Where had he even found a steak knife behind the bar?*

She'd taken the shaker and dumped it in the sink without a word, surprised that Miles didn't object. Thankfully the couple was in a good mood and visibly smitten with each other—the man with the salt-and-pepper mustache was so fascinated that the woman with sunburned shoulders didn't like arugula that Kate judged it to be a third date. While the early birds entertained themselves, Kate whipped up two martinis, served them, and turned to Miles, hands on hips. "We do not play around back here. Okay? So do you want to learn?"

Miles nodded and lifted his hand to his forehead for a slow-motion salute. If he weren't Miles Hoffman, Kate would have sworn he was embarrassed.

"Okay," she said. "We'll do this old-school. First of all," she began, "you need to know where everything lives." Kate pointed out the cubby that housed menus, above which were the shelves for glasses. "You need to know your stemware, measurements, instruments, and garnishes. It goes without saying that you use this cocktail stirrer to, you know, stir cocktails, but since you just used a steak knife to mix a martini, please take notes on everything I say so that we don't get scorched in our next LaBan review."

Kate waited for a smart-aleck response but Miles had fixed his eyes on the rack of glasses she was pulling from under the bar and so she continued. "Know your inventory. Don't eyeball liquor, use this." She held up a jigger. "You use the jigger so that when a customer says there's not enough brandy in his old-fashioned, you can hold this guy up and say, I know I poured two ounces in there because I used one of these. It's silly, but it—"

"Kate," Miles interrupted, and she braced for the reminder about how he could fire her whenever he wanted. "Thanks for doing this," he said instead. "I mean it. Thank you."

Thrown off, Kate pretended to locate a smudge of dirt on the polished wood of the bar and wiped at it furiously before responding. "It's not rocket science, but there are rules, especially here."

"Yeah," Miles grunted. "I hear Jo Hoffman runs a tight ship."

"Jo Hoffman runs a successful, efficient, and respected ship," Kate asserted. "Your mom is a legend."

Miles waited for the "but" that never came. Instead, Kate spent the next five minutes explaining proper maintenance and usage of the soda gun before taking him on a walking tour of the kitchen, the walk-in, the storage rooms, the linen stacks, and the ice machine in case Joey or any of the other barbacks called out sick. "Which reminds me: Don't call out sick unless you're dead because otherwise we will kill you. Every night in here during high season is a Saturday night. We expect to get pummeled but it's a group pummeling. It's one big traumatic bonding exercise with a cash prize at the end, but if one of us calls out sick, the rest of us get straight-up slaughtered. Working here is a team sport."

"And I thought we were just pouring drinks for tourists."

"Trust me, after Memorial Day Weekend, it's more like *Survivor* than *Cheers*."

When the couple asked for another round, Kate made one cocktail and had Miles mirror her every motion and measurement. She coached him through each step and explained that twisting the lemon peel directly over the drink released essential oils.

Kate handed her martini to the sunburned woman and Miles slid his glass self-consciously to the man with the mustache. They took sips and then switched, enjoying their intimate taste test.

"Hers is better," Mr. Mustache said, throwing Kate a wink.

"She's the master," Miles agreed, giving Kate a small bow that she refused to acknowledge as she searched for a fresh bar mop and began wiping down the well bottles.

"Let me show you how to enter orders into the computer," she said, pulling her ponytail holder out and redoing her hair into a top knot, ready to rumble.

An hour in, Miles leaned against the tiled wall of the kitchen while Kate demonstrated the proper way to load glassware into the dishwasher bins. "You're a good teacher," he said.

"I learned from the best—Mike Shapiro."

"Ah, Hot Mike."

"You know it," Kate grinned.

"Everyone learned something from Hot Mike—he taught me how to juggle."

"Women?" Kate joked as Miles grabbed three limes and rotated them through the air.

"Hey," Miles said, catching all three limes before gripping Kate's shoulder and letting his hand linger there. "Let's bartend the hell out of this summer. Like, let's be the new Hot Mikes."

Kate laughed as she nodded, finally understanding why Ziggy had remained friends with Miles all these years, and why countless girls had wept publicly over someone who would use a steak knife to mix martinis. He really was fun. Kate noticed herself showing off for Miles as the night wore on: She was more perky, joking around with customers, asking Danny the dishwasher how his brother was doing after a skateboarding accident had left him with a broken arm. She was paying attention to the moment, reveling in the possibility that Miles was watching her, admiring her ability to do a job well. Every time a customer celebrated her return to the bar, called her by name, Kate hoped that Miles had heard it.

When Miles asked her to watch him course out a large order with a fries substitute, she stood over his right shoulder and inhaled his sandalwood smell while he slowly pecked at the touchscreen. She watched as he readjusted the pour spout on the Belvedere and affixed it the way she'd shown him minutes earlier, using the trick Hot Mike had shown her. It was exhilarating having a new act on the Jetty Bar stage—an extremely attractive act who'd allegedly declined an offer to model for Ralph Lauren in high school.

At the end of the night, after Kate showed Miles what got wiped, wrapped, and tossed, she pretended not to notice his struggle with the industrial-size box of plastic wrap until he asked for help. Like everything else in hospitality, experience provided a better way to perform each task. Kate hadn't realized she'd mastered tearing plastic until she demonstrated it for Miles.

"You can do everything," Miles marveled as she covered the leftover olives.

"Just waiting on my MacArthur."

"I'm serious," Miles said, nudging her out of the way so he could attempt to copy her quick rips. "Your New York people must be dying without you."

"Ha!" Kate's disdain erupted from her lungs as reflexive as a burp. "Everyone at Artemis is doing just fine without me."

"Doubt it," Miles shrugged. "And I bet that jackass is struggling too." Chancing a glance at Kate's narrowed eyes, he added, "Ziggy told me."

"He's fine. They're all fine. I'm the one who's . . . back here."

Miles nodded sympathetically. He was more or less in the same position, but he had the funds to flee at a moment's notice and wake up tomorrow morning in a European hotel bed with an unconscionably high thread count. That knowledge kept him free from the despondency pinching Kate's shoulders up toward her ears and tunneling self-doubt through her brain like an apple core. Any time he began to feel claustrophobic, Miles reminded himself of all the Delta points and equity he'd accrued—it was a touchstone he'd relied on since college. The very idea of being in Kate's position, living without a parachute, made him wince.

"He already has a new girlfriend," Kate volunteered, keeping her eyes on the maraschino cherries she was wrapping.

"That doesn't mean anything, trust me." Miles wiped down the serving trays slowly so he wouldn't run out of a job to do. "You're just more honest than he is—you loved deeply so you're healing slowly."

"Love deeply, heal slowly," Kate repeated. "I've got to say, that sounds a lot more like Brené Brown than Miles Hoffman."

"I only did it once, and I promised I'd never do it again."

"You loved deeply?" Kate asked, shocked. "When?"

Miles nodded, smiling at the memory as he wiped down a serving tray that was sticky with residual Worcestershire sauce. "Long time ago. Anyway, Yates had a bunch of kids that boarded, and if you wanted to visit a girl in her dorm room, the two rules were door open and at least one foot on the floor. I learned it was safer to love the same way—door open with a foot on the floor."

Kate rolled her eyes like she had at the customer who'd asked for her number earlier in the night—half disgusted, half amused. She imagined Miles in high school—he'd probably fallen in love with some Italian heiress who was now professionally strutting up and down runways in Milan. From her online digging, Kate knew that had always been his type— physically exotic, financially familiar. And yet, as she ran the tap to rinse out the coffee dispenser, Miles's words flashed across her mind like a chipmunk darting across the street: *Love deeply, heal slowly.*

Coming of Age

After nearly a month behind the checkout desk—and despite having adjusted to wearing both a bra and non-stretch pants—Kate still found each shift at the library exhausting, especially the Thursday morning of Memorial Day Weekend after training the Prince at the Jetty Bar. Sitting behind the checkout desk alone was the opposite of slinging drinks next to Miles Hoffman. Last night, Kate had felt like a jaguar. This morning, like every morning at the library, she remembered she was just a heron.

Kate knew nearly every patron who came in, which meant she was obligated to politely ask each time-warped face for a life update—with a strained, feigned enthusiasm, of course—before glossing over her own plane crash of a career path that had led her to standing right here, ten feet away from an inexplicable ant farm. In just a few weeks, she'd seen most of her graduating class and privately gawked at how everyone had aged, which, Kate noted, had nothing to do with how they had (or hadn't) matured.

The star quarterback had gained weight but acquired manners, a wife with great reading taste, and two kids. The editor of the school newspaper was still pompous and was now a triathlete who came in just to use the bathroom during his workouts, flicking her a peace sign on his way to relieve his bowels. Louanne the fire marshal, who'd been in the same popular crowd as Bernadette, looked and behaved exactly as she had as a seventeen-year-old when she and her date had come over to the Campbells' house for prom pictures — tight-lipped, polite, all business, as if she were constantly in the middle of counting how many people were in any given room.

But the most stressful encounter Kate had experienced thus far was with Dahlia of the Navel Gazers, who was now, confoundingly, a new mother and appeared genuinely happy to see Kate. "Glad to be home?" Dahlia had asked, all chewing gum and maternal glow. It felt like a trick question, but Kate nodded, like she was savoring every breath she took in Sea Point.

"I love keeping up with you online," Dahlia said, her earnestness undeniable, and therefore alarming, as she smiled with her teeth and slid *Curious George* books across the checkout desk. "Your life got so exciting after high school — and your husband is so cute! We should all get together sometime — you know I married Jackson."

Kate nodded. Jackson Smith. The boy who'd asked Georgina on her first day in a new school how she felt about being the only Chinese girl in Sea Point, the boy Georgina had first called inbred, and then a dumbass, with such controlled affect that it was now insane, Kate realized two decades too late, that Georgina hadn't gone into comedy.

Smiling as she handed Dahlia Smith's books back to her, Kate cooed at the infant strapped to her chest and decided there was no need to correct Dahlia about her relationship status. She and Thomas would be back together soon enough. She had until Nessie's wedding to prepare for the ultimate comeback.

In the meantime, she would keep busy with her three-point plan. She already had two demanding jobs, and her reflection during *Freaky Freakazoid* workouts was looking less like a weasel drowning and more like a dancer practicing a new routine. After the always-chaotic Memorial Day

Weekend, Kate would begin her search for the perfect date to Nessie's wedding at the same place she would begin her search for the perfect dress to wear to the wedding—online.

"Mrs. Larsen!" Kate said now, smiling at the woman approaching the checkout desk. "How are you?"

"Kate Campbell! Oh my! Well, truth be told I'm embarrassed— I didn't know you worked here, or even that you were home." Mrs. Larsen blushed. "Don't mind these naughty ones on top." Kate looked down to see the raised gold lettering of a Danielle Steel novel.

Mrs. Larsen had taught eighth grade language arts at Sea Point Middle School and, more important, had let Kate eat lunch in her classroom the week she and the Navel Gazers had fought about which boy band had the best singers. Now in her late sixties, Mrs. Larsen retained the playfulness of a dark-haired Shirley MacLaine: sun-kissed skin, sparkly blue eyes, a dimple in the center of her chin so deep it could clutch a sunflower seed. Kate wondered if teaching kept Mrs. Larsen so youthful—or maybe it was all the Danielle Steel?

"I like to read the juicy bits aloud to Henry," she said with a wink. Henry Larsen was 80 percent deaf and everyone knew it because he was constantly taking out his hearing aids and leaving them in bizarre spots around town—the pear display at the Acme, the ATM, the men's room at the Coffee Cow, and by the mints at the Jetty Bar hostess stand. Everyone knew he was mostly deaf and no one was ever certain where those hearing aids might turn up next.

Henry Larsen appeared just then from the other side of the ant farm and collected his stack of presidential biographies from the nearest communal table. He made his way over, grumbling about how they should have packed sleeping bags if they were going to take all night. His gruffness was part of his uniform and his charm—he was a retired scallop man.

Mrs. Larsen tsked at her husband's impatience. "Hang on to your Grundens, Henry. I need to collect my holds. Do you remember Kate—"

"Yes, yes, I know who you are," Henry Larsen muttered, giving Kate half a wave.

You do? Kate thought to herself. She wanted to ask Henry Larsen who he thought she was, because she had no idea. Instead, she whipped around and eyed the stack on the back shelf of reserved books.

"I wonder how often John Green gets coupled with Danielle Steel," Kate mused, scanning the bar code in the back of each book. "Young Adult fiction is all about coming of age, and in Danielle Steel, it's all about—"

"Kablooey, Kate Campbell!" Mrs. Larsen interrupted. "I'm so tired of YA cornering the coming-of-age market. I am sixty-eight years old. I've taught middle schoolers for forty-four years. There is no way a bunch of teenagers deserve to monopolize coming-of-age. We are coming of age all the time, until we die—or else we're already dead!"

Kate grinned as she handed Mrs. Larsen her stack of holds. With that kind of conviction, she thought, maybe Mrs. Larsen was right. She had to be. After all, Kate was back in Sea Point, which would prove to be the intermission of her thirties before her great comeback of a second act. She would return to the city and grow up. Again. But differently. Better.

After clocking out for the day, Kate reached for her phone and reflexively checked her email. She hadn't received any important messages since leaving New York and yet her thumb still instinctively tapped the icon every time her phone was in hand.

But there, in her in-box, was Georgina Kim's name.

It was an incredible phenomenon to physically feel her heart stop and then hear it start again, the blood sluicing harder to catch up, like waves sloshing against the sides of a boat. Kate clicked the email, wondering if it was real or if spam could have become this targeted:

Hey Harriet,

How are you? I got your text last weekend and thought it would be a good time to let you know I'm coming back to Sea Point for Nessie's wedding and Zeke Miller's Rock the Boat thing. (How sad is that? I still can't believe it.) My wife hasn't been to Sea

Point so we'll spend all of August bumming around town and my
mom says you're back too—typical Sea Point, right? Everybody
knows everything! Anyway, I didn't want to just show up unan-
nounced and then we'd have to be all, like, polite at Nessie's wedding. Want to meet for a drink the Friday before the Monster's big
day? I get in late that Thursday night and then I'll be around until
the Wednesday after Labor Day.

Hope you're well,

G

Georgina was in Kate's hand, on her phone, in the front of her mind,
bigger than a billboard. This was huge. This was crazy. Kate read the
email over and over again as she clocked out with her punch card. She
suddenly craved an Oreo milkshake and decided she'd stop by the Coffee
Cow before her shift at the bar. Georgina was coming back and she didn't
seem to hate her, which meant there was still a chance that Kate could
finally make things right. Walking out of the library, Kate's face ached
from grinning: Georgina had called her Harriet.

Bones

Per Denise's instructions, Miles had been steeping tea for the Jetty Bar's special Memorial Day Weekend punch when he realized he'd ignored Ziggy's text for five days. At least, that was sort of what happened. More honestly, Kate had walked into the Jetty Bar, holding an Oreo milkshake and fuming that she'd just seen Ziggy on his back in the Coffee Cow kitchen. He'd been trying to resurrect Goldie's industrial dishwasher while yelling over to Kate to ask if she'd seen Miles. It was this vision of Ziggy drowning in dirty suds that inspired Miles to count up his days of negligence and arrive at the number five.

"You need to tell him," Kate spat, taking her stack of roll-ups to the opposite end of the bar. Less than twenty-four hours ago, she had demonstrated endless patience while teaching Miles proper shaker technique, and now she'd made it clear that she had zero time for him. An old vision of Kate Campbell returned to Miles then—the way she'd navigated the bleachers at high school football games, with her nose in the air, like she was better than everyone else. He'd forgotten all about that person until just now.

Ziggy didn't pick up the first time Miles called. Or the second. Or the third. But Miles knew Ziggy would eventually relent. He tried four more times in succession so there would be a record of his tenacity. Miles's deep roster of ex-girlfriends had always treated his missed calls like they were their own apology—he was just a good guy who'd made a mistake, and he was so, so sorry. By the time they picked up or called him back, they'd already forgiven him. A string of missed calls was annoying unless they were from Miles Hoffman, in which case, they were endearing—a rare piece of proof that he cared.

"Yeah?" Ziggy barked on the eighth attempt.

"Zig, I'm so sorry—we had this table of ten come in last night right before the kitchen closed and they ordered four rounds of whiskey sours and I—did I tell you I'm bartending with Kate at the Jetty Bar?"

"You know why I didn't pick up the first seven times?" Ziggy asked, interrupting. "Because I was up to my neck in old sink water that stinks, like really stinks, but because I thought you must be in some kind of crisis, I did what any friend does and stepped away from my own shit to help you with yours, and now what you're telling me is that you're tired from working a job that you picked up on a whim?"

Miles opened the door to the walk-in and stood inside the refrigerator for privacy. Kate had taught him so much during his first shift, not least of which was to take personal business off the floor and into the walk-in. Ziggy had never yelled at him before, at least, not since high school, and that was only on the ice.

"I'm really sorry, Zig, just let me make it up to you." Miles ignored the prongs of guilt stabbing his chest—how long was he going to dodge the truth? But he couldn't think that far ahead. Not yet. "I'll bring over dinner for you and Bev tonight—how's that?"

"I'd rather you just go through the books so I can figure out my life."

"I know. And I will. But I'm going day to day right now—not even—more like hour to hour, just trying to keep a lid on it."

"Okay," Ziggy said, audibly calming down. "I'll tell Bev you're coming over with dinner—she'll be happy to see you."

They hung up and Miles gave himself a moment to breathe in the walk-in, even though it was freezing. It was his second night working at the Jetty Bar and he was going to have to ask Denise for the rest of the night off—and for three orders of crab cakes and house salads to-go. *Oh well*, Miles shrugged, *what was she going to do, fire him?*

Miles locked eyes with a red snapper that was sticking out from the shelf and walked over to it, ran two fingers down the dead fish's body, admiring its scales. Chef would serve this guy whole, and people would pay to pick out all the tiny, translucent bones.

His phone buzzed and it was Chloe, again. She still called him at least once a week, sometimes yelling, sometimes begging, always on the verge of tears. The best thing he could do for her at this vulnerable juncture was avoid her if he wasn't going to marry her, which he wasn't. Miles looked back at the red snapper, its googly eyes staring him down. Chloe didn't like a dinner with bones, but having grown up here, Miles couldn't imagine a life without them. The bones made you savor the meat. The bones were what made the meal worthwhile. Chloe would never get that, just like she'd never get him. It didn't matter that she was a supportive partner and a gold-hearted human being—she wasn't what he needed.

Miles hit "ignore" and then, the voltage from Ziggy's call still ripping through his skin, he went one step further and blocked Chloe's number. Before he could stop himself, he texted Bell a question mark. She didn't respond but he knew she was there.

Green Light

And just like that, with the stiff tradition of the Queen's Guard, the blinking yellow traffic lights of the off-season resumed their tricolor rotation at six a.m. the Friday morning of Memorial Day Weekend, and thus commenced the high season.

Regardless of how he mentally prepared for it each year, Memorial Day Weekend hit Ziggy like a hurricane that weather forecasters had been predicting for weeks. He'd had plenty of time to hammer everything into place, but a hurricane didn't care about plans or preparation. A hurricane thrived on chaos, and Memorial Day Weekend was a four-day maelstrom. Starting the Thursday night before the long weekend, an onslaught of outsiders appeared on every street and rendered a left-hand turn on Ocean Avenue an exercise in futility. Impatient SUVs crammed with overheated parents, sticky-fingered children, and impulsively purchased jumbo-size beach snacks sped through crosswalks, yellow lights, and stop signs only to find themselves mired in the inevitable holiday traffic.

And that was only the beginning. After investigating the rental and claiming bedrooms, screeching kids stormed the beach like the Allied forces on D-Day. Each hour, they took ground, demanding sandcastles, a dip in the water, more goldfish crackers, a turn with the big yellow bucket. The adults who accompanied these small, needy people were similarly afflicted with zigzagging desires. Large men on direct orders from sleep-deprived spouses would stumble onto the beach first thing in the morning and assemble a row of chairs that would remain empty until the after-noon. Ziggy felt sorry for these people who thought life boiled down to a game of dibs, who seemed to derive more pleasure from the idea of the beach than the actual ocean. Hours later, after waiting in a lifetime of a line at the Coffee Cow because everyone said their pancakes were the best, the women baked in the midday sun, complaining of the heat, and the men held up hardback biographies to shield their phone screens as they texted those not present. "This stuff gets everywhere," they'd grumble about the sand.

The out-of-towners' oral soundtrack of griping, gossiping, and scolding competed over an even more offensive playlist: portable speakers. It never ceased to amaze Ziggy how many tone-deaf tourists decided that vacation was the perfect time to showcase their DJing skills, at the expense of ev-eryone else. Earphones were expected in every public setting except here, where the tin sound of competing '80s rock held the ocean air hostage and inspired Ziggy's most murderous thoughts.

Closing his eyes and listening to the harmonizing chorus of waves, wind, and gulls, Ziggy knew that this place would soon be a zoo of not-so-exotic suburbanites with pale skin, soft hands, and something to prove to their friends on social media. Soon, but not yet. He looked around and tried to soak in the final moments of peace. This beach, for at least a few moments longer, belonged to him.

After his all-day wrestling match with Goldie's dishwasher, and for the first time in months, Ziggy was actually, kind of, more or less caught up. Even the man cave at Daffodil Cottage was on hold until the eight-foot-long piece of enameled lava stone arrived for the bar counter. He had opened all the houses, given the green light to every commercial establishment in his care, and eventually shown Goldie's dishwasher who was boss.

For now, Ziggy was free—or as free as any small-business owner ever was. He knew the first emergency call would come soon enough. Until then, Ziggy focused on the warmth of the sun as he flirted with the idea of sleep.

"Your mom said I'd find you here," Kate said, blocking the sunlight with her head. "Can I sit or—"

"Seat's taken," Ziggy joked.

"Were you asleep?"

"No," Ziggy yawned. Behind his sunglasses, he watched Kate lather her face, neck, chest, and stomach with sunscreen. Beach culture was bizarre, even to him, and he'd grown up immersed in it. How was it appropriate to sit around in waterproof underwear with your parents, and your neighbors, and your friends, and wave to your former teachers as they waddled by in modest bathing suits looking for hermit crabs with their grandchildren? And then people—his peers—Ziggy himself— would play volleyball and all the things would wiggle and jiggle and jostle and how many times had he accidentally ogled breasts and butts and stubbled bikini lines because how could he not?

Kate squirted more sunscreen into her hand and as she bent down to lather her legs, Ziggy looked away but he still saw her in his mind. And even though he squeezed his eyes shut behind his sunglasses, he felt a visceral tug to reach out and grab her arm—and then what? He envisioned how her surprise might turn into a wrestling match like they used to have on this same beach, but then maybe it would turn into something else entirely, her skin slick from the sunscreen, her mouth still tasting like the Snapple lemon iced tea she'd just sipped, but where was this going— how was this—

Ziggy lay down on his back, and Kate scanned his torso behind her sunglasses. No one would have ever believed that Ziggy Miller would look like this, like a model with a hard, flat stomach and a small patch of blond hair between his pecks, a tiny bird's nest of spun gold. His nipples were just right there, in front of her, staring up into the cloudless sky like two dumb bull's-eyes. She fought the impulse to reach out and put her palm on his stomach, keep it there, like a teakettle on a flame. Kate blinked behind her sunglasses—*what was happening?* She looked left and right, as if onlookers would be able to read her thoughts, but the beach was deserted except for them. It was only after Kate imagined Ziggy reaching over and pulling loose the string of her bikini top that she stood up and wiped the sand off the backs of her legs.

"Paddleball?" she asked, terrified of her own mind's meanderings. She wasn't due at the bar until three and she'd been giddy with her short-term freedom until she'd started fantasizing about her oldest friend. It was just weird to think about him in that way—Ziggy Miller, who'd come over in first grade to stare at her pink urine in the toilet bowl the morning after her mom made her try beets. Ziggy Miller, who hadn't cried at the end of *Free Willy* but all-out sobbed until Zeke had taken him by the hand and led him out of the movie theater. Ziggy Miller, who was $116,709 in debt and didn't know it.

"Okay," Ziggy grinned, reaching for a paddle. "But can you do my back first?"

He stood up and handed Kate his sunscreen. It smelled like coconut and summer and bottled potential. Kate squirted a white puddle into her palm and then massaged it into Ziggy's back, between his shoulders, down the curve of his spine, over the taut skin of his hips.

"Whoa, perv!" he said when she ran her finger along the inside of the elastic band of his swim trunks.

"You don't want to get burned right on that line!" Kate said, echoing what Bernadette had always told her, back when her older sister had worn braces and run her own finger along the inside of Kate's bikini bottom. They both knew she was right, but Kate still blushed as she rubbed the white goop into Ziggy's skin.

"Want me to do you?" Ziggy asked.

Kate grunted, reluctant but very much over the burn-turns-to-tan mentality of her twenties. She handed Ziggy the bottle, who rubbed lotion all over the back of her body with quick, rough pats, like he was blotting a greasy piece of pizza. Kate could tell that he hadn't even tried to blend the sunscreen and that she probably looked like Casper from behind. His clumsy slathers also suggested she'd imagined any sexual tension between them.

They played paddleball for an hour, just like they had as kids, complete with full-body layouts and face dives, and pretended not to feel self-conscious in their waterproof underwear.

"Georgina wrote to me," Kate said, brushing a strand of sweaty hair out of her eyes before serving.

"Seriously?"

Kate nodded. "She's coming back for all of August so she can go to Nessie's wedding and your dad's Rock the Boat."

"That's great—right?"

"Yeah, we're getting drinks the Friday night before Nessie's wedding."

Ziggy nodded his approval. "Awesome. Maybe we'll get the old roller hockey set out from the garage. Also, I'm done with this game." Ziggy tossed the paddle into the sand and then collapsed, belly down, eyes closed on his threadbare beach towel. Kate followed suit, sighing with contentment as she spread out next to him. Ghost crabs scuttled by while seagulls gossiped down by the water's edge. Without saying a word, Kate and Ziggy thought the same thing: *Savor this.* Soon enough, the beach would be as packed as the Wildwood boardwalk, crammed with bad music and condescending chatter about how quaint the town was.

The rising heat melted all sense of time. Ziggy drifted in and out of thoughts, obligations, dreams, his dad's books, Miles's flakiness, the unbearable unknowing of his own future.

"I'm going in," Kate announced. Ziggy stood up and they ambled down to the water. "Want to come over for dinner Tuesday night?" Kate asked, wading in past her knees. "Invite Bev too."

"What for?"

"Just a we-survived-Memorial-Day-Weekend dinner party," Kate said. "And it's my birthday on Sunday, but I'm working at the Wharf through the weekend. These are my last few hours of sanity."

"Can I invite Miles?" Ziggy asked. It would be another opportunity to guilt-trip the Prince into action—when Miles had shown up at the Miller house with champagne and crab cakes, he'd made Bev's night and avoided any real talk about tackling Zeke's books. Kate jumped between the waves with notable grace and Ziggy watched her out of the corner of his eye. He remembered how she'd show up at his doorstep on a Saturday morning, Scrabble board in hand, still wearing her black leotard from dance class. And here she was now, gliding through the water like a ballerina, only in a bikini that he imagined peeling off.

"Already did!" Kate yelled over, before diving under a wave.

Of course she invited Miles already, Ziggy thought. She'd invited Miles before him because Kate and Miles worked together now. They had their own thing. Ziggy bit his bottom lip and reminded himself that he'd wanted Kate to like Miles despite his high school reputation. Reality cut in for a dance just then, because Ziggy remembered that Miles didn't befriend girls—he baited, dated, and ditched girls. "Well, let us know what we can bring," Ziggy said, forcing a smile. "Besides the cake my mom will insist on."

Kate laughed. "If it were anyone else, I'd tell you to stop her, but her frosting is better than the Wharf's."

"You know it's just whipped cream?"

Kate lifted her arms over her head and spun, drops of salt water ski-jumping off her elbows. "But it's Bev's whipped cream!"

They emerged from the water and Ziggy was about to suggest another round of paddleball but Kate began to pack up her stuff, mumbling about getting ready for work. Ziggy checked his phone—no missed calls, no frantic texts. Either everyone's appliances were behaving, or they were too jammed up to reach out.

"I'll walk back with you," he announced, and he too began to collect his towel, T-shirt, unread book, and bottle of sunscreen.

"Work?" she asked.

"Always," he responded. And it was. But for the first time in a long time, Ziggy was excited about the project he'd just thought up while watching Kate dance in the Atlantic.

Memorial Day Weekend

Everyone knew there were good nights and bad nights at the Jetty Bar. The Friday night of Memorial Day Weekend was shaping up to be a good night, possibly a great one.

When Miles and Kate began their shift, a group of men in their sixties came in and declared, "A round of old-fashioneds, and keep 'em coming!" The man who handed over his credit card explained that they were in town for a bachelor party—"fourth time's the charm."

One young, eager-eyed couple at seats five and six wanted to try the special rhubarb shrub cocktail that rang in at $22 each, and another couple in their forties announced with urgency, "We need four shots of your best tequila!" The same couple also requested seven Surf & Turf platters to-go, along with half a dozen appetizers to bring to their friends, who were saving their prime viewing area in the sand with beach blankets. Memorial Day Weekend marked opening night for the outdoor movie series, which meant *Jaws*. Although they were at the Jetty Bar for less than an hour, the woman and her spouse ran up a tab close to $600—and that was before their teenage son texted them, requesting two more Surf & Turfs.

Kate's body buzzed with adrenaline as she directed the heavy flow of traffic that, under anyone else's watch, would quickly end in a fifty-person pileup.

"Holy shit," Miles muttered under his breath as he entered another large order into the computer. "We're making money tonight," he gushed, swiveling his hips as he said it.

Kate grinned in agreement, and as she opened a new bottle of Belvedere, Denise called her name from the hostess stand.

"I need you in the kitchen," she said, walking toward her. "Danny had a family emergency."

"What?" Kate asked. "Is he okay?" Danny the dishwasher had never taken off work before—except when he had shingles, the summer after Kate's freshman year of college. It's not that he was never sick or hungover—but unlike Kate and her friends, he was a father of four and couldn't afford not to show up.

Denise shrugged and muttered that Danny hadn't offered details, but it had sounded as if he were crying. "I asked if someone died," Denise offered. "I'm pretty sure he said no."

"Pretty sure?" Kate marveled at the one-track mind of a restaurant manager.

"Does it matter?" Denise snapped. "He's not here, Joey asked off for his graduation thing, and we're all out of martini glasses."

That's when Kate stopped thinking about Danny and realized her great night was about to turn to stacks of dirty dishwasher racks. The bar was crowded with the buzz of anticipation, a bunch of giddy grown-ups acting like toddlers on a sugar high. It was going to be a late night that ended with vomit and spilled cocktails on the light-up dance floor downstairs in The Basement which, for Kate, translated into generous tips—tips that now she wouldn't see, because she was about to get paid the $13/hour wage of a dishwasher.

"I'll do it," Miles volunteered as he dumped a twelve-gallon bucket of ice into the bar sink. Kate hadn't even asked him to refill the ice, she realized with pride—he'd begun to see the insurmountable side work that was only visible to those with restaurant experience. After just a couple of shifts, he was demonstrating potential as a bartender, and it was because she'd taught him. Denise stood between them, her mouth hanging slightly open, hoping she'd misheard Miles.

"I asked Kate," Denise asserted, crossing her arms.

"And I'm saying I'll do it," Miles said, his voice even but forceful over the clinking ice cubes. He employed a distinct, son-of-the-owner tone Kate had never heard him use before during a shift.

Denise threw her arms up in a resigned *Whatever* and pushed the swinging kitchen door hard, yelling something at Jodi the line cook about shitty-looking kale.

"She asked *me*," Kate said.

"Yeah, and we both know why."

"Because you'll break the dishwasher."

Miles laughed as he quickly wiped down the bar and threw the dirty bar mop at Kate before squeezing past her. "Take no prisoners!" he called over his shoulder before disappearing into the kitchen.

"Kate!" the men in town for their friend's fourth marriage shouted in unison from the far end of the bar. This was why she avoided telling tourists her name—so they couldn't yell it like barnyard animals in heat.

"Another round?"

"Yeah, but also," one of the men said, beckoning her closer for a secret, "we want to send those lovebirds down there two shots of sex on the beach." Kate looked over at the young couple who were talking shyly, their empty cocktail glasses long since cleared. It was definitely a first date.

"No."

"Aw! Come on!"

Calculating in her head, Kate reconsidered. Maybe a round would help the couple out. But they could do better than sex on the beach, and so could she. If Miles had given her the opportunity to make more money, she was going to do just that. "They need after-dinner drinks—how about Macallan 12?"

"Even better!" the men cheered. "For us too!"

Before pouring, Kate added another $150 to their ever-growing tab.

The rest of the night, like so many nights at the Jetty Bar, was an exercise in dry-land drowning. The festive crowd kept ordering, tipping, declaring their love for one another, the Wharf, the Jetty Bar, the town of Sea Point, and, not least of all, Kate, their valiant bartender.

And so it wasn't until the end of the night, after she'd wiped down every bottle and counted out her bank and signed the necessary slips for Denise, that she saw the true generosity of Miles's move in the unprecedented stack of twenties she counted out at a back table. She'd never made this much in a night, not even close—then again, she'd never handled the bar on her own on a holiday weekend. Miles had given her the chance to earn this kind of money while he'd suffered in the kitchen. For whatever reason, the Sea Point Prince had fallen on his sword for her.

Strawberry Shortcake

After her first shower in more days than she'd care to admit, Bev Miller wrapped herself in the white linen bathrobe Zeke had given her on their thirtieth anniversary and headed downstairs to check on the cake. It was the Tuesday after Memorial Day Weekend and she'd made a strawberry shortcake for Kate Campbell's birthday cookout that night. The dessert was a bit of an inside joke because she'd always thought Kate looked like the Strawberry Shortcake doll. Touching it now on the cooling rack, Bev decided it needed a few more minutes before icing.

On her way back upstairs to blow-dry her hair, Bev screamed at the dark figure in the doorway before realizing it was Miles.

"I'm really sorry," he said. "I let myself in." Except for the Harry Leeper houses with their security systems and motion-sensor lights, no one in East Sea Point locked their doors during the day. Miles had always loved that—the trust inherent in an unlocked door. Jo called it foolishness. "I was just about to knock but then I saw you, and I thought you saw me."

Bev nodded and told Miles she wasn't sure where Ziggy was.

"Yeah, he's not answering his phone, which is why I just showed up." Sniffing the air, Miles asked, "What are you baking?"

Bev led him into the kitchen and, although he would have to wait for Kate's birthday party to sample the cake, she took great joy in offering him the contents of the refrigerator. Miles, however, was distracted by the fresh color in the corner.

"Hey!" he said, pointing at the wet canvas like he'd spotted an endangered species.

Bev shook her head. "Don't look at that—it'll hurt your eyes."

Miles stared at the canvas, trying to relax his gaze so his mind could focus on its subject. Chloe's parents were serious art collectors and he knew they'd have gone crazy for Bev's stuff. And now he was seeing it—the painting was of the busiest intersection in town from a magnified aerial perspective, like a seagull had painted it, perched from atop the four-way traffic light. It appeared abstract until Miles recognized it as anything but.

"You know you could make a killing with these," Miles said for the millionth time.

Bev rolled her eyes. "None of them are finished. Every time I think, 'Okay, this is it, I'll stop,' I look at it a week later and there are a dozen glaring problems just mocking me. If I sold them, other people would have to live with those mistakes, they'd have paid for an incomplete work, and that's just wrong."

"Where are the others?"

Bev ignored him and took out a carton of heavy cream.

"Bevvie . . ."

"Out there." She gave the faintest nod in the direction of the backyard but Miles knew where she meant. When he and Ziggy had taken the canoe out, Miles had peered through the garden shed's pollen-dusted window and seen the army of canvases lined up along the floor. Bev hadn't even bothered to protect them with a tarp, and all of Zeke's extra supplies were right there—rusted wrenches, a couple of saws, a propane torch, even a random toilet seat lid, all surrounding Bev's priceless work.

Miles tried to modulate his tone and reminded himself that Bev didn't know that she was $116,709 in debt, but she was sitting on a gold mine— *she was the gold mine*—if only she'd relinquish the idea of perfection.

"Can I sell the ones in the shed for you?"

"Sure," Bev said, "right after you settle down, marry a nice girl, and take over the Wharf."

"I'm working on it."

Bev's laugh started low but quickly grew louder. "I'm sorry," she gasped, "it's just—you—settling down—I mean, you can't even commit to Ziggy."

"I'm gonna look at the books tomorrow," Miles snarled defensively. In response, Bev stood up and turned on her yellow hand mixer. Over the whir, she sang the song from *Annie* about tomorrow being only a day away.

"He's focusing on me because it's easier than focusing on what he wants," Miles said. "It's not like QuickBooks is going to tell him whether or not he should keep the business going."

"Oh, no thank you," Bev said, her tone blasé, as light and airy as the whipped cream she was in the process of making. "I'm staying out of it. He's an adult, you're an adult. You guys are grown-ups now, even if you're both living at home and acting like asshats at the Wharf."

"You really don't know where he is right now?" Miles asked.

"No, I don't," Bev said, "but my default assumption for him and his father has always been the hardware store." Turning off the hand mixer, Bev dipped her finger into the bowl and ran a taste test she deemed satisfactory.

"I had a funny thought while I was making this cake," Bev said.

"Oh yeah?"

"Love is like flour," Bev said, staring at Miles. "I don't know how much baking you do, but if you start with a lot of flour, maybe even too much, and you tamp it down, pack it in, force it into too small a space, mix it with a bunch of other stuff, and then add heat, that love dries out and the whole thing you were trying to make just crumbles."

"Okay?" Embarrassed for Bev, Miles took out his phone to see if Bell had caved yet.

"I know you love Ziggy and that you want to do right by him, but what I don't know is how my Piney husband had an accounting system too complicated for a Wharton graduate."

Miles stopped trying to compose a witty text and looked up. Did Bev already know about the debt?

"For whatever reason, you still haven't put in the time to figure it out, and that's fine, but just tell Ziggy to ask Barry."

"Who's Barry?"

"He's married to Todd—SeaSalt Inn Todd. But Barry was a money guy before he retired at, what, forty, so I think he'd be up to the challenge."

"What's that have to do with love being like flour?"

Bev exhaled loudly and walked over to the three circles of cake. They were finally cool enough to ice and so she got to work, dropping a cloud of whipped cream into the center of the first circle and spreading it into a smooth surface.

"It's obvious you don't want to deal with Zeke's books," she continued. "Even Ziggy must know it, in his heart of hearts, buried under all that denial—and honestly, I don't blame you. I still have that ugly La-Z-Boy angled exactly how he liked it, even though, when he was alive, I constantly threatened to set the thing on fire."

After the first cake circle was completely iced, Bev stacked a second circle on top of it, dropped another white cloud in its center. "My point is that you can't tamp down who you are to try to fit into Ziggy's expectations of you. Help him the way that you know how or else the whole thing's going to crumble." Bev carefully added the third circle to the top of the cake stack. "People don't always express their love the way you want them to and that's okay—I don't want to crunch numbers, either." She dropped the last white cloud with a satisfying *floff* and spread the icing until all three stories of cake appeared as one. "You don't have to be the perfect friend," she said. "But you have to be honest—with Ziggy and yourself."

Miles forced a curt nod as Bev opened the refrigerator door and placed the cake on the center shelf. She returned to the counter where the yellow mixer sat, reposed, its two beaters up in the air at a 90-degree angle. Bev pushed a button and they popped out into her hand.

Offering him a beater, Bev added, "You both deserve to be happy." The whipped cream was better than the stuff at the Wharf, and their pastry chef, as Jo was quick to advertise, had won the James Beard Award *twice*. Miles had seen Bev pour in vanilla, but there must have been something else.

"Excited for the party?" Miles asked, eager to change subjects.

"I'm trying to be," Bev answered truthfully. "It's the closest I've felt to excitement since February, but the idea of attending a party without Zeke is just—"

"I'll be your date for the night," Miles interrupted. "I'll keep your drink fresh—actually, I'll be better than Zeke because no one will bug me to take a quick look at a leaky faucet."

Bev laughed genuinely, which Miles understood to mean an acceptance of his invitation. He would keep Bev company on her first social venture without her husband. Miles rarely felt proud of himself, but he knew Zeke would appreciate this gesture, wherever he was.

Summer Church

Sore and stupid with exhaustion from bartending through Memorial Day Weekend, Kate welcomed her mild Tuesday morning back at the library after the holiday. Bending down to pick up the pile of books from the Return drop-slot, she hung there, hinged at the hips, and stretched. It was hard to tell if her body felt this broken because of all the hours on her feet or because, as Henry Larsen had pointed out when he'd come back to retrieve his hearing aids from above the ant farm, she was no longer a spring chicken. People her age not only got pregnant on purpose but talked about trying to get pregnant with an unnerving casualness—as if forcing an acquaintance to envision a couple's strategies for deeper penetration was just what you did in your midthirties, along with complain about the mortgage and wonder aloud about refrigerator prices.

Kate had turned thirty-four on Sunday, which she'd celebrated with a few run-throughs of *Freaky Freakazoid*, followed by a quick walk to the beach with her parents, a long shower in which she even shaved her legs, and brunch on the back deck with her family before clocking in for her shift. At work, she wasn't the birthday girl but the bartender, and she was relieved.

Life in Sea Point didn't swing high and low the way it had in New York, but maybe that was also her twenties, or running in Thomas's elite social circle. She hadn't experienced a single night like the dozens she'd endured in New York—how many midnights had she left Thomas at a wild party and gone home alone, wondering why she hadn't had any fun? Kate had blamed herself for being awkward at such gatherings up until last night, when, driving home from work, with the windows down and the sea breeze drying out the sweat in her hair, Kate realized those parties hadn't been fun because those people were not her people.

Since Bernadette's original suggestion of a small get-together, the birthday party had spun out of control. What had started as an intimate dinner had expanded for the reason invitations often did in a small town—to avoid hurt feelings. As a result, Ziggy and Bev were attending, as were Miles and Jo, Patricia from the library and her professional lifeguard husband Chad, Goldie from the Coffee Cow, Gus and Gertie from the hardware store, and of course Bernadette, Rob, and Clementine.

Kate left the library and walked to the beach to read the first few pages of a controversial ARC predicted to blow up when it hit shelves in November. After only a few pages, she'd completely lost track of time and when she finally looked at her phone, Kate saw she was already five minutes late to her own party. Speed walking while strategizing how to excuse herself upon arrival to apply makeup, Kate turned onto her street and saw a pink balloon tied to her parents' mailbox. It was no doubt Bernadette's work—an homage to the birthday parties they'd had as kids. For a moment, Kate felt a pang of nostalgia, and then an overwhelming wave of self-consciousness: Why had she thought throwing a birthday dinner for herself at her parents' house would be a good idea? She'd have to ask Bernadette not to post anything—the last thing she needed was for Thomas to see how provincial her life had become. Before she could text her sister, however, Kate heard a voice calling her name.

"There's the birthday girl!" Bev Miller exclaimed, crossing the street while holding a beautiful three-layer cake decorated with white icing and fresh strawberries. It was the first time Kate had seen Bev outside since she'd returned home, and the sight made the rest of the evening inconsequential. Bev wore a flattering floral shirtwaist dress and she'd blow-dried her hair, which made her jagged DIY haircut look more avant-garde than worrisome. They hooked arms and entered the Campbell house together.

For the first several minutes, it was a blur of faces that Kate saw every day, and yet here they were, in her parents' house, excited to celebrate. She gave up on the notion of mascara just as Clementine rushed toward her holding a paper crown. Only moments later, Gertie nearly blinded her by thrusting two handfuls of rainbow confetti in Kate's face—which Gus then immediately vacuumed up with a portable dustbuster he must have brought for this very reason. Ziggy stood with Kate's dad on the back deck, and as Kate approached, Dirk exclaimed, "There she is!"

Ziggy smiled as he swirled the air with his finger. "Hear the music? I made a birthday playlist—you'll like it, it's mostly my dad's stuff."

Rob, Bernadette's husband, gave Kate a hug and handed her a beer before realizing she'd want something stronger. In moments like these, she and Rob had an understanding—he'd survived enough Campbell family reunions, weddings, and funerals to quickly stir up a vodka soda, complete with a lime wedge.

"We call these vod-sods at work," Kate said with scientific authority, clinking her glass with Rob's beer bottle.

"Don't try to take credit for that!" Miles yelled from across the room, allowing all eyes to drink him in as he made his entrance. "Vod-sods are what the twenty-one-year-olds order at the bar, and you make fun of them for it."

As the guests mingled, everyone made their way over to greet the Prince of Sea Point with an enthusiasm, Kate noted, that bordered on desperation. It wasn't because he had finally returned after so many years away, or because he was wealthy, or because he would inherit the Wharf, she suspected, but because he was so beautiful. People loved to attach themselves to a pretty thing. Like watching a movie on the big screen, or wandering through a museum, engaging with Miles felt like a temporary escape to a better place. Life was unfair in myriad ways, and not least because standing before Miles Hoffman felt like walking through an orchard on a fall day.

Kate looked around for her mom and sister, whom she'd yet to see.

"They had a last-minute thing to do," Rob said, reading her mind. "I saw them run upstairs, squealing about a red ribbon."

Jo Hoffman arrived then, toting a small gift bag for Kate and a wicker basket with wine and wildflowers for her parents. On Jo's worst days, she reminded Kate of Thomas's mother, Evelyn Mosby—insufferable as she roamed the floor of her kingdom, quick to point out imperfections. But most of the time, Jo struck Kate as wholly misunderstood. She was a person who not only loved to work but also worked in pursuit of love. Before Kate could get to her, Gertie leapt at Jo to ask how her Memorial Day Weekend numbers had been while Patricia begged for the designer of Jo's long khaki skirt.

"Actually," Jo said, "it's made of hemp—and it has pockets."

As Kate waited her turn, she heard someone whisper "Relax" in her ear. "Just chill," Miles instructed. "You don't have to welcome everyone—you're not at work."

She reluctantly followed his lead and returned to the back deck to join Dirk and Ziggy. Miles raised his beer and asked, "Ziggy, where ya been?"

Ziggy smiled but his eyes stormed. "Funny," he said, "I could ask you the same thing."

Kate ignored the tension between them by taking a deep sip of her vod-sod, and Dirk soon filled the lull by lecturing them on the history of American cheese: "So, apparently in the late 1700s, any cheddar that America exported to Britain was called 'Yankee Cheddar' or 'American Cheddar' and then in the 1860s, Dickens wrote about 'American Cheese' in his Uncommercial Traveller series, which was really only the beginning."

Stepping between Ziggy and Miles, who thumbed the labels of their beer bottles in uncharacteristic silence, Kate planted a kiss on her dad's cheek. He had proven once again to be the ultimate grill master: On the barbecue, burgers, hot dogs, scallop shish kebabs, and an array of colorful veggies sizzled in organized rows. Dirk pulled her close and kissed the top of her head. "Happy birthday, kiddo," he whispered in her ear. "It's nice to get to celebrate with you."

Rob appeared with another vodka soda, which softened the edges of the evening. Kate walked back inside to sit with Gertie, Jo, Patricia, and Chad in the living room, who were fuming over the newest abomination Harry Leeper had built next to the nature preserve. Not interested in such a buzzkill, Kate moved on to say hello to Bev and Miles, who were chatting in the kitchen with Gus—or, more accurately, listening to Gus yammer on about the new paint he'd just ordered. Dirk was still on grilling duty, lecturing Ziggy about the history of the pickle, and her mom and sister were—

"Back!" Bernadette panted, one hand under her barely noticeable baby bump as she and Sally appeared at the front door, beaming with a secret they refused to share.

"Perfect timing," Dirk announced, raising his spatula like the Olympic torch. "Dinner's ready." As Kate helped deliver plates to her guests, she overheard her parents on the deck, no longer grilling meat but Ziggy about the Daffodil Cottage man cave. Straining to hear Ziggy explain the benefits of enameled lava stone countertops, Kate found herself finally relaxing just before she heard a scream from the living room.

"What on earth?" someone shrieked. Kate exchanged an alarmed glance with Bernadette before rushing into the living room and seeing all eyes on Jo Hoffman. She had been holding court but was now inspecting her burger, the bun lifted, the lettuce, tomato, and onion pulled off to reveal the patty. In a frenetic mental scroll, Kate worried where her dad had bought the meat, and how long ago, and if—

"This is the best burger I've ever had!" Jo said. "Dirk?" She stood up and marched through the kitchen, gathering Gus, Miles, and Bev in her wake. Everyone crowded onto the back deck. "Dirk Campbell, I swear to God I'm going to poach you for my kitchen—how did you make this cheeseburger so perfectly medium rare?" Dirk's proud grin puckered his whole face so he looked like the happiest little garden gnome as he stumbled over a response about keeping the meat in the fridge until the very last moment. Kate felt the vod-sods nudge her into a new gear just as she heard Bev Miller behind her, encouraging Clementine to take small steps and use both hands.

The lights went out. In the dark, Kate turned around and there, her face aglow from thirty-four lit birthday candles, was her niece. Nothing but lashes, cowlicks, and baby teeth, Clementine teetered toward Kate carrying Bev's three-layer strawberry shortcake. While everyone sang and tried not to salivate, Kate crouched down so she was eye level with Clementine. Before blowing out her candles, she made a wish and felt grateful she'd get to keep it to herself.

"There's one more thing," Sally declared, flipping the lights back on.

Ziggy stood up. "Yeah, you should go see before it gets too dark."

Confused but curious, Kate followed Ziggy's lead. Behind her, the group hushed one another, and Kate felt a rush of nervous excitement pinwheel through her stomach. Walking toward the front of the house and squinting in the dusk, Kate couldn't see through to the driveway because there was a big wooden box with a thick red ribbon tied around it blocking her view. And then, with all of the locks, zippers, and buttons of her brain working in unison, Kate realized what was under the big red ribbon that her mom and sister had been squealing about before her arrival. The wooden box wasn't a container so much as a sacred offering: an outdoor shower. She froze just as Ziggy turned to face her.

"Come on," he grinned. "Let me show you."

"But now I have to live at home forever," Kate half-joked, gaping at the sight. To call it an outdoor shower was an understatement; it was art.

"I modeled it after the one at Daffodil Cottage," Ziggy explained.

"But when did you do it?"

"Over the weekend."

Everyone laughed and clapped. Before long, Zeke's name flitted between them like fireflies, how he would have been so proud of Ziggy, how much son was like father.

"But like Bev too," Sally pointed out. "I mean, this required plumbing skills but also creative vision." Everyone cooed at this astute observation, and Bev didn't fight the quiet tears that rolled off her cheeks.

"You're the best of both your parents, Ziggy Miller," Jo Hoffman called out, holding up her glass in praise of him. Everyone followed suit, and Dirk shouted, "Hear, hear!"

Opening the door of the shower, Ziggy explained that the panels were cedar, and before he could provide the origin story of the antique-looking hardware, Kate lifted her gaze. The fading sunlight, which would be gone within minutes, illuminated the stained-glass window that hung above the shower. "You did this?" Kate asked in disbelief.

"I thought you'd appreciate it," Ziggy confessed, shrugging as a growing splotch of red traveled up his neck. "Know what this is?" He pointed to a small blue-and-white tile, featured prominently on the inside of the door, right at eye level.

Kate nodded, speechless. She didn't know, but she knew. It was from the lobby floor of the Bluebell Hotel.

"I only had one piece left, but I think that kind of makes it more special."

Kate jumped on Ziggy then, hugging him so tightly that everyone behind them exchanged looks, but Kate didn't care. It was, hands down, the best gift she'd ever received.

As Scuzzy As It Gets

After punching out at the end of her shift, Kate looked around for Patricia, who had never reappeared after her phone call with the library board. It was the first Tuesday in June and half-past noon—Kate had lost track of time helping Mr. Garver, a new widow and proud AARP card-carrying member, sign up for a Gmail account so he could message with his daughter in North Jersey. The process would have taken only a few minutes except that the ancient public computer needed half an hour of coaxing just to open a new window browser. "This thing's older than I am," Mr. Garver had croaked as they'd waited.

Since it was Kate's day off from the Jetty Bar and she had consumed enough coffee to fuel a bus, she'd decided to ask Patricia if she wanted to grab lunch. Maybe it was a little premature, but Kate wanted to pick her boss's brain about which jobs she should apply for in New York.

"Come in," Patricia muttered from the other side of her closed office door. Kate turned the knob, let herself in, and was shocked to see Patricia slouching low in her chair.

"Everything okay?"

"Take a seat," Patricia said, and Kate's heart sank. Either she was fired or someone was dead. "Look, I'm not aware of the details," Patricia said, half-reading something on her phone, "or even if it's legal or possible, but apparently Harry Leeper is going to submit a proposal to the planning board to raze the building."

"What building?" Kate asked.

"This building."

"But this is the library," Kate said, confused.

"Indeed," Patricia nodded, eyebrows raised, "but libraries are buildings too and Leeper thinks the town would benefit more from fourteen luxury condos." Patricia tossed her phone across the desk. "Honestly, I should have seen this coming."

Patricia went into a quick summary of what Kate already knew: The library had few—but loyal!—patrons. The annual swell of summer guests who adored the library, who declared at the checkout desk that "this place feels like stepping back in time," didn't matter. They could acquire a library card by providing a driver's license or any government-issued form of ID with two proofs of a permanent address. This allowed the library to fine tourists for overdue or non-returned books, but it hardly compensated for the fact that the wave of summer visitors didn't pay taxes, which meant they didn't contribute to the library budget, which was unequivocally pitiful. The business model, if you could even call it that, was outdated. Kate instinctively glanced over at the two decrepit public computers.

"But doesn't the government own the library?" Kate asked.

Patricia cringed. "This isn't China." At Kate's bewildered expression, Patricia elaborated. "I mean, yes, librarians are civil servants and the library is funded by local taxes, but it's run by the board, and that board, as indomitable as we may be at Summersault quizzo, doesn't stand a chance if Leeper can persuade city council's planning committee that this block should be designated a redevelopment zone." Anticipating Kate's next thought, Patricia explained that the Ship Harbor library was only a fifteen-minute drive away.

"You have to understand," Patricia said as she inhaled, "redevelopment laws in the state of New Jersey are as scuzzy as it gets. The only reason why Leeper's able to raze historic buildings and get his McMansions greenlit is because he knows the right people on city council."

"How'd you find out?"

Peeling her stilettos off her feet, Patricia smirked. "Same way you find out anything around here—Chad was in the Acme and he overheard John and Frank—city council guys—talking about it like it was already a done deal. He called me right before I had the board call, and Stuart Skahill—he's on the board—said he'd just heard the same thing."

"Jesus."

"And if that weren't enough," Patricia continued, "Ms. Rose is retiring at the end of June."

"No!" Kate gasped. Clementine would be devastated.

"So first we'll break all the kids' hearts into a thousand pieces, and then Leeper will pave over those thousands of pieces with luxury Creeper condos, which you know will be uglier than a pig snout turned inside out."

Forgetting about lunch, Kate returned to her parents' house and spent the rest of the day researching redevelopment law. As much as she loathed Harry Leeper, Kate felt her frustration with Sea Point growing in her belly like a mushroom cloud. After all, the town voted down historic preservation laws year after year, and the town allowed Leeper and his like to come in and exploit, bully, and potentially convince them that condos and corporate-owned Airbnb properties were more important to Sea Point's future than their library. How was she going to tell Clementine that Ms. Rose was retiring and that her replacement would be fourteen condominiums?

She had to stop the Creeper, and yet Kate knew from Patricia's anger and the town's changing landscape that Harry Leeper would most likely get his way. City council, Patricia had wallowed, was stacked with businessmen who'd already enabled him to flout zoning regulations on most of his properties, and Donna McConnell was on the planning committee— she would be one of nine residents to vote on the library's future.

It was all so overtly corrupt, so double-dipped in self-interest that Kate's first impulse was to post a rant on social media, exposing the local crooks. She thought better of it, however, after remembering how Mr. Scoda's fiery post about dog poop on the beach had only inspired an endless thread of vitriol and finger pointing without any constructive reasoning. If Kate wanted to unify the town against Leeper and his cronies, she would need to do her homework and brainstorm solutions before going public. By the time her parents arrived home from chaperoning the Sea Point senior prom, Kate had traveled so far down the bizarre rabbit hole of arcane zoning laws that she almost didn't notice Ziggy's truck pulling out of his driveway after midnight. Almost.

Dovetail

Ziggy's excuse was that the enameled lava stone countertop had finally arrived.

His excuse was that his best friend was avoiding him.

His excuse was that his father had followed all the rules.

His excuse was that even after Kate's hug at her birthday party, nothing interesting had happened. Ziggy was convinced that if he didn't initiate the walk-offs, Kate would be just as happy to stay home and watch *Wives with Knives*. Maybe she just felt sorry for him or didn't know how to say no.

His excuse was that he worked hard during the day and he was growing more and more convinced that none of it mattered.

His excuse was that he couldn't fall asleep at his parents' place—all the night sounds were too familiar but altered, as if Zeke's absence had thrown the house itself out of sync.

His excuse was that so many of the women he'd met this summer were looking for a weeklong fling during their girls' getaways and family vacays, and the more he tried to ignore their messages, the more they texted absurd offers that guaranteed a fun time and a deep sleep.

His excuse was that his secret wasn't hurting anyone.

And so Ziggy spent most nights at Daffodil Cottage—sometimes alone, but often with someone from the Main Line or Mercer County who found his impressive residence almost as surprising as his extensive vocabulary. Ziggy's parade of tourists silently reasoned that his alleged profession as a plumber was a cover for something sexier—maybe he was a spy, or one of those crazy successful hedge fund guys who retired at thirty and had picked up plumbing as a lark. Regardless, the cute local with the film-set-ready mansion only made for that much better of a story the following day: Bikini-clad and a little buzzed on the beach, Ziggy's romantic flings would lean in and whisper what they told their friends, but the jealous screaming in response to the sultry details was always so loud that, even from several umbrellas over, a family of five would look up from building their sand castle and wonder if those shrieking girls had seen a shark.

As if to justify the women and his unsanctioned use of Daffodil Cottage, Ziggy spent the first few hours of his evening working on the man cave, which was coming along nicely, if slowly, now that he had discovered his affinity for hand-cut dovetailing. Oddly enough, it was because of Kate that Ziggy now spent the first half of his night with saws and knives. Ever since his friend Greg at the lumberyard had lent him his Leigh D4R jig for the outdoor shower, Ziggy had developed an obsession with dovetailing just about everything—only not with Greg's jig. He preferred to carve by hand.

"Why would you waste your time?" Greg had scoffed. "With the D4R, you can't tell the difference."

But Ziggy did notice the disparity and it wasn't a waste of time. It was a meditation to manipulate salvaged wood with the same control he wished he could exercise over his life. He was creating something useful and beautiful from discarded scraps and, with a little finesse, Ziggy had marketed his burgeoning skill.

Did the Daffodil Cottage owners care about the joinery of the drawers in the man cave bar? Nope. Or at least, they hadn't until Ziggy wrote to them and offered to hand cut them. "You had us at 'custom,'" the wife replied.

It was a small victory in a year of loss.

Zeke had died. Miles had shown up only to let Ziggy down. Kate had also reappeared, but she was so focused on her ex-boyfriend and New York that Ziggy knew his hours of carving were a better use of his time than pursuing her. Bev wanted to sell their house and Bernadette had suggested meeting with Clyde at Ocean City HVAC in person.

Securing the tailboard to his bench vise a little after midnight in the basement of Daffodil Cottage, Ziggy wondered if maybe he should have stuck it out at Cornell since Kate seemed to value formal education above all else, which made sense since her parents both held master's degrees. After dropping out, Ziggy had come home and aced the exam to become a licensed master plumber—earned his certifications with his eyes closed—but that wasn't the same thing as having an actual master's degree. No one thought plumbers were smart in a way that mattered. Ziggy wiped his forehead before pinching the top of the board with his thumb and forefinger. And yet, wasn't what he was teaching himself right now, at thirty-four years old, alone in a basement, a worthwhile endeavor to expand his mind? *I may not be a scholar but I'm not a turtle, either,* Ziggy thought to himself before pushing the saw well past the scribe line and cursing aloud.

His phone lit up with a text from Isla letting him know she was outside—perfect timing for a distraction now that he'd botched the tailboard. Flicking off the basement lights after climbing the stairs, Ziggy caught himself feeling at home as he switched on the kitchen overheads, then the table lamp in the hallway, and straightened the small watercolor hanging to the left of the front door. He imagined inviting houseguests into the living room, encouraging them to watch a movie on the gigantic television from the pristine white sofa, and offering them drinks from one of the two (soon three) custom built-in bars he'd installed.

With his hand on the knob, Ziggy caught himself wishing it again: that when he opened the door, his oldest friend would be standing on the other side. She'd ask about hand-cutting and he'd show her the tools, which she would pick up, one by one, always curious about everything. Ziggy ignored the flutter in his stomach that he'd trained himself to tamp down since first feeling it in the Acme checkout line—that sort of hope was dangerous, and Ziggy knew all too well that love meant loss.

Opening the door, Ziggy smiled through the screen at the woman he'd met earlier in the day, when he'd been summoned to retrieve an engagement ring from an Airbnb sink. Expecting a married couple, he'd been pleasantly surprised to see the behind-the-scenes of a bachelorette party—the puddles of clothes, the mountains of snacks, the palpable diffusion of responsibility. So many different perfumes clogged the air that Ziggy developed a headache while disassembling the P trap, but the women from Ohio were cute and funny, and Isla had slipped him her number on a dare from the kitchen as he worked in the master bath, so here they were. He appreciated the clear expectations almost as much as the company.

Ziggy pushed open the screen door and forced a smile. This woman didn't see a failing plumber or a lost son standing before her—only the proud owner of a glorious house. "Come on in," he said. "Welcome to Daffodil Cottage."

On the Line

June was the sneakiest of summer months: In the beginning, every barefoot step hurt, and then the lifeguards blew their whistles at five p.m. and it was over. When July hit with an explosive pow, the only proof of the past thirty days was the pair of lost sunglasses and the layer of calluses that made shoeless walks the default method of transportation. June was a slow burn, which Miles knew was not Chef's preferred method of heat.

"Fire six scallops, five swordfish, two steaks—one rare, one medium—and eight fries," Chef called out now, and as Miles dropped the meat into the scaling pans and began the clock in his head, Chef shoved a plated cheeseburger across the shelf. "Throw this back on for a minute." She didn't call him a stupid fucker, which was how Miles knew he was doing well.

It was the second week in June and Miles's fifth shift on the line, keeping his head on a swivel between foot-high flames and Chef's irascible perfectionism. The various meats with their range of cook times on the different size flames reminded Miles of his brief attempt to drum for his friends' band at Princeton—so many things happening at once, best not to think too hard or he'd invariably mess up his own rhythm. If he stopped to consider the scallops browning or the oil bubbling in the deep fryer, he'd choke. And that's what he loved about the kitchen: There was no time for thinking and no space for bullshit.

Jo Hoffman had lured Chef Natalie Prezzo, culinary ingenue, away from her uncle's restaurant in Richmond, Virginia, and then nearly lost her to a famous New York restaurateur after her first summer in Sea Point. What she lacked in height and experience, Natalie more than made up for in hair and attitude. Her high ponytail looked like it belonged on the back of a stallion and added three vertical inches to her five-foot frame. Quick-witted and lionhearted, Natalie's confidence afforded her endless creative vision. She was a body and mind forever in motion, timing and redesigning courses, so it required close attention to her face and a disregard for her bark to recognize that Natalie was not only a kitchen visionary but also a vision in checkered pants. The Wharf needed her more than Natalie needed the Wharf, which is why she'd been able to look Miles up and down a week before and simply say, "No." And when he'd pushed, she'd practically growled, "Over my dead body, Richie Rich. No."

No, he was not welcome to join the kitchen staff. No, she didn't care that he was willing to work for free. No, she didn't give a flying fuck who he was or that he would actually pay her to let him chop onions. "No," Natalie told him over and over. She turned him down so many times the first week in June that Miles started to call her Notalie behind her back.

It had started the Friday of Memorial Day Weekend, when Danny hadn't come in and Denise had told Kate to take over the dishwashing station before Miles stepped in and rolled up his sleeves. Danny didn't come back to work for a week, however, having thrown out his back at his day job as a landscaper, and Miles proved to be a half-decent dishwasher—in that he was marginally better than no dishwasher at all. That first night, while Kate made bank at the bar, Miles pushed racks through and learned to scream with his mouth shut after grabbing a still white-hot pan with his bare hand. When Emmy, a new server, dropped a bowl of oyster shells on the kitchen floor and Miles scrambled to clean up the mess, Natalie looked over and told him to move faster, he was in her way. It was only after he'd swept the remaining shards and returned to his station at the sink that he noticed the river of blood gushing from his finger and realized what was happening. Miles was falling in love. Hard.

He thought he'd experienced proud work days in San Francisco and understood the satisfaction of a cold beer after a beat-up round of real estate negotiations, but the nightly performance in the kitchen of the Wharf crossed the New York City Ballet with the World Wrestling Federation he'd loved watching as a kid. Between the tartar-encrusted silverware bins and thick cycles of steam from the industrial dishwasher, Miles learned the kitchen shorthand, the language but also the movements, the fragile balance of violence and beauty, independence, and cooperation, mighty T-bones coupled with delicate sprigs of rosemary. On the third night as Danny's fill-in, Miles wiped his brow only to feel an unprecedented mountain range of pimples on his forehead from sweating in clouds of condensation for ten hours at a time. His legs ached even though his entire workstation permitted him only a five-foot leash—except when he dragged the trash out back, hoisting hundred-pound buckets of lobster shells, cow parts, wine stems, greasy napkins, chicken skins, fish heads, and indeterminable slop into the dumpster.

Danny returned eight nights later, wincing every few minutes but refusing anyone's help—he couldn't risk losing the job. Miles reunited with Kate behind the bar, but after his first shift back, he had approached Denise with his request to work full-time on the line. "You are so strange," Denise had said, shaking her head. "Go ask Chef."

And Chef had said no. Miles persisted. He wrote her a heartfelt letter. He noticed she loved KitKats and brought in a gigantic bag, which he placed in front of her locker. Every time he helped Joey the barback run dirty bins to the kitchen, Miles saluted Chef, which she ignored.

But two days later, Ty, a quick-wristed meat-flipper, didn't show up for his shift. After the third night of Natalie cursing between each dupe, Danny told her that he'd heard Ty had started working construction for Leeper the Creeper, and so Miles was reluctantly brought on to the line. He'd started off prepping salads, but after a week of those, he asked Marcus to show him how to shuck oysters.

For a week straight, Jo Hoffman came home to find Miles hunched over a bucket in her pristine, barely used chef's kitchen, both hands bleeding through the shucking gloves, slowly working his way through several dozen oysters. "Are we having a party?" she'd joked. Miles had never taken extra lengths to do anything well. Good enough had always come easily, and he'd spent his life coasting downhill on a beach cruiser of well-oiled privilege. But there he was, glowering at Jo over the bucket, bleary-eyed but determined, and she had never been prouder or more confused.

If Kate was right when she'd told Miles that bartending was like being a rock star, the kitchen was a backstage pass he hadn't known he'd wanted. But Miles desired it more than anything, lusting after Natalie's impeccable knife skills, Marcus's deft shucking. And now, already halfway through June and getting in game shape for Fourth of July weekend, the biggest weekend of the summer, Chef was trying him out on the grill while Celia stayed home with some kind of unappetizing mystery rash on her face.

"Pull that cheeseburger," Chef barked, proffering a plate with her left hand while using her right to garnish the shrimp platter with lemon and a ramekin of cocktail sauce. It was a deep-fried dance-off with chaos, until they got slammed, or until too many entrées were sent back, which was when the stress level went from skyrocket high to completely bottomed out. The manic nature of a successful restaurant explained to Miles the ubiquitous drug use not only permitted but encouraged in most kitchens.

Jo Hoffman, however, did not run most restaurants and Natalie Prezzo did not run most kitchens. Drug use was strictly forbidden. Denise had a nose for her staff's tipping point, which is when she would wait by the dirty dish bins with a tray of tequila shots for all Jetty Bar employees. The shots couldn't always boost morale, but it kept the workers from walking out.

Chef peeked at the burger, gave it a "Good," and handed the order to Emmy, a server who Miles thought was cute but knew was barely twenty. Besides, the lapdog love looks Miles received from Emmy were nothing compared to that "Good" from Chef. The satisfaction he derived from plating a well-prepared steak shocked him each time—that swell of pride and exhilaration that coursed through his veins would be unnerving, embarrassing even, if it weren't so euphoric.

For the first time since his hockey days, Miles didn't have to wonder if his face or his mom played a part in his accomplishment. No one in this kitchen cared who he was beyond his ability to sear tuna. There wasn't time for giving him hell about his last name when there weren't enough hours in the day to yell at him for how slow he was, how dumb he was, what an absolute *puta* he was for prepping his station in the ass-backward order that he had.

In a bizarre full circle, Miles found himself thanking his childhood au pair every day. If Jo hadn't insisted on her boys growing up with Valentina, he would have been *follada* in the kitchen. Miles had always been embraced for exactly who he was, but here among the sharp knives and high flames, every day felt like a preseason tryout as he self-consciously but whole-heartedly attempted to prove himself worthy by learning the language—Spanish and Kitchen—as quickly as possible. Every time he sliced his finger with the eight-inch chef's knife, Miguel would hand him a tiny paring knife and say, "Trabaja con lo que sabes," which, fortunately, Miles knew was a dick joke—"Work with what you know." On the line, keeping up with the banter was as critical as keeping up with the dupes.

Miles wanted to do right by Chef expressly because Chef, unlike nearly everyone he'd ever encountered, cut through his bullshit like a hot blade through a duck breast—which is what made her "Good" about the burger so golden. She hadn't called him a six-foot shithead in at least two hours, and he knew he was improving every minute of every shift, even when he screwed up, which only made him greedy to learn more. His hands looked like something out of a torture movie—the number of times he'd grabbed scalding handles without a cloth, the blisters and burns, the calluses that weren't developing fast enough, and the big cuts he'd played off as nicks. After lifting, dumping, filling, and emptying every tub, bin, can, and bucket Chef told him to, Miles went home and practiced his knife skills by dicing garlic, deboning chickens, shaving broccoli rabe. He'd never tasted beer—*really* tasted beer—until after his first week in the kitchen when he'd sat with the rest of the crew at Summersault, not speaking out of pure exhaustion but way too wired to go to bed.

Until now, Miles hadn't believed in destiny any more than he'd believed in everlasting love. But suddenly he knew how he wanted to spend his life, and it was both thrilling and terrifying to look backward and see how unhappy, how unfulfilled he'd been. It took five hundred oysters and thirty-four years for Miles to discover a profession that wasn't a career but a calling.

Pitching

Lounging on the beach on a Saturday morning in mid-June, Kate looked down at her phone buzzing with a text from Bernadette: *Did you talk to Patricia?* The answer was no, so Kate ignored her sister and went back to swiping faces of strange men in search of a viable plus-one for Nessie's wedding. Giving up after another dozen swipes, Kate closed the dating app and opened the email that she kept revising on her phone but hadn't actually sent to Patricia.

For the past two weeks, ever since she'd learned of Harry Leeper's plan to designate the library block as a redevelopment zone, Kate had spent what little downtime she had brainstorming ideas to stop him. At the end of her shift at the Jetty Bar, Kate poured boiling water over the heap of leftover ice and mentally rewrote the language of a letter to the planning committee that always sounded more like a run-on complaint than a compelling argument. She needed to change course.

It was during an early-morning *Freaky Freakazoid* routine, between the ax throws and baking cookies, that Kate had swiveled her head through the air and straight into an idea: *Rock Star Readers.* Instead of imploring

the planning committee to think big picture, Kate realized she would appeal to the public. She would create a library event that Sea Pointers,
shlocals, and tourists would look forward to attending, and she would harness the energy of that event to galvanize the town against Harry Leeper's
fourteen condominiums. Ms. Rose's imminent retirement, as tragic as it
was, provided the perfect reason for the library to devise a "redevelopment" plan of its own.

As detailed in Kate's proposal, Rock Star Readers would provide an
hour of entertainment for children, but it would also serve as a time for
the community to learn about the library's uncertain future. It was by no
means an earth-shattering idea, but it was at least on par with the ant farm.

At the end of Kate's next shift, she asked Patricia if they could talk.

"Please don't tell me you're quitting!" Patricia exclaimed.

Kate laughed nervously, surprised and flattered. "Definitely not," she
said.

"Phew-wee Almighty with an armadillo bag to boot!" Patricia said,
throwing her arms in the air, her head back in a full-body hallelujah. Kate
couldn't be sure, but she was almost positive Patricia made up bizarre
phrases and then excused them as Southern colloquialisms. She'd googled
"This here is fishier than a crawfish up a snatch," which Patricia had said
when $3 had gone missing from the cash drawer. Even Google had been
mystified. "All right, darlin'," Patricia said now. "What's going on?"

"I don't know how to say this, so I'm just going to say it," Kate said,
making intense eye contact with the corner of Patricia's desk. "I have an
idea that could take the library to a new level, and possibly thwart Harry
Leeper, but only if you—I mean, if the board—well, you and the library
board—" The arc of her pitch was similar to her performance in pull-ups:
clear determination that waned into self-doubt that fizzled into just awk-
wardly hanging there, unsure when to let go.

"Kate," Patricia said too softly for any good news to follow. "We're on
the brink of being literally leveled with a wrecking ball. You've been here
six weeks. The other associates have all been here much longer, not to

mention Ms. Rose has *decades* on you, and she's never once asked to initiate a new program, but here you are, trying to rock the boat after a month and a half."

Kate nodded down at her lap, ignoring the pinpricks behind her eyes. She didn't do anything wrong, she reminded herself. It was okay to ask.

"Which is why I'm so proud of you!" Patricia said, throwing a pen up in the air. "This is what needs to happen! Women need to advocate for themselves, and other women need to listen! Yes, Kate, of course let's talk about it!"

Kate nodded, stunned. "Ms. Rose's retirement will devastate the kids and significantly decrease our patronage," Kate began. "We could fill that void with a brand-new program called Rock Star Readers that would ideally launch the first Friday in July, right before the Fourth, to maximize turnout."

Patricia nodded cautiously and so Kate continued.

"Rock Star Readers would feature hometown heroes—local celebrities, if you will, who would read their favorite book to the kids after briefly summarizing their career paths so that high school students or those looking to switch careers could learn a bit more. And then afterward, we'd have a little reception—I already talked to Goldie and she said the Coffee Cow could sponsor—but yeah, a little reception to encourage the community to discuss current events, including—"

"Harry Leeper destroying the town as we know it?"

"Exactly." Kate grinned. "We'd sustain current interest and generate new appreciation for the library as a public space to foster growth. Hopefully attendees would be willing to sign the petition I've been working on—I don't have it here; I'm still tweaking the language a bit."

"Petition?"

"A document explaining the Harry Leeper proposal and why the library should not be a redevelopment zone. Even if it's underused right now, people would hate to lose the library. The only reason why it could happen is if the planning board tries to keep the public in the dark about the vote until it's too late. But let's not let them—let's shine a light on what's at stake."

Kate handed over her one-page proposal.

"Once a smart kid, always a smart kid," Patricia said, putting on her glasses. Kate couldn't help but notice that Patricia bit her bottom lip as she read through the proposal. The wall clock ticked ominously as Kate waited.

Finally, her boss looked up and smiled. "Kate," Patricia said, tapping the paper on her desk with a square-tipped French manicured nail, "this is our Hail Dolly."

"Is that good?"

"It's the best shot we've got."

Several hours later, Kate sat in her childhood bedroom applying a second coat of mascara. Step three of Kate's three-point plan—securing the perfect plus-one for Nessie's wedding—was proving far more challenging than saving up money or developing her career.

"Do you like movies?" the former Division I baseball pitcher asked. Kate smiled politely, cursing her sister. Bernadette had helped set up Kate's dating profile, selecting a variety of flattering photos that suggested Kate was cool but not too cool, worldly but not elitist, pretty but in an unassuming way.

Go Fish, the most successful dating app on the market with more than a thousand viable men in a twenty-mile radius of Sea Point, asked Kate to wait as it found her matches. After several seconds, the app apologized and explained there was no one who met all her criteria.

After a slight meltdown on Kate's part that made Clementine ask if she wanted a lollipop, the sisters went through each filter and unchecked half a dozen boxes that Kate considered crucial and Bernadette declared absurd.

"It's just to get back in the habit," Bernadette had said gently. "The first guy doesn't have to be perfect."

"It would just be nice if I had someone to bring to the wedding," Kate tested out, staring at the discouraging screen. "I wouldn't actually date anyone who lives in Sea Point."

"Don't be ridiculous," Bernadette said. "You need to go to that wedding by yourself and show Thomas what an independent, confident person you are without him. Bringing some guy you've just met will reek of rebound."

Kate nodded, acquiescing to her sister without any plans of ditching her step three. Bernadette hadn't been single since eighth grade. She didn't know what it was like to walk into a restaurant by herself, let alone a wedding, with an ex and his new girlfriend in attendance.

And so here Kate was, on a date with a thirty-seven-year-old who still identified himself as a former Division I athlete on his profile. Kate considered all the other things that this guy, Mike, had probably been, formerly. An all-star in Little League? A bedwetter? A serial killer? She had been a lot of things, formerly, as well: a successful PR exec, a proud New Yorker, a happy girlfriend who didn't need to look for men online. But here she was. And here they were—two human bundles of emotional baggage trying to have a decent time with a total stranger.

If only the dating app provided footage of how these suitors treated their servers or what they did when there was a line at the bank. Did they shovel their own sidewalk or pay someone? Did they stop to read every historical marker in a city or give directions when a stranger asked? What were their feelings on Bagel Bites? TSA PreCheck?

Mike ordered them a second round as they continued to talk about movies like a couple of sixth graders stuck on a field trip bus. He liked *Fight Club, The Departed,* and anything by Tarantino, and Kate took comfort in these predictable answers. Mike was a roast chicken of a human being. Having called himself an architect online, he explained that he worked construction two towns over. Kate nearly choked on her wine when Mike told her he was considering a new job opportunity in Sea Point. "Have you heard of Harry Leeper?" he asked. Kate nodded politely as she swallowed bile. "He's got a ton of projects and is looking for more hands," Mike added, "so I may be in your neighborhood." He glanced over at her with flirty eyes and Kate ordered a third drink.

An hour later, Mike kissed Kate outside of Summersault, and pretty soon it was a full-blown make-out with Kate leaning against a parking meter and Mike's hands teasing the hem of her shirt. The former DI pitcher must have been a former something to many, many women because the man had moves. As her cab pulled up, Kate thanked Mike for the kissing. "And good luck in all your future endeavors!" she called over her shoulder, grinning. She was surprised at how fun it had been to do something that felt so former, even in the moment.

Ten minutes later, as Kate thanked the cabdriver and headed up her parents' driveway, she heard the front door shut across the street. Ziggy's familiar silhouette cut through the dark and Kate watched him head toward his truck. It was after ten p.m.

"Where are you going?" Kate yelled over, her words slurring.

"Emergency work stuff," Ziggy called out.

"But where are you *really* going?"

Ziggy forced a laugh. "My life is this sad and boring—it's just an emergency over at the High Tide Hotel. The toilet won't stop running and the guest is freaking out, says she can't sleep with that sound, and you know how Tucker is."

"Fine," Kate conceded. "But I know you have a secret . . . thing."

"Is that right?" Ziggy grinned. "I think you're the one with the secret."

"I made out with a former Division I pitcher named Mike tonight," Kate confessed, right before she burped.

After a slight hesitation, Ziggy smiled. "Good for you," he nodded, "but I was thinking about the secret up in your room."

Kate tilted her head for more explanation.

"You blast 'Freaky Freakazoid' every morning after your parents leave. Like, over and over."

Even in the dark, Kate felt herself blush, caught. How long had Ziggy known?

"I'm learning the dance to it," she whispered. "Don't tell anyone."

"I won't," he smiled. "As long as you don't tell anyone about my midnight rendezvous with Tucker's running toilet."

"Off with you then!" Kate yelled, waving goodbye as she skipped drunkenly toward her front door. And because her night had consisted of three cocktails and excellent kissing, Kate didn't notice when Ziggy made a right onto Ocean Avenue instead of a left toward the High Tide Hotel.

Resident Mansplainer

Miles was clocking in for his shift when he realized it was the last day of June. Once the schools had let out and families flooded Sea Point on a weekly-rental basis, the days started running together faster than the red, white, and blue of a rocket Popsicle in the sun. Every waking moment revolved around not drowning, not failing, not forgetting to set an alarm clock, and not accidentally setting that alarm for "p.m." instead of "a.m." after the fourth straight night of soberly stumbling home from work at daybreak.

At the Wharf and around town, July stalked all of them in broad daylight because the high season always attacked from behind, no matter how hard the locals tried to face it head-on. Miles imagined how much better prepared he'd be for the influx if he'd spent the last decade perfecting his chopping instead of his bullshitting. But at this point, the summer plunge was inevitable—he'd just have to kick like hell toward the light of September.

"Are you going on Friday?" Joey the barback asked as they dragged trash cans to the dumpster. Technically, trash cans were Danny's job, but technically, Danny's back was still a mess.

"What's Friday?"

"That thing at the library?" Joey said. "Rock Star Readers?" At Miles's blank stare, he continued: "Your boy Ziggy is the main attraction, at least for this first one. My sister is all excited to take her kids—they love Ziggy. Apparently my nephews keep singing 'Little Drummer Boy' but changing it to 'Little Plumber Boy'—but not in, like, an offensive way," Joey added, gulping nervously. Miles laughed to put him at ease. He realized that he must seem like an adult to twenty-five-year-old Joey, even though he remembered being twenty-five like it was last month. Actually, Miles was pretty sure he knew more at twenty-five than he did now—or at least, he hadn't been afraid of what he didn't know at twenty-five. Now in his midthirties, he felt like he was just getting started and already so far behind.

"Think you'll go?" Joey asked as they walked back into the kitchen and Miles washed his hands to resume his prep. He was a good guy, Joey, the second-oldest of six kids who'd just put himself through technical school. He'd graduated the Friday of Memorial Day Weekend, the night Miles had first taken over dishwashing duties. Now that Miles thought about it, Joey was an integral part of the equation—if he hadn't asked for the night off to graduate, Joey would have covered for Danny, which meant Miles would still be front of house and lost in the world.

"We'll see," Miles replied a little too curtly to hide his annoyance that Ziggy hadn't told him. And why hadn't Kate asked him to be a rock star? Misreading the source of Miles's sudden irritation, Joey began to explain how "Little Plumber Boy" was really, if you thought about it, a pretty profound compliment, and so Miles swiftly changed topics. "Your graduation over Memorial Day Weekend—what's your certification in?"

Joey puffed out his chest and said, "Sustainable energy," which Miles translated as permission to zone out. "I've been working on a business model and cash-flow projections," Joey continued, loading up a rack of champagne flutes and beaming with pride. "Given how things kinda fell apart over the winter, I figured I'd work one more summer here for fast cash and then launch in the fall, once I figure out the best strategy for moving forward." Miles nodded absently as he focused on turning his paring knife 90 degrees to slice away the oyster's adductor muscle. He considered asking what had fallen apart, but worried Joey would get the wrong idea, maybe misread his polite questions as invested interest. The last thing Miles needed was yet another obligation from which he'd then need to wriggle free.

Just then Miles heard Denise greet Kate at the hostess stand. He abandoned Joey, who was still blathering on about some acronym Miles didn't understand, to confront the decider of rock stars.

"Hey!" Kate called out from down the bar. She'd arrived not even two minutes ago and she was already deep into her station prep.

"Ziggy's your Rock Star Reader and not me?"

Kate surprised him by laughing. "You're ridiculous," she said, shaking her head as she continued to slice limes. "You've been back in town for, what, six weeks? How would I even introduce you? Novice bartender? Mediocre line cook? Resident mansplainer?"

Miles chuckled in spite of himself. She made a good argument. Raising his hands to signal no foul, Miles dug deep and found the white-flag language he was looking for: "You're right, I'm a jackass."

Kate nodded. "But you're becoming a more self-aware jackass, which is why I wanted to ask you something."

"If it's 'Would I make a more entertaining Rock Star Reader than Ziggy?' the answer is yes, one hundred percent."

"I can depend on him to show up," Kate said, "which is more than we can say for you."

Miles caught her words in the pit of his stomach. He hadn't seen Ziggy since Kate's birthday party a month ago, when he'd embraced the role as Bev's date in part to evade conversations he wasn't ready to have. Never before could Miles have spent a whole day in Sea Point without talking to Ziggy, let alone an entire month, but now the kitchen possessed him, the sizzling meats called to him like the Sirens. A newfound love was the perfect distraction from facing his best friend who, Miles knew, would make him face himself.

"For the record, I did what he asked me to do," Miles contended. "I showed up, I went through the books. I just haven't—"

"Please just tell him," Kate said, cutting him off. "Playing dumb doesn't come as naturally to me as it does to you." She wasn't wrong, but Kate Campbell could be so irritating when she was right. It made him miss Bell, who would never snort at her own joke the way Kate did now.

"Is that what you wanted to ask me?"

Kate's smile evacuated her face. She put down the bottle of honey she'd been squeezing into the mint julep remix she was perfecting and stared at Miles with such utter seriousness that Miles held his breath, suddenly fearing the worst.

"Would you go to Nessie's wedding with me?" Kate's dilated eyes reminded Miles of E.T. and made it difficult to process her question.

"What?"

They stood there, separately mortified, as Joey appeared with a bucket of ice but kept his head down as he dumped it and sprinted back into the kitchen. Miles bit his lip and examined a blister on the inside of his thumb. "Did you ask Ziggy?"

Kate looked away, surprised to find herself fighting back tears of rage or humiliation or both. She was a high school junior all over again, waiting in the dark outside her house, listening to the Prince of Sea Point and his Yates Academy friends laugh in his red Jeep about how chuck-able she was.

"Forget it," Kate said, turning her attention to the several bunches of mint in front of her. Destemming each leaf, she realized that she'd made the grave mistake of assuming that Miles would do her this solid. Before he had deserted her for a career in the kitchen, he'd let her think they were friends. Now Kate recognized that his amiability must have been Miles's way to get her to train him into becoming a viable bartender. With his flawless face and impeccable manners, the Prince of Sea Point had

charmed her with an almost sociopathic flip of a switch. Kate understood
how that sort of magnetism could be emotionally dangerous, but it was
also necessary for impressing Thomas at the wedding.

"I'm just surprised you didn't ask Ziggy," Miles said tentatively, watching her pick each mint leaf with unnecessary violence.

"No," Kate finally said, imagining Ziggy in his baggy overalls and steel-
toed boots, shaking Thomas's hand with dirt under his fingernails. "It
didn't seem like his thing."

"But it's mine?"

"It's black tie and full of rich people worried they're not rich enough."

"Fair," Miles sighed. "Did you ask Denise?"

"Her tux doesn't fit her anymore."

"You're hilarious," Miles deadpanned.

In theory, Kate had to ask her manager permission for specific nights
off, but in reality, Kate could do whatever she wanted. She was the Wharf's
MVP bartender, hands down, which meant she could be trusted to find
her own coverage. Miles, on the other hand, would have to ask for Chef's
approval, which was far from guaranteed.

"It's fine. Never mind," Kate said, raking the mint into a pile with her
fingers. "But for the record, I'm not trying to catfish you into dating me—
I know I'm not your type. I've seen the photos."

"Photos?"

"Of your girlfriends. You date models with IQs even lower than their
BMIs."

"Sick burn," Miles grinned, adding, "especially coming from someone
asking a favor."

Kate braved a glance at Miles and was relieved to see his brown eyes
sparkle with amusement—or maybe that's just what his stellar looks encouraged her to see.

"Please?" she asked.

Miles grabbed a mop and wiped down the bar, surprised by his own
reluctance. He typically said yes to just about everything, and Kate had

been a good friend to him. But Bell would hate it. Although she still wasn't responding to his texts, Miles held out hope she'd come around. If Bell heard he'd gone to a wedding as Kate's plus-one, it would give her grounds to continue her silence. And then there was Ziggy. Not that they'd talked about it, but he had built Kate an outdoor shower, which, in Ziggy language, was the equivalent of John Cusack posted up with a boombox over his head, even if he thought no one knew.

"Why don't you try Ziggy?" Miles asked, straining to sound casual.

"Never mind, forget it. I thought it could be fun."

Miles took a deep breath in as he tried to scheme up a solution in record time. Natalie would be on his ass any second if he didn't get back to his station, but he hated confrontation and he owed Kate. "You're right," he said, ignoring the questions flooding his brain and muting the concerns about Ziggy and Bell. "I'll go with you and make your ex feel like a fool—right? Or not a fool? Wait, do you want him to feel like a fool?"

Kate nodded. "I want him to feel just foolish enough that he fights you and wins me back—not physically fights you, just, like, breaks up with his girlfriend and asks me to dance . . . slash marry him."

Grinning, Miles extended his hand and said, "Game on."

Rock Star Readers

It was Rose's Last Stand. On Wednesday morning, a colorful banner hung above her green velvet chair and announced in gold-foil block letters: WE WILL MISS YOU! When Ms. Rose read the sign, she began to cough so violently that Louanne the fire marshal had rushed toward her yelling, "Cough it out! Keep going, that's it—nobody dies on my watch!" It was only when Ms. Rose pushed Louanne away that everyone realized she hadn't been choking at all but laughing.

Kate watched Clementine navigate her way to the front of the red apple rug and smiled as her niece gazed up at Ms. Rose with starry-eyed admiration. Children were so bizarre—Clementine was scared of her dad with a beard but adored a woman whose laugh sounded like she was trying to hack up a furball.

Bernadette stood on the other side of the checkout desk, exhausted from pulling an all-nighter to make the banner with three other moms. She'd approached Kate to ask for an update on Rock Star Readers, but her sister had immediately begun to blab about Miles reading the MVP accounting books and the rippled ramifications of Zeke's secret debt.

"Miles shouldn't have told you," Bernadette said, rolling her eyes and compulsively caressing her baby bump. "He needs to tell Ziggy what he knows, and you shouldn't have told me—especially when you know I've been working with Ziggy on the probate."

Kate shrugged. "I get why you don't like Miles, but he is torn up about it."

"I barely know him," Bernadette said, straightening her spine against the wall. "But what you just told me is disappointing."

"You do know him though," Kate insisted. "Or at least, you did know him—from the golf course?" Throughout high school and college, Bernadette had worked at the Ship Harbor Country Club as one of the women who drove around in golf carts offering beverages to members. It had been a competitive position—Bernadette had had to beat out more than a hundred applicants ranging from high school cheerleaders to Atlantic City showgirls. The coveted role of "quench wench" paid exceptionally well—plus tips—because the gig required an iron stomach for blatant ogling and incessant flirting from the older and often married male members.

Miles, unsurprisingly, golfed nearly every summer day with his overgroomed Yates pals. As a result, Bernadette and Miles, two years and one school apart, had crossed paths on the pathway many a time. Even if Bernadette had forgotten, Kate remembered—such was the sacred duty of a younger sister.

"I wonder if they still call them quench wenches," Kate mused.

"I wonder if he'll ever grow up," Bernadette countered.

Kate shrugged. "People change after high school," she said, thinking of herself as much as Miles. She had never dared to tell Bernadette about the most humiliating moment of her life with the red Jeep on the street. A prom queen wouldn't be able to relate to that kind of embarrassment, of not being marriagable or fuckable but chuckable. "He's surprisingly fun to be around," Kate contended. "And he came back to help Ziggy, so that counts for something."

"Yeah, except he hasn't actually helped at all and now he's involved you," Bernadette scoffed. Kate watched her sister text Rob. "It's our anniversary," Bernadette explained when Kate pointed to the sign that said all phones must be off during Story Hour. "Eleven years with Slobby Robby, can you believe it?"

Kate forced a polite laugh when all she wanted to do was slap that phone out of Bernadette's hand and remind her that she'd just been dumped after twelve years.

"Wait, what's she reading?" Bernadette asked, suddenly tuning in and squinting her eyes at the hunched figure in the green velvet chair. Kate redirected her attention as well and did a double take. To a rapt audience of toddlers and kindergartners, Ms. Rose was celebrating her final Story Hour by reading the opening chapter of Stephen King's *Pet Sematary*.

After the fiasco at Ms. Rose's Last Stand, time flew by in a blur of preparation, emails, and last calls at the Jetty Bar until suddenly the countdown was over. Kate woke in the dark on the morning of the inaugural Rock Star Readers event, thrumming with adrenaline and watching the day play out in her head. The launch would be a provocative kick in the community's pants during the busiest weekend in Sea Point, and once she stood up to the planning committee, there would be no going back. The future of the library hinged on enough people signing Kate's petition to fight Harry Leeper. It was strange to think that, in her ideal life, Kate would never have even come home for the summer, but here she was, spearheading the Sea Point movement against shortsighted development and she had never felt more ready for a fight.

Kate arrived at the library early and took a lap around the room, making sure the stage lights and risers she'd borrowed from Walter Beam and the Sea Point theater troupe were in place. As time ticked toward the opening, she thought of all the launches she'd helped orchestrate through Artemis PR. Unlike those, this wasn't a cover-up for bad behavior or a thinly veiled vanity project. This was about the future of Sea Point.

When the clock struck nine and Kate pulled open the red doors, the beautiful sight punched her in the throat. Ziggy stood there, beaming like an idiot, a little book with crumpled corners tucked under his arm. Around him was a sea of children, who squawked like agitated seagulls and were surrounded by eager-faced parents and caretakers.

As the buzz inside the library teetered on the brink of chaos, Kate felt a hand clamp down on her shoulder. Bernadette stood before her with Clementine in tow, and it was only then that Kate realized Bernadette was pregnant enough to have surrendered to her favorite (and least-pillowcase-y) maternity dress. Kate started to say as much, but Bernadette interrupted: "You did it," she said, her eyes wet. "You should be so proud. *I'm* proud— look at this turnout!"

After everyone settled into their seats, which really just meant all the kids were wriggling in a relatively contained, hopefully sustainable way, Kate hit the overhead fluorescent lights and Patricia took to the stage. "Despite my Southern notions of hospitality, I know how to keep things brief," she joked before quickly thanking Kate for her initiative, and introducing Ziggy. As the audience watched Ziggy mount the riser, Kate saw Miles appear by the entrance. The thicket of parents created a buffer between them so they just waved to each other, Miles offering an encouraging thumbs-up.

"Good morning, everybody," Ziggy announced, his face pink but his smile bright. Kate thought back to when she first ran into him at the Acme, and how his teeth seemed too big for his face. Now everything fit together just right—or rather, she'd adjusted to how he'd changed. Despite the dozens of adults staring at him, Ziggy addressed the kids, crouching down and staring past the stage lights to connect with each face. "I'm honored to be here and grateful to my friends at the library for inviting me to read to you. Now, who can tell me what a bull is?"

The red doors opened and even though Kate couldn't see who it was through the crowd, she looked at Miles, who grinned and mouthed, "Bev." As far as Kate knew, Bev hadn't ventured into town since Zeke had died. Ziggy did all the grocery shopping, ran all the errands. Today, she'd braved the public to support her son.

When Ziggy asked who already knew *The Story of Ferdinand*, a few dimpled hands flew up with authority. "But have you ever heard a *plumber* read it?" he asked mischievously, and the parents in the back giggled as much as the kids.

As Kate had requested, Ziggy talked a bit about what he did in his job and what he liked most about it. "I enjoy fixing things," Ziggy said. "I like seeing a problem and figuring out how to make it go away—raise your hand if you like doing that, too." All the little hands shot up. Kate looked down at her yellow flats and thought of Zeke. He'd have loved this.

"But sometimes it's nice to just appreciate something pretty," Ziggy continued. "Like a flower, which is how Ferdinand prefers to spend his time. Who here likes smelling flowers?"

A few tentative hands went halfway up. Kate was surprised to see how early kids learned to feel self-conscious. "Well, I *love* smelling flowers," Ziggy declared, raising his own hand to the ceiling and smiling as all the doughy hands in the audience followed suit.

Except for a wailing baby in the back and an embarrassed toddler up front who shat herself halfway through, the reading went exceptionally well. After Ziggy had stepped down from the stage, Kate helped more than fifty children become proud owners of their first library cards. She wondered if any of the kids would replace their baby dolls with books as she once had.

Finally emerging from the library and stepping into the sunlight, Kate was surprised to see there was still a large crowd on the grassy knoll by the parking lot, where Goldie had set up three coffee canisters. Ziggy had finished reading nearly an hour ago, but instead of just signing the petition and dispersing, people were standing in circles, talking animatedly with lots of hand gestures about how to take down Harry Leeper. As Kate approached, she heard Patricia clear her throat and raise her voice about the importance of petitioning the Sea Point planning committee. Her pump-up speech sounded like a mix of *Braveheart* and *Revenge of the Nerds*—with a touch of southern belle when she ended with, "We need Harry Leeper's condos as much as a canoe needs a trapdoor. But this place," Patricia hollered, pointing at the library behind her, "this place fixes more people than a buttered biscuit on a Sunday morning—so let's get to work!"

Kate circulated among the clusters of locals and tourists, answering questions and handing out pens as needed. Eleanor, who ran a small farm on the edge of town, shook her head and kept repeating, "This just isn't right."

Kate suffered a bit of whiplash as she did a double take at Bernadette and Miles standing together, talking politely. In the interest of saving her sister, Kate walked over and told Bernadette that Clementine was asking to go to the bathroom. "More specifically," Kate stage whispered, "she said she needed your help wiping."

"Thanks for that," Bernadette sighed. "Nice to see you, Miles," she called over her shoulder without bothering to look him in the eye. As polite as Bernadette was, Kate could always tell when she quietly disliked someone, and this insight into her well-behaved sister never ceased to thrill her.

Twenty minutes later, Kate was on her knees, collecting stray napkins off the lawn, when the magenta points of stiletto heels cut through the green grass at her fingertips. Kate looked up and up and up until she met Patricia's radiant face. "Drink this," she said, handing Kate a cup of coffee. Kate pointed to the full cup steaming next to her foot. "Yes, but you've earned *this*," Patricia said. Kate smelled the whiskey as Patricia raised her own cup to toast her: "You are my buttered biscuit on a Sunday morning."

Kate walked back inside the library just in time to witness two little boys run full speed into the ant farm. Miraculously, the glass held and the brothers, Ben and Theo, bounced back up like tennis balls. By the time she returned the brothers to their parents and ran her card through the punch clock, Kate calculated she had just enough time to dash home and shower off the morning sweat before her shift at the Jetty Bar. It would be another seventeen-hour day, but Kate was too overjoyed with the success of Rock Star Readers to feel the exhaustion.

Closing the bathroom door behind her, Kate turned on the shower before noticing how the sunlight streaming through the window landed directly on the scissors like an invitation. If the morning hadn't been such a triumph, or if Goldie's coffee hadn't been so smooth, or Patricia's so strong, perhaps Kate would have ignored the glint of possibility. Instead, she saw the scissors resting on the vanity as a sign that it was time to sever ties with outdated expectations and their inevitable dead ends.

Kate cut her hair with a stranger's impulse before realizing she'd been fantasizing about the bob for years—it wasn't spontaneous at all, just a plan she'd been waiting for permission to execute. Watching the curtain of hair fall, Kate smiled at her reflection and realized she was her own chaperone; she signed her own permission slips for this ongoing field trip into adulthood. If she could organize Rock Star Readers, she could cut her hair. And if she was going to win back Thomas, he would have to be on board with the person Kate was on her way to becoming, not the twenty-two-year-old girl waiting her turn in line when they'd first met.

Thirty minutes later, her short hair already dry, Kate pulled into the Wharf's employee parking lot. With four minutes to spare, her phone lit up with a new text.

PATRICIA: Well done today. Let's meet at 8 am on Monday to discuss your very bright future.

Black Powder

As he stood on a barge packed to capacity with explosives, Ziggy's debut at Rock Star Readers twenty-four hours earlier seemed like a distant memory. Every year, on this day, a dozen men paid an hourly wage boarded the flat-bottomed boat before sunrise to make the town millions of dollars in twenty minutes.

The biggest annual event in Sea Point, the Fourth of July had been Zeke's favorite holiday, which meant it would now be the hardest for Ziggy. He had known this ever since winter had started to thaw. Driving through the predawn darkness, Ziggy had anticipated the morose fog in his head and the sludge in his legs, but what he could have never predicted was the sight of Miles Hoffman waiting for him in the parking lot, holding three boxes of doughnuts and two hundred ounces of coffee because he always did know how to buy his way into the hearts of men.

As Zeke liked to say, anything was possible on the Fourth, and so Ziggy swallowed his worries with a glazed doughnut before getting down on his knees with a knife in his hand. There was so much to set up in the next twelve hours that there was no time for all of Miles's silly questions, and yet Ziggy took a break from unpacking the pallets to answer each one. Showing Miles the racks of cannisters and explaining they'd shoot off thirty-two thousand fireworks in just over twenty minutes was like watching a little kid learn about Santa's workshop—his excitement resuscitated the experience for Ziggy, too.

Billy Croce was the reason why Ziggy had spent every Fourth of July since high school on this barge. An accomplished pyrotechnician, Billy ran the Sea Point fireworks show but, more important, he had been Zeke's best friend. They'd grown up together, near Hammonton, and even though Zeke left the Pine Barrens when he was nine, he and Billy had remained close. As kids, they kept in touch via handwritten letters, and as teenagers, Billy and Ziggy saved their money to buy glorified boxes of rust with just enough tread on the tires and gas in the tank to get them through the woods and back again.

After high school, while Zeke helped his father with MVP, Billy developed a keen interest in fireworks that took him around the country to attend different conventions before ultimately earning his certification. For as long as Ziggy could remember, Billy had made a living by traveling up and down the East Coast shooting fireworks for major league baseball games and amusement parks. But ever since he'd joined the board of directors for Pyrotechnics Guild International a few years back, Billy's reputation had, as he liked to pun, "skyrocketed." Now Billy globe-trotted most of the year, attending various intercontinental conferences, judging competitions, and organizing PGI's own highly regarded convention, held every August somewhere in the Midwest. It was because of Billy's hunger to see what was new in the world of fire that Ziggy only saw his godfather once a year, on this holiday. No matter what opportunities tried to lure him elsewhere, Billy had always made sure he spent the Fourth of July in Sea Point with his best friend Zeke.

"I keep waiting for him to clap his hands and tell us to get to work," Billy said now, standing next to Ziggy on the perimeter of the loading site as the big men began to fill the long tubes. Ziggy nodded but didn't look at Billy, afraid to meet his eyes—it was too early in a long day. As they filled each cannister with explosives, the crew was careful to leave at least a foot of string dangling outside the tubes. When it came to fireworks, even the biggest hothead learned to appreciate a long fuse.

For Ziggy's high school graduation, Billy's gift, sealed in a stiff white envelope, was a handwritten note extending a lifelong invitation to come out on the barge on the Fourth of July, and for sixteen years, Ziggy had joined Billy and Zeke. In the past, the sun would rise as they chugged cans of Coke and ignored the sunburn seeping into their skin. Ziggy would listen to his father and Billy razz each other about long-ago errors and miscalculations—Zeke's high school mustache, Billy's ex-girlfriend— "*extorter* ex-girlfriend," Zeke had specified. They would laugh until someone took it too far, until someone else said to lighten up, until they all laughed, until it was finally time to start the show. Only in hindsight did Ziggy appreciate the sanctity of their Fourth of July tradition. Like a higher calling, preparing the fireworks and shipping out on the barge to light up the sky with his father and Billy was both humbling and transcendent.

But now Zeke was gone and Miles had just tried to put a six-inch jellyfish firework into an eight-inch tube. Billy looked at Ziggy to make sure that jellyfish didn't stay there. Even though the guys hustling around in gray XXL T-shirts loved a dirty joke, the barge was a place of serious business. If the tubes were loaded incorrectly, the consequences could be fatal. When Billy barked at Miles for applying the wrong firework, Ziggy was surprised to see Miles absorb the abuse quietly before apologizing to Billy and then to the group as a whole. Instead of making excuses like he usually did, Miles accepted responsibility. As a result, the crew softened toward the Prince just as Ziggy felt his resentment double. Miles could easily apologize for misloading a jellyfish but he couldn't own up to having avoided his best friend all summer?

Oblivious, Miles asked, "So how high do these things go?"

"If it's a four-inch shell, it'll go four hundred feet in the air," Ziggy explained through gritted teeth, "and if it's an eight-inch shell, it'll go eight hundred feet up."

"Can you tie the two together?" Miles asked. "And if you can, do they go six hundred feet up? How would that work?"

Ziggy shook his head. "It's just one shell that gets loaded into each mortar. If you want something to go six hundred feet up, you just use a six-inch shell, like this." Ziggy held up an orb. "We don't need to get into the details but each firework needs fuel and an oxidizer, so black powder is the—"

"I'm having physics class PTSD."

"This is chemistry," Ziggy said. "But what I need you to do right now is just take the four-inch cylinders over there and load them into the four-inch mortars."

"Sir, yes sir!" Miles gave Ziggy a salute and then a caress on the cheek that was so tender it was impossible not to laugh. The trouble with Miles was that he was the best company you could ask for, as long as you didn't ever actually ask for it. He showed up when he wanted to, when he was intrigued or had nothing better to do. Bev called Miles "an experience junkie" but Ziggy called him a flake.

"Why are these cylinders and those are balls?" Miles asked.

"The spheres are Japanese and make starbursts; the cylinders are European and send off whistles."

"Righteous. You know your stuff, Zig."

Ziggy considered using this opportunity to point out how they could have been working together all summer, but today wasn't about him, or them—it was about his dad and this town. Zeke wasn't here, but his voice was stuck in Ziggy's head like a relentless radio pop song: *Let's give them the best show yet!* It's what Zeke said every morning on this day. Other people set New Year's resolutions, but Zeke Miller set off Fourth of July fireworks. Tonight, Ziggy would give them the best show yet.

While Bernadette lay prostrate on the couch being pregnant, Kate moved purposefully around her parents' kitchen, trying her best to keep up with the dictates of her mother's dinner prep. She looked out at the back deck and saw her brother-in-law Rob standing next to her dad, doing nothing, as Dirk painted another coat of barbecue sauce onto ribs. Kate wondered if Rob even knew how to grill before realizing she was in a terrible mood and it was her sister's fault.

Superficially, Kate was annoyed because when Bernadette saw her short hair, her immediate response was the worst kind of deflection: "Do you like it?" That question had come on the heels of Dirk's response, which was a prolonged hug before asking if something bad had happened. When Kate's mother had seen her hair, she'd inquired, "Should we consider this our forewarning of another meltdown?"

Thankfully, everyone at the Jetty Bar had loved the cut, especially Miles, who'd gone out of his way to say that he found short hair on women "beyond sexy." Even better, when Kate caught her reflection in the Wharf's kitchen door's circle window, she relished what she saw—it had taken forever to take the risk, but she had been born to bob.

So it wasn't actually about her family's lackluster response to Kate's dramatic haircut. It was their lackluster response to Rock Star Readers, which was Bernadette's fault and why the Fourth of July was shaping up to be a shitty night. Kate had always known her parents wouldn't be able to attend the debut of Rock Star Readers, or any future Rock Star Readers, because Dirk and Sally Campbell taught summer school. But she'd assumed Bernadette would have filled their parents in on the success—*the immense success*, as Patricia had said—of the inaugural event. When she'd first arrived at the library, Bernadette had basically been crying with pride. But last night, Sally had asked Kate how the event had gone with the nervous energy of someone who thought maybe it hadn't gone at all. Bernadette hadn't bothered to send so much as a text to her parents, and so Kate had had to tout her own praises, which wasn't nearly as much fun as hearing her sister sing them.

Then today, when Bernadette arrived for the Fourth and their parents had asked her in person about Rock Star Readers, Bernadette had simply said "It was good" before asking for a seltzer.

Good? Kate thought. *Just . . . good?*

What about the record-breaking turnout? Or the hundreds of signatures Kate had collected to stop Harry Leeper? Patricia wanted to meet, and the local paper had reached out this morning looking for a quote about her efforts to fight the redevelopment zoning. Kate had practically started a movement yesterday, but suddenly the only thing Bernadette found worthy of discussing was the baby kicking in her stomach.

Pouring Bernadette her seltzer—"Can you throw a lime wedge in it?"—Kate sensed a murky tension she decided to tackle head-on.

"Are you mad at me?" she asked, returning to the living room.

"Why would I be mad at you?" Bernadette replied, offering Kate a tired smile just as Sally asked for help in the kitchen.

"Kate?" Bernadette called from the couch. Abandoning the boiling water on the stove, Kate jetted back to the living room, where Bernadette wanly lifted her head to ask, "On a scale of one to ten, how fat do I look?"

Kate turned on her heels without responding and then, standing alone in the hot kitchen, annoyance flickering, Kate called out, "You're not fat, you're pregnant, and you're setting a bad example for your daughter."

The timer for the corn went off just then, but Kate could still hear the "hrumph" from the couch. She reminded herself that Bernadette was dealing with surges of hormones, and there was all that stuff about baby brain, but right now it seemed like her pregnancy was just a convenient excuse to be a lousy sister with swollen ankles.

Across town in the late afternoon, Miles helped the crew pack up while Ziggy pulled Billy aside. He knew Miles would appreciate the opportunity to go out on the barge for the show. It was a big ask, a liability for Billy, but he agreed. "It's a barge," Billy said. "I think we can fit the Prince's scrawny hide."

They'd finished loading the tubes with just enough time for Ziggy to go home, wash off the day, and return before launch. In the parking lot, Ziggy was about to invite Miles back on board for the show when Miles looked down at his phone and said he'd better run—he needed to get to the Wharf.

"You don't want to come out on the barge?"

"I can't—they need me at work." Miles said it so casually that Ziggy, speechless at such sacrilege, headed toward his truck without a word. As he searched for his keys through dark spots of rage, Ziggy heard Ace of Base blasting and looked over to see that absurd Porsche convertible idling five feet away. "Hey," Miles called over, taking off his sunglasses and looking Ziggy in the eye. "I know we haven't talked, but I've been meaning to tell you"—he turned down the stereo as Ziggy held his breath, anticipating the long-awaited breakthrough: Here came Miles's overdue apology, his acceptance of responsibility, his commitment to go through Zeke's books and be a better friend.

Instead, the sentence that rolled off Miles's tongue hit Ziggy with the force of Harry Leeper's wrecking ball. "I wanted to tell you in person that Kate asked me to go to Nessie's wedding with her—not in a romantic way or anything, just to make her ex jealous. But I thought I should tell you that it really doesn't mean anything to me. Seriously." Five thousand pounds of forged steel knocked Ziggy out of his body, and yet he willed himself to remain on his feet. Demolished but standing, he dug impossibly deep to appear physically unfazed as the Porsche idled and Miles waited for a response that arrived as an enigmatic shrug.

It was only after the convertible turned left toward the Wharf that Ziggy allowed his knees to give way as he slid down the side of the truck until his back rested against the front tire. What Miles had nonchalantly tossed at him like a Frisbee had detonated like a grenade and landed Ziggy here: alone in a parking lot on what used to be the best day of the year.

As soon as Ziggy was driving on Ocean Avenue, it hit him even harder than he could have fathomed: He was supposed to go out on the barge and light up the sky and put on the show without his dad. The debris of anger in his head rose up like a cyclone and made it difficult to navigate the road, which is why Ziggy second-guessed himself when he passed the nature preserve and saw open space where there shouldn't have been any. Ziggy slowed down, his eyes tricking him: The sky was too big, that new

Creeper McMansion too prominent. Then he realized: His favorite tree was missing. The white oak was gone.

Pulling off to the side of the road, Ziggy stared at the scene from the opposite side of the street. His tree was a stump. This wasn't possible. This wasn't legal. He'd just patted the white oak two nights ago during a walk-off with Kate—who'd since asked Miles to be her plus-one. Miles, who couldn't be bothered to look at the MVP books, who was too busy at the Wharf to go out on the barge but free to accompany Kate to Nessie's wedding.

Gripping the steering wheel, Ziggy cocked his head and tried to see how this could have happened. He looked at the land with cold eyes, Leeper eyes. Envisioning the property line of the McMansion next door to the nature preserve, Ziggy now understood. The tree trunk, as wide as it had been, well-ringed as it was, had made the mistake of growing bigger—so big, in fact, that the circumference of its trunk had become enough of Harry Leeper's property to become all of Harry Leeper's property. He'd cut it down and no one had stopped him. Just as Ziggy knew no one had protected the white oak, he knew no one would notice him get out of the truck, lean his head against the stump, and sob. No one intervened because there was no one left.

Bev was at her easel when someone stormed through her front door with such rage that she knew she didn't have time to call 911 before seeing her son, a blur of limbs and fury, appear in the kitchen, his face so contorted with pain that she scanned his body for blood.

"What happened?" Bev asked.

"Let's go!" Ziggy exploded. "Let's just go!"

"Why aren't you on the barge? Go where?"

"He won," Ziggy continued to shout, pulling at his hair. "Let's go."

"Who won?" Bev asked, trying to catch up, desperate to understand her son, who was sputtering through tears.

"You were right. Before. Let's just sell to Leeper and leave." Ziggy used a fist to wipe his eyes. "He'll end up with all of it anyway and we've already lost everything. There's no point in staying. There's nothing for us here." That's when they both heard a high-pitched whistle—a girandola—and Ziggy realized Billy had been forced to ship out and start the show without him.

The sun had set and Kate was still at home trying to wrangle her impossibly slow-moving family when she heard the first firework explode in the sky. Walking faster with every hiss, whistle, and crackle, Kate led the way up the rickety wooden boardwalk and scanned the crowded beach for an empty patch of sand.

"Not there—it's too close to the water," Bernadette yelled from behind. They'd left the house late because Bernadette kept having to pee one more time. Now the tourists had claimed all the prime viewing spots, and they'd missed the first five minutes of fireworks. The dunes were off-limits so Kate marched toward the water, trying her best not to step on the blankets, toddlers, or liplocked teenagers. Kate wished she hadn't requested tonight off—at least at the bar she'd be getting paid to take orders instead of shouldering them from her sister.

Rob pointed out a small open space between two families who watched the fireworks through their phones. Once everyone was settled and Clementine had distributed glowstick necklaces with autocratic glee, Kate looked up and thought of Ziggy. He was out on the barge, sending up flares to his father.

"I heard something interesting yesterday after Rock Star Readers," Bernadette whispered to Kate between bursts of light.

"Oh yeah?"

"You asked Miles Hoffman to be your plus-one?"

Kate clenched her jaw. "Did he tell you that yesterday? Before I saved you?"

"So it's true?" Bernadette asked.

"Yup."

"Why?"

Kate shrugged, as petulant as an eighth grader.

"It would be far more impressive if you'd just go by yourself," Berna-dette said.

"Is that why you haven't done anything by yourself since you were fourteen?" Kate asked.

"Going to a wedding on your own is such a statement of confidence."

"Going with the guy who owns the venue isn't a bad statement, either," Kate fired back.

Bernadette picked up a broken seashell and drew lines in the sand by her sandaled feet. The sandals, Kate knew, cost more than Kate's entire outfit and had been a birthday present from Rob. "It's juvenile, Kate. You're bringing one rich kid to cancel out another rich kid. And it's not like Miles is your actual boyfriend, so I don't—"

If Clementine had begun to cry just then, perhaps the night would have been saved by distraction. But Clementine was in her grandfather's lap, singing to herself. And so the sisters continued their private battle on the crowded beach as the fireworks dazzled overhead. "Don't take it so personally, okay?" Bernadette said in her courtroom *I'm-always-right* voice, between booms and crackles. "Try to listen to what I'm saying: You're pretending Miles is something he isn't, and I think it's time you stop."

"That's it," Kate said, standing up and wiping the sand off the backs of her legs. "I'm gonna go."

"I just don't want to see you get hurt," Bernadette persisted. "You're only going to wind up feeling even more rejected. You focus so much on money with these guys, it's like—I mean, I know you're not a gold digger, but at the same time—"

"Enough!" Kate yelled. Clementine stopped singing. "You do not get to lecture me about relationships or money when Rob was just Slobby Robby, the rich guy with the pool, until the day you decided it was time to settle down. Or I guess just settle."

"What?" Rob yelled, cupping his ears. He hadn't heard what Kate had said over the fireworks, but Bernadette seethed. Her eyes sparkled with threats, but Kate kept going.

"You have gotten everything—everything!—you've ever wanted—the plush job you then quit to be the perfect mom, the husband, the body that bounced back in, like, a week, the big house in the nicest part of town. But in case you forgot, the first thing I wanted—really wanted—was to go somewhere that you hadn't touched, that you hadn't already peed on like a fire hydrant with your perfect dumb face."

"What?" Rob called over, thinking he must have misheard. "Bern, did you wet yourself again?"

"But I didn't get to go," Kate continued, struggling to breathe and fighting back angry tears. "Even though I tested in, even though I got financial aid. I went to Sea Point so you could go to Rutgers, full tuition, because you're not even that smart! You're just pretty!"

"Kate!" Sally interrupted, but she was too shocked to find more words. Dirk looked absolutely gobsmacked. Rob asked Kate to repeat that last part just as Clementine began to cry.

"Wow, way to live in the past," Bernadette scoffed before turning her back on Kate and looking up at the fireworks. Yawning, she added, "At least you think I'm pretty."

As a blue Japanese starburst dazzled onlookers, Kate decided Bernadette didn't deserve her mercy. "Actually," she said coldly, "I used to think you were pretty—now you're just fat."

Kate stormed off the beach and down the street toward home. As she walked through the darkness, fireworks continued to splatter across the sky. This is why she hated home. This is why she had fled to New York as soon as she could. Because Bernadette had been the Sea Point homecoming queen before she'd become the Sea Point PTA secretary and the hottest MILF in mommy-and-me yoga class. But Kate was not Bernadette. Kate had not returned home with a husband who wore Lululemon athleisure wear, or an app on her phone comparing their zygote to different-size fruit. She was not a small-town boomerang. The world had so much more to offer than the godforsaken Garden State Parkway.

It was after midnight when Miles emerged from the Wharf, the sweat from the night now a cold jacket he'd have to shower off. When the fireworks had started, most of the kitchen staff had ducked out onto the load-ing dock to catch a glimpse, but Miles had stayed put. The Jetty Bar was dead—he didn't have a single dupe because all the patrons had gone outside to the wharf to watch Billy Croce's show turn the sky into a pyro-technic Lite-Brite. Even Natalie had wiped her hands on her rag and given Miles a nod toward the open door before walking through it herself and joining her team—albeit while yelling to Denise about a squash blos-som delivery.

Miles wiped down his station. He'd never felt so at home as he had over the past couple of weeks in this kitchen, but tonight he was in the wrong place. He should have been out on the barge, standing next to Ziggy and taking credit for every four-inch cylinder that launched into the sky. He should have been honest with Ziggy about the books, told him about the debt, offered to devise a payment plan together. He should have been the loyal friend, the decent person, *the good man* whom Zeke had believed him to be.

Pulling out of the employee parking lot, Miles found himself cruising through Sea Point with the cabriolet's top down, desperate for an excuse not to go home. Early in the evening, he'd prepared seared scallops and broiled oysters for Pete Wells of *The New York Times*. Before Emmy had carried the plate out of the kitchen, Natalie had examined Miles's work and said with a sincerity that embarrassed them both, "Nice job." He was bursting to tell someone, anyone.

Miles texted Bell and asked if she wanted to meet him at the beach closest to the lighthouse, their old spot. As soon as he sent it, he felt an immediate twinge of regret: Their exchange was just a series of blue mes-sages sent from him, unanswered by her. Still, he stared at his screen, begging her to respond.

Five minutes went by before Miles turned up his music and released the brake. He'd drive to the lighthouse for no other reason than it was a destination across town and who knew, maybe Bell would show up.

Turning off Ocean Avenue, Miles did a quick loop past the lighthouse and around all of East Sea Point before heading toward Ziggy's house. If the lights were still on, he'd call Ziggy, ask him to come outside, and, in person, he'd tell him about the books. They'd figure out a solution together because Kate was right, Ziggy deserved to know.

Much to his relief, the Miller house was completely dark.

Miles was about to turn left to go home when he hallucinated. Looking right, he thought he saw Zeke's truck crossing the intersection one block down. After rubbing his eyes, Miles remembered that Ziggy drove that truck now, he wasn't hallucinating at all, and so he turned right and then left, just in time to see the truck pull into the driveway of Daffodil Cottage. Turning off his lights, he slowed the Porsche to a crawl and parked on the street. The distinct jangle of a woman's laugh floated through the dark like wind chimes, followed by the familiar groan of a rusted passenger-side door he knew all too well.

Cutting through the grass, Miles peered through the hedge, over the sleeping daffodils to the front door just in time to hear shoes on the crushed shell driveway. Maybe it wasn't what it looked like, Miles hoped. As if in response, Ziggy announced, "This is it!" as he stumbled up the steps. Opening the front door, his tongue thick with authority and whiskey, Ziggy didn't know the extent of his audience when he declared with a slurry, borrowed smugness, "Welcome to my humble home."

Part III

Part III

Hot, Cold, and Scalding

"**B**ravo," Patricia said to Kate in the library office first thing Monday morning. "Your hair looks amazing, Rock Star Readers was the talk of the evening at our Fourth of July party, and did you see *The Wind* this morning?"

Kate shook her head. If she'd had time to read anything, it would not be the local paper.

"So you missed this," Patricia smirked, holding up a copy of *The Wind* and watching Kate's jaw drop.

LOCAL RESPONSE TO DEVELOPER'S PLAN IS ONE FOR THE BOOKS, read the headline. Snatching the paper out of Patricia's hand, Kate couldn't believe her eyes: Splashed across the entire front page was an article about Harry Leeper's sneaky redevelopment attempt and the outpouring of public dissent in response, most accurately depicted by the 2,311 signatures collected over forty-eight hours. Below a cute photograph of Ziggy reading *The Story of Ferdinand* was a full rendering of the petition Kate had agonized over for weeks, tweaking the verbiage and the order of sentences as she worked behind the library checkout desk. The last line of the article was a direct quote from Arnold Nixon, chair of the zoning board and planning committee. "We represent the interests of Sea Point residents and they've made their voices clear—I'd say *loud* and clear, but you're supposed to whisper in the library."

Kate didn't realize she was wiping tears from her cheeks until Patricia passed her a box of tissues.

"So this is incredible," Patricia offered gently, "but I wanted to meet with you before that even happened." Kate looked up, confused, just as Patricia asked, "What's your dream job?"

"Oh. Ummm. I'm not sure."

"I know, I know, it's a daunting question," Patricia said as she sympathized, "but a very important one since I now owe you my livelihood. Besides, every young woman should have a list."

"I'm not that young anymore," Kate mumbled.

"Well, the alligator gets us all in the end, my dear. It's a matter of perspective—and skin care."

As Kate tried to understand the gnarls of her own thoughts, Patricia continued. "Maybe I should be clearer. Here's what I can offer you. If you're interested in library work, my friend from graduate school now runs the MLS program at Drexel, which, as you may or may not know, is top tier for the field and she owes me about three hundred favors. If you want to go back to PR, I can reach out to my high school roommate, who's a VP at H+K Strategies. If you want to try your hand at publishing, I have people at Random House, HarperCollins, and—"

"Those are in New York," Kate said, sitting up straight and paying attention.

"Isn't that where you want to go?"

"Yes," Kate said, grinning even harder now than she had at *The Wind.* "Definitely yes."

"Terrific," Patricia said, winking at Kate. "Make your list and leave the rest to me—I bet we'll have options by Labor Day."

The following night, Ziggy could not have been more surprised to see Kate's text asking for a walk-off. So she was, in fact, capable of initiating plans with him. For a moment, Ziggy wondered if she somehow knew

that Bev had sent one email to Harry Leeper and another to the accoun-
tant. Ziggy considered ignoring the text but decided it was now or never.
Soon enough, a different family would live across the street from the
Campbells. Their nights for walk-offs were numbered.

"Dude!" Kate yelled from across the street. "Where have you been?
Do you want a Popsicle? It's not really a choice; I grabbed two for the
road." Her unbridled enthusiasm cut through the dark as she tossed him
the treat. For a few moments, Ziggy escaped the weight of his present life
and appreciated that, twenty-five years later, the Campbells still stocked
their freezer with Creamsicles.

"You chopped your hair," Ziggy said, staring at her.

"And?"

"And you look different but also—I dunno—more you?"

Kate nodded, pleased with this assessment. "I have so much to tell
you!" Her pace matched her mouth as she zipped past the duck pond and
told Ziggy about Patricia's offer to network on her behalf and the blowout
fight with Bernadette.

"Wait, why did she tell you to go to the wedding alone?" Ziggy asked,
feigning ignorance.

"Because I asked Miles to go with me," Kate replied matter-of-factly,
as if she'd made a sound business decision. "Going with the Wharf's future CEO will drive Thomas *crazy*." The way Kate made Miles sound like
the strategic choice, the obvious pick—reminded Ziggy of his club hockey
coach when he announced the lineup, as if starting any other players than
the ones he'd named would have been foolish.

"But isn't he—"

"And I'm seeing Georgina that same weekend!" Running up to a rock,
Kate kicked it down the road.

"You never told me what happened between you two," Ziggy said.
"What was your big fight about?" He wanted to puncture her good mood,
bring Kate down to his level, but even so, Ziggy felt a twinge of guilt as he
watched her physically deflate: Her head sank into her shoulders first,
then her shoulders melted into her legs, into her sneakers.

"We disagreed," Kate answered just as they reached the lighthouse. She could hear her own shortness, her defensiveness turning over like an engine.

"Okay."

"Fine," Kate relented. "After college graduation, Georgina and I were going to work one more summer at the Wharf. I had two interviews lined up at a publishing house and one at a literary agency, but they were moving slowly, and then Thomas came to visit."

"Right," Ziggy remembered, "and he and Georgina didn't exactly hit it off."

Kate nodded. "Yeah, but she'd already met him the summer after our junior year and she didn't really like him then, so I knew not to expect chemistry."

"So if it wasn't about Thomas, what was the fight about?"

"It's bad," Kate replied, her voice dropping. She had cataloged each cruel word and then shoved the whole disgraceful mess into the back of her mind. The price of maintaining her self-image as a good person required letting go of Georgina. And this was fine, because Georgina had witnessed her insurmountable ugliness and so Kate couldn't exist in the same universe as that in which she'd said all those heinous things, just as Jekyll and Hyde couldn't attend the same party. It wasn't that Georgina had been unable to forgive Kate, but that every time Kate had looked at her best friend, she saw herself through Georgina's eyes and couldn't bear what she saw. In the name of self-preservation, or pride, or both, Kate had given up her georgeous best friend.

Ziggy cut in. "I'm waiting for you to say you tried to strangle her."

Kate found a rock on the edge of the street to kick. "Metaphorically speaking, yeah." She struck the rock and it didn't go as far as she'd wanted. "The summer after we graduate, Thomas comes to visit and we go out to dinner and he tells me I got a job. My mind starts whirring about how and why they would have contacted him but, hey, he's a Mosby, and his mom is well-connected in that world so who knows? So I shriek and ask him which job it was and was there an email or a letter or what, and he laughs at me, enjoying this moment where he knows the ending and I don't. And he's like, 'No, my mom thought you'd like working at Artemis'—and he slides me this formal letter from his mother. 'On behalf of Artemis International' blah, blah, blah, and my head is just swimming, and I'm skimming the lines, and then I see that they've offered me, no joke, Ziggy, twice the salary that publishing would have offered."

"So you take it."

"Yeah, I take it! I'm glad it makes sense to you too. I take it there on the spot—we leave the restaurant so I can call Evelyn and thank her and hit all the important buzz words—'honored' and 'opportunity' and 'grateful' on loop for five minutes. And then I text Georgina to tell her the good news and she doesn't respond."

"Maybe she was on her own dinner date."

"Close—I remembered she was bartending, and Jo has that rule about no phones on the floor, which was why Georgina hadn't texted me back. So I dropped Thomas off at home because he had already started med school and had some big test the following Monday and drove over to the Wharf. I run over to Jetty Bar, interrupt some tourists to tell her the good news, and her response is, 'That's cool but you didn't say yes, did you?'"

"Uh-oh."

"Yeah, but I was still so giddy. She'd been accepted to a bunch of MFA programs for creative writing, and I'd been sinking in unanswered emails, and now, finally, we could succeed together, at the same time. I said something like that to her, and she made this weird face and said, 'But you don't want to be in PR—you want to be in publishing. You want to be an editor.'"

Ziggy winced sympathetically. "How dare Georgina speak the truth."

"Exactly." Kate laughed, making fun of herself. "But of course I didn't see it like that. I told her how much they offered versus what I'd get paid in publishing, hypothetically, since no one had even hired me yet, and she just sort of shrugged and said something like, 'You'll never work in publishing if you're not willing to make sacrifices.' And that did horrible things to my brain so I just left. I walked outside to the employee parking lot and Georgina followed me, but she didn't apologize—she actually doubled down—so I started sputtering every mean thing I could think of."

"Because she wasn't excited for you?"

"I think, looking back, for our entire friendship, I always swallowed the fact that she could afford stuff I couldn't. Yeah, she didn't have her dad around and her mom worked long hours, but they had money—not Hoffman money, but money. They went to a different country every spring break, and it was always understood that her parents would pay for college, graduate school—any sort of education, which also meant rent, food, a car—all the stuff that's not included in tuition."

"Sure."

"I mean, if Georgina had earned my test scores on the PSAT, her parents would definitely have paid for her to go to Yates." Kate took a step outside herself and remembered she was talking to Ziggy. "Is it weird that I'm complaining to you about this stuff?"

Ziggy smiled. "Up until February, I would've defended dropping out of Cornell. But now that my dad is gone and I'm desperate, I think I should have tried to stick it out. I could have taken business classes that would have benefited us. Then again, if he was gonna die as early as he did, I'm really glad I didn't spend four years away from him."

"Yeah." Kate sighed, aware she was treading in foreign water where she, most fortunately, had never touched the bottom.

"Anyway, this isn't my story," Ziggy said. "Keep going."

"One time Georgina even said, 'My parents really value my education'—as if my parents, *my high-school-history-teaching parents*, didn't care about education."

"Oh boy."

"So it seemed pretty fucking unfair"—Kate felt herself growing angry all over again, her face starting to flush, her speech quickening—"for her to judge me about taking a job that would allow me to actually live like a professional adult."

"Right."

"So Georgina went on a rant about how she just wanted me to be happy and to pursue my dreams, and that twenty-two was the best time to be broke, but I was just fuming at that point. I mean, it wasn't even a rant probably, I think it was supposed to be a pump-up talk. She did say she believed in me at least ten times, but all I heard was her judgment. She kept repeating, 'You need to be true to yourself' and each time she said it, it felt like she was taunting me, because she was being so hypocritical."

"How so?" Ziggy held her gaze.

"So then I told her that she was just jealous," Kate said, ignoring the question. "Because I had a successful boyfriend who'd helped me secure a fantastic job while she was alone and pursuing the most impractical career path imaginable on her parents' dime."

Ziggy cringed. "I mean, that's not *that* bad."

"No, but I was just getting started."

"Uh-oh."

"Because then I said, 'Of the two of us, you're the one not being honest about who you are,' and I still remember how she looked like I was choking her, like every word I said was a finger tightening around her windpipe. So then I doubled down."

Ziggy's eyebrows were so worried that they touched each other as he stared down the street. Kate wondered if he was about to walk away from her—his body suggested he was considering it. She took a deep breath. "I said, 'For having a therapist for a mom, you should be more aware that you're projecting all this living-a-lie bullshit onto me because even though you have the world's most supportive parents, you are one hundred percent gay and one hundred percent hiding in the closet like this is Nebraska in the nineties and I've been so patient, waiting for you to stop being so pathetic'—I said that, I called her pathetic—and I said, 'I finally figured out why you haven't.'"

Kate was suddenly back at the Wharf, staring down her best friend in the employee parking lot, waiting for her punches to land. In a flat, emotionless voice, her hands coiled into fists, Kate had said, "Just admit you're in love with me. Just admit you hate Thomas, you hate the idea of me staying in New York, you hate that I got a job doing PR and that I'll never be able to publish your books—if you even ever write them—because you hate the fact that I love Thomas, not you."

To her shock, Georgina had sneered. Kate had leveled her by going low, and yet Georgina had delivered the final blow of the night in a prophecy destined to come true: "You're going to end up back here, alone and unhappy, because at your core, Kate Campbell, you are a pretentious, superficial, wannabe snob who only cares about being rich and popular." Georgina had said it with a soothsayer's calm, her dark eyes glimmering and furious. "You will never be happy, because you go after the wrong things. You are the one who is truly, deeply pathetic and I feel sorry for you."

"Jesus," Ziggy said, stopping in his tracks and looking down at his steel-toed boots.

"I gave notice at the Wharf that night," Kate said. "Denise said she'd heard about the fight and they were overstaffed anyway, so she told me no hard feelings and no reason to stick around for two weeks. I started at Artemis the following Monday and moved in with Thomas, and I heard through the grapevine that Georgina got into Iowa last-minute so she moved there. I think she kept waiting for me to say sorry, but I kept waiting for her to say sorry, and then so much time passed that it became this deep, deep wound that didn't get cleaned out and was just, like, totally infected and festering with twenty types of bacteria until it just—we just died."

"Friendship gangrene. And you haven't talked since?"

Kate shook her head. "She's married now, you know. I wasn't invited to the wedding. Obviously." Kate took a breath. "Did you know she was going to write a memoir called *The Only Asian in Sea Point* and the opening scene was going to be from her first day of school here? The fantasy was for her to become a bestselling author and I would be her editor."

"It could still happen."

"Yeah right."

"Well, unless I missed it, she still hasn't become a famous author and you still haven't become her editor—or anyone's editor. You could still go into publishing, too, if you wanted."

With a teenager's sense of theatrics, Kate stopped in her tracks, put her hands on her hips, popped her leg, and cocked her head. "Why, Ziggy Miller, you're the most optimistic plumber I've ever met."

Ziggy couldn't help but laugh. "Yeah, okay, I'm also the only plumber you've ever met."

"Speaking of which, and I'm sorry to ask, but could you look at the outdoor shower at some point?" Ziggy felt his stomach sink—he couldn't even successfully install an outdoor shower correctly. Could he do anything right anymore? But before he could pepper her with follow-up questions, Kate added, "I can't get it as hot as I want."

"Oh, that's easy," Ziggy said, his confidence instantly surging to 100 percent. "I just need to adjust the anti-scald valve—I can do it now," he offered as they rounded the corner of their block.

While Ziggy retrieved his tools from the back of his truck, Kate told him how she usually used the shower twice a day because she would come home so gross from the Wharf. "That's why I need it hotter," Kate explained. "During the day, the temperature is great, but at one in the morning, I want to crank that heat way up," she said, gyrating her hips in a comical move that seemed borrowed from Miles. Ziggy tried not to think about the fact that the two of them spent so much time together at work that Kate probably felt closer to Miles—she probably didn't even realize she was mimicking him now.

"Do you mind holding up your phone flashlight?" he asked, hanging his tool bag on the towel hook and feeling around for his screwdriver.

As Ziggy pried off the shower handle and took out the center screw, he explained each step to Kate—not because she asked or because it was particularly interesting, but because he was suddenly very aware of how close their bodies were in the small cedar box he'd built just for her. Ziggy could smell her shampoo, the faint tang of her sweat as they stood in the four-by-four space and grew aware of their breath. He might have been imagining it, but he felt like Kate was using the flashlight to look at him, not the valve, as he focused on rotating the small circle counterclockwise to increase the heat.

"A slight shift makes all the difference," he said. Reaching across her for his tool bag, Ziggy's arm brushed Kate's bare shoulder, making her jump. "Sorry!" Ziggy yelped. Fortunately, Kate had turned off the flashlight—his face was so hot that it needed its own anti-scald valve.

They parted ways quickly and said good night without looking at each other because it had been a strange phenomenon—too strange, in fact, for either of them to acknowledge. Everyone knew that, in the dead of winter, dry air lent itself to static electricity. But it was the height of summer in Sea Point—even at night, the humidity was so thick that tourists joked about carrying oxygen tanks on the boardwalk. Kate and Ziggy knew static electricity didn't happen this time of year, and yet, standing together inside the outdoor shower, they'd both felt the shock.

Gutting with Integrity

By the end of July, his eighth week on the line, Miles understood that most of the local college kids who worked at the Wharf didn't attend parties because they were too busy seating them, usually back-to-back and in the same section since the dining room was always slammed by 5:15 p.m. Weekends weren't days off but doubles, the major moneymakers when the kitchen door didn't have time to swing but instead took swift kicks from servers on either side carrying heavy trays and asking with shrapnel in their voices, *Did you get table 9 those creamers? Did Ben really call out sick? For the love of God, which dipstick drank the last of the coffee without making more?*

Having spent his own Princeton summers interning in major cities and traveling abroad, Miles found himself looking at the college kids in his hometown with fresh eyes, astounded by what he saw. His colleagues cursed, they complained, but they showed up on time and put in the work. Until now, Miles had failed to appreciate the high-season warriors he'd grown up with, the people in front and back of house who could tame even the hangriest tourists through fake smiles, quick service, fast appetizers, and the gift of improvisation.

Sea Pointers kept their knees bent twenty-four hours a day so that when the serving tray slipped, or the rain clouds opened up, or the filet got eighty-sixed, they could avoid disaster with a tight pivot, spinning the change as a positive development for their customers—or at least an entertaining show. This acquired skill set was the only reason such a small Jersey town could handle the endless sucker punches of summer—the power outages, the bad tippers, the screaming babies, the fighting couples, the hurricane winds, the electrical fires, the perfect beach days spent inside folding napkins, and the impossible nights when a table of ladies nursed their house wine for three hours. They were gritty but graceful, or maybe it was all the grit that had taught them such grace because when Miles messed up royally, no one razzed him. The small mistakes, on the other hand, required immediate torment.

It was just after one p.m. on a Wednesday and Miles was elbow deep in beef. He and Chef would prep for a few more hours until the rest of the crew trickled in from their other jobs. That was the other thing about Sea Pointers—the vast majority held down multiple side hustles. Every time Miles wanted to whine about his feet or his back, he thought of Danny, who spent eight hours landscaping in the sun, or Marcus, who delivered linens to restaurants in Ship Harbor until he clocked in. Even Emmy spent all day lifeguarding before arriving at premeal, still smelling like coconut sunscreen and sweat as she double-knotted her apron and prepared for another night of the male gaze.

As Miles chopped onions, Chef passed him with a grunt, waddling under the weight of a fifty-pound Atlantic salmon. He knew better than to try to take it off her hands—he'd made that mistake before. That was his problem, Miles knew—he offered help to those who didn't need it and avoided people who did.

He hadn't seen Ziggy since the Fourth of July, which had been three weeks and three eons ago. It was hard to believe but summer nights on the line smeared his sense of time. Cooking for hundreds of people each day had aged Miles with the same swift callousness with which he shucked each oyster. He loved every minute of it. Even when he hated it, he loved the way he hated it, because just when he was ready to chuck a saucepan into the dining room at the guy who sent his rare burger back three times, one of his teammates would save him by saying something morbid, crude, or hilarious—usually all three.

"Sorry to have to do this to your dad," Chef called over, scaling the salmon. At Miles's bewildered expression, she elaborated: "This guy is known as King of the Fish—and you're the Prince of Sea Point—so doesn't that make you two related?" Miles indulged her with a smirk as he stared at her hands.

"What happens after this?" he asked, the scales falling in front of his eyes.

"Gutting," Natalie answered, steadily moving down the salmon with her scaler.

"Can you teach me?"

"It's messy," Natalie sighed, waving him closer and showing him how to work the tool. "Everyone complains about how expensive the fish special is, but I've got to invest serious time into these big boys—scaling, gutting, filleting, skinning, portioning. The only way to enjoy a fish this fresh and this beautiful—see how plump and clear his eyes are?—is to do all the dirty work yourself. It's my responsibility to keep his integrity."

"Even after you gut him?"

"*Especially* after I gut him."

Miles nodded.

"And by me, I mean you." Chef handed him the fillet knife, and with her guidance, Miles tipped the blade into the belly of the fish.

Georgeous

"We did it!" Patricia shouted from down the street as Kate approached the library on the first Friday morning of August. "You did it! We did it! We all did it!"

Lifeguard Chad shoved the morning paper in Kate's face, but before she could read the headlines, Patricia announced, "He officially withdrew his proposal! Leeper the Creeper gave up! The library lives!"

All three of them jumped up and down, holding hands and screaming their heads off like schoolchildren. Their unbridled exuberance compelled every passerby to ask what happened, so that soon the same block that Harry Leeper had tried to redevelop grew crowded with locals congratulating one another, overjoyed by their shared victory. All it had taken, Patricia kept repeating to anyone who would listen, was a petition, some publicity, and Kate Campbell leading the charge.

It was such a remarkable start to the day that Kate nearly forgot what lay ahead, or whom she'd left behind. After all, she hadn't spoken to Bernadette since the Fourth of July. In their cold war, Bernadette had missed so many things—the string of successful Friday Rock Star Reader events, including Jo Hoffman's funny little kerplunks during *Blueberries for Sal*, and Gertie strutting around the library with a scepter and crown while Gus read *Where the Wild Things Are*. Kate had also organized a three-hour forum at the library to get feedback on what they could do better and what its patrons hoped to see in the future.

As a direct result of the forum and despite the imminent threat of Leeper's bulldozer, Kate had gone ahead and installed a suggestion box—technically a birdhouse from Holloway's Hardware—that she'd put above the water fountain in the back of the library, right by the bathroom for anonymity's sake. And while some of the suggestions were comical—"Free orange juice"—and some surprising—"Organize a speed-dating night"—and some just straight-up impossible—"Make the roof retractable for sunny days"—most of them were simple, direct instructions for how to make the library a more accessible, useful community space. Kate had started drawing up a few different proposals for the library board and had prayed it wasn't an exercise in futility—until this morning's joyful news.

Bernadette had missed all of this. She'd avoided the library, skipped the forum, and sent Clementine to Rock Star Readers each Friday with a neighbor. Now she was missing the celebration. Kate took out her phone to text her—after all, Bernadette had been the one to instigate Kate's involvement in the library—but then she thought better of it. This was her moment, her accomplishment, and if Bernadette wanted to share in it, she'd need to apologize first.

Even though the library was safe, Kate could hardly relax. It was the day before Nessie's wedding, and she had never been so jittery—she would meet Georgina at Summersault that night if she didn't melt into a puddle of nerves first.

Thankfully, Kate had Rock Star Readers to distract her. After five weeks, she finally had stage prep down to a science. Like the choreography for *Freaky Freakazoid*, what once overwhelmed her now came easily, naturally, and Kate could do the entire setup and breakdown in under an hour. This morning, Goldie was on deck to read.

As always, Kate had sent out an e-newsletter announcing Friday's Rock

Star, but no one could do PR like Goldie. For the past week, she had told every one of her customers that she wouldn't be working on Friday morning because she'd be over at the library. Her children and grandchildren were driving from Delaware for the occasion, "and you'll get yourself there too if you like these pancakes," Kate overheard Goldie tell a line of waiting customers on Tuesday afternoon when she popped in for a tugboat (four shots of espresso over ice because August was a beast). Multiply Goldie's pancake threat by the hundreds of patrons she saw each day, and that explained why there was a line around the block when Kate opened the door at ten o'clock.

"Stop looking so surprised," Goldie said, grinning. She glowed as she paced back and forth on the stage, welcoming everyone to come closer, even though it was already standing room only. It was funny to see the bottom half of Goldie, Kate realized, having strictly seen her from the waist up behind the counter at the Coffee Cow. Here she was, wearing flattering jeans, a white blouse, no apron, and leopard-print heels.

"I've been working at the Coffee Cow since I was your age," Goldie said to the audience of young children sitting before her. No one laughed because no one knew if she was serious or not. "I like working there because I like talking to people, I like taking care of people, and I like getting to eat French fries whenever I want." The adults in the room laughed at this while dozens of children silently decided that they too would work at the Coffee Cow when they grew up.

Holding up *Cloudy with a Chance of Meatballs*, Goldie explained, "I chose this book because it's my grandson's favorite and he's here today visiting, plus it's in line with my whole, you know, food theme." The morning flew by in goodwill and giant pancakes, Kate still riding the high of defeating Harry Leeper as she drove home from the library and got ready for her big night with her ex best friend.

When it was finally time to head to Summersault, each footstep agitated the butterflies in Kate's stomach. Opening the door of the bar, soft rock billowed out as Kate located the back of Georgina's head in seconds. They'd always had this, the extra sense of each other's whereabouts, and

Georgina looked up and whipped around in her swivel stool. Kate experienced an intense bout of déjà vu, a familiar moment of free fall that knocked the wind out of her. Still beyond breath, the former friends stared at each other from across the packed room, and then Georgina Kim smiled at her, that curtain-opening smile she'd first given her in Ms. Hesser's homeroom.

"Harriet!" Georgina stood up and walked toward her at a clip, her arms already outstretched.

In those split seconds, Kate registered that Georgina's hair was shorter and her teeth were extremely white. She was tan and taut with muscles, her jean shorts and flimsy yellow tank top leaving enough skin exposed to prove that Georgina's posts about mountain climbing were accurate reflections of how she spent her time. The moment before their bodies collided in a tight hug, Kate caught a whiff of vanilla perfume. Georgina still smelled like her best friend.

"You look amazing," Kate said.

"I love this short hair!" Georgina beamed, reaching out to muss Kate's bob.

It felt more like seeing an ex than Kate could have fathomed, but also like reuniting with a long-lost twin, and they kept finding reasons to touch each other, to ground them in reality, that this was really happening, here they were, together again. Too much time had gone by and yet their teenage shorthand remained intact, as did their ability to find the word the other fished for, the tendency to interrupt and finish each other's thoughts.

"So we're doing Long Island ice teas all night, right?" Georgina joked, alluding to a particularly messy evening their junior summer. They gossiped about high school classmates before moving on to the topical information about each other that they'd already gleaned through numerous searches over the years, until finally Georgina admitted as much: "Honestly, I almost feel up-to-date on your life, but only in a statistics-and-stalking kind of way."

The second round arrived just then and they skipped ahead to their existences behind the online veil to their actual state of well-being. Georgina was married to a woman named Liza she'd met six years ago at her rock-climbing gym. "This probably sounds lame," Georgina prefaced, "but from the moment I saw Liza, I felt like I'd always known her." Kate nodded and snuck a glance at Georgina's left hand, but there wasn't any gleaming diamond as she'd anticipated, only a delicate gold band.

Halfway through the second glass of wine, they waded into the sediment of their friendship.

"I'm sorry about Thomas," Georgina offered.

"No, you're not."

They both laughed. "No, I'm not," Georgina agreed. "I blamed him for a long time because it was easier than blaming you."

Kate felt the pull from the pit of her stomach, an apology as urgent as any upchuck reflex. "I'm sorry I said all those things. There's no excuse, but I was just so excited and then you—"

"Blew it," Georgina interrupted with a baleful smile. She patted Kate on the shoulder. "We were young and dumb and I think really upset about moving in different directions. I should have ridden your high instead of being all judgmental, and you shouldn't have outed me during a fight in the parking lot. Trust me, I've rewatched that interaction a million times in my head, hating both of us but also feeling sorry for us for not knowing better. We were so arrogant about what our relationship could withstand. But I guess that's your twenties for you—it's like how I never used to stretch and never got hurt and assumed I'd always be flexible—and now I'm dealing with all that fallout because things keep changing and my body hates me now and—I'm just rambling—"

"You're not," Kate said, "but you're right—about us being arrogant and both of us—God, it's kind of tragic, isn't it?"

"The time lost?"

Kate nodded. "I mean, Thomas and I broke up and got back together so many times and I wish—I just wish that had been us, you know? We should have just had a big fight and then made up and gotten back together. We were harder on each other—"

"Than we were on significant others," Georgina said. "Totally. I've thought the same thing. We were both assholes."

"I was the bigger asshole," Kate said, giving Georgina a knowing side glance.

"Yeah," Georgina agreed. "But we're here now, and I still like you."

"I still like you too," Kate said. Taking a deep sip of wine, she added, "He's coming tomorrow."

"I heard that. You worried?"

Fighting a proud smile, Kate said with a straight face, "I'm bringing Miles Hoffman."

Georgina leaned forward and gripped Kate's knees. "Please don't tell me you're dating the Prince of Sea Point."

Kate laughed and took another sip so she wouldn't have to see the concern on Georgina's face. "I'm not, but we're friends now." Kate considered telling Georgina about her three-point plan, about her hope to win Thomas back, but they'd just made up after ten years. Why get into another fight?

"That's sanctioned, I guess," Georgina offered half-heartedly. "Kate?" They spun their barstools to face each other. "You seem good."

Kate nodded. "You do too—how's the writing?"

Georgina let her forehead smack the bar with a dramatic thud. "I feel crazy most of the time, but I like teaching, and I keep getting scraps of work thrown my way, so it's going, I guess."

Kate remembered an optimistic notion that was not her own: "I told Ziggy how we'd planned on working together, how I'd be the editor to your bestselling books, and he was so cute and said it could still happen."

"He's not wrong," Georgina mused.

"We can work over email," Kate said, playing along. "I'll be back in New York after the summer." At Georgina's raised eyebrow, Kate elaborated. "Patricia is helping me with career stuff—I'm hoping to get a job in publishing."

"It won't feel weird, New York without Thomas?"

Kate resisted the bait. "I think the city will feel familiar but also brand-new."

"Like us?" Georgina asked, her eyes wide.

"Like us," Kate agreed, beaming. "Where's your engagement ring?"

Georgina rolled her eyes and shook her head, annoyed at the thought. "She got me the most obnoxious ring you've ever seen, so I never wear it. I told her I want to climb boulders, I want to live in Boulder, but I do not want to wear a fucking boulder."

Kate leaned into her best friend so their shoulders touched. "I've missed you so much," she thought in her head before realizing she'd said it aloud.

Rooney the bartender appeared and pushed two tall glasses of water in front of them. "Drink these, wouldya? Double Trouble has never looked so pathetic," he teased, his gold tooth catching the dim bar light as he grinned at them. "And do me a favor—don't insult me with your credit cards tonight. Seeing your dopey faces together again is more than enough."

Lying in bed an hour later, Kate ran the tape of what had just transpired with Georgina Kim. There had been no dramatic blowup, no screaming match, no ugly words slung. There had been no performance, no peacocking. They'd both apologized and what remained after all this time was the undeniable, irrevocable connection. The simplicity of that fact was so revolutionary, it almost seemed anticlimactic. And yet, Kate saw the truth on the blank canvas of her bedroom ceiling: She had her best friend back.

Well, one of them.

She'd resolve things with Bernadette after Nessie's wedding, once she'd proved her sister wrong.

Game Time

The following afternoon, Kate stepped out of the shower, took a look at the rented blue dress hanging on the back of the bathroom door that she'd need to shimmy into for Nessie's wedding, and wondered if she should just give in. Kate knew that if she called Bernadette crying—openly *weeping* with desperation—her sister would back-burner the animosity between them and come over to do Kate's hair and makeup with professional finesse.

But for the first time in a long time, Bernadette was in the wrong and needed to apologize, so Kate was on her own for getting ready. She'd done far harder things alone this summer—like wait on that guy at the Jetty Bar who, when she'd told him the Special of the Day was Ipswich fried clams, had jeered, "Do you even know where Ipswich is?" If she could handle that, she could handle this. With the strategic eye of a seasoned general, Kate reached for the comb and began her attack.

"Wow!" Miles yelled from the front porch as he stumbled back several steps, pretending Kate's appearance had physically blown him out the door. "Vengeance has never looked quite so . . . vengeful."

"I'll take that as a compliment."

"As you should. And this short hair," Miles said, reaching out to touch Kate's locks, "I know I've said it before, but it's badass."

"So is that," Kate said, nodding at Miles's car. She'd specifically asked him to pick her up in the Porsche so they could make a low-key spectacular entrance as they rolled into the Wharf and idled in line for valet parking. Even though they'd both used the staff parking lot all summer, tonight was about being seen.

After so many blurry months of rushing through the employee side entrance and clocking in, wiping down every bottle, marrying all the ketchups, making it a double, splitting the check, brewing coffee, dumping creamers, clocking out, and then clocking back in, it was weird for Kate to walk through the front doors of the Wharf in a floor-length dress with a Prince on her arm.

As soon as they entered the pre-ceremony cocktail area, Kate locked eyes with Thomas, but before she could decide what to do, Mrs. Drew, Nessie's mom, was throwing her arms around her and making introductions to cousins who chirped like parakeets about what a cute little town Sea Point was while Miles stood by her looking hot and engaged in the cousins' nonstop platitudes. As she pretended to listen, Kate chanced a quick glance at the woman next to Thomas and clocked Wally, the delicate and flexible woodland nymph she'd seen online, only now in 3D, wearing a slinky teal dress and incredible earrings.

Miles rubbed the small of Kate's back but when she turned to look up at him with feigned adoration, it wasn't Miles at all but Thomas, right there, right next to her, with Wally, who was smiling too genuinely for Kate's liking.

"How are you?" Thomas asked, leaning in for an air kiss as if she were a great-aunt.

"Hey!" Kate said, her voice cracking as it flew out of her mouth, high-pitched and trying too hard.

"I'm Wally," the pretty nymph said, flashing a mouthful of beautiful teeth.

"And I'm Miles," the Prince announced, reappearing with two cocktails in hand.

Kate pretended to examine her drink as she watched Thomas's skull slowly rotate up like a crane lifting something especially heavy. Miles was only a few inches taller than Thomas, but Kate still remembered Thomas lounging on his midcentury couch telling his college friends, "I'm only comfortable if I can see the tops of everyone else's heads." There was no way he could see the top of Miles's head. And now, as Kate assessed her ex, she saw that his hairline was receding. Rapidly.

"I guess we should go find seats," Miles suggested, steering Kate by the waist and guiding her toward the wharf. Just as she'd hoped, Kate caught Thomas staring at Miles's hands on her body.

"It's about that time," Thomas agreed, withdrawing the case from inside his black jacket. "Hope you guys remembered your sunnies." He smiled at Kate as he slipped the shades onto his face.

Gripping Miles's arm for balance, Kate stood in her designer dress while suddenly understanding what Janet Leigh had experienced in the shower of the Bates Motel. Those sunnies drawn meant the knives were out. Even through his polarized shields, Kate felt Thomas's gaze stabbing her through the heart.

Five or six Decembers ago, Thomas's favorite sunglass brand had announced a limited-edition collection, the Superba, with only one hundred pairs made in North America, and Thomas had become obsessed with owning a pair. Exploiting every ounce of every type of resource she had—dipping into her savings, taking the LIRR in the middle of a workday, calling not one but two college acquaintances she hadn't spoken to before or since—Kate had incurred all kinds of social and physical injuries to procure the sunglasses currently shading Thomas's eyes from hers. The night she gave them to him, he'd put them on immediately, thrown her on the bed, and kept her there the entire evening, all while he wore his new Superbas. It had been ridiculous and funny and fun. It had been the best of what they'd been together.

Miles grabbed Kate's hand and shook her from the memory. Leading her outside to the actual wharf behind the Wharf for the start of the ceremony, he whispered, "Breathe—you're doing great."

He pointed out two empty chairs but someone called Kate's name—it was Georgina and her wife, several rows back. Liza's smile lured Kate like a fishing hook. "Sit with us!" Georgina mouthed, gesturing to the open seats next to them.

"Kate Campbell at last," Liza said, leaning across Georgina and extending a hand. She wore her copper-red hair in a long fishtail braid, and the bold curl of her smile made Kate understand that this was Georgina's person, the gentle soul to hug all of Georgina's sharp edges. "We've got some catching up to do," Liza whispered and Kate nodded enthusiastically, wishing she'd remembered to pack gum or mints for the ceremony. Reunions required so much close talking.

"Altoid?" Miles asked, plunking his hand on her thigh and offering her an open tin full of assorted pills in every shape and color. "Make sure to go for a white circle—I can't remember what half these guys are." Reassurance flooded Kate's system—not just from Miles's pillbox as she picked out what she hoped was a mint—or his knee squeeze, but from her own foresight to invite this charming, handsome man who had already burrowed underneath Thomas's thin skin. She felt like a Super Bowl champion coach recalling the choices he'd made during the draft—she'd chosen well.

"Can you believe I married such a ginger?" Georgina asked as the groom and his men marched down the wharf and stood at the end of the dock. "She's like you but with, like, an almost-too-bright filter slapped on."

Kate grinned as she shook her head at her lap, nervous to look at Georgina, scared she would just *poof*, disappear, and she'd wake up from this dream. But then Georgina reached out and squeezed her hand three times, which somehow, at least for now, said all that needed to be said.

The bridesmaids paced themselves down the aisle wearing variations of the same lavender dress and the traditional expression of the sartorially oppressed. The layers of foundation caulked on each of the bridesmaids' faces was now beading in the August sun but could not hide their aggrieved relationship to their body-clinging gowns. Pat Benatar was right—love was absolutely a battlefield, and there was no greater proof than the POWs who now stood at the end of the dock, to the right of the groom, arranged from smallest to largest because there is always humiliation in war.

The music changed and everyone stood like well-trained shih tzus.

Nessie Drew radiated a nubile confidence as she stood between her parents at the back of the wharf, her chin tilted slightly up as she took her first step down the aisle in an off-the-shoulder white gown.

"It's a Vera Wang," Georgina whispered, "which surprised me more than if she'd opted for a space suit."

Kate tried to disguise her chuckle as a cough. Nessie seemed to have gone from rebel child to conventional bride without any fallout—perhaps everyone needed their own self-designated rumspringa in order to grow up and toe the line.

The ceremony was brief—barely fifteen minutes—and soon the three hundred guests were throwing peony petals at the newlyweds as they raced back down the wharf toward their future marital bliss and a cadre of overenthusiastic wedding photographers.

Afterward, merging into the bottlenecked aisle, Kate overheard Miles debating Liza about personalized vows while fitting the definition of perfect wedding date. Kate noted he was objectively the best-looking guy in attendance, and the only person who would be more aware of that fact than she was Thomas. In a meek attempt to hide her wicked grin, Kate reapplied her lipstick and silently congratulated herself on a plus-one well picked.

Although Nessie's traditional ceremony had been surprising and more than a little disappointing, the Loch Ness monster came out of retirement at cocktail hour: There were six stations, each one offering a full bar but also a different specialty cocktail to honor a meaningful place in Nessie and Rye's relationship. There were mai tais to represent their annual trip to Maui, a whiskey neat from their Christmas in Osaka, a pisco sour to commemorate their hike along the Inca Trail and up Machu Picchu.

"To be clear," Nessie announced before disappearing for golden-hour photos, "this is just an extremely bougie version of Theta's infamous 'Around the World' parties!" Several of the bridesmaids whooped and cheered from their lavender casings.

"I mean, if that's the game—" Kate began.

"And it's Nessie's day—" Georgina hedged.

"It just seems like the right thing to do," Kate shrugged, catching Wally's eye from across the outdoor tent.

"Wait," Liza said, finally catching on. "Do you mean we're trying *all of them?*"

As the twelve-piece band implored guests to join the dance floor, Kate, Georgina, Liza, and Miles swiftly traveled around the world on empty stomachs. An hour later, Kate didn't notice that the best man's speech dragged on for twenty unfunny-inside-joke minutes or that Thomas kept looking over at her. In fact, after the Cuba libre—because of course Rye had proposed on a seawall along the Malecón—Kate didn't notice anything except that she was having the best night ever. "I'm worried about the bridesmaids' hair," Liza said, swaying. "They just look so flammable, don't they?"

And then the band took a break and a DJ took over.

Kate was chugging water when she heard the triangle. She thought she'd imagined it, but the familiar intro grew and Kate knew—*she knew*—and so she pretended that she didn't. She continued to chug with a denialist fury.

The beat dropped.

The Theta girls at tables three, four, and five screamed with recognition and scurried to the dance floor just as Nessie appeared on the band's empty stage in a mini black leather dress, knee-high boots, and what appeared to be a studded dog collar around her neck. Amid the gasps of her great aunts and uncles, Nessie yelled into the microphone: "If you are female and physically able to dance, I DEMAND your ass on the dance floor now!"

Georgina grabbed Kate's wrist and took the water glass out of her hand. "I love this song!" she yelled, yanking Kate toward the growing crowd of dancing guests.

Given the circumstances, she knew her refusal would not hold, and so Kate surrendered to yes.

Her shoulders automatically hiccupped in time. The floor was half full of wholly drunk women jerking their limbs every which way, waiting for the singing so they could belt out the lyrics into one another's open mouths like some kind of holy communion.

Kate had secretly practiced these steps every day for four months. She had them down, and she was five international drinks deep.

Before she could stop, she was starting.

Her muscles found their proper home among the airwaves, each step, each second, drawing a larger divide between Kate and the Thetas. Not everyone was on the floor, but every pair of eyes found Kate's body, the figure that kept moving to the music, not pausing to fix a strap or put up her hair or murmur something to a friend. She was in it, and she couldn't stop, and she both had no idea and was fully conscious that three hundred wedding guests were gaping at her.

She heard multiple cat whistles and woops when she Baked the Cookies just right. When she put a snake in her neck for the Fila, Nessie shrieked with glee, and Kate was forced to look left and take a full inventory of the stares. Most people were up from their seats, lining the perimeter of the dance floor—even the Thetas had stopped to circle around her, their feet planted, and their molars visible. The song hit its bridge and Kate popped her hip, ready for the hardest part of the sequence.

Kate threw her head back, sank to the floor, remembered to smile just as the choreographer had said to, as if this weren't work but joy in motion, which it was. She'd practiced and practiced and now she was the master of her *Freaky Freakazoid*.

Kate jitterjabbed left. She jitterjabbed right. She did the Biz Markie and she wopped the hell out of the wop and then marched to a stop, just like in the video. When the routine ended, right before the final chorus of the song, Kate reached for Nessie, which was the signal for everyone to pretend that what they'd just witnessed wasn't a big deal and to join her on the dance floor. Georgina, Liza, and Miles rushed toward her, tongues flopping sloppy exaltations as they moved their bones in time with the music.

"Holy shit, Kate!" She felt two hands clamp down on her shoulder and turned around. "What the hell was that?" Thomas yelled. His Mayflower blue eyes were bright, entertained, elated. It took her a moment to identify the golden beam of his gaze: She'd surprised him the way she used to surprise him before his chosen family became their only friends and she'd tried too hard to fit in. Now, Thomas was looking at her like he hadn't seen her in years. It was her fearlessness that Thomas had first fallen in love with—the way she had been so honest about who she was before slowly succumbing to whom she thought Thomas wanted her to be. Still panting, beads of sweat collecting at the base of her bra, Kate realized that she'd shrunk over their decade together—not into Thomas's shadow but into her own. She would have never felt free enough in their apartment to have rehearsed that choreography—Thomas wouldn't have cared, but she would have worried that he'd privately view it as a waste of time.

Nessie and Rye hurried over along with Mr. and Mrs. Drew—a haze of hairspray, bouquets, and boutonnieres. "The Bravermans just asked if you did bat mitzvahs!" Mrs. Drew shrieked. "They thought we'd hired you to dance like that—a ringer!"

"Sounds like you've got a real career ahead of you," Nessie joked. As everyone continued to jostle her, touch her, tell her how amazing it was, Kate and Thomas continued to stare at each other.

"But seriously," Thomas said, cutting through the group's messy chatter, "where did that come from?" There was a hungry glimmer in his eye, but before Kate could answer, Miles swooped Kate up in his arms. Twirling through the air and laughing, Kate knew she was exactly who and where she was meant to be.

Her three-point plan had paid off and hand-delivered to Kate the love of her life—in a tux, no less. But as Kate flew and Thomas stared, she knew he was the love of a past life, not the one she'd discovered this summer, the one in which she'd saved the library, taught a Prince how to bartend, taken nightly walks with her oldest friend, reunited with her soulmate after more than ten years apart, and secretly mastered her own *Freaky Freakazoid*. In Thomas's gorgeous blue eyes, Kate found her reflection and knew she was no longer the person she'd dissolved into in New York. She felt a pang of heartache until she realized it was gratitude.

American Cheese

After Nessie requested everyone take another journey around the world, Kate found herself in Seoul when she realized Miles was missing.

"Is your fella intimidated by your dance skills?" Mr. Drew garbled, eliciting polite laughter as he approached their table. "I saw him heading"—he hiccupped—"toward the kitchen to hide." Reeking of soju, Nessie's father announced to the group that they'd converted the Wharf's private dining room into a cheese room. He puffed up like a blowfish as he listed the hard cheeses he'd had shipped directly from Italy, soft cheeses from France. "How many weddings have you been to where there is a whole *fromage* room?" he asked Kate, clinking her shot glass and nearly tipping over from the exertion.

Watching Mr. Drew toddle off in search of a new audience, Georgina linked her arm with Kate's. "Don't you wonder if weddings were always such competitions?" she asked. "Like, do you think the real reason why Queen Elizabeth imprisoned Mary Stuart was because she heard her cousin had a *fromage* room at her wedding?"

"I'm gonna go check it out," Kate announced. "Wanna come?"

"If I start eating cheese, I'll stop drinking," Georgina said, and Liza nodded in agreement.

What Mr. Drew hadn't explained was that a *fromage* room was so extravagant in part because the space had to be temperature controlled. Goosebumps rose on Kate's skin as she entered. The room was empty except for a large man standing in the corner, his broad back to Kate as she watched him pour a silver bowl full of blackberries onto his plate. His black blazer was working overtime, every fiber gasping as it continued to stretch from shoulder to shoulder.

"Oh my God," Kate said, stepping fully into the room.

"Something else, isn't it," the man clucked with shared admiration. "Nice moves out there, by the way—ever do private dances?" The man laughed and Kate felt a slight wave of recognition. He must be a local, but she couldn't place his face.

"Try that one with some of the fig spread," the man said, chewing loudly as he pointed to a soft cheese.

"If you insist." Kate grabbed a small plate and then, upon further consideration, swapped it for a full dinner plate.

"You look familiar," he said, cramming a cracker into his mouth. "Are you from here?"

Kate nodded. "I'm Kate Campbell—I grew up with Nessie."

The man expressed his approval by licking cheese from his fingers, and Kate noticed a gold class ring on his pinky that looked a little tight. "I met the Drews a few years ago," he offered. "Tremendous people." After wiping his hands on the white tablecloth, the man gave her a flirty wink and took two steps toward her before introducing himself: "Harry Leeper."

The temperature in the room, controlled as it might be, felt like it dropped twenty degrees.

"*You're* Harry Leeper?" Kate asked. Before she could stop herself, the impact of having traveled around the world gurgled up her throat to the tip of her tongue. "You ruin everything." It sounded dumb, melodramatic, even as the words charged past her lips, but she was thinking of Ziggy's tree, the white oak that was now just a stump, and the Bluebell Hotel, and all the bulldozed bungalows. She was thinking about the library and how he'd planned to level it for fourteen condos.

"Jeez, tell me how you really feel," Leeper quipped, eyeing Kate up and down. "Actually, don't, because this is a wedding, and we shouldn't talk business at a wedding."

"It isn't business. You exploit people."

"Some would call that progress," he said, shrugging. "There are perks to a free market—no doubt I've given your parents' property value a nice little bump."

"It's short-sighted greed." Hearing herself speak, Kate realized she was trembling with anger.

"Is that right?" Leeper's eyes narrowed as if ready to pounce. "I think there's a supply-and-demand argument to be made," he said, rocking back on his heels. "I never force anyone to sell me their outdated, mold-ridden clapboard house." Kate watched him, frozen in her tracks, as he put down his cheese plate and blew his nose into a napkin. Leeper smiled at Kate as if this exchange were all in good fun. "People are grateful," he added.

"People are desperate."

"And what about this place?" Leeper said, lifting both hands to marvel at the Wharf. With unsparing theatrics, he gawped at the high-arched ceiling, the views of the water. "Hard to believe, but the Wharf as it stands didn't always exist. And those lodges on the other side of the parking lot, which, by the way, wasn't always a parking lot—those lodges were built on ground that city council was considering protecting."

"The Wharf employs half the town, especially in the winter."

"I employ my fair share."

"Undocumented workers you pay less than minimum wage under the table."

"And? I'm giving the man a fish and teaching him how to fish at the same time. My guys have families to feed."

Kate rolled her eyes, less frustrated with Leeper than she was with herself. She didn't have an answer to that.

"I pay my men enough," Leeper said. His eyes rested on the low neckline of Kate's dress. "Campbell. You're the girl behind the library petition."

Kate was pretty sure she only said, *That's right, motherfucker*, in her head.

"Here's the thing, Katie—I can't do anything on my own. Hate me all you want, but you're giving me too much credit. I can't ruin anything without a whole lot of cooperation. Same with Jo Hoffman. Same with anyone trying to do anything. And at least I'm not like everyone else around here who only offer jobs to college-educated white girls with a BA in self-righteousness."

Kate gawked at the words as they hung in the air between them. Pleased with her expression, Leeper smiled and took a small bow. "See you on the dance floor, sweetheart."

Kate stood there, enraged and shaking as she spun on her heels to face him. "The library is only the beginning," she called out, hoping he didn't hear the quiver in her voice. "People are going to stop selling their houses to you."

"Ignorance is not your color," Leeper grinned, turning around and meeting her eye. "Not too long ago I got a very nice email from Beverly Miller."

Kate's stomach dropped. Her heart clawed at her chest like a caged animal trying to escape. Bev would never do that. Ziggy would never do that. They wouldn't be the Millers if they could be so duplicitous.

"Anyway, I should get going—Donna has some friends she wants me to meet from the planning committee." Leeper winked again and turned to exit. "Enjoy the cheese," he called over his shoulder.

Kate stood in the *fromage* room for an unclear amount of time, paralyzed by the shock of so many conflicting realities. Her throat begged for air as she shivered in the cold, but she remained until a couple appeared and began rapidly undressing each other, oblivious to Kate, the cheese, the fact that this was not their hotel room. Kate slid past them undetected, annoyed that she had forgotten the most obvious fact about weddings: They were expensive excuses for fancy dresses and bad behavior.

Forever and Over

After Kate had been swept up in her *Freaky Freakazoid* fan club, Miles found himself dateless and drunk, which was just the cover he'd needed. Without a second thought, he popped into the kitchen to say hi to the crew and tell Natalie he'd rather be spending his night getting yelled at by her than attending this wedding. Natalie told him how much she cared—not at all—and to stop tickling Joey the barback, who was carrying a heavy bin of dirty dishes and entirely defenseless. Reluctantly dragging his feet back to the party, Miles decided the night was beginning to feel a lot like way too much, and so he veered right and asked the valet to bring his car around.

He texted Kate three times and waited for the band's cover of Tom Petty's "Free Fallin'" to wrap before he reentered the Wharf in search of his date. Surveying the bacchanal from the doorway, Miles didn't see Kate anywhere, but he did spot Thomas. He allowed his eyes to linger on Kate's ex-boyfriend, who stood in the narrow hallway to the left with the secret good bathrooms most patrons didn't know about. Thomas was leaning into a woman who was not Wally but was, in fact, Kate.

The reception had turned that corner in the night where one either went home and took Advil or stayed out and embraced the consequences. As Miles approached them slowly for eavesdropping purposes, he watched as Thomas fixed his eyes on Kate and asked her with seductive conspiracy, "What's our plan?" From several feet away, Miles recognized Thomas's endgame: He wanted Kate back—not in any real way, but he needed to see the worshipful sparkle return to her eyes when she looked at him before he could return to New York with Wally. Like Miles himself, Thomas had an eye for whatever was off-limits and nothing appealed to his competitive nature more than apparent indifference or the threat of losing control.

Kate cut through Miles's evaluation just then by shooting him an all-too-familiar three-quarter grin. In her glittering green eyes, Kate telegraphed that everything Miles had just thought about Thomas Mosby—she'd understood it, too. Her *Freaky Freakazoid* performance seemed to have snuffed out whatever flame she'd been fanning all summer, and somewhere between baking the cookies and going around the world, Kate had freed herself from the former love of her previous life. Miles realized that, like a well-fed cat, Kate was simply curious to see how many ways she could make a mouse squeak.

"I've got the car out front," Miles said, clearing his throat.

"You guys are already heading out?" Thomas asked, one eyebrow arched in disbelief. As Kate and Miles nodded, Thomas followed up. "Want to grab a nightcap somewhere?"

Wally appeared and put her hand on Thomas's stomach in the classic territorial move of the social media age. At this nightcap suggestion, Kate saw Wally poke Thomas in the back.

"Come on," Thomas pressured, squeezing Wally's shoulder. "One drink—how about that place we went, Kate? The Rumble?"

"The Ramble," Kate corrected. She hated that he knew about it, that he could reference a spot intentionally left off every *48 Hours in Sea Point* list. The Ramble was where clusters of locals, shlocals, and perennial vacationers congregated to escape the likes of Thomas and Wally. Live music wafted through the open windows of the parlor room at the Ramble, and even the off-duty line cooks swaying outside on the wraparound porch would take a break from pining after September to sing along. So many empty cocktail glasses bounced against knees to the beat of the music that the ice cubes added another layer of percussion, another dimension of togetherness.

"That place was great," Thomas reminisced, staring at Kate, his knowing gaze daring her to remember. They'd walked the two miles back to her parents' house on the beach that night, stumbling into the dunes to make out, giggling like children with extra pocket money. The moonlight had painted the sand in silver, and the beach stretched ahead of them like the design of their lives—infinite with possibility. How many times, Kate found herself wondering, had Thomas told her he loved her on that walk? On all the walks? For the first time since April, Kate found herself able to appreciate their shared history. They'd walked next to each other for twelve years and they had loved each other—imperfectly, but they had—and they probably always would.

Checking his phone, Miles shook his head. "It's too late. We won't even make it to last call."

"Small towns," Thomas moaned. "I'd invite you to our Airbnb but there's no booze there," he lamented with visible tact.

Miles shrugged. Even though he knew Kate would be angry at him for ruining his perfect debonair-bachelor image, he confessed, "I'd invite you to my place but I live with my mom."

To Miles's shocked pleasure, Kate laughed at this admission with the big, openmouthed guffaw of a Freaky Freakazoid. And then she couldn't stop because this whole night was for dilettante adults and such a silly, immature spoof on real life. The person she cared most about wasn't Thomas at all, but the woman two hundred feet away, dangling her legs over the wharf and looking out at the water with her wife. And yet, right now wasn't about Georgina, either. "Yeah, me too," Kate said. "It's actually kind of amazing, living with my parents. So many good snacks."

"Can I talk to you for a sec?" Thomas asked, before walking outside and beckoning for Kate to join him in the secluded courtyard where Nessie and Rye's "First Look" photo shoot had taken place hours earlier. "Why don't you want to hang out?" Thomas asked, once he closed the French doors behind them. They were by themselves for the first time since April. "I thought this would be a good opportunity for us to catch up, learn to become friends. You know I want you in my life."

Kate thought of Wally's yoga profile picture, the timeline, the planned ambush at the diner. She bit down on her anger and mustered, unconvincingly, "That's flattering." The face Thomas made as a response was not. Even a hint of condescension, a whiff of patronization, sent him into an indignant rage. Kate did not miss those prolonged tantrums.

"Want to hear something ridiculous?" she whispered. Thomas leaned forward and, under that familiar scent of his pricey hair putty from Vancouver, Kate smelled their apartment on his collar, the essence of their life together. Remembering what was ridiculous, Kate took a step back. "I've spent so much time analyzing how I must have disappointed you and what I could have done differently," she said. "Maybe I should have left Artemis, or complained less about going to things I didn't want to go to, or made more of my own friends instead of just latching on to yours—"

"That's not—" Thomas interrupted. "That wasn't—"

"But now that all seems so stupid," Kate said, dropping her voice. "And obvious in a clichéd kind of way—like, of course I'd blame myself, that's the easy thing to do. Because what was harder to reconcile was all the ways you disappointed me."

"Um, okay." Thomas ran a hand through his hair and started to walk away but Kate called him back.

"You know the best part about you being here?" she asked, not waiting for a reply. "Knowing that you're leaving."

Thomas started to turn but then whipped around and cupped her face in his hands, leaning in so close and so quick that Kate thought he might kiss her. "You can hate me, and I get it, but Kate, seriously—" He moved even closer so their noses nearly touched. "We grew in different directions and we weren't happy. *You weren't happy.*"

Staring into Thomas's kaleidoscope eyes, Kate surrendered. He was right. She hadn't been happy—or, at least, she'd been so much happier these last few months. In their story together, she'd settled into the footnotes. Since leaving Jane Street, her actions had driven every chapter. She could be angry about the time lost or thankful for the future saved.

Thomas shook his head and let go of her face. "Do you know how much I didn't want to break up with you? How much I didn't want to hurt you, or piss off my mom, or lose you in my life?" Kate croaked an indecipherable response and Thomas continued. "They haven't replaced you at Artemis, and my sister still won't even—it was the hardest thing I've ever done," he whispered. "And it was shitty how I did it—I know that. But we're both happier now and I just thought—"

He wasn't sure what he thought, it turned out, but Wally looked pissed as she approached them with her arms crossed and announced she wanted to go. Watching them quietly argue, Kate realized she wasn't sad or envious or angry—just exhausted. Thomas was right and Kate was relieved: They were over, but he would stay with her forever. Accepting both truths for the first time, Kate interrupted Wally to kiss Thomas on the cheek. She left them in the courtyard and walked back inside alone.

Kate's Step Four

After Thomas and Wally muttered hasty farewells—the all-night fight between them visibly ticking up on the Richter scale with every step toward the exit—Kate told Miles she was ready to go home.

"Well-played tonight," he said, downing his drink. "I think you really—"

Miles was still speaking when Kate stood up on her tippy toes and kissed him. Its soft force pleasantly surprised him and so he kissed her back.

"You taste like a whiskey ginger," Kate mused, her eyes still half-lidded, stunned by her own impulsiveness but pleased with the results. Miles looked equally dazed, bordering on confused, and so before she could second-guess herself or apologize or make a self-deprecating joke, Kate asked, "Can I show you my step four?"

"Is that some kind of euphemism?"

Kate shook her head, laughing. "I had this three-point plan for winning Thomas back," she divulged. "Step one was saving up money, step two was building my career, step three was getting a hot date—ta-da, thank you."

"Your three-point plan has a step four?"

"Only as of a few hours ago—I figured that if I did win him back, I needed my own place so he wouldn't know I lived at home."

"But you do live at home."

"Do you want to see my step four or not?" Kate asked, pretending not to see Miles's hesitation as she led him to the valet.

Despite the half-dozen drinks in his system, Miles insisted on driving. Kate considered shaming him but she was too drunk for good judgment and bad things didn't happen to men like Miles Hoffman anyway. If he were stopped by the police, which he wouldn't be, Miles would drive away with a warning and a "welcome back" because the Prince of Sea Point enjoyed certain privileges—specifically all of them. If Miles had crashed, which he didn't, his mother would have hired the best lawyers and they would have settled before going to court. The truth of this was woven into the seam of the machine, like the hidden compartment in the convertible's trunk that held a wad of cash, a backup phone battery, and that pink fanny pack containing a few illicit drugs of choice. People went to prison for possession of far less, but Miles Hoffman's biggest concern when a police car pulled up behind them at a red light was that hooking up with Kate was a bad idea.

As they turned onto Ocean Avenue, Kate almost told Miles about the Millers selling their house to Harry Leeper on the sly. Such acidic betrayal burned in her chest like tequila—or maybe it was just all the tequila coming back up, the inevitable motion sickness of going around the world twice. Either way, if Kate thought about Harry Leeper or Ziggy Miller right now, she'd lose her nerve and ruin the night.

"Turn left up here," Kate directed as they drove toward East Sea Point, and when she didn't hear the click of Miles's turn signal, Kate repeated herself.

"I heard ya," Miles said, making the turn.

"Then why didn't you use your blinker?"

Miles slowed down for a bump in the road that turned out to be a bushel of runover tomatoes—tragic, August-specific roadkill.

"I don't want people knowing my business."

"Your turn-signal business?" Kate balked in disbelief.

"Any of my business."

They passed a raccoon raiding a trash can on the side of the street.

"I wonder if you're bad at sex," Kate pondered aloud with the same concern that had made her ask Chef the day before what made the impossible burger possible.

"Excuse me?"

"I mean, good communication is pretty key to good sex," Kate said, enjoying the freedom of exploring her uninhibited thoughts. "So if you don't like communicating, it just gives me pause about what you're like in bed." Kate grinned in the darkness and looked over at Miles, whose mouth gaped open. "Make a right up here, on Lighthouse."

With a dramatic fluttering of his right hand that may have even involved spirit fingers, Miles flicked on his turn signal.

Andrea was a radiologist who'd asked what Ziggy was drinking at Summersault a little before eleven p.m. She'd shown up with a handful of wedding guests, but it was only at last call that Andrea realized her friends had since left. "Want to keep hanging out?" Ziggy asked, groping his pockets for his key ring. "I've got a place not far from here."

They were halfway to Daffodil Cottage when Andrea's conscience surpassed her carnal desire and she started sputtering about a boyfriend. Ziggy nodded and asked where she was staying—he could drop her off.

"God, you're hot," Andrea slurred. "Chivalry is not dead." Ziggy should have withdrawn his offer when she said the address—the Creeper McMansion next to the nature preserve—but it was after midnight and he'd already offered. Besides, it was only a ten-minute drive from the bar, five minutes out of the way.

For the rest of Andrea's long, relatively happy life, she would recall this ride as the strangest left-hand turn of an evening. The cute plumber she'd politely chatted with at the dive bar suddenly transformed into an environmental lunatic with the rage of the Hulk, ranting about trees and

greed and global suicide and blood on all their hands, pontificating with
his arm wagging out the driver-side window of his truck, the floor of which
was covered in so many Butterfinger wrappers it made Andrea nervous.

"Here we are at the white oak massacre," Ziggy announced, pulling up
to what Andrea had considered a very nice and clean Airbnb. "Enjoy your
oxygen-deprived vacation—and the boyfriend!" Ziggy waved with a glee-
ful, glassy-eyed smile that compelled Andrea to feel around in her bag
until she wrapped her fingers around the bottle of pepper spray. *Why were
the locals always so angry?*

Ziggy switched gears and sped away. On his drive home, he imagined
the yellow hallway light Bev would have left on for him, and the foil-
covered plate of cold chicken on the kitchen table, and the decibels of
silence as he stood in the bathroom looking at the mirror, staring at the
worry lines around his eyes and mouth that were quickly turning his face
into his father's. The hangover that awaited him at dawn would be sadis-
tic. And if Bev was still awake, she'd ask him how he was, which he
couldn't quite handle at the moment.

Ziggy gunned it to Beach Avenue and hung a right toward Daffodil
Cottage. He slowed down and allowed the truck to crawl up the seashell
driveway, already feeling a deep peace at what awaited him—the white
sofa, the endless options on TV, the framed photographs of people he'd
never met on the bookshelves he'd built with his father. It wasn't his house
but he and his dad had poured their hearts into it. They had actualized
their own dream for another family, and that should count for something.

There would be the beers he'd left in the refrigerator last time, when
he promised himself the next time would be the last. Awaiting his arrival
in their frosty green bottles, the beers called to Ziggy like breadcrumbs
leading him home to his own empty house. Except that when Ziggy
crested the hill, he saw that the house wasn't empty at all.

Miles was a good sport when Kate removed the house key from under the
conch shell, and didn't say anything when she punched in the code on
the keypad and shrieked with surprise when it worked. She pushed open

the door and let herself into Daffodil Cottage with the demonstrated en-titlement, the mockable privilege of a drunk white girl with a "good idea" on a Saturday night.

"Henry Louis Gates would have some choice words right about now," Miles said. Back at the Wharf, Natalie and the kitchen crew would be hosing down the floors, doing final checks before locking up for the night. His hands twitched at the thought, but here he was, the plus-one accom-plice. As Kate groped the walls for a light switch, Miles stood in the center of the living room, hands on hips, and wondered what he was doing there.

"We have beer!" Kate announced, her face illuminated from the re-frigerator light.

Carrying a six-pack into the living room, Kate felt like a one-woman parade. Tonight, she'd defied all the rules, flouted them, which meant it was time for music, and she knew just which playlist she wanted.

"We should call Ziggy," Miles said, avoiding her eyes.

"Ziggy can never know we were here," she said, moving toward him. She opened her mouth to explain the conch shell, the walk-offs, but Miles had put his beer down on the coffee table and was walking toward the basement door, using an outside voice to wonder aloud about Ziggy's progress on the man cave. If Kate didn't know better, she'd think he was trying to prolong what was going to happen next, and if they both hadn't been so preoccupied trying to capture each other's attention, they would have heard the tires on the driveway, the heavy boots on the front steps, the low groan of the screen door.

"Sorry to interrupt," a voice growled from the threshold, "but what the fuck?"

Burning Rings of
Fire and Water

"**I** used the conch shell key!" Kate blurted out.

"Why are you here?" Ziggy yelled.

"I'm really sorry, we were at the wedding and—" Kate looked at her feet on the white shag carpet.

"But I never told you the code." Ziggy looked at the open beers on the table—from the six-pack he'd bought—and moved swiftly across the living room to slip coasters under the sweating bottles. But the rings were already there, set.

Miles looked down at his tuxedo jacket and tried to smooth out the unnecessary creases the night had caused. He should have left Kate at the wedding, gone home, taken a hit, and slept off everyone else's problems. Ziggy turned to him. "You just went along with this?" he asked too softly.

"What was I gonna do?" Miles asked, eyebrows knitted together, hands up at the referee who'd just blown the whistle. He took a deep breath, allowing his instincts to guide him toward a peaceful solution. "I think we either drink these beers or just go home. No point in getting bent out of shape about—"

"Of course not," Ziggy scoffed. "No reason to get bent out of shape over anything, ever, right, Miles?"

Miles's eyes narrowed and his lean body condensed, preparing for impact. "Don't get mad at me, Zig. This wasn't my idea. I was just trying to be a good friend to Kate."

Ziggy snorted. "Sure."

"What's that supposed to mean?" Kate interjected, her eyes pinging back and forth while her body remained frozen. Both men were practically kicking up dust with their hooves.

Looking from Kate to Miles, Ziggy sneered, "You didn't go tonight to be a good friend to Kate any more than you came back to Sea Point to be a good friend to me."

"What are you talking about?" Miles muttered, his goodwill suddenly wicking off him.

"You came back to prove to your mom that you could run the Wharf and you—"

"That's ass-backward," Miles said, raising his voice. "I came back here to do both, like I told you from the beginning, but if you'd just—"

"Stop," Ziggy said, cutting him off. "Stop lying."

The room itself seemed to clench, bracing for the inevitable blow.

"Everyone's drunk, everyone's tired," Kate whispered. "We should all go home."

"Nice playlist," Ziggy deadpanned. When he looked at Kate, she blushed. It was the playlist of Zeke's favorite songs that Ziggy had made for her birthday barbecue. "How'd your performance go?"

Kate blinked at the sudden shift, the distant memory of her dance at the wedding, how free she'd felt, how powerful. *"Freaky Freakazoid?"*

Ziggy tilted his head, confused. "No," he barked. "Your attempt to trick your ex-boyfriend into thinking that you had the perfect boyfriend and, apparently"—he used both hands to gesture at the immaculate living room—"the perfect house."

"It was step four of her three-point plan," Miles offered unhelpfully.

Ziggy ignored him and continued to stare down Kate. "Maybe you'd be less of a mess if you could be honest about what you wanted," he hissed. "You want money and status and trips to Mexico and Cannes with people you don't even like and—"

"Whoa, Ziggy," Miles said, touching Ziggy's shoulder.

"You know what?" Ziggy swiped Miles's hand away. "You two deserve each other."

"Right, because you've got it all figured out," Kate snapped, her arms across her chest. "Except that your business is failing and instead of dealing with it, instead of trying something new, you're giving up and selling your house to Leeper."

Miles laughed and the noise sounded unnatural amid the taut air, like a broken bone sticking out from flesh. "You can't believe everything Goldie tells you," he said to Kate, who ignored him.

"What are you even doing here?" she asked Ziggy. Sure, she'd broken the rules and Ziggy's trust, but so had he, and he'd done it first. How could he not have told her they were going to sell their house? That her parents were going to walk out their front door and see yet another Leeper monstrosity staring at them from across the street? How could he sell to the guy who'd chopped down his white oak? Who'd tried to bulldoze the library? If the Millers could sell out to Leeper, anyone could, and a lot of people would. The boys on the back of the bus had been right all along: Sea Point's inverted heart really would become America's ball sack.

Speechless, Ziggy turned to Miles. "We're selling the house because you never bothered to do the one thing I asked you to do."

Miles glanced at Kate, who looked as sick as he felt. He took a hard swallow. "I did look at the books. The day after I got them from your truck."

"What?" Ziggy's voice broke in disbelief.

"He took out a line of credit to pay for Yates," Miles said, adrenaline steering him to a place of calm. "The interest on the credit spiraled into a massive debt."

Released into the atmosphere, the truth quickly consumed all the oxygen in the room. Miles felt both sick and liberated. Unsure what to do, he kept going. "I didn't know how to tell you that Zeke owed over a hundred thousand dollars, and that as soon as you or Bev try to make a move with the house or the business, the bank would show up and demand their money, which is $116,709."

Ziggy stood there, trying to absorb the hit. Kate stared at her bare feet and wished she hadn't been so quick to have kicked off her heels. Meanwhile Miles studied his best friend and realized that, all this time, he had been wrong in his calculations.

If Miles hadn't known Ziggy pronounced "lilac" as "lilock," and was right-handed but left-footed; that he loved mystery novels and HGTV, he might not have noticed the way Ziggy's eyes didn't flicker at the sum but darted at Kate. If Miles didn't know that Ziggy Miller preferred his bananas still a little green and that he blushed if deploying even the palest of white lies, then Miles wouldn't have clocked how Ziggy's nostrils flared at the words "massive debt," or that his neck had turned into a patchwork of red when Miles had said "Yates."

And that's when Miles saw what he'd overlooked all summer: It was the same combination of subtle physical clues that had made them the Richard Brothers in the hockey rink. Miles understood his best friend better than anyone, and it was their connection that made Ziggy seem like a stranger as they stood in the living room of Daffodil Cottage and stared at each other. All the truths of their friendship allowed Miles to see the lie.

"You knew," Miles said, his voice as flat as the ocean on a windless morning.

"Knew what?" Kate asked, confused.

"You knew," Miles repeated, gaining momentum, his hands curling into fists.

Ziggy scratched his eyebrow as he stared at the ground. "I didn't know what to do," he finally said. "And I knew you would. I knew you'd figure something out. But then you didn't." Ziggy dropped his arms to his sides, resigned to his own confession, and Kate finally understood what they were talking about: Ziggy had always been aware of Zeke's debt.

"I'd know what to do?" Miles fumed. "You mean, like, write a check?" Miles asked. The thing was, Kate realized as Miles spoke, that he would have. If Ziggy had asked, Miles would have done it in a heartbeat. After spending the summer with Miles at the Wharf and Ziggy on their walk-offs, she knew they'd do anything for each other, just like she would do anything for Georgina. Or Bernadette. Even if they weren't speaking right now, if Bernadette needed her, Kate would jump through any ring of fire to help her.

But Ziggy never asked. Ziggy followed. He endured. He suffered in silence and waited for the wind to change, Leeper to offer, the bank to forget. Kate wanted to kill him.

"I can't help someone unwilling to help himself," Miles delivered like a clean upper cut. "It's like you never grew up. You just stayed here and got to hang out with your dad all day, and then he dies, and instead of facing the fucking facts, you dump all those stupid books into my lap and hope that I'll make the problems go away." Miles sat down on the white sofa. He took a long sip of beer in an otherwise suffocating silence and then, either encouraged by the hops or a fresh wave of anger, he jumped back on his feet.

Outrage stretched Miles vertically, so that, even from several feet away, he seemed to tower over Ziggy as he continued to process the night's revelations aloud. He took a long sip of beer in an otherwise suffocating silence. "Newsflash: I'm not a magician, or your sugar daddy, or the fucking Godfather. I'm your friend. Or, at least—this is a lot of shit, Ziggy, it really is. All you had to do was grow up and ask. Instead, you dump books in my lap and sneak girls in here like it's your house—yeah, I've seen you, buddy. Not quite as stealthy as you thought you were—'*Welcome to my humble home*' my ass."

Each sentence hit like a string of punches, making Ziggy's ears ring. He could barely breathe but he had to make it stop, he had to shut Miles up, and now Kate knew about the girls, and it was enough, enough, enough. He had no doubt that he'd regret pitching this one, but he did it anyway. The night was already torched. Ziggy looked at Miles, then to Kate, and then back to Miles. "You never even told her about Bernadette, did you?"

The air, thick with new information and pulsing with resentment, felt like a fourth presence in the living room of Daffodil Cottage.

"What about Bernadette?" Kate asked, but it wasn't a question.

His eyes locked on Ziggy, Miles addressed Kate. "He's just trying to change the subject."

"What about Bernadette?" Kate asked again, her voice rising.

Miles sighed, annoyed, and reached for his beer before looking at Kate. "It's not a big deal," he said, rolling his eyes like Kate was nagging him. "We had a thing forever ago. It doesn't matter."

"Except that you're still obsessed with her," Ziggy interjected. "And you took Kate tonight only to get Bernadette's attention."

"What is wrong with you!" Miles bellowed, standing up and taking a step toward Ziggy. "Just because you're miserable doesn't mean you can drag everyone down with you. This isn't how you treat your friends!"

"What would you know about friends?" Kate said, confusing both of them. Turning to look at Ziggy, she enunciated each word. "He told me about the debt forever ago—a few days after he went through the books."

"What?" Ziggy asked, feeling dizzy. The hits kept coming.

"He figured out Zeke's line of credit for Yates and told me that he wasn't sure what to do about it," Kate ranted. "And I went along with it because I assumed he'd eventually screw up the courage to tell you. Instead, he just picked up more hours to avoid you. We didn't need him behind the bar—or in the kitchen, for that matter. As always, the Wharf is overstaffed. He wasn't helping his mom, he was helping himself."

"Nice," Miles said, shooting Kate a look so disgusted, she knew in that moment they'd never be friends again. Miles backed away from her and returned to his seat on the couch, covering his face with his hands.

"So you knew all summer too?" Ziggy asked, looking at Kate. "You knew how trapped I was and you never once thought to talk to me about it? And now you're here, indicting me for thinking about selling my parents' house because I have no trust fund"—here he turned to glare accusingly at Miles before returning his icy gaze to Kate—"and no father who knew that Yates was too expensive. No father who is still alive, still working, with health benefits and a retirement plan. I don't have any of that, Kate. But you want to be pissed at me for thinking about selling to Harry Leeper instead of letting this debt bury me alive?"

Silence reverberated against the walls as the three of them reeled, struggling to process. After several beats in which Kate could hear her heart in her ears, she watched as Ziggy stood up and walked toward the front door. "Good luck getting what you want," he said to the water ring on the coffee table. He twisted the knob and Kate could hear the trees rustling outside like concerned neighbors, tittering about all that noise coming from Daffodil Cottage. Miles reached for his beer as he and Kate listened to Ziggy speed down the driveway in reverse, a cloud of seashell ash rising in his wake.

"Is that true?" Kate finally asked, her voice warily testing itself, like an ice skater inching out on a frozen lake. "About Bernadette?"

"Jesus, Kate."

"When?"

"Does it matter?"

"Yeah, to me it does." She gritted her teeth. "Ziggy was right—you were using me."

"We used each other."

Kate's mouth puckered as she stared at her full beer bottle, and she imagined hurling it at Miles. Of course he'd used her for her sister.

"Ziggy was right about you too, you know," Miles said slowly, standing up and taking his time buttoning his tuxedo jacket, slipping his phone into his pocket. "You've been having this pity party since you came back, like Thomas robbed you of his family fortune, which is just like how I remember you from high school." A mix of embarrassment and surprise forced Kate to look at him—did he remember that time in front of Ziggy's house, all the boys in the red Jeep?

Miles laughed to himself and the sound pricked her skin. "I was in a different grade, at a different school, and I knew your PSAT score because that's how much you bullhorned about yourself," he continued. "It's like you ran your own publicity campaign to ensure everyone knew you deserved to be at Yates."

Kate reached for the beer bottle on the coffee table, but instead of throwing it at Miles's head, she walked to the kitchen and poured out the contents, rinsing the basin of the sink so it wouldn't smell like old hops. Miles watched her as she kept her back to him. Eventually, Kate turned the water off but refused to turn around and face him.

"That's the thing that pisses me off about you, Kate," Miles sneered before tipping up his own beer bottle and drinking the rest of it in three long pulls. He wiped his mouth with the back of his hand. "If Ziggy had the Mosby name and the Mosby money, you would have been all over him this summer. But you want the rich dude in the Porsche and, you know what, you're welcome for delivering that guy on all fronts tonight."

Kate stared down at her trembling hands on the edge of the sink. She wanted to hit him and she wanted to cry and she wanted him to take it back, say that he didn't mean it. But Miles meant it, and they both knew it.

Dennis and Bell

Miles fluffed the cushions of the white sofa where he had briefly sat as the night had turned to shit. He returned the coasters to their stack, collected Kate's beer bottle from next to the sink, turned out the lights, locked the front door to Daffodil Cottage, and returned the spare key to its rightful place under the conch shell. *Everything has a home,* Kate had said his first day at the Jetty Bar. Walking down the driveway to his car, Miles took out his phone with purpose.

Ziggy told Kate about us, he texted Bell.

She hadn't answered all summer. But now he saw those heart-palpitating dots. Based on her slew of rhetorical questions punctuated with expletives, Bernadette was not pleased. He asked if he could come over and explain, and he was not entirely surprised when she said yes — there was a code when it came to sisters.

Bernadette Campbell opened her front door holding two mugs of chamomile tea. She wore a plain white V-neck T-shirt that barely made it over her pregnant stomach, plaid blue boxers that undoubtedly belonged to her husband, and a familiar expression of annoyance that Miles still read as a love letter. She looked exhausted and frustrated and adorable—the way she'd looked the entire time they'd secretly dated the summer after his senior year of high school.

"What seems to be the problem, officer?" Bernadette asked, sitting down on her front stoop and offering Miles one of the mugs. She spoke in the distinct tone of an old friend who happened to know what he looked like naked and which scene in *Homeward Bound* always made him cry. Bernadette smiled and Miles surrendered to what she'd been to him, what she'd always be—that door closed, no feet on the floor, love deeply, heal slowly kind of love.

"So were you just up at two a.m.," Miles started. "Waiting for me to text you?"

Bernadette rolled her eyes. "I put my ringer on in case Kate needed me."

Except for the briefest of interactions—from across the packed church at Zeke's funeral, in the crowded Campbell house during Kate's birthday, and on the lawn after Rock Star Readers—Miles and Bernadette hadn't seen or spoken to each other in almost two decades. He'd texted her sporadically—from San Francisco, from Chloe's bed, and all the girls' beds before Chloe's—but she'd never responded except once, many years ago, to say: *I'm engaged. Be good out there, Dennis the Menace.*

"You look beautiful," Miles said now, looking her in the eye.

Bernadette shook her head. "Let's skip your Jedi mind tricks, okay?"

"But you do."

"Is my sister okay?"

Miles nodded. "She had a great night up until about an hour ago."

"What happened an hour ago?"

"Too much for me to explain. But I need your help."

"No, you don't."

"I have no idea what I'm doing," Miles declared. "And the only thing I like doing is working in the kitchen and thinking about you."

"So go work in the kitchen," Bernadette said, ignoring the second part.

"Come on, Bell," Miles whined. "You're the only person I've ever loved."

"No, I'm the only person who's ever rejected you."

"See? You get me."

Bernadette sighed, but Miles saw she was smiling. After all this time, she still knew exactly who he was and she loved him anyway. Their connection was so clear, an embedded history as undeniable as handprints in wet cement. They had bonded the way you only get to once, the first time, before the past turns your trampoline heart into a bit of a minefield.

Twenty years earlier, Bernadette had returned to Sea Point after her junior year at Rutgers with one goal in mind: to make as much money as possible as a quench wench at the golf course. She had no time for Miles Hoffman and his crew of overfed jocks who had just graduated and were spending their summer day-drinking on the back nine and making jokes about the ball washer.

But then Miles's friend Trevor thought it would be funny to scatter hundreds of condoms in the rough and, as quench wench, it was Bernadette's job to collect them. As she crawled through the sand, alone and humiliated, she did a double take at the golf cart speeding toward her. Miles hopped out and was suddenly at her side, on his hands and knees, apologizing to her as he cleaned up the condoms, apparently too embarrassed to make eye contact. That was their only interaction for a few weeks, but every day on the green felt like a slow dance toward the inevitable until the Fourth of July, when the golf course hosted a members-only party and Bernadette signed up to work it because time and a half was time well spent.

Through the catered appetizers and divorcée flirtations, Miles kept Bernadette in his periphery, even after the fireworks began and everyone else looked toward the sky, which is why he saw Scooter Bennington pretend to lose his balance just as Bernadette was walking past with a tray of cotton candy. Scooter's hand was still mid-grope when Miles's fist connected with Scooter's weak chin and the middle-aged state senator went flying across the fairway, his loose neck fat wobbling like a turkey gobbler in slow motion, the fear in his eyes so bright that Bernadette could see it through the dark.

As Scooter threatened to press charges, Bernadette disappeared and locked herself in the employee bathroom. She knew coworkers had been assaulted in the past and that management hadn't done anything about it except put the employee on probation. It was part of her job, she'd signed up for it, hadn't she? Bernadette snuck out to her car without getting the okay from her boss and saw, to add insult to injury, a parking ticket on the windshield. Except that it wasn't a ticket; it was a note from Miles Hoffman saying in his cramped handwriting that he hoped she was okay, he'd looked everywhere for her, and here was his number just in case.

She called him that night and they met at the foot of the lighthouse, talking and not talking until sunrise, when they went to the Coffee Cow for pancakes during the hour when the diner was full of fishermen. Most things in life had come easily enough to Bernadette and Miles, prom king and queen at different schools in different years, but nothing had ever come as easily as the connection between them.

And then, after a whole summer together, Bernadette had asked Miles to meet her at the lighthouse and swiftly ended the relationship. "If we break up now, we can meet other people and stay friends," she'd explained through tears as he stood there, refusing the rejection. "We should slut it up and then marry each other."

"No," Miles had fought back. As the light above them rotated through the dark, Miles argued it would never work. "We love each other now, we should be together now." Bernadette relented, relieved to keep him and terrified to lose him, which is what happened a month later when hundreds of red roses were delivered to her apartment at Rutgers after Miles had cheated on her with a girl from his residential college and decided she was right, they should "slut it up." Bernadette had ignored him ever since, but over the years, her ice had melted into a fondness for the first boy she'd given her whole heart to, even if it had ended in disaster.

"What I have always liked about you," Bernadette said now, taking a sip of tea, "is that despite how much you try to hide it, you like to work hard. You just tend to do it for the wrong reasons." Miles shrugged and pressed his palms against the cool wood of Bernadette's porch floor. Leaning back on her elbows, Bernadette absently caressed her stomach and continued. "Even if you are the Prince of Sea Point, you're allowed to be hungry. You're allowed to want to prove yourself."

Miles nodded, turning an idea over in his head. "Have you heard of the CIA?"

Bernadette tried to hide her shock by gulping her tea. "You want to be a spy?"

"Close. Culinary Institute of America. Natalie went there—the chef at the Wharf."

"Interesting," Bernadette said, patting his knee before struggling to her feet. "Well, you can certainly afford some trial and error in the name of happiness, which might just be the greatest of all your many privileges." After taking in a deep breath of sea air, Bernadette announced she was going back to bed.

"Can I come with you?" Miles was mostly kidding—Bernadette was markedly pregnant, after all. "I can give you a prenatal massage—strictly platonic."

"He knows you're here," Bernadette said so coolly that Miles winced. She ruffled his hair. "If you want to be happy, go be happy."

Bernadette held out her hand for his mug and told him to go home. They'd never be anything, but there'd always be love there. Timing wasn't important when it came to relationships—timing was everything, and theirs had been off. Miles heard her bolt the door from the inside and tried not to take offense. She was right, he should go home, but instead, Miles stayed on Bernadette's front porch and watched the sunrise bloom through the trees before getting in his car and driving to the place where he belonged.

Pedialife

The sun was already high in the sky when Kate's bedroom door swung open to reveal no one. The door thwacked against the wall, waking her up, but no one entered. Instead, Bernadette stood in the safety of the hallway. From a distance, she found Kate's bloodshot eyes amid the gutter of her face, where mascara, tears, sparkly eye shadow, liquid eyeliner, and dried sweat had swirled together in an interesting design that Bernadette knew better than to comment on.

"I'm sorry and I brought you breakfast," Bernadette announced from the neutral zone, holding up a white paper bag from the Coffee Cow and a liter of Pedialyte.

Despite the gong in her head and lead in her bones, Kate dug up the strength to lift her arm and summon the delivery closer. She had no words for her sister and, even if she did, her mouth was so dry it felt taut with cobwebs. Bernadette twisted the top off the Pedialyte and handed the bottle to her sister, who took it without making eye contact.

"It was a long time ago," Bernadette said, standing next to the bed while Kate sat up to guzzle electrolytes.

"Sure was," Kate croaked. She shoved her hand into the bag and withdrew the egg and cheese supreme that might save her. "You should have told me."

"You were seventeen. We weren't, you know, equals. Friends. You were stressed about applying to college."

"Ziggy knew," Kate said. "Everyone knew except me."

Buying time, Bernadette looked down at her lap. She felt older than her thirty-eight years but also childish for having been caught. "Ziggy only knew because he saw us once. And I told Rob when he and I got serious. And now you, obviously."

"I love how your big life secret is that you dated a male-model millionaire."

"He never actually modeled—can you move over?"

Kate groaned and rolled over. The sisters lay on their backs, next to each other, staring at the ceiling fan as it rotated the thick August air.

"The embarrassing thing," Bernadette exhaled, "is that I loved Miles Hoffman. Like, legitimately, first-love loved him."

"I bet he couldn't write poetry like Derek Urgar."

"Oh Derek," Bernadette sighed. "To be clear, I love Rob, I love my family, I love being at this point in my life. But that history with Miles—it's complicated in a dangerously sentimental, alternative-universe, disgustingly romantic kind of way."

"Speak slow and in small words, please."

"It's pretty weird to work your ass off for years only to then become a mom," Bernadette said. "The skill set doesn't transfer and your new client is your only client, and she's never grateful, never impressed by anything except your milk production, which, in case you forgot, was not my forte."

"What's that got to do with Miles?" Kate asked.

Bernadette drew in her breath and twisted her mouth like she did whenever she was working out a problem in her head. "These days, I spend most of my time hanging out with Clementine, who is more or less a belligerent drunk that I created." She sighed, resigned to her lot. "And that toddler, who still pees her pants at least once a week, determines when I get to take a shower and also has the nerve to dictate my social circle. If she likes Claire, I've got to spend two hours on Saturday with Claire's mom. If she suddenly doesn't like Claire, bye-bye Claire's mom. It's all very weird, motherhood, how it fucks with your identity. Or maybe it's just getting older, I don't know. Even just trying to make a new friend in your thirties is way more nerve-racking than dating in your twenties."

"I haven't made a single new friend since I've been back," Kate confessed.

Bernadette shimmied under Kate's soft bedsheet. "And then, boom, Miles shows up and sends these flirty texts that allow me to pretend I'm still that cool girl with all that self-possessed agency, all that—I dunno—potential energy that single women zing around with. There's a real lightness to that existence—the one you have now—even if it doesn't feel like it. You have so much freedom."

Kate chanced a look at her sister out of the eye that felt less like a sinkhole. "Janis Joplin says freedom's just another word for nothing left to lose."

"And Ludacris says the grass is always greener."

Kate fought back a laugh but relinquished a small smile. "So you were having an emotional affair with Miles all summer?"

Bernadette shook her head. "I never responded to the texts. I told Rob about them, even showed them to him because I was aware of how much I liked the attention and it scared me. But I didn't block his number. I didn't tell him to stop. And then when he told me you'd invited him to the wedding, it exposed my own insecurities, and you're right, I should have told you. I'm sorry."

"But? I know there's a but."

"But I still think going to the wedding alone would have been a better idea. It's two separate issues. I think I saw you taking Miles as a failing on my part."

"You? How?"

Bernadette let out a heavy sigh, reached into the white paper bag, and withdrew a crabby fry. Without letting on, Kate marveled at her sister's impeccable ordering skills. "When you came back, you were a shell of yourself, but I knew we'd build you back up, and by the Fourth of July, I thought you'd gotten to this great place—everything you'd done at the library, basically running the Jetty Bar, cutting your hair even though Thomas liked it long, spending all that time with Ziggy, an actually decent guy. You've been busy but also, at least from my perspective, happier than you ever were in New York. But then this silly wedding—"

"I did the *Freaky Freakazoid* dance in front of everyone."

"Miles told me you were amazing," Bernadette said.

"And I made up with Georgina," Kate added triumphantly.

"Jesus. Well, you missed two colossal Clementine temper tantrums, so there. How's Georgina?"

"Really good. I wish I'd reached out years ago."

"See, that's my whole point!"

Kate closed her eyes and rubbed her temples, as Bernadette's voice ricocheted inside her brain. "What's your point?" she asked.

"Georgina, unlike Thomas, is worth fighting for," Bernadette declared like it was her courtroom opening statement. "*That's* a love worth fighting for. The only time Georgina has hurt you was in the name of holding you accountable. Thomas, on the other hand, wanted you to be someone else and, worse yet, he made *you* want to be someone else. And I know you think coming home has been one long exercise in regression, but trust me, you've grown up more in the last four months, living at home, than you ever did while playing house with him in the West Village."

"What's that got to do with feeling like you failed me?"

"Kate," Bernadette said, rolling onto her side to face her sister, "listen to me. You are my favorite person. You're Clementine's favorite person. You're Ziggy's favorite person if you'd just open your eyes to it."

Kate nodded as Bernadette combed the short pieces of hair out of her face with her fingers. "I wish you could see you the way I see you," Bernadette whispered. "You know you're my best friend, even if I didn't tell you about Miles when you were sobbing on the couch about what to write for your personal essays. But you've got to be your own favorite person before anyone else can take care of you, even me."

Kate nodded.

"Come on, you need to sit up," Bernadette said.

"I will."

"No, now, because Mom's going to freak out about that."

Kate sat up and saw that her tears had collected in two shallow pools of black makeup on her mother's antique pillowcase.

"Hey," Bernadette said, perching her chin on Kate's shoulder. "How's Ziggy doing?"

"Oh my God!" Kate yelped, suddenly remembering. "Harry Leeper!"

Labor of Love

A week after the blowup at Daffodil Cottage, Ziggy was back at the scene of the crime, installing the last of his cabinets in the basement. The man cave was finally finished. He imagined his dad sitting back in one of the antigravity Japanese massage recliners and telling him it was a job well done. Instead, his dad was gone and Ziggy was so pissed at him that he kicked his tool bag across the floor. Completing a project of this magnitude was cause for celebration, but the only people who cared were in Italy, awaiting the bill, which he had yet to break down in order to add up. Assessing the cost of his work struck Ziggy as a quiet existential crisis: How did labors of love compute into dollars and cents?

Since the previous Saturday, Miles's meanest lines kept finding Ziggy in quiet moments—*you never ask for help; you just followed me around and then your dad*. Ziggy had spiraled until he'd climbed into his truck on Monday morning only to find Bev already in the cab, waiting for him.

"I'm not getting out until you tell me what's going on," she'd said. They'd driven all over Sea Point, Ziggy's eyes on the road and his heart in his throat as he told Bev about the Yates debt, how Bernadette had discovered it back in February when she'd alerted Freedom Bank to Zeke's death, and Ziggy not dealing with it, and then the fight at Daffodil Cottage.

"Oh my," Bev sighed.

"That's all you have to say?"

Bev put up her hands in surrender. "We went through hell in February, and we're still in hell, which means owing a ton of money doesn't really scare me the way it would have before. Loss trumps debt, which is why I'm more concerned about you and Miles."

"He said I just followed Dad around."

"And?" Bev asked. Ziggy pulled up to a red light and looked over at his mother. "You did follow Zeke around. It's only an insult if you think it is—I bet Miles would have killed to follow Zeke around or, better yet, his own dad."

"He said I was passive, that I didn't ask for help."

Bev nodded thoughtfully. "Well, you didn't ask him and you didn't ask me, so I think he has a valid point. But who cares?" At Ziggy's pained expression, Bev elaborated: "Just because you didn't before doesn't mean you can't now. Growing up is just one long effort to course-correct the best you can."

And so Ziggy had taken the first step.

Todd and Barry had sounded overjoyed when Ziggy called SeaSalt Inn and asked if he could take Barry up on his offer for a bit of money advice. The two of them had sat at the bed-and-breakfast's immense dining room table while Todd scurried about and tried to ply Ziggy with a blueberry pie still warm from the oven.

"QuickBooks is a solid choice," Barry said, licking his blueberry-stained fingers before opening his laptop. "But after you called, I did a bit of research, and there are a few great programs designed specifically for plumbers and general contractors that I thought we could look into as well."

Barry's casual use of "we" landed squarely in Ziggy's chest. He hadn't been part of a we since February. It was the aural equivalent of a hug he desperately needed, and as Barry showed him a few different accounting programs and explained what he'd found to be the positives and hang-ups of each one thus far, Ziggy felt that old flutter from the Acme checkout line before recognizing it as hope. For the first time in a long time, he thought he might be okay.

"They're here!" Kate announced to Patricia in her office. The proposals Kate had submitted to the board had fallen on receptive ears, and now the woman from FedEx wheeled in four brand-new computers for public use. Even more exciting and thanks to an anonymous suggestion from the suggestion box, the library would launch a paid internship program next year, when six Sea Point High School juniors would earn a generous stipend to spearhead their own community-centered initiatives. At the end of the summer, Patricia would offer her extensive professional network to the interns, just as she'd done for Kate. White girls with a BA in self-righteousness wouldn't be the only ones getting a leg up anymore.

After a *New York Times* reporter learned of the Harry Leeper battle, the paper ran a feel-good piece titled, "The Little Library That Could," which mentioned the future internship program and encouraged other libraries to do the same. The press was gratifying but it was the work of developing the program itself that kept Kate moving and exhilarated as August charged on. In fact, she was so excited about providing a launch point for her fellow Sea Point herons that Kate almost forgot that the summer was ending.

"I swear these fancy poodles won't turn on until you buy them dinner," Patricia said now, intimidated by the sleek laptops. Kate laughed and showed her the power button. "Don't get too high and mighty with me just yet," Patricia said. "I've got news."

After their fight in Daffodil Cottage, it was easy for Miles and Kate to ignore each other at work. There was no dignity in August, not even for a

Prince. Each moment was a grueling quest to survive, an ongoing test of human strength, will, and courage. Miles called August the Blackout because he would wake up each morning and have no idea what he'd done the night before—and then he'd get up and do it again.

The Blackout was made all the more horrific because halfway through a Saturday-night humdinger in the middle of August, Miles realized with the same confidence with which he now shucked that he was not only in love with cooking but also the cook. Somewhere between the 500-degree flames and the freezing walk-in refrigerator, he'd fallen hard for Chef and, true to her name, NOtalie was having none of it.

After watching the sunrise from Bernadette's front porch, Miles had driven straight to the Wharf kitchen and sharpened his knives before taking out his phone and looking up the application for the Culinary Institute of America. He'd never felt as giddy as he did standing alone at his station, composing the application's required Statement of Purpose in his head. And then Natalie had walked in, unrolled her knives in preparation of her daily gutting, and all he could think about was how he wanted to be her sous-chef for life.

It made sense for all of these epiphanies to occur during the Blackout, because the Blackout was the love child of bonkers and bananas, which was why Miles looked up and realized Zeke's Rock the Boat was a week away and he hadn't spoken to Ziggy in nearly a month. He had seven days to make things right and tomorrow wasn't good enough—he would get to work on it today.

Turtled

Five days before his father's Rock the Boat party, Ziggy knew he didn't have time but he went anyway. On the drive out of town, he counted three new HARRY LEEPER CONSTRUCTION signs and considered using his chain saw to cut them in half. But it wouldn't do any good. Leeper had won. Sea Point was becoming something else. There was no point in trying to keep up and so he wouldn't. He'd call Clyde at Ocean City Plumbing and pray they wanted to buy out MVP. Barry thought OCH would bite, but he also said there was a path forward if Ziggy was willing to consider some unconventional ideas about how to keep MVP afloat. But Ziggy wasn't willing. The year had been hard enough, Ziggy had determined, and the last thing he needed was to risk further failure. If OCH made a respectful offer, Ziggy would take the money.

He and Bev could sell the house to Leeper and move somewhere else, start over. He'd heard good things about Asheville, or maybe Portland, Oregon, or maybe he'd go international for a while, go see all the things his dad had never seen, listen to his favorite musicians live. The future would require a sit-down conversation with Bev, but she was doing better now that she'd started painting again. Life was devastating and heartbreaking and hard, but it was buoyed by love and dappled with both comic relief and joy where you least expected it. With enough sunlight and the right angle, shattered glass always glittered.

Paddling out in the canoe, Ziggy wondered how long this place would exist; how long before Harry Leeper and his kind found the legal language and deep pockets to redevelop the Pine Barrens. A year? Five years? And when Leeper kicked the bucket, someone else would climb into the backhoe, turn over the ignition, and keep on going. The campaign of concrete was the myopic story of humankind but it was no longer Ziggy's problem. He was done.

The Mullica River buzzed with life and so Ziggy ignored the first splash, assuming it was an osprey diving into the water for breakfast. But the splashes continued, and grew louder, which is when he craned his neck and saw Miles gliding toward him in a sleek orange kayak.

"Ahoy, asshole!" Miles shouted, holding up his paddle and startling a pair of mallards.

"What are you doing here?"

Miles ignored him and looked up at the sky. "I had a dream about your dad last night. Woke up crying. Went to your house to apologize but the truck wasn't there so I checked Bev's shed, saw the canoe was missing, Sherlocked my way here."

"Whose kayak?"

"Jo Hoffman's," Miles said.

"What do you want?" Ziggy stared at Miles's hands on his oar, unable to make eye contact.

"Look, Zig, I'm sorry," Miles said, pleading with his whole face. "I'm really sorry things got so out of control."

In the silence that followed, the water dripping off the oars fell like sand in an hourglass.

"It's like you enjoyed watching me struggle," Ziggy said, watching the drops. "I mean, you told Kate instead of coming to me." He looked up and met Miles's gaze. "You said you wanted to help but you came back to prove to your mom that you're not your dad and to prove to Bernadette that she should have picked you, and meanwhile you kept pushing me off as I begged for your help and—"

"Excuse me?" Miles interrupted. "Begged for my help? More like dumped a bunch of books in my lap and assumed I'd figure it out, when you already had and you couldn't just say it. How different would this summer have been if you'd just said, straight-up, one, Zeke messed up, two, we're in debt, three, I need you to help me figure this out—instead of hoping I'd just pay it off behind your back and make everything bad go away."

"That's not true." Without looking at Miles, Ziggy began to paddle back to shore. Of course, one man in a kayak can move far faster than one man in a canoe built for two. Miles beat him to dry land.

"Look, we both messed up," Miles insisted from the riverbank, speaking quickly because soon Ziggy would no longer be a hostage in a boat. "I should have told you about the books and you shouldn't have waited for me to tell you. But the stuff with my mom—"

"Dude, you're thirty-four. Don't you think it's time you stop blaming your mom?"

Miles looked like he'd been slapped across the face. "Fuck you."

Ziggy's laugh was more of a snarl. "You're the Prince of Sea Point. You roam the Earth saying 'fuck you' and then you're mad when no one takes you seriously. Especially Bernadette—or either Campbell for that matter. You're cheap entertainment for both of them—always were, always will be."

Ziggy had finally reached the shore, and he stepped past Miles to pull the canoe onto the riverbed. As he did, he felt the air buzz just in time to see a body in motion as Miles lunged at him. Tripping backward over the red canoe, both men stumbled in ungraceful slow-motion before landing with a splash in the river. Miles emerged first and jumped on top of Ziggy, punching him in the gut. Ziggy gasped and then managed to swing at

Miles's face, connecting with his cheekbone in an obliterating punch that knocked Miles into deeper water, his feet no longer able to touch the bottom. Miles held his breath, waiting for another blow, but suddenly Ziggy was gone. Touching his hand to his face, Miles's cheek came out to meet him, already swollen. He looked behind him and didn't see Ziggy, just the stern of the red canoe before it disappeared, the current carrying it around the bend at a clip. And then Ziggy's head popped up five yards away, swimming with urgent strokes after the canoe. Miles launched himself off a rock and followed the canoe down the river.

Several minutes later, gasping for air, the boys held the canoe with one hand and treaded water with the other. "I really don't like to think about what's in here," Miles confessed.

"Snakes," Ziggy said.

"Shouldn't we just get in?"

"No paddles," Ziggy grunted. "They're back where you ambushed me." He rocked the side of the canoe toward him and Miles followed suit. Using all their strength, they tipped the canoe until it turtled. The boys ducked under water and reemerged inside the hollow space where they normally sat.

On the slow journey back to shore, neither Ziggy nor Miles said a word as they blindly fought the current in unison. They kicked and they kicked. Finally, their feet could touch the ground. They took a deep breath and left the dark hollow of the upturned boat before emerging back in the vibrant world to which they belonged.

Warm summer air greeted them as Ziggy and Miles silently lifted the red canoe onto their pallbearing shoulders and carried it to the MVP truck. They worked to load it and then returned to the riverbank. At the water's edge, they sat until the sunlight faded behind the trees. Together, as brothers, they grieved.

Legacy

Billy Croce picked up his house phone on the fourth ring and was so surprised to hear Ziggy's voice that he choked on his peanut butter and jelly sandwich.

"I'm sorry I bailed on the fireworks," Ziggy said. "Can I stop by?"

When he wasn't traveling internationally, Billy lived in the slipshod bungalow he grew up in, among the pines that he and Zeke ran through as kids. The front door was a peeling dark green that Ziggy thumbed with interest before the door swung open.

"To what do I owe the honor?" Billy asked, hugging his godson.

After a quick tour of the small house Ziggy hadn't stepped in for decades, Billy led him through the kitchen and out to the back porch, where the corrugated roof was thick with mold but kept the rain off the two brown La-Z-Boy chairs that looked out on the looming woods. Billy tossed Ziggy a beer and invited him to sit down in the slightly newer-looking of the two recliners.

"Did you know my dad was in debt?" Ziggy blurted out.

Billy's eyebrows alone proved that he did not. "Debt?" Billy asked. "From what?"

"Yates."

Billy nodded at his beer, fiddled with the metal tab.

"He hid a hundred-thousand-dollar debt from me," Ziggy said, taking a long swig. "And technically I was his business partner."

Leaning back in his chair, Billy stretched out his legs, visibly weighing his words. "Sure, but you were also technically his son."

"Either way," Ziggy muttered, "I'm dealing with the fallout."

Billy took a deep breath and tapped his fingers on his armrest. "I know he was old school about those accounting books and, I mean, let's face it, Zeke wasn't much of a businessman since he barely charged his friends, and he had a lot of friends. But as your dad, he had one job—I know because he told me so himself—and that was to give you better options—a bigger life—than what we had."

Staring into the trees, Ziggy said, "Well, since he's not here, I was hoping I'd get your blessing to sell MVP to Ocean City HVAC. They made a decent offer to buy it—or acquire it, I guess is the business term for it."

Billy chuckled as he looked over at Ziggy. "Do you want my blessing or my help?"

For thirty-four years, the only person Ziggy had felt comfortable asking for help was his dad. But Zeke was gone and Billy was here.

"Help," Ziggy mustered after several beats. "I'm asking for your help."

The thing about a small town is that it tends to get smaller the older you get. Joey the barback waved to Ziggy as soon as he entered the Coffee Cow, where they'd arranged to meet the following Monday—Labor Day. After Goldie delivered two coffees, Joey launched into the business pitch he'd perfected over the last two years at Tech before Ziggy cut him off. I'm sorry," he said, "but I just don't understand how a certificate in sustainable energy is going to help me."

"It's a certificate in HVAC and sustainable energy," Joey corrected him. "So I already know a thing or two about heating, ventilation, and air-conditioning—most of the stuff you do on a daily basis."

"Okay, so—"

"But it's not just me," Joey interrupted. "I've teamed up with some friends I met at Tech—one does computer stuff and the other does business marketing stuff—we're trying to take on Ocean City HVAC." At the prospect, Joey beamed devilishly and Ziggy laughed.

"Then what do you need me for?"

"Your name." At Ziggy's confused look, Joey elaborated. "It's hard to launch a brand-new business without any built-in credibility. Everyone around here knows and trusts MVP."

Ziggy nodded slowly. His dad and grandfather had sacrificed so much for that legacy, Ziggy's true inheritance, and he'd almost squandered it all at Daffodil Cottage. It still made him shudder to think of all the fallout if he'd ever been caught, all the trust lost. Despite his misfortunes, Ziggy knew he was lucky.

"Billy told me about the debt," Joey said, withdrawing a professional-looking binder from his satchel. "This is the business model and here are the cash-flow projections I've been working on for the last six months— I thought I could walk you through them, if you're interested. The plan is tight enough and the numbers are sound enough that I've actually got a few different banks competing for the business line of credit—we'll go with whoever comes up with the lowest interest rate, and I'm confident we can roll the outstanding balance into that line of credit."

There it was again, Ziggy thought: We.

He flagged Goldie for more coffee and tried to harness the wings in his chest. Joey's plan was more comprehensive than he could have hoped for. "So what would I do, besides let you use the company name?"

"I don't have my license as a master plumber or half the certifications you have."

"Oh." Ziggy felt an unfamiliar swell of pride.

"Which is why you'd be, joking aside, the MVP of MVP," Joey said, smiling. "And we'd need to compensate you for it—I figure you'd get a signing bonus and your first year's salary up front—we could roll it into the loan from the bank."

The number Joey scrawled on the corner of a syrup-stained napkin was several times larger than what Ziggy had expected. He snarled, "I don't need your charity."

Joey stared down at the counter and scratched his ear nervously. Like Ziggy, he had a propensity for blushing. "You know, if your dad hadn't died—"

"We'd be the competition?" Ziggy quipped facetiously.

Goldie arrived with a fresh pot of coffee and a warning look that told Ziggy to ease up and listen to what the kid, who wasn't a kid anymore, had to say.

"Not quite." Joey squirmed on his barstool. "Look, you know I work with Kate, right? At the Jetty Bar?"

Ziggy focused his eyes on the silver tines of his unused fork, not liking where this was going. He and Kate hadn't spoken since Daffodil Cottage a month ago. He didn't know if she was still going to come to his dad's Rock the Boat party the next day. He didn't even know if he wanted her to.

"She told me about how you and your dad renovated Daffodil Cottage and the other places around town," Joey said. "I was thinking, we could expand MVP so that it was plumbing and HVAC but also general contracting. We could give Harry Leeper a run for his money, except we'd actually do solid work—like what you and your dad did at Daffodil Cottage. You've got the experience and the trusted name; I've got the banks competing to give me money, a hunger for this thing to succeed, and enough business savvy from Tech to navigate the launch—"

Ziggy looked out the window at his bustling town on the last busy day of the summer. He closed his eyes and wondered what his dad would want him to do. Joey had clearly thought this through—he had an immediate plan and goals for the future. It was impressive. Overwhelming but impressive and, if Ziggy was honest with himself, exciting: It would be a dream to do more projects like Daffodil Cottage.

"What I was trying to say before, about your dad, if he hadn't died," Joey said, cutting through Ziggy's thoughts with choppy nervousness, "it's just . . . I really admired him."

Ziggy nodded. "Thanks."

"Yeah, but—well, so"—Ziggy looked over and saw Joey searching the counter for words—"I used to cut school a lot," Joey said, squinting at the memory. "In high school. And one time I was walking out of the Wawa when I should have been in class, and your dad was like, 'Get in the truck.'"

Ziggy leaned forward, hungry for any story about his father.

"And I was a punk for sure but I wasn't dumb enough to say no to Zeke Miller, so I got in the truck, and we ended up just driving around for a while, talking about nothing and everything, my siblings, the Phillies, he was kind of obsessed with some instrument from Zimbabwe? And then, well, so, the thing is—"

"Joey, for the love of God, spit it out."

"I guess what makes this feel full circle," Joey said, sitting up straight on his barstool, "is that when he dropped me back off at school, your dad said that when I got my degree, he'd give me a job."

Ziggy let the idea sink in.

"I'm not trying to be dramatic, but I've thought about it a lot," Joey continued, "and it's kinda like he'd always planned for us to work together."

Rock the Boat

The Tuesday after Labor Day Weekend, a conga line of cars pulled up to the ferry's loading dock. Kate sat in the back of her parents' car with Bernadette, Clementine, and three freezer bags full of mint chocolate chip ice cream, nervous to see Ziggy but knowing she had to go. She couldn't miss Zeke's Rock the Boat.

Behind the Campbells, Miles and Jo sat in her black Range Rover with several thousand dollars' worth of seafood and alcohol in various coolers. Behind them were Gus and Gertie in the '89 blue Volvo that Gus kept in perfect condition, and behind them were Georgina, Liza, and Dr. Kim on bicycles, talking to Goldie through the window of her old blue Honda, which was filled to capacity with coffee, cookies, pastries, and pie. Patricia and Chad rolled up in his beach cruiser, Louanne in a Fire Department Jeep, and Billy on his motorcycle. Todd and Barry arrived on foot with Rafael and Roger, the Great Danes of SeaSalt Inn, wagging their tails and proudly sporting faded yellow MILLER VALUES PLUMBING T-shirts.

Ziggy was already aboard, too busy with logistics to consider that this was his dad's final wish. After today, he didn't know what his dad wanted for him or Bev. But right now, there were speakers to blast, a boat captain to thank, and locals pulling into the packed parking lot, carrying cooler after cooler, as if his father's Rock the Boat were a town-wide holiday, which maybe it kind of was.

Bev had brought one painting aboard and hung it below the wheelhouse. It was a portrait of Zeke. Unlike most of Bev's work, there was nothing impressionistic or conceptual about it. He smiled back at her from the canvas, tickled as he'd been the day she'd woken up and decided to paint him for their twenty-sixth anniversary. The portrait wasn't an abstract corner of his face or a close-up of his forehead or the cleft of his chin. It was Zeke Miller, smiling back at her in his MVP work shirt. The portrait had been in the pile of paintings she'd stored in the shed, convinced they weren't good enough to live anywhere else. The blue behind Zeke's face was from that damn La-Z-Boy chair he insisted on sitting in, but no one had to know that. Bev felt a hand on her shoulder and assumed it was Ziggy, but it was Miles and Jo Hoffman, who stared past her at Zeke's likeness.

"Would you look at that," Jo gasped, with awe in her voice.

"Thanks for coming!" Bev mustered, her voice a little too high to sound authentic. It had been a tough morning in an impossible year. The loneliness had nearly pulled her under—some days it had, but ever since she'd picked up her paintbrush again, she could hear her husband say, "Atta girl," and so she kept going.

"Bev, my mom and I talked it over," Miles said, deep and formal. "And before this party gets started, we wanted to present you with an offer. You don't have to say yes right away, but please don't say no until you've really considered it."

Before Bev could find a proper response, Jo took over. "I understand and respect why you don't want to sell any of your paintings, I really do." Jo took a deep breath and stole another glance at Zeke's portrait. "But they are wonderful, Bev, truly, and we were hoping to share them with more of the community."

"What are you saying?" Bev asked. Locking eyes with Jo, she realized this was the most face-to-face interaction they'd had in decades, since the boys were small. She'd been intimidated by Jo for as long as she could remember, but now all Bev saw was a familiar struggle tugging at the corners of Jo's mouth. Learning to live was a lot like learning to paint: understanding shadow, exploring gradation, appreciating bright, fleeting light.

"I'm saying," Jo said gently, "it would be a great honor if you'd let me rent them from you, monthly, and display them at the Wharf. You could take them back whenever you wanted, and you would retain full ownership of them, but we could compensate you for sharing them with people who find your talent as staggering as we do."

"Oh," Bev said, astounded.

"We can discuss all this later," Jo continued, her eyes dancing with goodwill. "But knowing how proud of you Zeke was, today seemed like the right day to broach the subject."

"And for what it's worth," Miles interjected, "I think he'd want you to say yes."

Bev nodded, and this time when she felt a hand on her shoulder, she knew it was Ziggy. "Something to think about, huh?" he asked, grinning ear to ear. Ziggy looked more like Zeke every day, and it was both eerie and a comfort, those familiar blue eyes.

The crowd of locals clambered aboard, and Ziggy pressed "play" on his phone so the ferry lit up with music. Not only had Walter Beam trusted him with the theater company's speaker system for the day, but he'd even volunteered to set it up first thing this morning. Zeke couldn't be here and so all of his friends were—a compiled choir of voices, keys, strings, winds, and drums from every corner of the world. The playlist was thirty hours long, they wouldn't get through half of it, but Ziggy didn't care—he'd suffered enough loss without trying to cut any of his dad's favorite bands. Today they would traverse the Delaware Bay six times in three round-trip journeys to the soundtrack of his father's life.

Greg from the lumberyard appeared carrying several wood benches and arranged them in a circle. "For the storytelling portion of the program," he called over to Ziggy. "Well, storytelling and roasting. And I've got some roasts ready to go—did I ever tell you about your dad and the glue gun?"

"Avert your eyes!" Billy interrupted, yelling to Bev and Ziggy with the grin of a high school boy who'd gotten his hands on an illegal amount of fireworks. He and Greg rolled up a crate that looked quite similar to the cannister-filled crates Billy loaded onto the barge every Fourth of July.

Ziggy looked up and saw Kate, who was holding what looked like the entire Acme stock of mint chocolate chip ice cream in her arms. Before he could think of what to do, he watched her walk toward him with none other than Georgina Kim and a woman who was presumably her wife.

"Hey," Kate said sheepishly just as Georgina bum-rushed him with a hug.

"How's my favorite keeper?" Georgina asked, tussling Ziggy halfway to the ground because sports teammates were teammates for life. When Georgina allowed him to come up for air, Ziggy and Kate moved toward each other, and their limbs dovetailed in a hug neither had anticipated. "I'm sorry," Kate whispered into the crook of his neck, where shirt met skin. "I'm really sorry, Ziggy." They held on for a moment, and then another.

"It's okay." Before pulling away to greet the newest arrivals, Ziggy tousled Kate's short hair as a way to say they'd talk more later.

"Anchors aweigh in ten minutes, people!" Miles yelled. He'd scampered up the metal ladder and, at his announcement, everyone clapped and hollered. Amid the crowd, Jo watched him with pride. He'd approached her the day before about his attending CIA. She'd never seen him so excited—he said he dreamed of Shun knives, that he woke up depressed on his days off. Jo followed her son's gaze now, aware that he was running at full speed to greet a brunette carrying a tall stack of dishes, and Jo was more impressed than surprised to see Natalie Prezzo, her chef, who rolled her eyes at Miles's exuberance before ordering him to find serving spoons for the containers of antipasti stacked so high that they hid most of her face.

As usual, Kate was one step ahead of Miles and already inside the ferry's kitchen, wielding a pair of oversize tongs like a weapon as he approached.

"I'm sorry," Miles shouted at the sight of her. She walked toward him and snapped the tongs so that they nipped at his shirt, which inspired him to add, "I was a jackass."

Kate surprised him for the hundredth time that summer by saying, "So was I. Let's just—let's just be good to each other. And no more using."

"No more using," Miles agreed.

"Friends?" Kate asked, extending her hand.

"Good friends." Miles shook it, his eyes twinkling, and pulled her in for an anaconda hug.

The Rock the Boat ferry blasted its horn three times as it took off for Delaware. Somewhere among the waves, Ziggy grabbed Miles's arm and dragged him to an inside cabin. "I want you to meet Joey."

"Is this a joke?" Miles asked. "Joey's my barback—he will stick his hands *anywhere*."

"Correction," Ziggy said, putting his arm around Joey. "He *was* your barback, but now he's my business partner." As Joey and Ziggy worked in tandem to catch Miles up to speed on the future of MVP, Ziggy's heart felt like a pipe full of water on a freezing December day: ready to burst. He wished his dad were here to see how things were working out before realizing that he was.

Halfway through their first return to Sea Point, Miles rounded everyone up to commence the roast. "But before the roast, we toast," Miles shouted out, walking from person to person and distributing a new Rock the Boat mug. Miles had put the MVP logo where the year was usually prominently displayed, giving everyone aboard a way to have coffee with Zeke Miller for many mornings to come. Ziggy hugged his best friend for a long time before clinking his mug with Joey.

"To MVP," Ziggy said.

"To Zeke," Joey added.

The roast wasn't much of a roast at all. As funny as some stories were, the moral was always the same: Zeke helped me. He saw me, he was kind to me, and he fixed what needed fixing. On the second trip to Delaware, Miles insisted on a dance party like the one where Bev and Zeke had met, so that's what they did. They danced for their friend, with their friends. They moved their feet in time to the music because on this boat, on this day, no other time mattered.

The three round trips transpired in a tear-soaked blur. The collar of Ziggy's navy blue MVP T-shirt was stretched out from him using it to wipe his eyes—and he wasn't the only one. By the time the ferry left Delaware on its final trip home, all of its passengers had runny noses, bloodshot eyes, and heavy, happy hearts. After the sunset, Billy set off fireworks, lighting up the dark with a dazzle of color that Zeke would have loved. Standing next to his mother, Ziggy could hear Zeke whistle his approval. He was here, and he was hollering at his best friend to give them the best show yet. Billy must have heard him too because Ziggy saw him salute the stars right before he turned the night sky into Zeke's grand finale.

It was late when the ferry docked for the last time back in Sea Point. The revelers rallied to make fast work of unloading while Ziggy went around, thanking each person for coming. Bev passed by with her portrait of Zeke and a lightness in her step that Ziggy hadn't seen since the Before, but here it was in the After.

Bev and Ziggy drove home in exhausted silence. They sat at the kitchen table drinking room-temperature water out of their new MVP Rock the Boat mugs. Wholly depleted with their eyes half-closed, they kept remembering the best parts of the night. Retelling the stories from the boat kept a quiet energy pinging between them, a kind of hope for the future that they each silently feared would be gone in the morning. Bev would rent her paintings to the Wharf. Ziggy and Joey would grow out MVP to include building contracts, renovations, restorations, and remodeling jobs. They would keep the house and pay off the debt. They were going to be okay. Zeke had left them the tools to save themselves.

"I can't stay awake," Bev eventually confessed. As part of their nightly routine, she reminded Ziggy to lock up as she climbed the stairs to bed. Ziggy had just turned off the lights when he heard a knock.

Kate Campbell stood outside the front door, her eyes pleading as she asked, "Walk-off?"

Despite his body's silent yelp, his own desperate need for sleep, Ziggy called out to Bev that he'd be back in a bit.

"I'm sorry about Daffodil Cottage," Kate said once they were in the street.

"I know. It's okay," Ziggy said. They began to walk and then Ziggy stopped in his tracks. "But how did you know the code?"

Kate bit her lip, both embarrassed and proud. "You said it was built the same year the Bluebell opened and the *Titanic* sank and I just—it made sense that you and the owners would appreciate—the code would be— how do I put this?" Kate stopped stammering and closed her eyes as she collected her thoughts. "It made sense to celebrate the beginning as a way to honor how far it's come."

"That's a helluva guess. What if you'd been wrong?"

"It's not exactly like I was thinking straight," Kate said. "And along those lines, I'm sorry I asked Miles to the wedding instead of you."

"That—it doesn't matter."

Kate turned and faced Ziggy. "I just got a job offer at a publishing house in New York," she said, and began to walk again. "Of course they called today while I was on the ferry without reception."

"Whoa," Ziggy forced himself to say. "Congratulations."

"The wedding would have been more fun with you," Kate said before she could stop herself. They looked at each other and she shook her head. "I'm saying all of this in the wrong order." Her eyes were serious and a little sad as they stared off into the distance. "Today was really nice and, I don't know if you'll think this is strange, but I think your dad was there. Like, I *know* your dad was there."

"Yeah," Ziggy agreed, stuffing his hands into his pockets. "Me too."

They walked in silence until they reached the lighthouse and then they walked on, past the entrance of the nature preserve, the Leeper McMansion. Without saying a word, Kate hoisted herself up and sat on what remained of Ziggy's white oak. The stump was just tall enough that Kate's feet dangled off the ground and Ziggy remembered what she'd been like as a kid—quiet, obsessed with books, vicious in Scrabble.

"You know how turtles go in one direction their whole life?" Kate asked.

Ziggy nodded.

"Well, we're not turtles," Kate declared, her voice defiant, almost angry. "I never wanted to move back here," she said, her voice wavering in the quiet. "I was supposed to be a big-time editor, a New York success story from Podunk, New Jersey."

"That can still happen," Ziggy offered, stretching his calf on the edge of the curb.

"You're not getting it," Kate said, jumping off the stump and walking into the nature preserve. Ziggy swore this would be the night they encountered a skunk but said nothing so Kate would continue, which she did. "I got into Drexel's library science program too—Patricia knew the director and they pulled strings—and I'm going to do that instead of New York, and you know why?"

"Because you're not a turtle?" They were deep into the nature preserve now and Ziggy heard different creatures moving out of their way, scampering up trees and dipping into the marsh.

"Exactly," Kate huffed. "I'm allowed to change my mind about things, even really big things."

"So you're moving to Philly."

"It's not that far," Kate argued, and if they'd known each other a little less, Ziggy wouldn't have detected the nervous hitch in her voice. "I'll probably come back most weekends to help Bernadette with the baby and—"

Ziggy took a step toward Kate. He found her in the dark and let his hands sweep through her hair like he'd envisioned doing on every walk-off. He'd been a turtle for long enough, and so he cradled Kate's face in his hands and leaned in.

Her lips on his felt exactly like that airborne exhilaration Ziggy experienced right before he capsized the canoe, but also like collapsing in the sand after a morning of bodysurfing—profound satisfaction. Kissing her for the first time felt like the one time he'd gotten lost in the Pine Barrens and discovered a secret swimming hole. Everything about being this close to her was wonderful and terrifying and electrifying and the only thing he'd wanted all summer.

Ziggy pulled back to make sure the kiss was okay, they were okay, and Kate smiled as she hugged him tight. "Did you know herons have wingspans twice the size of their bodies?" Kate asked, as if they'd been in the middle of an ornithology discussion. "Your dad told me that the day I found out I couldn't go to Yates," she said, taking a step back to create space between them. "He stood in my front yard and said he'd gone to Sea Point High and that the cool thing about herons is that for how tiny they are, they have an incredible wingspan—up to six feet."

Ziggy let out a breath he'd been holding since February and heard it slow roll into a laugh as he watched Kate mimic Zeke's flying heron impression from all those years ago. She stretched her arms out to the sides and flapped them with big dramatic swoops. Between her own giggles, Kate tucked her chin into her neck and dropped her voice to sound like Zeke's: "They tuck their necks into an 's' shape, like this here," she gruffed, her body still flopping in motion. Cheeks still tear-stained, they laughed until Ziggy begged her to stop swooping.

On the day of his father's Rock the Boat party, Ziggy found himself so happy that he didn't quite trust it, and so he pulled Kate back to him. He felt her heart beating against his chest. "Hot dog," he whispered in disbelief. The whole day had been surreal, and Kate looking at him this way while their arms dovetailed made it all the more dreamlike.

Still sitting on the bow of the ferry, Billy Croce decided he'd set off one more firework in Zeke's honor. He lit the mortar, and the black powder inside followed down its intended path of magic. When the gold starburst filled the sky, all of Sea Point looked up to watch the glitter rain down.

Even through closed eyes, Kate and Ziggy could see the starburst cut through the dark—the same way they could feel the lighthouse beam, the white oak stump, all those concentric rings of light and time, loss and love. They didn't have answers yet, but they had a sense of direction as they hurled themselves toward the unknown and leaned into each other.

"Did you hear that?" Ziggy asked.

"It's a skunk," Kate whispered. "I know it is."

They froze as a creature rustled amid the reeds before it emerged from the marsh and stepped into the silver moonlight.

It was not a skunk.

An animal as familiar and preternatural as time, it had been there all along, waiting for them to notice. Ziggy opened his mouth, but Kate squeezed his hand to keep quiet—there was no need for words. They would be each other's witness for what was to come—whatever that turned out to be. Staring in quiet awe, Kate and Ziggy watched as the creature slowly bent its legs in thoughtful preparation. And then, in a flash of blue and a blur of feathers, they heard a decisive *swish* as the heron doubled its size and took flight.

Acknowledgments

Thank you to my agent, Becky Sweren, who helped grow the first seeds of Sea Point into something exciting. You continue to be my professional partner and big-picture godsend.

Thank you to my editor, Whitney Frick, for believing in this project, being an invaluable teammate, and using your enthusiasm, tough love, and keen eye to strengthen *RTB* by exactly one billion percent.

Thank you to the entire team at Dial Press and Random House, particularly Sarah Horgan for the turtle-power(!) cover art, Ted Allen and Muriel Jorgensen for the lifesaving copyediting, Ellen Weider and Madeline Hopkins for the outstanding proofreading, as well as Rose Fox, Maria Braeckel, Carrie Neil, Barbara Fillon, Debbie Aroff, Jess Bonet, Taylor Noel and Madison Dettlinger, Denise Cronin, Avideh Bashirrad, Andy Ward, and legal tiger Matthew Martin for the invaluable support and insights.

Thank you to my mother and sister, who both took turns editing this book. Ninny and her Mini made these pages so much stronger, in ways large and small. (For those interested, Caroline was less abusive and more efficient, but also not as emotionally entrenched as my mom, to whom I read the entire book aloud because you can't spell "Mother" without "S-A-I-N-T.") Thanks also to my brother, Zach, who didn't edit this book but did save lives in Temple's COVID ICU throughout the pandemic and still managed to ask how the writing was going. Thank you to my dad, whose ever-present support and patience is as crucial and calming as a walk in the woods. Thank you to Shilpa Samudrala and Enoch Kraycik for making the twins happy. On the off-chance that they learned to read during quarantine, thank you to James Winkfield, Clementine Clampett, Bodhi Bear (king of kings and gentle sir), Billy Jr., and Mary Jane.

Thank you to Iyi and Uncle Murphy as well as Aunt Kathy, Uncle Craig, and the rest of my extended kin for the unwavering support and enthusiasm. The older I get, the luckier I feel to be part of this family.

Thank you to the friends who read early drafts and/or received all sorts of frantic texts from me throughout the publishing process. You weighed in on the sticky stuff and helped quell the quills of my nervous-porcupine heart: Nick Hiebert (multiple drafts, holy homie!), Ellie Doig, Kerry Rose, Shilpa Hegde, Claire Lombardo, Sara Corbett, Vanessa Haughton, Charlotte Hastings, Hope Hall, Joani Walsh, Emma Van Susteren, Kat Narvaez, Jamie Nash, Tomás Pagán Motta, Casey and Drew "Pastry Face" Degen, Joe Paulsen, Lindsay Givens, Juliet Larkin-Gilmore, Alicia Berenson, Jen Denholm, Bernadette Doykos, Megan Rooney, and the Wes-Laxers of yesteryear.

Thank you to Kerry Rose, Chris Dorbian, and Goose for keeping me well-fed, socialized, and energized during the first several months of the pandemic/drafts of this book.

Thank you to the BTBs of my dreams—Scott Larkin, Jody Gilmore, Juliet Larkin-Gilmore and Decker, Natalie Larkin-Gilmore and Seamus—now move on up here for some Maine Justice!

Thank you to my beach friends, with particular affection for and appreciation of the magical Jodi Schad, Elizabeth Degener, Lindsay Givens, Ashley Fowler, Molly and Sarah Bernstein, Andrew Phelan, Kate

Conaboy, Meghan Protasi, the Laudemans, the Mullocks, Joanie Kelley, and the entire staff at Mayers Tavern, Givens Circle, Enfin Farms, the Chalfonte Hotel, and Louisa's, with a special shout-out to the OG renegade who puts the "art" in "heart" wherever she may roam, Louisa Hull.

John McPhee's everlasting gift, *The Pine Barrens*, influenced this book—or at least I hope it did.

Thank you Kathy DeMarco Van Cleve for saying "yes!" when the gatekeepers had already said no, and for inviting me to remember how much fun a classroom can be.

Thank you to the experts who helped me: Matthew Levy, Dr. Melvin Singer, Alicia Berenson, Austin Hoggan, Mike Valenti, Zack Mullock, Alex Laudeman, Chris Arnone, Caitlin Speers, Lisa O'Rear, and Teddy Pickering.

Thank you to my incredible SoPo neighbors and Willard Beach dog posse, as well as Scratch Bakery, Omi's coffee, Drillen Hardware, Tandem, and the entire state of Maine for welcoming me during a pandemic and making my adventure north feel less like an experiment and more like a homecoming.

Thank you to Izzy Deane and her most wonderful dad for enchanting a girl and her goat. It's been the happiest dream.

Thank you to YOU for choosing this book when the incredible reading options are endless.

On losing loved ones, John Prine said, "Realizing you're not going to see that person again is always the most difficult part about it. But that feeling settles, and then you are glad you had that person in your life, and then the happiness and the sadness get all swirled up inside you."

In addition to Sandy Tattersall and my grandmother, the more recent years have filled my heart with new swirls of happiness and sadness:

We lost my former White House boss, Peggy Suntum, to whom every Bruce Springsteen reference is dedicated. (I always meant to set her up with Sandy, so I'm hoping they're listening to The Boss together now.)

I will forever miss but be so grateful for my favorite nonagenarian spitfire, Charlotte Amelia Croce, and her loving canine companion, Billy Croce, who was my emotional rock from 2017 to 2020. While promoting the first book and writing this one, I spent more time with those two life-affirming goons than anyone else. Thank you, Carmen Croce, for giving me a key to "Billy's house."

My mom's cousin Debby Wetzel Wallace was one of my biggest cheerleaders—she was all heart, clever creativity, and enthusiasm. Losing her so suddenly was devastating, but one time she dressed up as a dough-nut and I prefer to think of that.

Last but the opposite of least, Sophie Christopher played a major role in this book in that she was my motivation for getting it done. If I could write a book, I told myself, maybe I could go back to London and see Sophie again, the effervescent, young, and fun publicist who took the work seriously but never herself. We spent only three days together but she made an impression that lasts a lifetime, which is why this book is dedicated to her and the legacy of kindness, joy, and optimism that she leaves behind.

May we find the bright lights we've lost in the stories we tell.

Rock
the
Boat

Beck Dorey-Stein

A Book Club Guide

Discussion Questions

1. What did you think of the town of Sea Point? How did the setting affect the read?

2. How does the book explore ideas of home and family?

3. When Kate and her sister Bernadette are at their parents' house, they "regress as teenagers." How does Kate's personality change during her time in Sea Point? Do you find yourself acting differently when you visit your hometown? What do you think it means to be "grown up"?

4. Who was your favorite character and why?

5. Why do you think Miles, Ziggy, and Kate have grown apart at the beginning of the novel? What mistakes do they each make in terms of their relationships with one another, and how are these remedied?

6. Why do you think Jo is initially hesitant to cede ownership of the Wharf to Miles? How does Miles change and grow throughout the book?

7. At the start of the novel, Kate wants nothing more than to move back to Manhattan and win Thomas back. How do her priorities shift? What do you think the author is trying to say about the components of a happy, successful life?

8. What roles do class and privilege play in the story?

9. Ziggy reflects that "the path he'd walked his entire life had left him utterly lost." How are these characters forced to choose new paths? Have you ever had to make a change in your life after realizing you were on the wrong path?

10. What did you think of the book's ending? Were you surprised by who Kate ended up with?

Quiz: Which Sea Point Job Would You Have?

How do you spend your spare time?

    A. Figuring out how to optimize every area of my life.

    B. Reading.

    C. Tinkering around the house.

    D. Experimenting in the kitchen.

    E. Painting.

What do you look for in a work environment?

    A. An efficient place where things run smoothly and we're generating maximum profit.

    B. A quiet place with smart, passionate colleagues.

    C. A place where I feel important, knowledgeable, and confident in solving problems.

    D. Fast pace, thrilling workdays, high stakes—but you can leave it all at work when you go home.

    E. A calm and inspiring atmosphere where I have the space to be creative.

How does your most satisfying workday end?

    A.   Business has been strong, and we've felt that our fingers are on our customers' pulse.

    B.   The community has come together and I've guided readers toward their perfect books.

    C.   Everything in the house is running smoothly and efficiently.

    D.   With a shift drink, a sweaty brow, and full-body exhaustion.

    E.   I've expressed myself and put something beautiful on a canvas.

Mostly As: Like Jo Hoffman, you're the ultimate boss. The Wharf would be lucky to have you in charge.

Mostly Bs: Like Katie, you're comfortable around books and community. The library is your ideal workplace.

Mostly Cs: Like Ziggy, you love to work with your hands and solve problems for people. You'd be a fantastic plumber and contractor, designing and building your own Daffodil Cottage.

Mostly Ds: Like Miles, you've found your match in the high-energy environment of the Wharf's kitchens.

Mostly Es: Like Bev, you're a creative spirit and a born artist. Keep channeling your energy into your paintings—you never know what they might sell for!

QUIZ: Which Sea Point resident are you?

What's your dream job?

    A.   Anything involving books!

    B.   CEO . . . or maybe cook?

    C.   Builder/plumber

How do you like to spend your free time?

    A.   Dancing in my room or out with friends.

    B.   Partying and jet-setting.

    C.   Working with my hands and relaxing.

Are you a planner?

    A.   Absolutely—I've got a three-point plan for everything.

    B.   Not really—I tend to sit back and things just fall into place.

    C.   Yes and no—I like blueprints, but it's harder when it comes to my future.

What do you do when you have a crush?

A. I devise my strategy for getting together—then plan our bright future as a couple.

B. Text them intermittently for years just to see if anything's still there.

C. Not much.

How do you break up with someone?

A. We're not broken up. We're getting back together just as soon as I . . .

B. I let them think it's their idea.

C. I don't do exclusivity in the first place. No relationships, no breakups!

Mostly As: You're Kate!

Mostly Bs: You're Miles!

Mostly Cs: You're Ziggy!

PHOTO © CHARLOTTE HASTINGS

BECK DOREY-STEIN grew up in Narberth, Pennsylvania, and taught high school English for three years before serving as a White House stenographer from 2012 to 2017. Her first book, *From the Corner of the Oval*, was a *New York Times* bestseller. She now lives on the coast of Maine.

beckdoreystein.com
Facebook.com/BeckDoreySteinAuthor
Instagram: @beckdoreystein

About the Type

This book was set in Electra, a typeface designed for Linotype by W. A. Dwiggins, the renowned type designer (1880–1956). Electra is a fluid typeface, avoiding the contrasts of thick and thin strokes that are prevalent in most modern typefaces.